# IN THE CREASE

## TONI ALEO

Editing by: Lisa Hollett of Silently Correcting Your Grammar.

Cover Design: Regina Wamba

Cover Picture: Sara Eirew

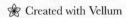 Created with Vellum

# Dedication

*In case you didn't know*
*Baby I'm crazy 'bout you*
*And I would be lying if I said*
*That I could live this life without you*
*Even though I don't tell you all the time*
*You had my heart a long, long time ago*
*In case you didn't know.*

*Brett Young "In Case You Didn't Know"*
*Wren and Jensen's song.*

# Prologue

ive months earlier…

WREN LEMIERE FELT AWFUL.

The kind of awful where you felt like you were dying.

Not that she had ever been the victim of an almost-death, but she was pretty sure it felt like what she was feeling.

Why she came back home to Colorado when she was this godforsakenly sick was beyond her, but then she hadn't felt like death when she got on the plane. It was once she got off and for the following three days that the death hit her. She didn't know what was going on, but she just wanted some drugs to make the excruciating nausea go away. That was all. Just some drugs.

Holding her face in her hands, she inhaled a deep breath before letting it out in a whoosh, begging the turning of her gut to stop. She wasn't sure what she ate or what bacteria she picked up, but when she found out whatever did this to her, they would suffer. Slowly and painfully. It was probably Vaughn, her brother's best friend. He was a walking cesspool. Ugh. She had never been so sick in her life, she swore it, but then again, that time she had the flu, she was sure she'd thought the same.

Either way, she was dying.

Plain and simple.

"Ugh," she moaned as she swallowed back the bile that was threatening to come up her throat. When the door opened and the doctor stepped in, she cried out in relief. "Please, give me something. Anything. Knock me out if you have to."

Ryan Churner laughed. They had gone to school together, dated briefly, but they'd been just kids. Now, he was married and happy—with lots of kids of his own. Wren, though, was living the single, carefree life. Much to her mother's dismay. Her mother wanted grandbabies, and since her brother, Wells, was gay, it was easy to say it was Wren's job to give her mother babies. Which was not going to happen. Wren would suck as a mom. Plus, she couldn't find a decent guy to love her large ass. So that left her brother, and Wells could adopt. Yeah, he should do that. Take some of the pressure off her. She needed to call him about that.

"I'm afraid there are no drugs for what you have."

Wren threw up her hands. "It's a virus?"

He laughed. She didn't like the sound of that laugh. Or the way he said, "Um, no."

Her face wrinkled in confusion. "Then, what?"

He grimaced a bit before looking up at her. His dark blue eyes held her gaze as a grin pulled at his lips. "When was your last period?"

She shrugged. "Like six months ago. I have polycystic ovary syndrome, though." She added while pointing at him, "Not sure that's in my chart."

He nodded. "It is, but I hadn't realized it had been that long."

"Yeah." She had maybe two periods a year, possibly three. It was a problem, but her problem. One she was blessed with when she was younger. Her PCOS kept her a little on the thicker side and also wreaked havoc on her hormones, but she managed. She wasn't going to let it bring her down or dwell on it. She already did that enough.

"Okay, well, are you in a relationship right now?"

She shook her head. "No."

"Are you sexually active?"

"Always," she said with an exaggerated wink. Then she paused. "Wait, I'm not hitting on you."

"I know." He laughed and she grinned, though, it was brief

before she felt a wave of queasiness. "But your pregnancy test came up positive."

Wren could only blink as her body went cold. She started laughing because surely, she'd heard him wrong. "You weren't this funny when we were younger."

"I'm not joking."

"I'm sorry?"

"Your pregnancy test came up positive, but sometimes with PCOS, you can get a positive result. So I want to do an ultrasound."

"For what?"

"To see if you're pregnant."

"Pregnant? Me?"

"Yes."

"But…really?"

"Yes," he said with a smile before he stood, walking to the door. "Well, usually when you have sex, a baby can be made as a byproduct of all that passion."

"But…" She trailed off, her heart jumping into her throat. Surely that wasn't the case. She couldn't be pregnant. They'd used protection. "I have sex with condoms, and I'm on birth control."

"Are you consistent with your birth control?

She shrugged. "Sure."

He raised an eyebrow. "That's not believable, Wren."

Her face wrinkled more as he called out to the nurse. Sitting there, she tried to remember when this could have happened. She was home last month and had seen him…a lot and all of him, but they'd used condoms. Hadn't they? Shit.

Soon a cart was brought in, and she was asked to take off her pants. It was all a blur, lying there with a drape over her bottom half and Ryan shoving some damn probe up inside her. Staring at the ceiling, she didn't know what to think. She hadn't even thought this was a possibility. With her PCOS, it was supposed to be hard for her to get pregnant. Not to mention, she didn't want to be a mom. She would suck as a mom. And he would suck as a dad. They were selfish.

"Yup, there it is."

Turning her head, she looked at the screen to see a little peanut. Seriously, a peanut, or at least, that's what she assumed it was. But in the middle of the peanut was a little flicker. It was so small, almost undetectable, but she was sure she could see it. Was that the heartbeat?

"That's it? I'm pregnant?"

"You're pregnant."

Blinking hard, she gasped. "Oh, fuck."

\* \* \*

"I'M PREGNANT."

The words felt funky.

"I am pregnant," she said to her reflection in the rental car's visor mirror. "We're having a baby." She tried saying it while waving her hands. But that felt weird too.

Holy shit, she was pregnant.

She was almost thirty. She had a good job, and she was in a good place. It was not even the least bit expected, nor was it good timing since she wasn't thirty yet, nor was she married. But it was fine. They would get a quickie marriage, and bam, they'd be good. No one would have to know she was pregnant before they decided to elope. It would be fine. Everything would be fine; her inheritance wasn't in jeopardy.

But, shit, she didn't want to move back to Colorado. She would have to because he wouldn't be able to leave his job. He owned the damn firm, while she was contracted by the Nashville Assassins, the professional hockey team back in Nashville, Tennessee. Her gig was awesome, so damn awesome, and she loved it, but it wouldn't work. She'd have to be the one to move. Damn it. She'd finish out the season for sure, but that meant she couldn't sign the five-year extension that was sitting on her desk back home. With the lovely bonus that was going to pay off her car early. Damn it.

She wasn't sure how he was going to take it, but they were good. They had known each other their whole lives. Been fucking for years, so it was time. She loved him. Ish. Kinda. Well, obviously a little since she continued to sleep with him, but he was a cool dude. And even if marriage was the last thing she wanted, she knew she had to do it.

She needed the money from her inheritance that her dad was holding, which had been passed down from her grandfather. When she turned thirty in October, it would be hers. The only catch was she couldn't have a baby out of wedlock before she was thirty. It was stupid, and it was barbaric in her opinion. But it was what her grandfather had written up, and her father was standing behind it. It was annoying, to say the least, but if she wanted to pay off all her debt and live pretty damn comfortably for the rest of her life, along with providing a comfortable life for Wells, she had to do what she had to do.

She just hoped *he* didn't let her down.

Getting out of the car, she swallowed hard as she walked toward the doors that read *Washington, Fieldsman, and Barnes.* When she opened the door, she was greeted by the receptionist, and Wren shot her a quick, curt smile. She was nervous. Why was she nervous? Crap, was she going to puke?

Yup.

Dipping into the bathroom before his office, she threw up the rest of her guts and sat there shaking her head. "You're lucky I love you, kid."

Wow, that was quick.

Wren had never seen herself as a mother. She'd thought she was going to grow old with lots of money and dogs. She hadn't seen love or babies in her future. She'd seen lots of fucking, but that was about it. She didn't have the best luck in love and really hadn't imagined this coming, but now, she saw herself holding a baby.

Problem was, she still didn't see him in her picture.

But that would change…right?

Surely.

Crap.

Washing her mouth out and then popping some gum, she walked out of the bathroom and right into another person. "Ah!"

"Crap! I'm sorry, Wren."

Wren clammed up. Shit. "Hey, Shanna. What you doing here?"

"I had to see Bradley. What are you doing?" her best friend for her whole life asked.

Dammit, Wren hated lying to her.

"I have a meeting with him. He has to go over my contract for the Assassins."

Shanna lit up. "Cool! Are you still coming for dinner tonight?"

Wren was shaking. Why was she shaking? Shit. "Shan, I texted you. I had to move my flight up, remember?"

"Oh, yes. My bad. Next time."

"Of course," she said before Shanna embraced her. Squeezing her eyes shut, Wren knew she would have to tell her. But Bradley had wanted to keep them under wraps. Plus, Wren knew how over-protective Shanna was of her baby brother. Wren had known better, but the dude was hung like a horse and hot to boot. She just hoped she wouldn't lose a friendship over this. But Shanna would be excited. They'd be sisters like they'd always wanted, and there'd be a new baby. Shanna would love that.

Right?

Right.

*Don't freak out. This is fine.*

Saying goodbye, Wren waved as she walked toward his office before knocking on the door. "Come in." As she opened the door to the huge, posh office, he stood behind his desk, looking every bit as gorgeous as the day was long. His suit was pressed and clung to him. His light brown hair was brushed to the side, while a bit of stubble dusted his jaw. She only saw it because the sun was kissing it, shining on it ever so sweetly. He was a good-looking man, beautiful even, but still, she couldn't see herself married to him. Shit.

Wren smiled though, and when Bradley looked up, heat filled his gaze. "Hey, you."

"Hey," she said, shutting the door as he came around the desk to her. Gathering her in his arms, he kissed her hard on the lips, dipping her back slightly as she clung to him. This had to work. He was a great guy.

Pulling back, he kissed her nose. "You look hot."

She laughed, waving him off. "I look and feel like death."

"Still?" he asked, concern filling his handsome face. He was a year younger than her, and growing up, they'd called him the baby. Though, he didn't look like a baby. When he had first kissed her, eons ago, she hadn't expected it. And even though they had both been with other people over the years, they somehow always gravitated back to each other.

Always.

But that was about to change.

"Yeah. I went to the doctor today."

Moving his thumb along the inside of her palm, he smiled. "Is it contagious?"

She shook her head, her face filling with heat. "No."

"Oh, good," he said, gathering her in his arms and pressing his lips to hers. "So we can take this discussion to the couch."

She stopped him as he tried to pull her to where she knew they would likely have all kinds of hot sex, but she needed to get this out. "Not yet."

His brows pulled together. "What's wrong? Don't feel up to it?"

She swallowed hard. "It's not that. It's…um…" Inhaling deeply, she met his gaze. The gaze she had known her whole life. Though right now, she felt like she was going to puke, her nerves were so bad. "I'm pregnant."

She watched as his eyes widened, his jaw dropping before he dropped her hands. "Pregnant?"

"Yeah."

He only blinked. "Is it mine?"

She nodded. "You're the only guy I've been with for the last six months."

He blinked once more, his eyes burning into hers. "Are you sure?"

She gave him a deadpan look. "I think I'd remember if I happen to fall, pussy first, on a cock other than yours."

He didn't laugh like she wanted, nor did he look her in the eye. Instead, he chewed his lip, looking anywhere but at her. "So, no other chance it isn't mine?"

Her brows drew in. "It's yours, Bradley."

Turning his back to her, he walked away, going to the windows as he looked out of them, his hands folded across his chest. "I didn't expect this. We used condoms."

"I know."

"And you're on birth control, I thought."

"I am, though I don't take it as often as I should."

He looked over at her. "So you trapped me?"

She glared. "You'd better be joking."

He didn't answer; he just looked away as her heart started to speed up.

This didn't feel right.

As he started to pace, she watched him, her blood beginning to boil. She didn't like his comment, nor did she like the way he wouldn't look at her. Clearing her throat, she watched him as she said, "Okay, well, I know this is a lot at once, and it's a lot for me too. But we have something that could pose an issue—my inheritance."

His face wrinkled up as he snapped, "How does that have anything to do with me?"

She glared at the side of his face. "It has to do with you because your baby is inside of me, and I'm not thirty yet. So if I have this baby before I turn thirty and I'm not married, I'm fucked."

"Then don't have the baby."

Her jaw dropped. Actually dropped, almost catching flies. "Excuse me?"

Still looking out the window, he shrugged. "Go get an abortion."

"What?"

"Listen, I don't want this. I don't want a kid, and fuck, this is going to mess everything up."

Her heart was in her throat. "Mess up what?

Turning to her, he yelled, "I'm marrying fucking Fieldsman's daughter."

It was as if he'd hit her. Reaching out, she braced her hand on the window. He had been seeing the girl, but he swore it wasn't serious. They were just cool; it was *business* as he said. But marriage? "What? You said you didn't want to get married."

"I know, but I have no choice."

"You do. You can marry me and help out the mother of your child."

"No, I can't. I was going to tell you tonight, that we had to break this off. For good."

Drawing in a breath through her nose, she shook her head. "Wow."

"Yeah. So listen," he said, walking around her and to his desk, but she didn't move as the tears gathered in her eyes. "Go get an abortion. It's for the best. Here, this should cover it."

When she opened her eyes, he was filling out a check before holding it out to her. Shaking her head hard, she muttered, "I don't want your money."

"Take it, Wren. Please. I can't have this fuck up what I've got going for me. I'll have more stock in this firm once I marry her."

Her lip started to tremble. "But I'm having your baby."

"I don't want it," he said simply. "I don't want any of it. She will get pissed. She's already so jealous and thinks I'm fucking around."

"You are!"

"I know, but not anymore. So, please, get rid of it."

"I can't."

"Wren, come on!"

"You can't do this. We've known each other our whole life."

"I understand that. So please do it."

"No."

"Don't be stupid, because I'll deny it. You fuck around. Everyone knows it, and I'll deny the kid is mine. You'll have to take me to court to prove it. But by the time that happens, you'll already have it before your thirtieth birthday, so you'll be fucked anyway. Just do the right thing. Get rid of it, Wren."

She wouldn't let her tears fall. Not for this fucking douche. "I thought I knew you, you selfish asshole."

The words didn't even faze him. He glared at her. "I thought I knew you. How could you let this happen? We were never serious. We were just fucking."

Looking down at the ground, she bit into her lip to keep the tears from falling. Yeah, he was right, but she thought she'd meant more to him than just a fuck. "Just fucking, huh?"

"Yeah, it isn't like we love each other. I mean, come on. You're not even my type."

"Your type?"

"Wren, come on," he said simply, holding his hands out. "You're not trophy wife material."

She was going to deck him. "I can't believe this."

"Just take the check."

He held it out once more, and her eyes landed on it through her tears. She should take it. It really was the only option, yet she knew she couldn't.

Meeting his gaze, she swallowed hard as she shook her head slowly from side to side. "No."

"Wren, don't be an idiot."

"No."

"You're being fucking stupid—"

Standing erect, she stepped over to him, her eyes burning into his and completely cutting off his words. She was sure her eyes were full of heat, full of rage because his words shook her. To the core. She wasn't sure who this man was, but he sure as hell wouldn't be the father of her child. Over her dead fucking body. "Fuck you, Bradley. I don't need your money or even you. So. Fuck. You."

And with that, she walked away.

With no clue what she was going to do now.

Except for the certainty that she wasn't killing her baby.

# Chapter ONE

*J*ensen Monroe's heart was in his throat.

And it had been there throughout the whole series thus far.

Standing between the pipes on the other end of the ice, he watched as the Assassins trickled shots at the opponent's goal. His heart was pounding, almost choking him as he watched the Capitals take possession of the puck before starting toward him. Dropping into his stance, his eye on the puck, he watched as a player passed it back to the defensemen, who took the shot. But Jensen saw it completely, batting it away. Unfortunately, it didn't go to one of his players, instead to another Capital, but Jensen was there, blocking each shot as it came in.

He had to be.

He had to help his team win.

The whole series up to this point in the Cup run hadn't been easy. Everyone thought it was, though. The Nashville Assassins were being called a shoo-in, the sure winner because of how much they had dominated, but no one knew the truth. That Lucas Brooks was on one bad hip but still giving his heart. That Jayden Sinclair sat up night after night watching tapes of the other team just to make sure he could give the team the best direction. That Vaughn Johansson barely slept because his nerves were eating him alive. That Coach hardly went home because he wanted to make sure everything was right for the following day. Everyone was working, everyone was full of nerves, but they all had one goal.

The Cup.

And boy, did Jensen want it. With Tate being out, Jensen worked day and night, making sure he was prepared for every game. He was doing well. He could do better, though, even though everyone said he was better than great. He was his own worst critic, and because of that, he pushed himself harder to be the best. All that was in the past now; all that mattered was this game right at the moment. The game that could win the Assassins the Cup if they could beat the Capitals, and boy, did he want to. The Caps were up by one after a shitty goal that went off his back, but it counted, which meant the Assassins had to score to tie it.

With only three minutes.

He could do this.

They could do this.

The Capitals had been relentless. Being down three games to one would do that to a team. They were desperate. They wanted to take the series back to Washington, they wanted to prolong this, but that wasn't going to happen.

Jensen wanted the Cup.

His team wanted the Cup.

It was their time.

The Cup was meant to be in Nashville.

He watched King bank the puck up the boards to a waiting Sinclair before he got off the ice, Reeves taking his spot. When he threw the puck to the net, it was batted away just as Mason came, sending it back to the blue line. But Reeves's shot was blocked, and when the defense tried to clear it for fresh bodies, Sinclair flung himself to the ice, keeping it in before passing it, from his knees, to Johansson. Jensen held his breath as Johansson shot with his wicked wrister, right over the goalie's shoulder in a picture-perfect moment.

Throwing his hands in the air, Jensen looked up at the ceiling as the Luther Arena went insane. It was so loud Jensen swore he wouldn't hear for the next three days. Which was more of a reason why they needed to win, now. The period ran down in almost a blur. No shots on goal since everyone was battling against the boards and then lots of turnovers Jensen was sure Coach would be livid about.

And he was right.

When they got into the locker room, Coach reamed the team out for them. Jensen was leaned back in his locker, an ice-cold towel over his face as he inhaled deeply, letting it out slowly, almost in a meditative state. Everyone knew not to talk to him. He was busy. In his mind, he was watching the always-moving puck. He was trying to see through the bodies that almost always clouded his brain on game day, and he was trying to stay ahead of the game. It was a mental game, being a goalie, but it was a game Jensen lived for.

Ever since he was old enough to remember, he'd never wanted anything else but to be a goalie. He could still see himself in his father's way-too-big gear. Waddling around the house as his parents laughed. He had dreams, goals, and when the time came for him to come to the States from Canada and live those dreams, his parents didn't even bat an eye. They found the best family to take him in and sent him off to Colorado. Their only son. But thankfully, the family they sent him to was amazing, and soon they became a part of Jensen's family. A part of his life. He met his two best friends there, he fell in love there, and above all, he became the goalie he was right now, there.

Because of that, he was going to win.

For all of them.

The fifteen-minute break was gone in a blink of an eye. Again, he was between the pipes, staring down the ice at the Capitals' goalie, who seemed to be staring back at him. He didn't know the guy, nor did he want to at that moment. This was war, and their goalie was the enemy. All that mattered was winning, and as the puck dropped, Jensen begged his heart to be somewhat controlled as he watched the puck and the two teams start to battle.

Because the next goal would win the game.

For the next five minutes, Jensen felt like the kid from *The Mighty Ducks*, waiting for the puck to come his way. But it never did. They either stayed in the Capitals' zone, or they battled in the middle before the Capitals turned it over. The Assassins weren't playing for fun, they were out for blood, and Jensen guessed the ass-reaming from coach had been a doozy. Not that he could recall a bit of it.

Leaning on his legs, he watched as the puck snuck out to the defense at the blue line. Karson King shot hard as Brooks screened, but it went wide. Anderson was there, sending the puck back to the point where Jordie Thomas shot. Like had been happening the whole series, Brooks was hit. The guy was taking a beating, but he never went down. Somehow the goalie blocked it, but then the rebound was right there. Jensen heard himself scream or something, he wasn't sure. But before he could even finish whatever he was saying, Brooks top shelved it over the goalie with ease.

Jensen swore time stood still.

Gloves, sticks, and screams filled the air as he threw his stuff off before sprinting toward his brothers on the other side of the ice, who were all lying on Lucas Brooks. Jumping on the top of the pile, he heard Lucas groan, but he didn't think anyone cared as they all hollered out in excitement. Tears and confetti started to fall within seconds as the Assassins chant filled the arena. Before he knew it, Jensen's eyes had fallen shut, tears leaking out the sides as he squeezed someone.

They had won.

The Assassins had won the Stanley Cup.

When he stood to his feet, Vaughn Johansson, his best friend for as long as he could remember, attacked him from the left, wrapping his body around him like a koala just as Jensen did the same, both of them falling to the ice as they cried out.

The noise was deafening in the arena, but he could still hear as his best friend said, "You did it."

"We did it," he reiterated as they hugged tightly once more.

"Can you believe it?"

"No." He laughed.

"This is better than sex!" Jensen really laughed at that. "No, that's a lie."

"I figured!"

"Oh my God, we won!"

"We won!" Jensen yelled back as they both shook each other like two schoolboys. But then, that's what moments like these were made of. Men turned back into boys because they had achieved their dreams. Since Jensen was a small boy, he had wanted the Cup. Skating on the frozen pond back in British Columbia, Jensen used to act like he was defending the goal for the Cup. Now that dream was a reality.

The next few moments, Jensen was convinced would be a hazy memory for the rest of his life. All he would remember would be the tears and the smiles on all his brothers' faces. How Jayden rushed to the other side of the ice where his wife stood with their little boy behind the glass. How Lucas waved to his family in the boxes. He watched as Vaughn rushed to his fiancée, kissing her hard on the lips, though she tried to get away since she was working. How everyone was screaming to their loved ones as Jensen just stood there.

But he had no one.

His parents couldn't make it because his dad's diabetes had gotten so bad that his legs were giving him issues. The doctors had gotten it under control, but his mom wouldn't leave his side, which was understandable. Thankfully, he knew they were watching. Though, he did miss them more than he could ever put into words. He knew he would see them in a few weeks.

With his Cup.

Jensen's throat was tight as he looked around the arena, all the fans going nuts, the guys clinging to each other as Jayden took pictures with the commissioner and the Cup. It was so much shinier in person. Jensen had seen it on the internet and even at events, but he had never been this close to it. Soon, he would touch it.

As the crowd roared, Jayden picked it up to do his victory lap, but to Jensen's surprise, he carried it over to Lucas Brooks before yelling, "For the last time, brother. This is all you, Brooksie, you earned it." The team all yelled out for the veteran forward before he took the Cup, holding it above his head and kissing it. Jensen clapped along with his team, their fans, and their families as Lucas did his lap, tears gushing down his face. When he came back to the team, Jensen assumed Lucas would give it back to Jayden. But instead, he paused in front of Jensen.

"We couldn't have done this without you, Monroe. Take your lap."

Jensen reached out, taking the Cup before looking back at the guy who was Tate Odder's biggest fan. He'd felt like Lucas held a bit of animosity toward him since Jensen had taken Tate's spot after he went out with an injury. But looking into Lucas's eyes, all Jensen saw was love and admiration. Bringing the Cup up, he shook it wildly before kissing it and doing his lap. It was all such a blur, like it wasn't even happening, and then it was over. It almost felt as if he hadn't even done it.

But he knew he had.

Handing the cup off to Jayden, Jensen felt a grin grow on his face before someone called out, "Monroe, media."

He was watching as Jayden was skating with the Cup, tears welling up in his eyes as he stopped in front of his wife and son.

Shit. Jensen was going to cry.

Swallowing hard, Jensen skated to where Brie Soledad was standing, tears in his eyes, but he wouldn't let them fall. He couldn't; Vaughn would give him shit for days if he cried on camera. Before she could ask anything, though, they embraced. She had become a pillar in his life the last six months. Engaged to his best friend, newly pregnant, Brie was just as much a sister as Vaughn was a brother. Jensen was vying for the baby to be named after him, though, Vaughn had said no way in hell. Jensen was pretty sure he could change that. He had his ways.

Kissing his cheek, she backed up, a grin on her face as she yelled into the mic, "Jensen Monroe, congratulations."

Holy shit, he still couldn't believe it.

They had won.

"Thank you, Brie."

"Your goals against average is only .940, setting a new record. You saved 1,033 shots this run, almost beating the record of Tim Thomas. They say the Vezina Trophy is yours. Tell me, can life get any better?"

As he looked up, meeting Brie's happy and excited gaze, he said, "No, it can't."

He actually paused, waiting for God to strike him down for lying.

Because even in that moment, with all the confetti, the undying love from the fans, his boys cheering him on, and the tears in Brie's eyes, Jensen knew things could be a lot better.

Yeah, he had just won the Cup. Had made records, and might win the Vezina Trophy, but at the end of the day, unlike everyone else in the arena, he had no one to share it with.

Because of that, the moment was almost ruined.

Almost.

\* \* \*

"WELL, CRAP."

Wren turned side to side in her full-length mirror, staring at her reflection.

Or better yet, her ever-growing belly.

Biting her lip, Wren furrowed her brow as she ran her hand down her stomach. "Really? I bought this to hide you, kiddo."

She wasn't sure what she expected, for her belly to talk back or what, but one thing was for sure, the many tunics she had bought to hide her stomach were not working any longer. She had done so well the last six months, hiding the fact that she was very much pregnant. Today, though…today, her little baby had decided it was time to make its debut.

And that wasn't good.

Because she still wasn't married.

Letting her head fall back, she looked up at the ceiling because if she didn't, she'd look at the counter where her brother's wedding invitation sat. A wedding invite that showed a date a month from today, and her presence would be expected. She thought about trying to get out of it, but she was pretty sure Wells would kill her dead if she didn't show. So would her parents, but she just couldn't face them. Any of them.

Closing her eyes, she could see her trust fund slipping away since there was no way she could keep this a secret when she went home. She had always been a thick girl, but she didn't look fat any longer. She looked pregnant. And since she was, that made sense, but that was beside the point. She couldn't believe this was how her life had played out. She didn't know what she thought would happen when she walked out of Bradley's office, but a part of her had thought he'd call her back.

But he hadn't.

He married his partner's daughter three months ago, and boy, did that sting.

It was like she meant nothing to him. By now, she wouldn't think it would still hurt so bad, but it did. It hurt terribly, and she hated him. Oh, did she hate him. He wasn't the man she'd thought he was. But then, what did she expect? He never committed to her. Only wanted sex. Just like everyone else. She wasn't trophy wife material. No one wanted the fat girl long term. They just wanted to bury themselves in her fluff and keep it moving.

Fuckers.

Pursing her lips, she looked back at her reflection. She wanted to see the fat girl everyone else saw, but she didn't. She never had. Even in school when people called her fat, she'd find herself so confused. She thought she looked normal. Did she love food? Hell yeah, but she wasn't huge by any means. Nor was she skin and bones either, and with her curves, she was beautiful. Dark as night hair, big, green eyes that had flecks of darkness in them. Darkness that leaked from her soul, probably. Her face was round with bright pink cheeks, but even with the loveliness of her face, her eyes fell down to her protruding stomach.

"That's a problem." She pressed her lips together as her little nugget kicked hard on her bladder. "Not you, kid, but the fact that you're showing."

She had a session with Tate Odder in a little over an hour, and since no one at work knew about the baby, she really didn't want to go to work with her child on full display. But as she took herself in, she was discovering she might not have a choice. Which was bad. She couldn't let it get back to her family that she was pregnant without a husband. She knew she should just let the trust fund go, but she couldn't. She had so much debt, and she couldn't let Wells down. As much as he said he didn't need the money, she knew he did. Their parents hadn't paid for college because they knew the money would get to the kids. So instead, they stuck them with debt and told them they'd pay for the books. Wells made decent money as a hockey player, but he wanted a family too, and the money would help.

But for that to happen, she either needed a husband or for her brother not to be gay—which would never happen since Wells had been gay since he was like three.

So she needed a husband.

One who would want to claim a kid that wasn't his.

She considered pulling a *Wedding Date*, but unlike the popular movie, in this day and age, you couldn't trust some dude on the internet. He'd kill her and steal her baby or some crazy shit. Asking Vaughn, her brother's best friend, hadn't been the greatest idea either. Not only did he say no, but she knew it would have turned out badly in the long run. He was too immature to keep a secret like that, and she knew that no matter what, she would never fall for him.

Wren had a reputation for being a hard-ass with no soul, hating love and all that jazz, and she knew why she was like that. For the simple fact that she always fell for shitty dudes. She couldn't control her emotions, and she always found herself in love with a guy who had no intentions of loving her back. She was fat, she was too blunt, and she was too close to her brother and his friends. She was never good enough, which led to heartache because all they wanted was sex. And that was why she only slept with guys.

God, she was a mess.

A pregnant mess.

Rolling her eyes, she reached for her oversized kimono that was covered in pregnancy books before throwing it on and shaking her head.

Her belly wasn't to be hid.

Fuck.

* * *

"How's it going, Tate?"

Tate Odder look uneasy as he sat across from her. His body was taut, his blond hair falling in his blue eyes as he looked around the room. Anywhere but at her. As with everyone else, her office wasn't his favorite place. As the team therapist, she wasn't the most popular person to talk to, but she did her job, and people ultimately loved her for it. Especially, her boss, Elli Adler. Elli thought the world of her and trusted her completely with her boys. Due to that trust, Wren worked hard to make sure that everyone's mental health was intact.

But Tate wasn't doing well. His injury had left him pretty messed up physically and mentally, and it was her job to help him see through it all.

Running his hand through his hair, he shrugged. "I'm hurting. Every day."

"How does that make you feel?"

"Frustrated. Angry. I hate it. I miss the ice, but they won't let me on it until I'm healed more."

"I can understand your frustration, then. You love the ice."

"I do. And I want back on. Desperately."

"Can you tell me why you feel that way?"

Exhaling hard, he shook his head as he looked down to the ground. She felt so bad for him. Stupid injuries. "I feel whole on the ice, and I feel like an asshole for not being whole with my wife and children."

"You're a hockey player, Tate. The ice is part of your life."

"Yes, but my wife and children are a part of me too."

"I can see that, you know that. So why do you feel like you're not whole?"

He looked away once more, inhaling sharply before shrugging. "I think I'm jealous."

"Jealous?"

"Yes, I have a good ten more years left, and I feel like my spot has been given away. That Jensen Monroe has come in and taken over. He won the Cup for us, and I know I should be proud of him —and I am—but I'm jealous. That should have been me."

Hearing Jensen's name, Wren felt the hair on her arms stand to attention. She had been going back and forth over whether she should call him. Ask for his help. He was Wells's other best friend and a great guy, but Jensen… Jensen, yeah, no.

Chewing on the edge of her pen as her stomach moved and wobbled from her crazy kid playing soccer with her bladder, she met his gaze, a small smile on her face. "The jealousy, is it full of anger?"

"No," he said quickly, shaking his head. "I don't hate him. He's a good guy, but I wanted it to be me."

"That's understandable."

As he bit his lip, the little gap in his teeth made Wren smile as he shook his head. "My wife wants me to retire."

Wren paused, her pen falling to her bottom lip. "How does that make you feel?"

He looked down, trailing his fingers along his scalp. "I think she might be right."

"Want to elaborate a bit?" she asked after he paused for a good long moment.

"She's worried that I'm going to push myself too hard, and then, what if I die or I can't play with my children. That's not okay with me—or with her."

"But will it be okay with you to be without hockey?" Wren agreed with his wife, but she needed him to get to that point on his own.

Slowly nodding, he looked up. "I can get a job within the sport.

Or something. Maybe as a goalie coach. I know a lot, and Elli would hire me."

"You do, and I'm sure if you talked to her, she would."

"Yeah."

"Is that something you think you want to do?"

"I go back and forth. Sometimes yes, but then no. I don't know."

"That's to be expected, your wariness of the new path. It's a big decision."

He nodded in agreement just as the soft bell on her desk rang, ending their session. He looked up, and she smiled with a shrug. "I can go another thirty if you want."

He shook his head. "No, I'm good."

He slowly stood up, reaching for his crutches. She stood, taking his hand before shaking it hard. "So let's make your goal for our next session to think more about the retirement."

Tate nodded. "Okay."

"Talk to Audrey and the kids about it."

He smiled. "The kids will want me to."

She smiled back. "I'm sure. Okay, I'll see you Friday?"

"Yup, have a good day, Wren."

"You too, Tate."

As she watched him leave, her heart broke for him. He used to stand so tall, so sure of himself, but now, he walked with a limp on crutches, and his shoulders always seemed to be down. A sullen look covered his face, and it sucked.

Man, she hated injury.

When the door closed, her desk phone started to ring, and she groaned. She needed to put a phone on the little table by her chair since she was getting to be very lazy. Walking over with a louder groan, she stepped behind her desk, grabbing her phone. "Hello?"

"Hey, honey. How are you?"

Wren smiled. "I'm good, Momma. How are you?"

"Stressed. Your brother's wedding will be the death of me."

"Is he still stuck on the glitter-dropping doves?"

Elaine Lemiere laughed. "Yes, though your father is completely against it."

"I'm sure. So he's coming?"

"Yes, thank goodness."

It was no secret that Wren's father didn't agree with Wells's lifestyle. He had tried to disown Wells, but that didn't work out well. Wells was the kind of guy that was hard to get rid of. His personality was infectious, and he had a great soul. Plus, Wells was her father's best friend, so things were a little tense. Despite everything, though, Wells still loved their father with no reservations. It was kind of beautiful in a way, and she was glad her father would be there.

"Will he walk him down the aisle?"

"Wren, stop." Wren snickered as she fell back into her chair. "When will you arrive?"

Her laughter stopped as soon as the words left her mother's lips. "I don't know yet."

"Can you come early? I may need help."

"Momma, I'm sorry, but I have to work."

"Oh, true. That's fine."

"Yeah. Sorry."

"Don't be. I'll hire someone."

"Good idea."

Hanging up with her mother, Wren set the phone on its base before leaning back in her chair and embracing her stomach in her hands, rubbing her thumbs along her stretched dress that she wasn't sure was hiding anything. But no one had asked, so that was good. As she went through idea after idea in her head, tears began to flood her eyes. She knew that losing her trust fund shouldn't be that big of a deal, but it was.

When a knock came to her door, she looked up as Brie Soledad poked her head in. "Hey, you."

Wren smiled. She had become close friends with Brie over the last couple months. Brie was engaged to Vaughn and pregnant and just a great girl. Wren loved her, which didn't happen a lot when it came to whom Wells, Vaughn, and Jensen dated. She usually hated anyone they hooked up with or tried to marry, but she had liked Brie before her relationship with Vaughn had started. Wren had worked with her for the last two years—Brie in the media department, while Wren did her thing in the health department, and they'd always found themselves getting along. Now, it was like they were going to be sisters, and that was awesome. Brie was a wonderful person, and Wren loved her brother, Rodney. He was hilarious. "Hey."

"Wanna go to lunch with me, Vaughn, and Jensen?"

Wren shook her head. Not only was her dress a little too tight for her liking, but she had more clients. "I have a full afternoon."

"Boo, you suck."

"I know. Eat some food for me."

"Want me to bring you something back?"

"No, I'm good."

Brie grinned. "Cool, text you later?"

"Yeah, sounds good."

When her phone started ringing, Brie looked down and then waved. "It's Jensen. See ya."

The door shut before Wren could say bye, not that she was going to.

Because at that moment, her mind was flooded with thoughts of Jensen.

Jensen Monroe.

Crap.

# Chapter TWO

*I*t wasn't that Wren didn't like thinking of Jensen. No, she thought he was a pretty stand-up guy. Compared to Vaughn and Wells, he was the only one who actually stopped the other two from terrorizing her through her teenage years. She could still remember the day he showed up to their home. He was only thirteen at the time, but even then, he was gorgeous. Like, movie-star gorgeous. She almost didn't believe he was real when he walked in. Unlike Wells and Vaughn, he was stockier, thicker, and he had this hard look to his face.

It was so sexy.

And on top of that, he was just a good person.

She heard him on the phone with his parents constantly, speaking French. At the time, she'd found it so intriguing that she'd sit outside his door and listen. No clue what was going on, of course, but she loved listening to him speak. He loved her parents, too, and did everything he could to do whatever they needed. Unlike the other billet boys who came through, Jensen worked his ass off—on and off the ice. So, of course, her parents loved him and only wanted him. Wells and Vaughn were already best friends, but Jensen fit right in with them. He was a silent presence, but they respected him, and soon all three of them were inseparable.

When Jensen would go home for a month in the summer, everyone missed him, and the mood was down. He'd call and talk with Wells and her parents, but the only time he spoke to Wren was when he was keeping Vaughn and Wells from tormenting her. When he was in a room with her, he didn't speak, but she always felt his gaze. Especially after she turned fifteen. He was eighteen then, and she swore he had a thing for her, but he never acted on it. He was so hot and cold that she didn't know what was up. Then he started dating some girl back home, and she figured he wouldn't ever be interested in her, and she made herself let it go.

Her stupid little girly dream of him had been good, but it was completely a dream. They were two different people. He was quiet, she was loud. He was kindhearted, she was hard-hearted from the years of fuck-ups she had been involved with. Plus, he was a sexy god of a man, and she was thick and frumpy. He was way out of her league. Yet, in their adult years, he had always looked at her and treated her like she was gorgeous. But he still never acted on anything. It was frustrating and insane, but that was Jensen.

The quiet, nice guy.

He wasn't the type to fuck around for fun. He wanted lifetimes and eons from a woman. Wren wasn't that girl. But she sure wouldn't mind getting in between the sheets with him. He had to be hung like a horse, he was so big and sexy, and Lord, she was hot. Fanning herself, she looked around her office and let out a breath. It had been a long six months without sex. Since she felt dirty getting a dick inside of where her child was growing, she hadn't gotten any in a while. Add in the fact that her kiddo slept on her bladder, and it was easy to say Wren wasn't the nicest girl to approach. She needed ice cream, some dick, and a back rub like none other. Alas, she was single, pregnant, and probably out of ice cream.

Reaching for a pen, she wrote on her notepad to pick some up on her way home. Though, both she and the notepad knew that wasn't going to happen. When she left work, she went home and went to bed. She was exhausted all the time, and she wanted nothing more than an ice cream delivery service. Maybe the ice cream man could be sexy and have great hands... Wow, that was a porno waiting to happen.

She should write that down.

Before she could, though, her cell phone rang. Glancing at the screen, she groaned when her mother's picture popped up. She loved her mother more than life itself, but lying to her was taking its toll. And twice in one day, crap.

"Hey, Momma."

"Hey, Wren, are you almost done for the day?"

"Nope, got lots to do before I head home."

"Oh, well, I'll be quick, then." She cleared her throat as Wren leaned back in her chair, running her other hand along her rounding belly. It was like one day she woke up, and it was there. She had been thick, but nothing was popping out of her. That wasn't the case anymore, and if she were smart, she'd jump on either not going to the wedding or finding a fake husband.

Lord. She was in a mess.

"Two things. Are you sure you can't come a week or two early before the wedding?"

Wren groaned. "Momma, I told you, I've got so much work." Lie. "And the flights are expensive." More lies. "And I have to watch Vaughn's dog." That was straight pulled from her ass. "And yeah, I don't know."

"Wren, it's your brother's wedding. He needs us."

"Hire someone," she suggested for the nine hundredth time. "There is no reason for you to be doing this."

"I want to."

"Well, then you hire people to help you."

"Ugh, fine. You're being a brat."

Wren closed her eyes. She was always the brat. "I know. I'm sorry. I'm so busy."

"I know," her mother said as an exhale. "It's annoying."

Wren laughed. "Sorry."

"If you can pull it off, please try."

"I'll try," she lied. "But don't get your hopes up."

"I won't," her mother promised. Though, Wren knew she would probably start looking for flights and buy her one. Damn it. "Also, Shanna came by."

Wren squeezed her eyes shut. "Man, I've been meaning to call her."

"Wren, she's been your best friend since you two were little. I don't understand what is going on."

"Mom, I'm swamped here." Wow, the lies were pouring out of her like water. "Since I got my bonus, they've been working me to death."

"She's your best friend."

And also the sister of the fucking douche who didn't want

her baby.

"I know I'll call her."

"Promise?"

"Yeah," she tried, her face scrunching up as the tears welled up in her eyes. She was the biggest liar ever, and there was a special place in hell just for her. Damn it.

"Oh! One more thing—"

"I thought the last thing was the last thing."

"No, listen, are you bringing someone?"

Wren let her head fall to the desk. "I don't know."

"It's tragic to show up alone."

Shaking her head, she pulled her brows together. "I don't care."

"Lord. My daughter, the spinster."

"And proud of it. Okay, I gotta g—"

"Try to find a date?"

"Mom—"

"Please. For me."

"Mom, really? I don't need a man."

"I know, but I want you to be happy."

"I am happy."

"Please."

"Ugh, okay."

She was pretty sure they both knew that was a lie too.

While her mom just assumed she wouldn't bring anyone, Wren actually would be bringing a husband.

If she could find one.

Why was Jensen's face in her head?

Shit.

* * *

"How much?"

Wren's eyes widened at the six figures the lady quoted over the phone.

"And that covers just the week?"

"Yes, ma'am."

"Okay, does he have a golden cock? Can I use said golden cock for the whole week?"

When the lady laughed, Wren felt like she must have thought

Wren was joking.

She wasn't.

"No, ma'am. If you would like to have intercourse, it's up to the escort's discretion how much he charges."

"Can I at least look at it? Maybe fondle it?"

Her laugh was a lot more curt this time. "No, ma'am."

"Hmm. So, I'm paying for what, then?"

"A husband. He'll schmooze your family, he'll act like you hung the stars and the moon. Everyone will be completely convinced. I've seen this guy at work. He's gorgeous and one hell of an actor."

Covering her face, Wren scrunched up her lips. "And if I need him later, for different events?"

"We'll have to check his schedule, and future events will have different rates."

"More money."

"Yes, ma'am."

"And no golden cock."

"No, ma'am."

This was not her life. She was not on the phone with an escort company, trying to get a husband. This was ludicrous. Was she really this desperate?

Yep. She was.

Squeezing her eyes shut tightly, she asked, "And when do I need to book?"

"As soon as possible since the date is so close. He actually just had a cancellation."

"She found out she had to pay extra for the golden cock?"

"Ms. Lemiere, his penis is not golden."

"For over a hundred grand, it better be," Wren muttered as she ran her hand down her face, leaning on her elbows. Looking down at her desk, a picture of Wells, Jensen, Vaughn, and her at her graduation stared back at her. She hadn't been honest with two of the three, and she'd really thought that maybe Vaughn would go for it. Act like her husband. But that was dumb of her. He loved Brie, and he wouldn't break their trust to help Wren out. No matter that she'd known him before he even knew how to use that cock of his. And she couldn't tell her brother. He had such a mouth on him, he'd let it slip on accident. But then...there was Jensen.

Clearing her throat, she shook her head. No. She couldn't ask him. But could she spend a hundred grand for a fake husband to get more money? What if the investment didn't pay off? God, this was insane! "I'll call you back."

"Sounds good, Ms. Lemiere."

Hanging up, Wren let out a sound of distress as she let her head fall to her desk once more. Man, she was in a mess, and she really needed to talk to someone.

Sitting up, she hit Brie's number. "Hey."

"Hey, got a minute?"

"Yeah, I mean we're waiting for our food. What's up?"

Shit, that was right.

"Crap. I forgot you were out."

"It's fine. It's Vaughn and Jensen. They're fighting over who would look better naked by the Cup. You're actually saving me."

"It would so be me," Wren heard Vaughn yell, and she wanted to laugh, she did, they were idiots. But she felt a panic attack coming.

"I have abs. You have fluff," Jensen spat back.

"Lies!"

"Can you walk away for a minute?"

"Oh, yeah," Brie said as Vaughn's and Jensen's voices started to fade into the distance. "What's up?"

"So, hypothetically—"

"Okay, hypothetically."

"So, if you were going home to your family for a wedding and you were pregnant and had no husband, would you hire a husband for over a hundred grand, or would you ask a friend?"

Brie paused, and Wren held her breath. "Why am I hiring a husband?"

"Because you can't go home without one."

"Why?"

"'Cause you're pregnant."

"So?"

"So, if you're pregnant and have no husband, you won't get your inheritance." As soon as the words left her mouth, Wren shut her eyes. She prayed that Brie had been really drunk the night they went out and talked about this, but knowing her luck, she hadn't been.

"Hypothetically."

"Yes."

"And this isn't you?"

"No. God, no." The lies just kept piling up. "It's a client."

"Oh, are you allowed to tell me that?"

"Hypothetically, remember?"

"Oh, yeah. Okay, I don't know."

"Brie, that's not helping me."

"Yeah, hmm. I think I'd ask a friend. Babies are expensive."

"This is true," she agreed, thinking of that one time she went to the baby store and ran out because it was too overwhelming. The prices, the amount of stuff… Yeah, it was tough.

"Yeah, I'd ask a really good friend."

"Okay."

"Yeah, like Jensen."

Wren paused. "I can't tell my client to ask Jensen."

"I know, but if this client who apparently has a wedding to go to and is pregnant, which is kind of mind-blowing since I've been hanging out with the client almost every day and the client never said anything, Jensen would be the best."

"You don't know the clien—"

"Wren, you can't lie to me," Brie said, her voice full of compassion.

The jig was up.

"It all makes sense now. The sickness, the moodiness, your weight gain."

Biting her lip, she gasped. "Are you calling me fat?"

"I'm calling you pregnant. I don't know what's going on and I'd love to know, but since we're probably going to play this little game until you're ready, just know that you should ask Jensen. He'd lay down everything to help you."

"You think so?"

"I know so."

Wren closed her eyes, her heart jackhammering in her chest. "Is he single?"

"Yes."

Wren bit her lip so hard that she tasted the metal of blood before she nodded. "Okay."

"Okay."

"Don't say anything."

"I won't."

"Thanks."

"Anytime. So, dinner tomorrow, so we can discuss how this happened?"

"Ugh, do I have to?"

"Yes, ma'am. Without wine."

"Don't remind me."

"How far along are you?"

Her face scrunched up as she muttered, "Six months…?"

"Wren!"

"I know!"

"Lord, you've waited till the last minute."

"I know."

"Goodness gracious, girl."

"I know."

Brie clucked her tongue as Wren sat there, feeling like an idiot. "Well, I look forward to our date."

"I don't."

Brie laughed, her voice so carefree and happy. And, if Wren were married to the love of her life who didn't want to kill their child, she'd be all happy and shit too.

Probably.

Maybe.

Damn it, was she seriously going to ask Jensen?

Crap.

* * *

JENSEN ROLLED his eyes as Vaughn laughed from the gut. "No, really, dude. I would look better. My dick is bigger."

"You have a shrimp dick, you cocky shit. Shut up," he shot back as he leaned back in his chair, letting the sun hit his face. They were at his favorite place, Hattie B's, on the patio and enjoying the summer air. He was ready for a summer of relaxation and his trip home before he went to his buddy Wells's wedding. It might seem like he was busy, but he wasn't. Those were the highlights of his summer. The rest of the time, he'd be lying around. Watching HBO Go. Alone. It was slightly depressing.

"You're delusional," Vaughn laughed as Brie sat down, tucking her phone in her purse. "Where'd you go?"

"Phone call." She looked a little stunned, and Brie never looked stunned. She was usually ready for anything. Except Vaughn. He kept her on her toes.

"Wren? It's weird you two are buddies. Isn't it weird?" Vaughn asked Jensen, and he shrugged.

"I don't think so."

"Neither do I. You just don't like that she tells me all your old stories from when you were a kid," Brie said.

Vaughn glared. "I do not."

Jensen crossed his legs as the couple held each other's gaze. It seemed like eons ago that the two of them were at each other's throats about everything. Now, they were just in love. With a baby on the way. Something no one ever expected from Vaughn. He had always been the playboy. They thought he'd knock some chick up, but never the one he wanted. Or loved. It was nice, seeing his boy grow up, even if Jensen was green with envy.

"Told ya."

"Whatever. What did she want?"

"Stalker."

"I am not. I just want to know."

"Well, I'm not telling you."

"Is she okay?" Jensen found himself asking, and they both looked over at him. Vaughn gave him an annoyed look, while a small smile played on Brie's lips.

"She's fine."

"Okay, cool," he said simply, even though he really wanted to ask more.

Jesus, Wren Lemiere would be the death of him.

His best friend's little sister had always had him in knots. He'd thought she was beautiful from the moment he met her. When he came into the Lemiere home so many years ago, he remembered his eyes falling right upon her. She was eleven, with dark green eyes, and dark hair that fell along her chin. She wore a tank that only went to her belly button, her little gut poking out from her jeans in almost a Winnie the Pooh sort of way. She looked up at him, a little curve to her lip that he knew would be his downfall—and it was. His whole life with the Lemieres, all she had to do was smile at him like that, and he was putty in her hands. He would do anything. Go

IN THE CREASE | 33

against his best friends to keep her safe. He cared for her. More than he should have, but he did.

But he felt like he couldn't hit on her or try to be with her when he lived with her parents. There were plenty of times when they were growing up, sharing an adjoining bathroom where it would have been way too easy to take her in his arms and press his lips to her thick ones, but he didn't. That was disrespectful in his eyes, and he respected Elaine and Winston Lemiere like no other. They took him in, and they loved him as their own. So he kept to himself, despite his need for her.

When they got older, he had started dating Ophelia, and then he married her. Like a dumbass. After that, it just didn't feel right around Wren. The timing, him, her... Instead, he was stuck pining for a girl that, in reality, he wasn't man enough to be with.

Again, depressing as hell.

Now, he just worried for her. He still spoke to Elaine weekly, and she thought something was up with Wren. Since Wren wasn't one to reach out to anyone, he wasn't sure, but she wasn't acting like her normal self. She basically only spoke to Brie, which he found odd since she had a best friend back home who was her world. Then she had him and Vaughn in Nashville with her, but she never reached out. But that was Wren. She kept him in knots—twenty-four seven. And the sad thing was, he wasn't even reaping the benefits of her.

Instead, he sat across from his two in-love friends while he stewed in his own self-pity, wallowing about being lonely.

He was pathetic.

When their number was called, Vaughn hopped up to get the order and returned in a flash, laying the scrumptious food in front of all of them, and they dug in. Jensen was halfway through his hot chicken when Vaughn pinned him with a look. "So, bro."

Jensen rolled his eyes. This was bound to be insightful.

"Yes?"

"I know you don't think we brought you to lunch for shits and giggles."

Jensen laughed. "I thought you enjoyed my company."

Brie smiled as Vaughn shrugged. "Kinda, but we have business to discuss."

"Oh Lord."

Still giggling, Brie shook her head. "We also enjoy your

company."

"Thanks, Brie."

She winked sweetly at him as Vaughn rolled his eyes. "As I was saying," he said very dramatically, and it was so Vaughn. He had been this way since they were kids. Because of that, you either hated the dude, or you loved him. Jensen was part of the latter group. He'd take a bullet for the idiot. Also for Wells, and especially Wren. "So, I need you to change days with me for the Cup."

Jensen's face scrunched up. "I'm going home with mine."

"I know, I figured, but hear me out," he said, holding his hands up, probably because Jensen's face read nothing but annoyance. They had discussed this a thousand times before picking dates. "We can both celebrate the Cup back in Colorado the week before Wells's wedding."

"Isn't that what I said from the jump?"

"He did," Brie added, and Jensen held his hand out to her.

"No comments needed from the peanut gallery." She scoffed, and Vaughn grinned back at her before holding a finger up. "Yes, but that was before I got confirmation that I can rent out the rink. Now I can, so please switch me?"

"I'll have to move my flight."

"I'll pay for it."

"And my flight to Colorado?"

"That too. Please."

Rolling his eyes, Jensen was aware they both knew he would say yes. That was what he did. "Yeah, that's fine."

Doing a fist pump, Vaughn let out a whoop. "You rock."

"And you're a three-year-old."

"He is," Brie agreed, to which Vaughn bit her exposed shoulder. Crying out, she smacked him as she laughed. "Stop."

"You like it," he challenged, and Brie grinned.

"I do."

"Get a room."

When Vaughn beamed back at him, Jensen almost regretted the words. "On to my next thing."

"Jesus."

Brie snickered as Vaughn went on. "I know this is going to be hard. Like, really hard on you. But, buddy, I'm sorry to say, we bought a house."

Jensen just stared back at him. "Okay? Why is this hard?"

"Because you're not moving with us."

He rolled his eyes. "Jo, we haven't lived together for six months since you moved in with Brie."

"I know, but we were across the hall."

Jensen laughed. "I'll be fine without you guys—"

"Now, I know this comes as a shock, but we're having a baby, and we need space for us and the baby."

"I know—"

"Now, Jenny, I know this is going to be difficult, putting space between us—"

"You know we lived apart for years, right?"

But Vaughn went on. "Just know I will always and forever love you as my brother, and nothing will change. Not the space, the new ball and chain, or the baby."

"Are you done?"

Brie apparently thought this was hilarious since she was basically choking she was laughing so hard. Which wasn't anything new. Vaughn might be an idiot, but he was a funny one. As always, Vaughn was unaffected as he said, "We'll never be done, Jenny, never."

"Okay," Jensen said, rolling his eyes again. "Listen, this is awesome. I'm happy for you guys, and let me know when we need to start moving stuff."

"You're such a good man," Vaughn proclaimed before clapping his hands together. "This weekend good for you?"

Laughing, he just shook his head at Vaughn's antics. "Yeah, man."

"Thanks, Jensen."

He smiled over at Brie. "Anytime."

Rolling his eyes, he went back to eating as a grin played on his lips. He wanted nothing more than for his friend to grow and be in love. Brie was that for Vaughn. They were moving and having a kid, and it was great. Vaughn needed that. So did Wells, who was getting married the following month. Both his best friends were living life, happily and to its fullest. Meanwhile, Jensen was stuck.

He didn't know how it happened, or even why, but it had. He wasn't interested in anyone he met, and he didn't just want to fuck around. He wanted someone to love him for him. The quiet, weird guy in the corner. The one who would lay down his life for anyone he loved. He had redeemable qualities, but for some reason, no one wanted them. They just wanted to have sex.

He didn't want Netflix and chill; he wanted Netflix and breakfast, lunch, dinner, snacks, and more.

Hmm, he should copyright that.

Taking a huge bite of his chicken, he felt his phone start to vibrate. He pulled it out, seeing that it was a text from Wren, as he chewed. Like always when she texted him, his heart sped up, and his palms went clammy as a lump formed in his throat. Or maybe that was the chicken, he wasn't sure. Either way, he slid the notification over so that his text thread with her opened up before he read her message.

*Wren: Are you free anytime this week?*

His brows pulled in. This had never happened before. The girl was seriously radio silent unless you were in her face or you texted her first.

*Jensen: For you, always. What's up?*

*Wren: I need to ask a favor. But I want to discuss it in person.*

*Jensen: Just let me know when.*

*Wren: What if it's a lot to ask?*

*Jensen: Let me be the judge of that.*

*Wren: Okay, tomorrow? Lunch at the Southern?*

*Jensen: 12?*

*Wren: Perfect. It's a date.*

A date. No. Wait. It was right there. The word. And then she sent a kissy face emoji.

Holy shit, he was going on a date with Wren.

Was he overthinking this?

No. She said it.

But, wait.

Crap, he was reading into this. She was being playful.

But Wren wasn't playful.

Shit.

"Why do you look like you just shit your pants?"

Looking up to his best friend, Jensen just stared at Vaughn. "I think I just did."

# Chapter THREE

*Vaughn: You told Brie.*

*Wren: Yes.*

*Vaughn: Why do you get to tell her, but I had to keep it a secret for the last million years?*

*Wren: Okay, dramatic Dallas, it's been six months, relax, and it's my place to tell, not yours.*

*Vaughn: But I've had to lie. To everyone, mind you. Mom, Dad, Wells, Jensen, Brie, all for you.*

*Wren: And it didn't kill you. Btw, I love you for it. Thank you. You're the best other brother ever.*

*Vaughn: Don't suck up to me.*

*Wren: LOL, but, wait, when did she tell you?*

*Vaughn: Today. She came home and told me because that's what couples do. They talk a lot and have sex, lots of sex.*

*Wren: I hate you so much right now, but what did you say?*

*Vaughn: Ooh, that's cool.*

*Vaughn: What was I supposed to say?!*

*Wren: That you already knew? Now you look like a liar when this comes out.*

*Vaughn: I know! That's what I'm saying!*

*Wren: Sucks to be you.*

*Vaughn: I hate you.*

*Vaughn: And you're not hiring a male gigolo.*

*Wren: I think the proper title is male escort.*

*Vaughn: Either way, you're not bringing a whore to our brother's wedding.*

*Wren: Dream ruiner.*

*Vaughn: Crybaby. Suck it up and tell everyone the truth. Then get me the name of the fucker so I can kill him.*

*Wren: He doesn't matter, and I hate you.*

*Vaughn: Back at you, and you're taking the blame if Brie gets pissed.*

*Wren: What else is new? Send it my way.*

*Vaughn: Good talk. Love you.*

*Wren: Yeah, yeah.*

Rolling her eyes, she set her phone down as she looked around The Southern restaurant. It was busy, like always, but the food was to die for. So were the cocktails, but yeah…that was a depressing thought. Before Vaughn had texted to bitch at her, Jensen had said he was running late, which was fine. It gave her time to prepare. It was a little bit of a feat for her to prepare to tell her friend that she needed him to lie to his family and hers by claiming to be the father of her child and her husband. She should have given herself more time. But she really didn't have it.

Wells's wedding was coming up fast.

When her phone started to sing "Hello" by who Wells confirmed was the queen of all music, she chuckled. Her brother had some crazy radar when it came to her thinking of him. "Brother."

"Sister. We have beef."

"Filet mignon or porterhouse?"

"Tube," he deadpanned, and she snorted. "Mom said you aren't coming up the week before the wedding. The boys are bringing the Cup. You have to be here."

She pinched the bridge of her nose. "I said I wasn't sure."

"Well, be sure. Blow off work and come."

"I'm in charge of over thirty-five players' mental health, I can't blow them off."

"Half of them have gone home, and the other half can be on call."

"Wells."

"Wren. Really. I need my sister through this."

"Through what? You want this!"

"I know, but I want you there."

"I'll try. Let me work on some things."

"Thank you."

"You're annoying. Like Mom."

"Bet you won't say it to her face."

She gasped. "Never."

"Thought so. What are you doing? Working?" he teased and she smiled. Her brother was probably the most amazing person on the planet. He was beyond funny, the realest guy ever, and captivating. She loved him so much. She always turned to him for advice, and it was killing her to lie to him, but she wouldn't put that on him. He had enough to worry about: his wedding, being one of the only openly gay players in the league, and all the other stuff that came with that. So Wren had kept the last six months to herself—well, except for Vaughn. She told him, but it wasn't like she'd reached out to him.

No, it was her. Alone. Doing it all, and she was fine with that. She was strong.

"Actually, I'm meeting Jensen for lunch."

"Ooh, for what?"

"That is none of your business, my dear brother."

"Finally gonna tell him you think he's hot and you wouldn't mind hitting it?"

"Shut it."

"You two would make hot kids."

Well, let's hope that Bradley made them too. Fucker.

"Wells, be real."

"Everyone knows you two dig each other."

"No, they don't! I don't even know that, and you don't—shut up," she sputtered because, while her brother always teased her about it, she didn't believe it. If Jensen was feeling her, why didn't he ever try anything? She'd flirted with him relentlessly after his divorce, but he never flirted back. He'd been tight-lipped, and that had been the perfect time to have a roll in the hay for fun. He probably thought she was too fat to be a trophy wife too.

Fucking douche. God, she hated Bradley.

"Ha-ha, you know nothing, Wren Lemiere."

"Ugh, you sound like Brie and Vaughn. Always with the *Game of Thrones* references."

He chuckled. "Stop hating, and binge-watch."

"No, I refuse."

"You suck."

"So do you."

"Always," he teased, and she snickered. "So, I'll see you in a couple weeks."

"Don't get your mind set—"

"See you in a couple weeks! Toodle-oo!"

The line went dead, and she swore her eyes were going to get lost in her head. That guy was an idiot. Toodle-oo? What the hell? Laying her phone down, she reached for her water since she had dry mouth like a desert, just in time to catch a glimpse of Jensen coming through the door.

Crap, she wasn't ready!

But it didn't matter because when he saw her, his face lit up as he pointed to her from the hostess stand before coming toward her. God, he was majestic. So damn big, unlike the stocky thirteen-year-old she remembered. He had grown over thirteen inches his freshman year; she remembered that because her mom was worried his skin would snap, he was growing so fast. His shoulders were massive and thick through the tank he wore. She knew from seeing him at the pool that he was ripped like no other, but it was his eyes that always got her. He had the darkest set of brown eyes she had ever seen. They were like two pools of deep, dark chocolate that always seemed to be a shade darker when he looked at her. His face had hard angles, his nose was broad, and his jaw was covered with dense, coarse hair—and those lips. Thick and scrumptious.

Yeah, she had a thing for Jensen Monroe, and she was pretty sure she was in a whole lot of trouble asking for him to pose as her husband.

But she had no choice.

Reaching the table, he had a smile pulling at his lips as he leaned over and kissed her cheek. Closing her eyes, she inhaled sharply, his musky scent tantalizing her core. "Hey."

"Hey," he muttered as he moved back, sitting down across from her. "Good to see you."

"You too."

"It's been a while. I didn't even see you at the Assassins' Cup party."

"Yeah, I was busy."

"Oh, that sucks."

"Yeah, Elli was not happy with me, but I've been under the weather lately."

His brow furrowed in concern. "You're okay?"

He reached for his water as she nodded. "Yeah, fine. Now. Thanks."

She giggled nervously as the waitress came up to take their drink orders. "Water is fine."

"Me too," he said with a grin that, of course, the waitress swooned at. Who wouldn't? He looked like an underwear model.

And Wren didn't miss the way the girl looked back at her, like, "Wow, you're with him?" Some would be offended, but having grown up with three very good-looking brothers, she was used to it.

After ordering her food, Wren leaned on her elbows. "I'm starving. Sorry to make you rush."

"No, it's fine. I love this place, and I always get the same thing."

"Don't like change?"

He shrugged. "Why mess up a good thing when you got it?"

"Touché, Monroe." He sent her a grin, and she smiled back sweetly. "So, what's up?"

"Nothing, just Cup stuff."

"Which is awesome."

He smiled shyly. "It's a lot."

"I hear you're all over the place."

"I am. Lots of interviews. We went to the White House, which was cool."

"I saw that on Facebook. So amazing."

"Yeah, I can't wait to take the Cup home."

"I bet."

He nodded before shrugging. "Other than that, I'm boring."

"So am I. It's okay."

"Boring people have more fun."

"Totally agree."

"But our friends are not boring. Did you hear Brie and Vaughn are moving?"

"Yup."

"Apparently, I was supposed to be torn up about it."

"Of course you were." He laughed and she chuckled. Vaughn was so dramatic. "But I'm guessing not."

"Not having to listen to those two go at it? No, I'll be good."

"You can hear them?"

"Yes, they are so loud. It's obnoxious."

"That is hilarious."

"Says you, the person that doesn't have to hear, 'Call me The Legend!'"

She laughed so hard she almost spat out her water. "No! You're lying."

"Ask Brie. It's pathetic. His ego is beyond words."

"He's your best friend."

"I know. I love the fucker." They shared a small laugh as he leaned on his elbows, taking a swig of his water. This was them. They were easy, which was why he would be perfect for this. "So, what's up with you?"

She swallowed hard, not ready to ask. "Like I said, boring as hell over here."

He scoffed as their food was brought out. "That was quick."

"Yeah, y'all came in at the perfect time. It's the start of my shift," the waitress said with another flirty smile.

"Awesome, perks to being late," Wren said, and Jensen laughed a little as he reached for his fork.

"I was actually watching *Game of Thrones* and lost track of time. Which is totally unlike me."

She groaned loudly. "Jenny! Come on! We were the last to get on the *GOT* train."

"I know, fucking Vaughn and Brie."

"Assholes."

"I hate them."

"All of them."

They shared a comfortable smile before digging in. The food was perfection as always and hit all the right spots. Kiddo was a happy camper, which meant so was Wren. When Jensen pointed his knife to her, she looked up, surprised. "Am I in trouble?"

He laughed. "No, but Wells said you might miss our Cup day back home."

"Between him and my mom, I'm going to scream. Everything is so up in the air."

"But it's his wedding and our Cup day, you have to be there."

She exhaled loudly. "I know."

"So you will."

"I probably will. I gotta figure some things out."

"Like what?"

She swallowed hard before running her tongue along her teeth, cleaning out a piece of kale.

That was hot.

Looking up at him, she felt her heart in her throat as her mouth went dry. Man, he was pretty, but besides that, things were good between them. It wasn't like with Vaughn. He was an idiot, but he was her idiot, and he wouldn't care one way or another when it ended. She would for sure never fall for the guy, but it was way different with Jensen. He had a soft soul. A sweet heart. He was a good guy, and she could fall. But she sure as hell didn't want to burden him with something that would hurt him in the end.

But it was either ask him or hire a gigolo.

Damn Vaughn.

"Um, stuff."

He laughed. "Wren, it's me. Come on."

"Actually, that's why I asked you here."

He drew his brows in. "Oh, so not because I'm awesome company? I'm starting to think I suck."

He laughed and she smiled. "You're amazing company, you are, but I need to talk to you about something. Or better yet, ask you for basically the hugest favor ever."

He looked a little defeated in a way, but it was gone before he shrugged. "Shoot."

She bit her lips as she nervously played with her hands. How was she going to say this?

"Wren, stop fiddling with your hands, and talk to me. You're making me uneasy."

She laughed anxiously. "Well, Jensen..."

"Yeah, Wren?"

She looked up, meeting his sweet gaze, and then in a burst of word vomit, she said, "See, the thing is, I kind of need you to marry me and act like the father of the kid I'm pregnant with so I can get my inheritance. And I swear, you'll be off the hook in like four months. I just gotta have the kid, and then you can run. I'll pay you, and we can act like it never happened. You don't have to even kiss me, maybe like a smooch on the cheek here and there so my mom and dad think we're in love. And I'll take all the blame when we end it. I'll say I cheated like a dumb whore or something, and they'll believe it. The thing is, you have to lie, and I know that really isn't your style, but yeah, please?"

When his jaw dropped, she snapped her mouth shut as his eyes bored into hers.

Well, that was one way of asking him.

\* \* \*

"I'M SORRY, WHAT?"

Jensen's heart stopped. He was pretty sure somewhere in the rambling mess his best friend's sister had just muttered, she'd said she was pregnant. But maybe he'd heard her wrong. Because Wren, pregnant?

What?

No.

"Which part didn't you get?" she asked slowly, and when her eyes started to cloud with tears, he was out of his seat instantly, coming to her side. Bending down to his knees, he looked up at her. Thank God the place was clearing out. "No, you can stay in your seat," she tried, but he ignored her, taking her hands in his.

"From the beginning. Not the rambling. Tell me what's going on."

Her bottom lip trembled as she looked down at the table. "I'm pregnant."

It was as if he had been slammed in the chest. With the biggest hammer. Like, a Thor hammer. Yeah, that was big enough to cause the devastating ache that burned in his chest. Biting his lip, he nodded his head. "Okay. How far along?"

Her face scrunched up as she swallowed hard. "Six months."

His jaw dropped for the second time in the past five minutes. "Six months."

"Yeah." She tried to look at him, but it was only for a second before she looked away. "I know, it's bad."

"By whom?"

"It doesn't matter. He's scum."

"Okay, no one knows, I assume."

"No one," she said, swallowing hard. "Well, Brie and Vaughn. But Brie just found out like last night."

He blinked, looking down at where he was holding her hands. They were so small in his own hands, but what killed him was he hadn't even noticed. He'd seen this girl plenty of times recently, and he'd never noticed she was with child. How? How did that happen? And why was she hiding it? "Jenny, can you go to your seat? People are staring, and all I want to do is hug you, which would probably make me cry because I'm an emotional mess."

Ignoring her wish, he stood, pulling her out of her chair and into his arms. She went more willingly than he expected before she wrapped her arms around his ribs, her head digging into his chest. Leaning his chin on top of her head, he closed his eyes as he held her tight. He wasn't sure how this had happened—well, he knew how it happened—but it wasn't like Wren. Of course, she fooled around, everyone knew that. But she wasn't the type to get pregnant. He was pretty sure when they had all talked about one day having kids, she had been the one who said she didn't want any.

So he was a little confused and a lot pissed at whoever the douche was who'd knocked her up. Where was he? Why wasn't he with her, being the father, or hell, her husband. Because if Jensen had knocked her up, he'd be right there, right beside her.

But that would never happen, he guessed.

Pulling away, she looked up at him with those beautiful green eyes and smiled. "I'm okay."

"You sure? I've got all the time in the world."

She smiled before patting his chest. "You don't know how much I needed just that. Really. Sit down."

He squeezed her biceps before going back to his chair, sitting down and running his hands down his face before looking over at her. "So, where is the guy?"

She shook her head curtly, her eyes blazing with fire. "He isn't involved."

"Why?"

"He didn't want it. Told me to get an abortion."

His veins caught on fire. "Excuse me?"

"Exactly. He's a fucker, so fuck him."

"Who is it? Do I know him?"

"No."

"Well, let me know him, so I can kill him."

"No. I don't want to bring him up. He isn't a part of my kid's life, he is dead to me and my child. In my eyes, my child doesn't have a father."

His blood was boiling. "That's not right, Wren. He needs to own up to his fucking responsibilities."

"No, he's a douche. Fuck him, I'm fine without him. Well, not really, because obviously, I'm here asking you to marry me and act like the father."

He didn't like that, not one bit, but before he could tell her that, her last sentence hit him full force, and he muttered, "Oh, so you did say that."

She nodded sullenly. "Yes, and I know it's a lot to ask. We'll have to lie to everyone, tell them that we had a one-night stand back in like December. That we both decided it was just a silly night, thought nothing of it, but then I popped up pregnant and didn't tell you until now."

Again with the Thor hammer in his chest. Gasping, he took in a needed breath. "You've thought this out."

"Yeah, well, I had this plan with Vaughn, but he was in love with Brie, and it didn't work out."

He glanced up at her, his eyes narrowing a bit. "You asked Vaughn?"

He loved his best friend. He did, but man, why would she ask him first?

She must not have noticed the annoyance in his eyes because she waved him off. "Yeah, he would be easy, and everyone would believe that he slept with me. It's Vaughn. Plus, he would lie and have no cares in the world about doing it, you know? But you're a good dude, and you love my parents. I know it will be hard for you to lie to them, and it's unlike you to sleep with people without wanting something more."

Oh. Well, that made sense. She was right, it would be something Vaughn would do. "Yeah, I mean, it makes sense. But will they believe that we did this?"

She chewed on her lip as she shrugged. "I think if we sell it, yeah, which is why I have no issue paying you for your time and your effort. I think five million would be good, right? Is that okay?"

He shook his head. "I don't want your money, Wren." Looking down at the table, he inhaled. "So it's because of your inheritance, right? That you need me to do this?"

"I have to be married if I'm pregnant. The baby is due in September, and I turn thirty in October. There is no way I can hide this. I mean, I'm huge."

He looked over at her. "No, you're not."

She smiled sheepishly before standing up and pulling her shirt back against her stomach so it clung to her extended abdomen. That fucking hammer hit him again as he drank her in. There were moments when they were younger when Jensen thought about putting his own child in her. Watching her belly grow, but he never got that.

And he never would.

"I am," she laughed, letting her shirt go before she sat down, brushing her long, dark hair off her shoulders. "And because of that, I need to be married."

Still breathless, he nodded. "But won't Winston and Elaine be pissed you got married without them knowing?"

She nodded. "They're gonna be pissed about a lot of things, but at least I'll be married and to the 'father' of my child."

Looking down once more, he tried to collect his thoughts, but it wasn't fucking working. This was too much all at once, and he almost couldn't believe it was happening. "Wells will kill me."

"I won't let that happen." He looked up to meet her gaze, and she shrugged. "I know it's a lot to ask, and I'm sorry, really I am. But Vaughn told me I can't hire a male escort, and I'd rather it be someone who knows my family, knows me, because it will be easier. I'm comfortable with you, and we can act like we're desperately in love."

He wouldn't have to act.

But he didn't miss that she felt she would. Swallowing hard, he held her gaze as he asked, "And we'll end it once the baby comes?" When she went to answer, he held up his hand to stop her. "Do you know what it is?"

She nodded, a little grin pulling at her lips. "A boy."

He closed his eyes, looking down as he drew in a breath, his heart aching in his chest.

Yeah, this was way too fucking much to take.

"But to answer your question, yes, maybe we'll end it like a week or two after. I don't know. We can discuss the timeline in more depth later. But don't worry, we wouldn't have to live together unless, for some reason, my family decides to pop in. We can pick a place, maybe put some things in one of our apartments to make it look like we live together there. And I'll take all the blame, I'll ruin us, but I just want to make sure that no matter what we stay friends because I'll basically owe you everything. It's mainly when we go home to Colorado that we have to look like we are truly in love, and then when the baby comes, 'cause I'm sure my mom will be here, and wow, I'm rambling again." He swallowed hard once more as he nodded, taking in everything she was saying. "No one will hate you, though. I'll take all the blame. I just need you to marry me and be my kid's father for five months, tops."

"Will we really get married?"

"Yeah, 'cause I have a feeling my dad will check."

"And we'll get divorced?"

When he looked up, her eyes were wide. "Maybe not divorced but annulled. I think we'll be in the right time frame. You wouldn't have to be divorced twice. I thought about that. I know you don't want that."

Looking away, he wrung his fingers together and thought about it for a moment. He had loved Wren almost his whole life. He had seen himself with her more times than he could count. This was his chance. He would be hers, and she would be his, but it would be a sham. All a fake love kind of thing. He would do anything for her. Anything. But could he do this to himself? It was essentially setting himself up for heartache and pain. Because watching her leave would be his downfall, and he wouldn't be able to stay friends with her. Even if she claimed it would only be a week or two of them being "in love" as she kept saying.

It would break him.

More so than when Ophelia left him.

Looking up, he ran his hands along his face and took in a deep breath before meeting her gaze. "When do you need to know?"

Her mouth parted. "What?"

"When do you need an answer?"

Her eyes widened as she shrugged. "As soon as possible since the wedding is in a month."

He nodded before getting up and pulling his wallet out. Throwing a hundred on the table, he went to her, kissing her cheek. Lingering longer than he should, he whispered, "I'll be in touch."

Pulling away, he turned and headed out because if he didn't, he'd say yes to her terms.

He'd be damned if he was going to set himself up for failure.

He'd done it once.

And he wouldn't do it a second time.

# Chapter FOUR

"*I'm pregnant, Jensen.*"

*His brows came in. Confusion racked his body as he stared into his wife's dark brown eyes. "But...really?"*

*Her eyes filled with tears, though not happy ones as she slowly shook her head. "But, it isn't yours."*

Sitting in his car, Jensen looked around the parking lot of his apartment complex and wasn't sure how he'd gotten there. He was thinking too hard. Why he was thinking of the end of his marriage would forever plague him. He didn't do that anymore. He hadn't in a really long time. Ophelia didn't want him, couldn't be with him, and that was fine. He forgave her, but sitting across from Wren, hearing everything she was saying, it all came back. With a vengeance.

Wren was pregnant.

And she wanted him to pose as the father and her husband.

Pinching the bridge of his nose, he was completely surprised he hadn't screamed yes at her. It was his chance. She would be his. But he knew it would end. Much faster than it began, and he might lose his family in the process. Winston and Elaine Lemiere were fiercely protective of their children, including him, but something like this, knocking up their daughter and then marrying her behind their backs, that would throw one hell of a wrench into their relationship.

And then there was Wells.

Fuck. Wells might kill him. He would usually be the one Jensen would call to talk something like this out. When Ophelia had told him she was pregnant by a guy at her work, Wells was the first one Jensen called. He loved Vaughn, he did, but until recently, Vaughn didn't do love and relationships. Plus, Wells and Jensen just had a different kind of friendship. Jensen was the one Wells came out to when they were sixteen. Wells told Vaughn the following day, but Jensen knew first. They trusted each other, they loved each other like brothers, but this… This could ruin all of that.

But he couldn't leave Wren hanging. Wouldn't Wells want Jensen to help her? He understood the whole inheritance thing. It was dumb, and her grandfather was an idiot in his opinion, but it was what it was. With Wells giving up his portion since he decided to "stay gay," as his father put it, Wren felt she had to get all of the money for both of them. Jensen would do the same thing in her position, but could he do this? Could he lie to the faces of the people he loved as much as he loved his own parents?

It was for the girl he had always loved.

Though, he couldn't forget—she didn't love him.

She just wanted a quick fix. Marry him, make him the "father," and then ship him off at the end. Not only did he hate the way she was thinking, but he also didn't like that she wanted to take all the blame. He would be the victim again, and man, what an ordeal it had been back then. Everyone all up in his business, trying to make sure that he was okay. It was suffocating. Plus, what if Winston and Elaine felt bad and stopped talking to him?

And what about the baby?

Would he be considered a deadbeat dad?

Fuck.

Throwing his door open, he got out, keeping himself from reaching for his phone and calling Wells. He wanted to, so badly, but he wouldn't do that to Wren. Heading into his condo building, he chose the stairs to burn off some of the crazy that was making his brain hurt. It didn't work, though. All it did was burn his legs, and when he reached Brie and Vaughn's condo, he prayed she hadn't cleaned out the fridge yet.

Knocking on the door, he could only hear Tricksie, their dog, going crazy, but no sign of them.

"Hey, buttface, we're over here."

Turning, he found Vaughn in the doorway of his condo. "What are you doing?"

"Packing," he said simply, pointing to the box. "How'd your *date* go?"

"Don't," was all Jensen said as he went by Vaughn and to his fridge, reaching for a beer. Pinning Vaughn with a look, he said, "So you knew?"

Vaughn's brow lifted. "Knew what?"

"That Wren is pregnant."

Vaughn's mouth snapped closed as Brie said, "Yeah, she told me last night."

Jensen pointed to Vaughn, his eyes on Brie. "She told him like six months ago."

"What?" Brie asked, looking at Vaughn. He just shrugged, looking every bit like a kid caught with his hand in the cookie jar. "I thought you didn't know."

He cleared his throat. "No, I did."

"And you didn't tell me?"

"I couldn't."

"Or me," Jensen added.

Vaughn threw his hands up. "I couldn't. She made me swear."

"Why'd she tell you?" Brie asked, leaning on the bar as Jensen did the same, wondering what his best friend would tell his fiancée.

"Um, well, she wanted me to marry her and act like the father."

Oh, Vaughn went with the truth. His buddy was growing up. "Really? But we were together."

"I know," he said quickly, holding his hands up. "Thanks, jack-ass," he spat at Jensen before going over to his soon-to-be bride. "She was going to pay off me and you. But I said no, because I only love you and wouldn't hurt you like that."

Her eyebrow quirked. "Pay you? How much?"

"Why does that matter?"

"Because if it's a lot, then take it."

"Brie!"

She snickered, her eyes bright. "I'm kidding."

Vaughn rolled his eyes while Jensen let out a long breath. "So, now, she's asked me."

They both looked over at him. Vaughn shook his head. "I told her not to."

"Why!" Jensen and Brie said at the same time.

Holding his hands out like it was obvious, he said, "Because, duh, I knew what she wanted. She doesn't want forever, dude. She wants a quick four months, tops. Then you divorce, and we all know how you are about that. Next thing you know, we find Jenny on the ground, drowning in a pool of his own tears, and I'm standing above him, unsure what to do because I don't do man tears, and yeah, no. I told her no. For you."

Rolling his eyes, Jensen glanced at Brie. "You're marrying and having a kid with this fool?"

"He's really great in bed."

Vaughn glared. "You know it's true!"

"I'm a big boy. I can take care of myself," Jensen added dryly, but Vaughn shook his head.

"With anyone else, yeah, I totally agree with you, but this is Wren. Wren Josephine Lemiere. You know I know how you feel about her. How you've loved her since the moment she told you something about hammering something or some stupid shit like that—"

"Hammering something?" Brie asked, and Jensen nodded.

"It's a really great story—"

"It's wack and dumb."

"It is not," Jensen snapped, shaking his head. "It's a great story!"

"Well, out with it, then," Brie said before Vaughn could complain more.

Jensen smiled. "We were working on some houses for Nate-Way1, and she comes over in these short as sin shorts and an even tighter shirt." His lips pursed as he could see her vividly at that moment. "She was stunning, beautiful, and, of course, I was already crushing hard on her."

"He's crushed on her since we were kids."

"I have," Jensen agreed. Though, Brie was just grinning, enraptured by the story. "She was standing there, just looking pretty on her phone, and I asked her to hand me a hammer. She looked at me with this grin and said, 'So you can bang the hell out of that nail?' and I'm like, 'Yeah, that's what you do.'" When Vaughn rolled his eyes, Jensen glared, but he couldn't help the chuckle that left his lips. "She laughed and laughed, and then goes, 'I was trying to be suggestive, Jenny, come on.' She walked away like it was nothing, but I swear I fell in love with her at that moment."

Brie blinked. "Because she made a joke about a nail?"

Two peas in a pod, Vaughn and Brie were, but before Jensen could reiterate how much Wren meant to him, Vaughn said, "Don't listen to him, he's a weirdo. But know he loves the chick, and she is going to break him if he does this. Like, in two. For real, bro. Don't do it."

Jensen set him with a look. "Like you said, it's Wren. I can't not do it. She needs my help."

"Let her tell the damn truth!"

"You know how much that inherence means to them. They were spending that money even when they didn't have it. They need it. Both of them."

"That's her own damn fault."

"Vaughn." Vaughn looked up as Jensen glared. "They both gave you a lot of money when that whore took all of yours. That was on credit cards, I know that for a fact."

"That's not fair."

"And you never paid them back."

"They told me I didn't have to!"

"Because they knew this money was coming," Jensen said simply. "I can't not help, but I sure as hell don't like how she wants to end it."

"That's what I'm saying, dude. She's gonna break you."

Biting his lip, Jensen stared down at the counter, trying to think it through. "What if I came up with my own terms?"

"What terms?"

"I don't know," he said simply, shaking his head. "But some-thing…something so I don't get hurt."

"You gonna tell her you love her? Because unless she says it back, you're gonna get hurt."

"Shut up," Jensen said, waving him off before he started to look for a pen and paper. "What if I did it for the chance that she would, though?" he said once he found a pen. Looking up, he met Vaughn's worried gaze. Brie stood beside him, her face twisted with her own concern.

"What if that backfires? What if she says she's trying, but she doesn't?" she asked slowly. "We all know how Wren feels about rela-tionships."

Swallowing hard, he nodded as he found some paper. "But what if I can change the way she thinks?"

"Jensen, come on. That's insane. It's Wren. You're walking into a clusterfuck, dude. This could be so bad," Vaughn tried, but Jensen was shaking his head.

"Or it could be so good."

"So you're gonna play daddy to some douche's kid?"

Holding the paper and pen in his hand, Jensen met his best friend's gaze, tears clouding his eyes as he nodded slowly. "What if this is the only chance I get?"

Vaughn's shoulders dropped. "Jenny. Come on."

But Jensen shook his head, heading toward his room and shutting his door.

He understood Vaughn's apprehension, hell, he had some of his own, but he knew from the moment Wren had asked for his help, he was going to help her.

He just wanted it on his terms.

* * *

STARING down at the sheet of notebook paper that had his terms listed, Jensen felt his heart in his throat. That was, until Tricksie licked half his face off before scooting beneath him to look down at the paper too. As she inhaled very dramatically, taking after her father, he smiled.

"I'm with you, girl," he muttered as she leaned her head up, licking his jaw.

Tricksie was as annoying as her father, but like he did with Vaughn, Jensen thought the world of her. She was a good girl, and he'd probably miss her more than he missed Vaughn when they moved. He wasn't sure how he got stuck watching her while they ran some things over to the new house, but he didn't mind. She was nice company.

"What should I do, Tricksie?" She whimpered up at him, cuddling against his chest. "Yeah, I don't know either."

As he stared down at each bullet point, he knew Wren wouldn't like it. As Vaughn had said, she might even agree just to get through it, but might never intend on sticking to their agreement. She wouldn't screw him, but she wouldn't even try to entertain his terms. She was a hard sell, Wren was. She had been hurt a billion times by assholes who only wanted sex. She had never in her life been loved right by a man. She always fooled with the guys who wanted to hide her since she was a little heavier or who just plain wanted to fuck her. No matter how many times everyone told her she was attracted to douches, she still went after them.

And got her heart broken.

He knew this, and he knew going into this wouldn't be easy, but he had no choice.

He had to help her.

When his phone sounded, he looked down to see that it was his mom. His lips curved as he answered, "Hey, Mum."

"*Mon chou*, how are you?"

Usually, if he couldn't get ahold of Wells, he'd call his mom for help. But even he couldn't ask her for help on this. She would lose her mind and probably call Elaine. "I've been better."

"What? What do you mean? You just won the Cup, you're coming home in a couple weeks, and we're having a big party. You should be happy."

"I mean, I am, but I'm in a predicament."

He could basically hear the gears in her head turning. "What do you mean?"

"I can't really talk about it, Mum. I'm sorry."

"Are you okay?"

"I'm fine."

"Are Vaughn and Wells okay?"

"They are," he answered with a smile. They were as much her kids as he was. "I'll figure it out."

"I can help."

"I know," he said softly, running his hands along Tricksie's dark fur. "I gotta do it on my own, though."

"Okay. Well, like I always say, follow your heart, okay?"

He nodded, pressing his nose into Tricksie's head. His heart said to do it, not to look back and just to help her. But his brain was begging him to make sure he protected that crazy thing that was his fragile heart. His heart had a habit of making him look like a dumbass. "Okay, Mum."

"Good, now the reason I'm calling," she said, clearing her throat. "You're sure Wells isn't upset we can't come to the wedding?"

Jensen laughed. "Yes, Mum, everyone knows Dad isn't up to travel. It's fine."

"I'll send him lots of money."

"He'll love that."

"And some glitter. Elaine said he wants doves with glitter or something."

"Of course he does," Jensen said, shaking his head. His best friend was very eccentric and awesome, and shit, what if Wells hated him because of all this? "It's fine, I promise."

"Okay, good. Are you sure I can't help?"

"Yes, Mum. Thank you."

"Sure?"

"Yes," he laughed, and she chuckled softly. Man, he missed her.

"Fine, well, I'll let you go, but call me if you need me."

"I always will."

"Good, I can't wait to squeeze you!"

"Me either, Mum," he laughed as they said bye, and he hung up. Throwing his phone onto the bed, he looked down once more at his notepad and exhaled loudly.

"Follow my heart," he said aloud, which made Tricksie look up at him with her big brown eyes. "My heart leads to her."

And he wasn't sure if that was a good thing or not.

* * *

THE FOLLOWING DAY, Wren leaned back in the plush chair as Brie set her with a look. Wren had somehow gotten wrangled into coffee, which she felt was a bit annoying. Brie was relentless when it came to getting information, but apparently, after their dinner, there was still more info to get. In Wren's mind, though, Bradley didn't exist, and the baby was given to her by the stork.

"The stork did not impregnate you." Brie glared as she leaned back in her own chair, not showing a bit but still wearing a shirt that claimed "Don't eat watermelon seeds. This happens." with an arrow pointing to nothing but her vagina, but Wren wasn't going to be the one to point that out. "Tell me the truth."

"You don't know him," Wren said, frustrated since they had been on this subject for probably seven hours. "He doesn't matter."

"Was he a boyfriend?"

"No."

"A friend?"

"Kinda."

"And he didn't want it?"

"No, told me to get an abortion, tried to pay for it, and said if I keep it, he'll deny it's his."

"What a fucking fucker. I'll kick him in the taco because there is no way he has a dick. Asshole."

Wren laughed. "You're insane. You'll never know him."

"Thank God." Brie shot her a serious look. "And he better thank his lucky stars you aren't telling anyone who it is because the boys would kill him dead."

"Oh, I know. He doesn't deserve to get his ass kicked by them. They're men, he's scum."

"Agreed."

"He hasn't even reached out, nothing."

Brie rolled her eyes, shaking her head. "Such shit."

"Yeah, but whatever. I'm good. We'll be fine."

Brie smiled, sitting up as she looked across the table, leaning down over her little cup of tea. "So, it's a boy?"

Wren's lips curved as she nodded. "Yeah."

"Have you thought of a name?"

She shook her head. "I just call him kiddo."

Brie beamed. "That's nice."

"Yeah, but I might need to come up with something better. Kiddo Lemiere doesn't really have a ring to it."

"This is true."

They shared as laugh before both sipping on their tea. Licking her lips, Wren glanced over at Brie. "I asked him. Jensen."

Brie nodded. "I know."

Her lips parted a bit because she hadn't expected him to tell them that she had spoken with him. But then, Vaughn was his best friend. Before she could ask what was said, Rodney, Brie's brother, came to the table. "I need twenty dollars."

Brie's face twisted in confusion. "I just gave you twenty."

"I know, but I need more. I want to buy something for Phyllis."

"Rod, you've bought enough stuff for her."

"Brie, please," he whined, and like Wren knew she would, Brie pulled out a twenty and gave it to him. "You rock, thanks!" Before he turned, though, he glanced to Wren. "Are you getting fat?"

"Rodney!" Brie exclaimed.

"What? She is!"

Wren laughed. "I'm having a baby, Rod."

"Oh, cool. Brie's having a baby too. She's gonna get fat."

"Thanks, brother."

"But you look super pretty today."

"Thanks, Rod," Wren laughed as he trotted away, and when she looked to Brie, she was beet red. "He's like a Sour Patch Kid sometimes, huh?"

"Seems that way," Brie said, shaking her head. "I'm so sorry."

Wren waved her off. "It's fine. How's he sleeping?"

"So much better since you recommended that new drug," Brie said, an expression of relief covering her face. "He wasn't doing well for a minute there."

"With Down syndrome, it's tough. You can't tell what's the Down syndrome and what's anxiety. Plus, I think he has a little more anxiety than what he's letting the doctor in on too."

"I do too," Brie agreed, leaning on her hands as she watched her brother buy mounds and mounds of candy. "But he's doing so much better now. They're saying we might be able to travel, so I think before the season starts, we're gonna take him to Harry Potter World."

Wren beamed. "He'll love that."

"I know. All three of us running around with cloaks and wands. I already told Vaughn he's wearing one."

Wren laughed. "And he will because he loves you two."

Brie nodded happily. "I'll be big and pregnant, but it will be fine."

"Yeah, you'll have a blast."

"Will kiddo be here?"

Wren swallowed hard. She hadn't realized that. Before the season started, she'd be a mom. Holy shit. Breathing in deeply, she nodded. "September third."

"Wow. That will be here before we know it."

"Yeah," she said nervously. It was cool when she didn't talk about the little guy growing in her because she could pretend it wasn't real. But once she did, anxiety ate at her core. Would she be a good mom? Would she suck? But more than any of that, it scared her that she would be doing it all alone. "Hopefully, I'll have a husband by then." Brie nodded as Wren watched her. Sipping on her tea, Wren looked over her cup to her friend and asked, "And so Jensen talked to you guys about our conversation?"

Brie shook her head. "Don't do that to me, please."

Wren's face twisted. "Do what?"

"Put me in the middle. I can't tell you what they say, the same way I can't tell them what you say."

"You told Vaughn about me being pregnant," she pointed out with a smile. She wasn't mad; she understood Brie's loyalty to Jensen. He would do the same for her.

"You didn't tell me I couldn't."

"So they told you not to tell me what was said?"

Brie shrugged as she looked down. "Yeah."

"Wow. Jerks."

Brie scoffed as Wren shook her head. "Is he gonna do it?"

"Wren…"

"Sorry!" she said, holding her hands up. "But in your opinion, do you think he'll do it?" When Brie just looked back at her, Wren glanced away. "Fine."

"Just be patient."

She shook her head. "I expected him to just say yes, and I'd be good. I didn't think I'd have to wait."

"Wren, you're asking a lot."

"And I offered him five million bucks! Plus, I'm pretty sure I lied for all of them a lot when they were younger. Like when they were all shitfaced drunk, and I told my mom they had food poisoning. And then I started acting like I was puking to make it seem like we all had it."

But Brie was just staring at her. "You offered him five million? Shit, Wren, I'll marry you and be the father."

Wren laughed hard. "You're silly."

"How much are you getting?"

"A lot."

Looking a little awestruck, Brie shook her head. "Obviously. No wonder you're doing all this."

"Yeah, it's gonna set Wells and me up."

"Wow."

"Stop looking at me like that," she laughed, and Brie smiled.

"Really, though, no one has met me. I can so go do some of that special effects makeup and look like a guy. It would be easy peasy!"

"You're such a dork," Wren snorted as her phone went off. Reaching into her bag, she pulled it out to see it was a text message from Jensen. Her heart picked up speed before she slid the notification over and read his message.

*Jensen: Can we meet? Today, if possible? I can come by your office or your place. I don't want to do this in public, though.*

Shit. What did that mean?

Hovering her fingers over the keyboard, she felt her heart beating so hard that it made her vision fuzzy. Brie was going on about growing a beard or something, but Wren couldn't pay attention. She read the message once more and then swallowed hard before typing back.

*Wren: I have an opening at one, but it's only for about thirty minutes.*

*Jensen: That's fine. I'll see you then.*

*Wren: Okay.*

She went to tuck her phone back into her purse but then paused, bringing it back up.

*Wren: Okay, I lied. I have a full hour, but I figured I'd need some time if you said no before my next client.*

*Jensen: I'm not gonna say no.*

Oh! Yay!

*Jensen: But I'm not saying yes either.*

What? What the fuck?

*Wren: Oh, okay, so I guess I'll see you in a bit.*

*Jensen: Yup.*

Pursing her lips, she sucked in a deep breath as she started to gather her things. Brie looked up at her expectantly, and Wren exhaled. "Jensen is coming to my office to talk."

Brie nodded. "Cool."

"Though, I'm sure you already know what he's going to say."

"Actually, I don't. So call me later?"

Wren glared. "I thought you knew!"

"No, they talked, I listened, and then Jenny went to his room for like nine hours. No one knew what he was doing."

Wren thought that through. What in the world was going on? "Well, I guess I'm about to find out."

"Well, good luck, and don't forget my offer."

Wren snickered. "I'm not kissing you with a fake mustache."

Brie held her hands up. "Then, no mustache. I can contour the shit out of my face to look like a dude."

Shaking her head, Wren sent a quick wave to Rodney before leaving the coffee shop. But the grin on her face was gone once she reached outside because in a matter of hours, she'd know what Jensen had meant.

And she wasn't sure she'd like it.

\* \* \*

JENSEN WAS PUNCTUAL, unlike the day before.

The knock on her office door came right at one, and she called, "Come in."

He opened the door, and she swore she had to look away to keep from drooling. Though that only lasted a second before she glanced back up to drink him in. He was wearing a tee with fitted shorts that hugged his thighs and some sneakers. His head was covered by an Assassins ball cap before he pulled it off, tucking it into his back pocket the way he had done when they were kids. "Hey."

"Hey, come on in." He nodded, coming toward her desk and to the seat she was pointing to. "Have a seat."

But he ignored her, coming around the desk to kiss her cheek softly. "You look pretty today."

Her lips curved. "Twice in one day. I must be on a roll."

He smiled. "Who else was complimenting you?"

"Rodney, after he called me fat."

Jensen scoffed. "You're not fat."

"I feel huge."

"You don't look it," he said simply, walking back around, but before he sat, he pulled out a little yellow sheet of paper, holding it loosely in his hands. He looked nervous, and he was chewing on his lip before he inhaled sharply. "You've done absolutely nothing with this office."

She laughed. "I have pictures of the people I love," she said, pointing to her desk, and he shook his head.

"Elli Adler's office is a shrine."

She nodded. "I know. Maybe when I have the baby, I'll be like her."

"I thought you hated the yellow in here."

"Oh, I do. I want to change it to white, but they won't let me. Says it bores people," she said with a grin.

"Better than black, which I'm sure you've considered."

"So many times."

He laughed. "I remember when you painted your bedroom black. Man, Elaine was pissed."

"I thought she was gonna skin me alive."

"And then when she found out we helped, I feared I wouldn't be fed."

She laughed. "Yeah, but you were."

"And you're still alive."

"Thank God."

A silence fell between them as they both stayed locked in each other's gaze, small smiles on their faces. "So, I'll get to it," he said suddenly, moving to the edge of his seat.

She did the same, holding her breath as he unfolded the paper. As he ran his hand over his mouth, she said, "Okay."

He nodded. "So I basically hate all your terms."

Her brows came in as she let out the breath she was holding in a whoosh. She hadn't expected him to say that. Sounding like there was a frog in her throat, she croaked, "Okay?"

"So here are mine." His hands were shaking, and he wouldn't look at her as he started to read. "I want six months."

"Six months?"

"You had said two weeks after the baby comes, that's not okay with me. I want a full six months."

"For what?"

"To make you fall for me."

When he looked up, she was sure he found her gawking at him. "Excuse me?"

"I don't want another failed marriage. If I do this, we do this for real. I want us to move in together, I want us to make love as husband and wife, and I want us to try to make this work."

Did he say make love? Her head cocked to the side, and then

she started laughing. "You're kidding. You're funny. Wait...you're not kidding?"

"No. I'm serious."

"Jensen—"

"If I'm going to lie to my second family, to my own family, I want it to be worth something."

She was flabbergasted. "I said fake husband, Jenny, not real."

"I understand that, but you're asking someone who has been divorced before. I don't want that again. If I'm going into this, I want it to be real. And if at the end it doesn't succeed, at least I tried and you tried."

She could only blink, her mouth hanging open. "But we're not into each other like that."

"Says who?" he asked, swallowing hard, his Adam's apple bobbing up and down. "I am extremely attracted to you. I have known you my whole life, and I...um..." He bit his lip and then shook his head. It was almost as though he was holding something back. "I feel this could work. At least, we should try for the baby's sake."

Confused, she shook her head. She felt like everything was going a hundred miles a second and she was holding on for dear life. "What? For the baby?"

"Are you sure the father is out of the picture?"

Her voice was sharp. "Completely."

He nodded. "Then my last term is that you let me be the father."

Wren's eyes widened. "I assume you mean not a fake father."

"Yes, I want to be the boy's dad. I want him to grow up and think I'm his father. When he turns eighteen, we can tell him the truth if you want, but he would have my last name, and he would be mine." His voice was strong, his gaze holding hers.

Breathless, she could only stare at him, unsure why he would want this. "Why, Jensen? Why would you want to be the father of a kid who isn't yours?"

Looking down, he inhaled shakily before nodding his head and meeting her gaze once more. "Because not only is it your kid and a boy needs a father, but I can't father children of my own."

# Chapter FIVE

"*I'm sorry, Mr. Monroe, and we are unsure why, but your sperm count is void. You aren't producing sperm, which is the reason you two are not successful in getting pregnant.*"

*Jensen's heart stopped as Ophelia clutched his hands, gasping loudly. Closing his eyes, he looked down as tears flooded the space behind his lids. Failure. Utter and disgusting failure racked his body. They had been trying for a baby for the last six months with no luck. Really trying. Ophelia was good, ready to go, and now they knew he was the issue.*

*He couldn't produce.*

*Shit, was he even a man?*

*"Can you fix it?" his beautiful wife asked. Jensen felt she knew he couldn't speak. He couldn't believe this. All they had ever spoken of since getting married was having lots and lots of kids. He wanted that. He wanted the kids, the dog, and the wife, along with the awesome career. He wanted it all, but now that was an unlikely goal.*

*Looking over at her, he memorized her face. The dimple in her cheeks, her long blond hair, her pointy nose. Her eyes were a soft shade of hazel and really added to her face, but at that moment, her brow was furrowed, her eyes intent on the doctor.*

*He understood. She was scared.*

*So was he.*

*"We can try some drug treatments, but I think I want to give it another six months. See if this is something that can fix itself. The human body is an amazing thing."*

*"But we've already waited six months,"* she complained, and Jensen squeezed her hand.

*"And we can wait another,"* he said simply, meeting her gaze as a tear ran down his cheek. He hated looking into her eyes and knowing he was the reason they couldn't have babies. Did he think he would produce in the next six months? No, but that was because he hadn't produced yet. They had been actively trying for six months, but they'd been having sex without protection for a year.

*Jensen couldn't have babies.*

*Heading out of the office with pamphlets on what to eat and natural ways to boost his sperm count, Jensen held his wife's hand, his heart in his throat. He couldn't believe this was happening. All they wanted was a family. A big family. They were decent people, he had just gotten signed to the Wild, and he was going places. They could finally afford a baby and then some. They had plans, names, everything. Yet, no baby.*

*Closing his eyes, he stopped abruptly. When he opened them, he met her worried gaze, and his heart melted. Man, he felt like utter shit. He was failing her.*

*"Ophelia."*

*"Yeah, babe?"*

*"If you want to get a divorce, go find a man who can give you children, I understand. I know it's all you want."*

*Her face fell as she shook her head. "No, I love you. I don't want to be with anyone but you."*

*He leaned into her, closing his eyes as their foreheads met.*

*The sad thing was, he had believed her.*

*Wholeheartedly.*

But that was a long, long time ago, and as Jensen watched Wren's face twist in horror, he prayed she'd want to go along with what he wanted.

"Oh, Jensen. I had no idea."

"It was a long time ago. I'm completely over it." And he was, not that it didn't still sting that his wife had gotten knocked up by someone else and left him. Something like that put a dent in a man's pride.

"Was that why she left you?"

"Yeah."

"You should have let me run her over with my car."

"She was pregnant."

"So? Whore."

"I couldn't give her what she wanted, I don't blame her. I was hurt and I was pissed, but still."

"No but still! It doesn't matter. If she truly loved you, she should have stood beside you!" she said, her voice rising as she ran her fingers through her hair. "Jesus."

"You're right."

"I am. And fuck her. Stupid whore."

"It's fine. It's been over ten years, I'm good."

"Well, I'm pissed right now."

"I can see that," he said, his lips curving as he looked down at his hands. Swallowing hard, he glanced back up at her, his heart in his throat. "Wren, I'm asking you to do what she didn't."

She looked up, her brows to her hairline. "What?"

"To stand by me. And I'll stand by you."

Her lips parted. "But, Jensen—"

He held up his hands, stopping her. "I don't want to end this and have you take the blame. I want it to work. If it doesn't, then at least we can say we tried. But I refuse to be a deadbeat dad. I want to be there for him and you. Always. And I think what I'm asking for is fair."

She was shaking her head. "I don't want that, though. I don't want a real husband—"

"Not yet, but maybe in the next six months, you will."

Her lips pressed together as she looked down at her growing belly. Maybe he had come on too strong, but he didn't think there was any other way to be but straightforward. If she wanted this, then this was how it was going to be. His heart was jackhammering in his chest. Sweat had broken out along his forehead, and everything was tingling. His whole body. Holy fuck, he was doing this.

"I would be a good father to him. I'd love him as if he were my blood."

Her lips curved down in a pout as she nodded. "Oh, Jensen, I know. I know that with all of my soul."

He nodded, choking on his own heart. "I'd be a good husband too."

She met his gaze, her eyes wide and so damn beautiful. "I don't doubt that, but it isn't what I want. I don't want that life. I don't even think I'm gonna be good at the whole mom thing, but a wife too?"

"You'll be great," he said simply, and her eyes widened, full of tears.

"I don't know."

He almost didn't move, but he knew he had to. Standing up, he dug into his pocket for the ring that was his grandmother's before walking around the desk to her. Going down on one knee, he held the ring up to her as she turned in her seat to look down at him. Her eyes were wide, wild, and full of fear.

The last time he had seen her look like that was when Vaughn dared her to jump off a bridge that was ten feet above the water. She didn't want to do it, but Wells and Vaughn had, and boy, were they taunting her. Coming up beside her, Jensen had said he'd jump with her. Together, hand in hand, they did it. And just like then, he wanted her to jump with him once more.

"This is my grandmother's ring, I thought you'd like it."

She glanced at the ring. He knew it was nothing special, just a vintage gold band. Ophelia thought it was ugly and didn't want it, so he had bought her a different one, but he was pretty sure this ring was more Wren's style anyway.

As she glanced up from it, a smile covered her gorgeous face. "It's so elegant."

"I agree, and I'd really love for you to have it as a symbol of my promise to stand beside you and be there for you. Maybe even be able to love you."

"Jensen," she tried, but then she shook her head. "Really, this is what you want? With me? Someone who could possibly never love you back. You deserve more than that. Find a woman who will love you and adopt a baby or something."

But he shook his head. "I believe God puts you in situations for a reason. This boy needs a dad. I can be that for him and more. I'll be his mentor, his best friend, and I will love both of you—till my dying day, if you let me. I can't be your mentor because I'm pretty sure you're smarter than me, but Wren, I've always been your best friend. You know that."

"Jenny, Jesus, you're killing me here," she cried, her eyes getting lost in his soft gaze.

"I know we can make this work."

"I don't know that," she admitted, her eyes holding his. "And I don't want to hurt you."

He could see it in her eyes. She didn't want that, and neither did he. But he refused to go into this without his terms. Because if he did, he'd get hurt. A hundred percent, he would. Clearing his throat, he shook his head. "You won't, as long as you try."

She looked to the ring and then back at him once more. He could hear her heart pounding, or maybe that was his. He wasn't sure, but his eyes stayed locked with hers as she went from the ring to him. Finally, she asked, "Can I have some time? To think it over?"

His heart dropped into his gut. Was he that awful? He was basically going to give her the world, why wasn't she taking it? Dropping his hand, he nodded. "I mean, yeah, you gave me time. I think that's only fair."

"I'm sorry. I just want to be sure I'm doing the right thing."

"No, it's fine."

"Jenny, I can see it on your face. You're not happy with me."

He got up, shrugging as he tucked the ring back into his pocket. "I'd give you the world, Wren. All of it."

"Why? Why would you do this? For the kid?"

"For you."

And with that, he turned, walking toward her office door. "You know how to get ahold of me."

"Yeah," she said to his retreating back before he opened the door and stepped out.

Catching her gaze once more before he shut the door, he shrugged. "And, Wren, I don't make a promise I don't intend to keep."

"I know."

He nodded. "And I hope you'll do the same."

Her lips started to quiver, and she nodded. "I know, that's why I'm asking for time to think this over."

He smiled. "Or to see if the gigolo is still available?"

Her face broke into a grin. "That too." He nodded, but as he went to shut the door, she called, "Thanks, Jenny."

He shut the door and then leaned against it.

That hadn't gone the way he'd assumed it would.

But then, what in his life ever did?

He had come to Nashville on a whim. Traded because he wanted so desperately to be loved and cherished on a team. At first, he didn't think that would happen on the Assassins, but it had. Not only on the ice, but in the locker room. He had friends, he had brothers, he just fit, but it wasn't what he'd thought would transpire. He'd thought he'd come here and play backup to one of the greats, Tate Odder, and just get by. People would like him, but he wouldn't be that big of a deal. Instead, he became a sensation. He established relationships with charities, supported them however he could, and then helped his team win the Cup. And now, he was asking a girl to marry him.

A girl who didn't love him, apparently.

A girl who didn't want to be in a relationship.

A girl whom he had known his whole life.

A girl who didn't know he loved her.

Yeah, he was an idiot. But if it worked, if he got Wren to agree and to try to love him, he would love the hell out of her.

And the baby.

Both of them.

With his whole body and soul.

He'd walk through fire for them. He just needed the chance.

That was all.

* * *

PINCHING the bridge of her nose, Wren leaned on her elbows as the door shut and her heart thumped loudly in her chest.

"What in the fuck just happened?"

Sitting up, she looked around her empty office and still couldn't believe what had occurred. She'd thought it would be easy. He'd say yes, they'd get married, and play along until the end. But no, Jensen came out of left field with a real marriage proposal, and he wanted to be the father of her child. What in the fucking world? That was the last thing she thought he'd ever want.

Since it was the last thing she wanted.

She had gotten used to the idea of being Mom and Dad to the kid. He'd have uncles, he'd be fine. But now…now, Jensen had gotten into her head. Wells was nowhere near her to help, and Vaughn was about to have a baby of his own. It would leave Jensen as the main uncle anyway, but that didn't mean he had to be the daddy! Did it? Shit. Also, what happened if Bradley decided he wanted to be a daddy. What would she do then?

Man, all she'd wanted was a fake husband.

That was all.

Instead, she got Jensen fucking Monroe ready to make an honest woman out of her. Be her child's daddy—and make *love* to her.

Holy shit, he wanted to make love to her.

"'Cause Jensen doesn't fuck, he makes love, you dumbass!"

What the hell was she going to do? How in the world was she going to make this kind of decision? When he said he'd give her the world, she didn't doubt that. Jensen was just that guy. He was good, he was kind, and he had a heart of gold. The problem was, while he was fully in, ready to love her and her kid, she was standing there saying, "Whoa, buddy, not even what I wanted." She didn't want a husband. She hadn't even wanted a kid until kiddo popped up. She thought she'd suck at being a mom—she still could—but she knew damn well she'd suck as a wife.

She never grew up playing house and doing that sort of thing. She was too busy running around with the boys and doing boy stuff. She was one hundred percent girl and loved girl things, but she always loved boy things too. Like having sex with lots of people. It was awesome, and she never got hurt. There was no reason that she couldn't live that life just because she was a girl. No one ever wanted her for long, which was fine because she was always moving on anyway. But it would kill her if she went all in with Jensen and he decided he didn't want her either.

Was that why she was stalling?

Was she scared?

Fuck, she was.

Soon, she was moving. She dialed Vaughn's number, even though, really, he was the last fucking person she wanted to speak to. But he was all she had because Brie would be all lovey-dovey. She really wanted to call her mom, Wells, or even her dad, but that would pose a bit of a problem. So, Vaughn it was.

"What do you want?" he answered gruffly, and she rolled her eyes.

"Oh, shut up. Brie isn't mad at you, no one is mad, so it doesn't matter. Get over yourself. I need you."

"You're lucky I love you. What's wrong?" he asked, tone gruff and completely overdramatic.

"Jensen just left here."

"Okay? And by the way, I thought I said don't ask him."

"You said I shouldn't."

"I said don't."

"No, you said shouldn't, and it doesn't matter because I fucking did."

"Now who's dramatic?"

"I hate you so much, and I don't even know why I call you."

"Because I'm filled with such amazing relationship advice."

"Yes, Vaughn, that's completely it," she said dryly, rolling her eyes. "Anyway, Jensen just came at me with a real proposal and wants to be the dad to my kid."

"Ugh, Jenny." Vaughn clucked his tongue. "I told you not to ask him. Ha. I bet you thought he was gonna lie down and do what you wanted, huh?"

"Whoa, not lie down, I'm not a dick. I just thought he'd be game."

"Oh, no. If he's gonna do it, he's gonna do it right."

"I don't want right, I want easy!"

"Well, sweetheart, better get that gigolo on the line."

"You are being no help," she said, her eyes filling with tears. "Jo, I don't want to hurt him. He's ready to be all in, and I'm over here thinking about who I should fuck tomorrow."

He scoffed. "You're a damn liar. You're over there freaking out because you know if you go all in with him, you won't be able to control yourself. Especially with Jenny. He's so cute and shit. Girls would die for the guy."

"You don't know my life," she snapped, and he laughed some more.

"No, but I know you. And I know you think he's hot, which is step one to getting into bed with him. I, for one, know he's hung, and that's step two to getting you hooked. Next thing you know, you'll be riding him, screaming that you never want anyone but him."

Wren couldn't help but squint at his stupidity. "There is something mentally wrong with you. You need help. I can schedule that."

"No, you need help. You know I'm right."

"You're not."

"I am."

"Not."

"Am," he said simply, and then he sighed. "Wren, either take it or leave it, but I can promise you, no man will do the job better than Jenny. That's him, he's made for this shit. He's wanted to be a dad since like forever, and with all that shit that went down with that bitch, it broke him. He was good to that whore he loved. He's a good dude, he just keeps getting shitted on. So don't shit on my boy, or I'll take you out."

She knew that. And that was the problem. "You couldn't take out a dog, you loser."

"Your insults can't mask the fact that you know I'm right."

"Vaughn, I would never admit to the fact that you're right."

"It's okay. We both know."

"We don't."

"We do, just do me a favor."

Annoyed, she asked, "What?"

"Don't hurt him. If you do this, do it for real. Go into it with an open mind. I'm not saying you'll fall for him right off the bat, he's a little awkward, but try. Because he—"

Wren's brow rose. "He, what?"

"Nothing. Listen, don't hurt my boy, okay? Please."

"I don't want to. You forget he's my boy too. I care for him like you guys do."

"I know, so consider that too. Because if it did end, he'd do everything to make sure you guy's relationship stayed intact. Even if it hurt him. Not just for you, but for the kid."

"That's what I just don't understand. It's not his place to love my kid."

"But why have a kid grow up without a dad when there is a man who wants to take the position?"

"Because it's not fair to him!"

"Or you're waiting for the real dad?"

She laughed, hard. "No. Not even kind of."

"Then, what's the problem? If it were me, I'd marry him."

She blinked. "Not sure how to take that."

"Take it whatever way you want, just don't hurt him."

"I don't want to, Jo, that's what I'm saying! How do I do this without hurting him?"

"How do you know you're going to hurt him?"

"Because I don't want what he wants."

"How do you know?"

"Because I do!"

"How, Wrenny? Have you ever had a man really be there for you the way Jensen is?"

She paused, her heart jumping up into her throat because she hadn't. Never. Jensen was there for her more than Vaughn ever was. No matter what she needed, Jensen would be there. He was good like that. So much like Wells, Vaughn was a flighty one, but Jensen, he was there whenever she needed him. There wasn't a time she could remember when she had called him for a ride after a night of drinking that he didn't show up. Even when he had just gotten married and had just moved to Minnesota, he still came home to help move her in to her new apartment with Wells. Whenever anyone needed him, he was there.

Clearing her throat, she admitted, "No."

"Exactly."

She bit her lip, looking up at her ceiling to keep her tears at bay. "So you think I should do it?"

"Hell no. I know for a fact that you're gonna break the dude. Because no matter how much I want to believe you'll try, you won't fully give yourself to the guy, and in the end, he's gonna be crushed."

Not what she wanted to hear. "Whatever, Jo. It's not like he loves me. You're acting as if he does." When he didn't answer her, she paused. "Right?"

"That is not my place to say."

"When has anything not been your fucking place to say?" she snapped back, rolling her eyes. "And please, Jensen loves me? That's as preposterous as it sounds. It's Jensen Monroe, he can date supermodels."

"But instead, he asked you to marry him," Vaughn said simply. "So what do you think that means?"

Biting the inside of her cheek, she shrugged because she didn't want to accept what Vaughn was implying. That was crazy. They were friends. Close friends. Sure, she thought Jensen was hot, but she didn't love the guy like that. She didn't love anyone. Well, that was a lie, but the last time she fell for some douche, he knocked her up and ran, so yeah, she wasn't stupid. Was she?

Man, maybe she was in need of therapy.

Pinching the bridge of her nose once more, she muttered, "That he's a nice guy?"

"Yeah, go with that."

"Jo!"

"Wren!"

"I don't know what to do, and I...I'm... Fuck, I'm freaking out."

"Well," he said, clearing his throat, and she wanted to wring his neck. He was always so blasé about everything except when it had to do with him. "You know, Emma, Jensen's mom—"

"I know who that is."

"Just saying. But she always told me to listen to my heart. So maybe try that."

"Has that ever worked for you?"

"Well, my heart didn't start talking until Brie came along, so I guess it does."

If she weren't so annoyed and didn't want to kill Vaughn, she would have swooned. Instead, though, she grumbled, "Fine. I'll try that."

"Good luck finding it in that black mass of a soul of yours."

"I hate you, Vaughn Johansson. So damn much."

"Love you too, sugar!"

Hanging up the phone, she threw it down before shaking her head and letting it fall to her desk. It landed with a loud thunk that echoed through her office. She couldn't breathe since her kid was crushing her lungs, but she really didn't care. Staring at her belly, she slowly shook her head.

"Well, kiddo, Mommy is in a pickle."

Unfortunately, her stomach didn't talk back with wise, amazing advice.

"I'd be stupid not to do it. But I'm scared. I don't want either of us to get hurt, and if I can't get over my own issues, I'll do exactly that. But he'll act like it's no big deal. He'll treat me the way he does now, and he'd love you. He'd love you so much. I've seen him with kids. I've seen the way his eyes light up and how he basically falls to the ground to play with them. He's always wanted a big family because his was so small." Moving her hands along her stomach, she sat up, leaning back in the chair as tears started to fall down her face. She had no clue what to do, yet a grin came over her face as her hands moved up and down her belly. "He's a good man, kiddo. Good heart, a beautiful, amazing family, and I've known him my whole life. So there really isn't a question, is there? I should say yes. Right?"

Still nothing. But then, she knew she was on her own. Though, if she did this, she wouldn't be on her own any longer. Jensen would stand beside her. Which was weird but kind of nice too. But still, weird. Plus, the whole making love thing was still freaking her out. She was a thick girl, but now, now she was really a little fat, and she wasn't sure how he would feel about that. What if he didn't like her body? What if he decided he couldn't do this? What if...

Stop, Wren.

It's Jensen.

Even so, she had no clue what the fuck she was going to do.

Man, she really needed her mommy.

# Chapter SIX

apping a pen to her lips, Wren stared at her computer screen where she'd typed the pros and cons of Jensen's proposal. She always did this. With everything. It was how she chose her college, how she chose her first car, and also how she decided to move to Nashville for the Assassins job. Even when she found out that Bradley wasn't going to be there for her, she wrote out a list of pros and cons for keeping the baby. The list was way con heavy, but the pro outweighed it all.

She loved it.

The baby.

Unlike her last list, though, she was finding out that this one was pro heavy. Which she didn't like very much because she was doing everything to talk herself out of saying yes to Jensen. Which was why she had rewritten it over nine times. But no matter how many times she did that, it always came out in Jensen's favor. Yet something was holding her back.

Vaughn's words were playing with her head too. She stayed up all night thinking about how he'd insinuated Jensen had feelings for her. She played with the idea, even giggled like an idiot, but it all just seemed so unreal. Jensen obviously wanted to do this because he cared about her and wanted to help. He didn't have an ulterior motive. It was Jensen. What you saw was what you got.

Right?

When a thought came into her head, she took the pen between her lips and typed it quickly beneath the con list.

**Con**

**I don't want to be married.**

**Someone, probably Jensen, would get hurt.**

**Or me. I could get hurt.**

**I could fall in love with him, and he would leave me.**

That last one stung a bit, probably because it was what most likely would happen. Why was this so hard? *Just say yes! No! Say no! Just kiss him and see what happens.* That was an idea. Couldn't be married to someone she couldn't kiss.

Right?

Glancing back to the con list, she started to type.

**Not sure how he kisses now. It has been a good many years.**

Nodding her head, she looked to the pro list, and her heart sped up.

**Pro**

**He would love the kiddo.**

**He would be a great dad.**

**He's probably good in bed.**

**He's loyal.**

**He's nice.**

**He's not a douche fucker like that asshole.**

Bradley. As much as she didn't want to think of him, she found herself doing just that. Ever since Jensen had come into her office only two days ago, her mind kept sneaking back to Bradley. Why? She wasn't really sure, except for the fact that when she went home with Jensen for the wedding, she'd probably see Bradley. She wasn't sure how he'd take seeing her with Jensen. Would he out them? Would he care? She wasn't sure, and if she was going to do this, nothing could expose them. She'd want it to go smoothly for Jensen. For her too. Obviously.

It worried her. To the point that she had dialed Bradley's number numerous times just to see what he would do. What he'd think. Why she cared was a legit concern, but at the moment, she wasn't thinking about that. He shouldn't matter, but she couldn't shake that he would somehow get in the way. She couldn't have that. Going into this with Jensen, she would have her own insecurities and self-destructive ways to do them in. She didn't need the worrisome specter of Bradley to add in there. He had made it clear, through many texts, he wanted nothing to do with her or her child.

Swallowing hard, she glanced at the clock on her laptop to see that she still had plenty of time before Tate Odder came in. Before she could chicken out, she reached for her office phone and dialed Bradley. She hadn't spoken to him on the phone in six months. She wasn't sure how this was going to go, but she had to make sure he was completely out of the picture. His secretary answered on the third ring.

"Bradley Washington's office, this is Brenda. How may I help you?"

"Yes, Brenda. It's Wren. Can you put me through, please?"

"Oh, Wren! How are you? I haven't heard from you in ages."

Letting out a small laugh that had no laughter in it whatsoever, Wren nodded. "Yeah, been superbusy, and I wish I had time to catch up, but I'm on a time crunch and have a quick question for Bradley."

"Sure, hun. One second."

Wren bit her lip as she waited, and then his voice filled the line. "Wren, why are you calling me?"

She was a little taken aback. "Well, hello to you too."

"I told you not to call me, not to reach out. I'm a married man now. I love my wife."

"Good for you, but I feel like we need to talk—"

"Unless you're calling to tell me you had an abortion, there is nothing to talk about. I told you, I can't do this. I'm not sure what you want, but you look pathetic. Take the hint, I don't want you. You were just an easy lay."

*This motherfucker right here...* Her lips pressed together tightly, her eyes filling with fire. Taking in a calm breath, she said, "Bradley, I was calling to ask you—"

"There. Is. Nothing. To. Talk. About. Don't call me ever again."

Then the line went dead.

Holding the phone from her ear, her eyes started to well with tears before she slammed the receiver down and covered her face. She must have startled the kiddo because he went crazy, kicking her hard in the liver, but she couldn't pay him any mind. She just didn't get it. Was she pathetic? Was she so much of an easy fucking lay that he thought he could treat her like that? Why was she lying for him? She should put his ass through the wringer. He was fucking lucky that she needed her inheritance and that Jensen was offering to be a father to her kid because Bradley didn't deserve shit.

But his words stung.

An easy lay?

Really? Was she that pitiful?

Gasping for breath, she reached for the phone before she knew what she was doing and dialed her mom's number. When her mother's cheerful voice filled the line, she almost hung up, but she knew her mom would call her back. Closing her eyes, Wren sucked in a deep breath, but before she could say anything, her mother's voice was full of panic.

"Oh, Wren, why are you crying?"

Gasping for breath, she shook her head, squeezing out the tears. "How'd you know?"

"You do that hiccup thing when you're crying. What's wrong?"

And with that, Wren let go. Her tears were coming fast and out of control as she held one hand over her face, inhaling quickly before shaking her head. "I can't tell you."

"Oh, yes, you can. You can tell me anything."

"Mom, am I a whore? Like, legit a whore? Ask Daddy. Am I?"

Her mom was stunned. Wren knew that, and she wasn't sure why she'd even said that. Maybe for the reassurance that the way she had been living her life was okay? Because, not two days ago, she was cool with her life choices, but now, now she felt dirty. How did she let him do this to her? Was it the hormones? Crap, her kid was making her a tragic little crybaby.

"Oh, baby. No, you're a good girl."

But Wren wasn't listening. Sobbing, she shook her head as she squeezed her eyes shut. "No, Mom. I'm a fucking easy lay, and that's why I get these shit guys because I can't keep my vagina in my pants."

"I didn't realize it was detachable. That's a talent."

"Mom!"

"Sorry, I'm sorry. I hate when you cry. You're so much prettier when you smile."

Man, these pregnancy hormones were no joke. Rage filled her from the tip of her toes to the top of her head as she cried out, "But, Mom! I'm not a trophy wife."

"Well, love, who the hell cares?"

"I do! I want to be worthy—"

"Of what? Trash? Because anyone that uses that term is trash. You're a beautiful, smart, semi-kind girl."

She didn't miss the *semi*, but they both knew Wren had a mean streak. Though, her mom's words weren't helping. It was pity party time for Wren Lemiere. Pull up a chair and grab some popcorn. "But, Mom, I'm fat."

"You're not fat, baby. You have fat on you, that doesn't make you fat. You've got fingernails too. Does that make you a fingernail?"

"Mom! I don't need your nine-year-old logic right now. I feel worthless."

"Why, baby? That is insane. Who did this? I'll kill them."

Biting her lip, Wren closed her eyes and shook her head. Why was she doing this to herself? Fuck Bradley, he was the worthless one. She wasn't dirt like him, but she couldn't stop crying.

"Baby, tell me what's wrong. Is it a guy? I'll kill him."

"No, Mom. I can't tell you."

"Yes, you can."

"I can't."

"Why?"

"Because I don't even know what to tell."

"The truth."

"The truth is a clusterfuck, and I'm a mess, Mom. A lonely, hot mess."

Her mom made a sound of distress before clucking her tongue at her. "Then call Wells. He'll call me, and then we can talk."

"I know, which is why I can't tell him!"

"Well, I don't like that you've figured this out."

"Mom. I seriously love your humor on any other day of the week, but not today, please."

She sighed heavily, and Wren could just see her, sitting in her easy chair, rocking as *Judge Judy* played on the TV. Her mom didn't do sadness well; she was full of life. Always smiling and happy. She was probably coming out of her skin at Wren's attitude, but she knew if she'd called Wells or her dad, they'd be on the first flight out to kill someone. Man, she had really gotten herself into a shitty fucking place.

"Fine. Call Shanna."

"Fuck no," Wren muttered. "Last person I need right now."

Which was the biggest lie imaginable. She really could use the advice of her best friend, if that's what she even was anymore, but Bradley was Shanna's brother. Shanna wouldn't be any help because Bradley never did anything wrong. Really, he was a poor excuse for a human being, and his family would be sickened if they knew the truth. She should tell them. Jerk.

"Vaugh—" Her mother stopped. "Wait, no, don't call him. He'll crack more jokes than I do. You know who you should call? Jensen." Wren groaned. Hadn't he been topic enough? "He would listen, and he would come over, be there for you. He wouldn't tell a soul either. Such a good boy, my Jenny is. Call him. He'd be there for you without any questions."

She knew that.

She knew that with all her heart.

So why wasn't she calling him?

Because the second to last sentence under the cons list was playing with her head.

*I could love him.*

But would he love her?

Or would she just be the easy lay, the non-trophy wife, the fat friend with a kid who needed a father, that he felt bad for?

* * *

"WHY AM I HERE?"

Jensen threw an annoyed look back at Vaughn as he stretched between the pipes in the middle of the Assassins' arena. Jensen needed his happy place. His sanctuary, and being between the pipes was just that. His home. He needed the grinding of the ice from his skates. The smell, man, he needed the smell. It had only been a few weeks since they had won and finished the series, but Jensen missed it. He missed his home because if he stayed in his apartment another second, he was going to lose his fucking mind.

Letting out a long, annoyed breath, he said, "I need you to shoot pucks at me so I stop thinking."

Vaughn thought that over. "Maybe it's a no?"

"Surely, she'd text me or call."

"Or she's a coward and is taking the easy way out. Maybe she called the gigolo."

"I will take the dude out at the wedding."

Vaughn sputtered with laughter. "That would make the gay wedding a billion times better."

"You're not funny."

"What? I'm hilarious! Can you imagine, you're standing there, and she walks in with him. Bam, you yell, 'He's a gigolo!' And then I could be like, 'Cue the glitter doves.'"

Jensen just stared at him, no emotion on his face. "The fact that I question my friendship with you should be a warning sign."

Vaughn waved him off. "Nah, it's part of my charm."

"Or you're annoying as shit."

"Really? No one has ever told me that," Vaughn said, moving the puck back and forth. "But really, it's been like two days."

The longest two days of Jensen's life. He just didn't get it. He'd laid it all out there. Short of telling the girl he loved her with everything inside of him, he basically offered her the golden ticket. If Vaughn were in his head, the dumbass would say "Cue the Oompa Loompas from the factory" because Jensen was Willy Wonka. Crap, he was starting to think like Vaughn. Maybe he should distance himself from that guy. His crazy was rubbing off on him, but that was beside the point. A distraction from the fact that Wren Lemiere was holding out on him.

"I don't get it, you know?"

Vaughn looked up. "You don't get why Wren, our best friend's little sister, who has a supershitty track record with dudes and who had decided just to fuck her way through life, wouldn't want to commit to a guy she considers someone special to her?"

Jensen glared through his mask. "Brie said that?"

He scoffed and then nodded. "Yeah, 'cause, like you, I don't get it. You're basically handing her the golden ticket." His eyes lit up. "You're Willy!"

Yup, Jensen was losing his mind. "Please don't start singing the song—"

But Vaughn was already humming, though he stopped once Jensen threw his mask up, glaring. "Done."

"Thank you."

"But for real, man, I told her—"

"Who? Wren?"

Vaughn paused. "Yeah, I told you. I talked to her."

"No, you didn't."

"Oh. Did I tell Brie that?"

"I'm not Brie!"

"Well, no shit. I don't want to do you."

"Oh my fucking goodness, you two-year-old! Focus! When did you talk to her?"

"The day you left her office."

"What did she say?"

Vaughn shrugged. "That she didn't want to hurt you."

Jensen's face twisted in confusion. "So she thinks she will?"

"Yeah, 'cause she's Wren."

Jensen chewed that over. "She's not a bad person, though."

"No, but she's Wren. I don't know. The female version of me, or what I used to be, just smarter."

"Way smarter."

"Yeah."

Shaking his head, Jensen lowered his mask. "Whatever, let's play."

"You sure you don't want to hug?"

"I will take you out by your knees. Shoot."

So he shot. Over and over again. With each shot Jensen blocked, he tried to figure out why it was taking Wren so long. He got it. If she didn't want to hurt him, then fucking don't. It was that easy. Just be honest. He knew her, she knew him. She was comfortable with him, and he with her. He wanted to bang her; she liked to bang. He would be a great husband, great father, and yeah, she didn't know how to do that stuff, but it would be okay. They'd figure it out together. He just needed her to get her head out of her ass and follow through with what she'd asked for. She was the one who wanted this. Not him. Well, he did, and she may have wanted a "fake" husband and father, but he wasn't rolling that way. It was his way or no way.

Shot after shot, Jensen took, only letting a few through here and there until his hands were aching and his groin was dead. But in a good way. It was a great workout, just what he wanted and needed in a way. Dropping his gloves, he lay on the ice as Vaughn did the same, sliding toward him. Looking over, he found Vaughn watching him.

"What if she says no?"

Jensen shrugged. He hadn't thought about that. "Then that will suck."

"You know it's 'cause she's scared. She's such a pansy. This whole 'I hate love' shit is wack. She doesn't hate it, she loves it. It just keeps fucking with her."

"Because she chooses shit to fall for."

"Wells tells her the same thing constantly."

"She doesn't listen."

"She's stubborn."

"Yeah, but I like that."

"You like everything about her."

"I do, except that she's making me wait for her to decide what the hell she's doing."

"Have you reached out to her?"

"No. I'm giving her space."

Vaughn nodded, tossing his gloves in the net as Jensen slowly undid his goalie pads. "Brie said the dude, the father of the baby, told her she wasn't trophy wife material."

Jensen glanced over at him, his brows furrowing as anger shook his body. "What the fuck does that mean?"

"Probably a dig at her weight."

"She's not even big. Thick, yeah, but she's been thick her whole life. She's a strong girl."

"Yeah, but dickheads don't see that."

"I fucking hate dickheads. Give us good guys a bad rep." Vaughn agreed as Jensen threw off his pad, starting on the other one. "I was thinking about that time, out at NateWay1 when I fell for her—"

"Dude, please don't tell me the story again. It's sickening."

"I'm not, asshole. Listen," Jensen said, a grin pulling at his lips. "Also, remember I helped you write out messages in sausage on pizza for Brie."

"Hey, that was sweet."

"And so is my story of the hammer on that hot—"

"Please don't."

Jensen smiled for the first time in the last two days. He could still see her hair blowing in the summer breeze. It was one of his favorite memories. He loved the sweat dripping down the backs of her thighs and the wide smile on her beautiful, round face. "I should have told her I had a thing for her then."

"That was right after Ophelia, though."

"Yeah, but I knew," he said simply. "I always knew. I was just too scared she wouldn't have me."

"Why? You ain't ugly."

Jensen smirked. "I'm aware, but I couldn't shake that I wasn't man enough for her."

"Dude. Really? It's not like you're the only dude who can't have kids. Plus, not all women are like that whore. Especially Wren, she wouldn't do that to you."

"Still, it fucks with you."

"I get it, but still."

"Yeah, but then again, I've always been scared Wren didn't see me as any more than just a brother."

"Maybe she thinks the same thing?"

"Probably. My fault."

Vaughn nodded. "You know, way back when, before I admitted to myself that I loved Brie and wanted her, knocked her up, and all that jazz, my best friend told me that his dad always told him, 'You can't be a coward and be in love. You're not allowed. You gotta choose one before you're a coward and alone.' And you, my friend, have been the coward and alone, a perfect example of that. Ready to change it?"

Jensen laughed. "Wow."

"I know, I'm amazing."

"And cocky as fuck."

"Oh, yeah, totally that."

"So I should call her."

"You should go to her office or her place." Vaughn sat up, looking down at him. "And you say, 'Woman, you're marrying me, and I'm gonna be that baby's daddy! And you're gonna love me!'"

Jensen sputtered with laughter as he sat up. "Yeah, we both know I'm not gonna say that."

Vaughn shrugged. "Hey, worth the try."

Nodding, Jensen sucked in a deep breath. "Yeah, but you're right. And please God, don't let that go to your head."

Looking over at him, Jensen found Vaughn grinning. "Too late."

* * *

"So she's pretty booked?"

Wren's assistant, Leah, glanced up from her computer. "I mean, she has like a fifteen-minute window between the appointment she has now and her next, but everyone is coming in today since they are either leaving or going on vacation."

Jensen nodded. The food he was holding from The Southern was burning his hand, and the flowers he held in his other hand were making him want to sneeze, but he didn't care. He was going to see Wren. "Can you put me in for those fifteen minutes?"

She looked skeptical. "She usually eats—"

He held up the food. "I know, I'm trying to surprise her."

Her brow perked and then she smiled. "Yes, Mr. Monroe, I'll put you in."

"You rock, Leah. If she doesn't tell you that enough, it's true."

Her face reddened before Jensen flashed her a winning smile. "You're sweet. Have a seat, it shouldn't be much longer."

"Thanks," he called back to her before taking the seat that was right in front of Wren's office door. His chest hurt, his heart was pounding so hard, but he had to know. Right now. Yes or no, if they were doing this. God, he hoped she said yes. But a part of him was pretty sure she was going to say no. He didn't know why, but he just felt it. She was a hard sell, and he understood she didn't want to hurt him. They had too much history, but man, he really wanted this. He did. More than he thought he would.

Not to mention he was pretty sure it went past more than him just wanting to help her.

He wanted her to love him.

Biting the inside of his lip, he tried to inhale and exhale slowly as he waited for the door to open. He felt jumpy. Almost like he had a couple of weeks ago during the play-offs. He felt like he was watching game five all over again. He really didn't want that feeling. She was Wren. His buddy's baby sister and he knew her. He shouldn't be nervous, but then it *was* Wren. Someone he had been very awkward around for most of his life.

He was pretty sure the only time he wasn't nervous around her was when he was married to Ophelia. But that was only because he was trying to let Wren go. To love only Ophelia. He should have known that would have happen, though. He'd always had a place in his heart for Wren. Ophelia was constantly a little jealous of Wren, and it was probably because he would drop everything to help her. Wren knew that, so why was she holding back?

When the door opened, he stood just as Tate Odder came out. "Monroe."

Jensen smiled. He hadn't seen Odder in a while. "Odder, how you doing? Any news on when we can start training together?"

Tate looked away and then shook his head. "No, sorry. No news."

Jensen's shoulders dropped. "Well, that sucks. I'm excited to get out there with you."

Tate looked apprehensive as he nodded. "Me too. I'll see you?"

"Yeah, see ya," Jensen said since Tate was already walking away. Huh, that was weird.

Taking a deep breath, Jensen pushed the office door open just as Wren looked up, her eyes widening. "Jensen."

She looked beautiful. Her hair was up in a bun, her makeup soft but bringing out her eyes gorgeously. She was wearing a low-cut dress or shirt, he wasn't sure. All he knew was her boobs looked great and, crap, he was staring. Was his mouth open? Shit, it was. She stood and the dress was loose, but he could see her bump. Her child. The child that could be his.

Moving her hands across the baby hairs along her forehead, she then ran them down the front of her dress, nervousness coming off her in waves. "I wasn't expecting you."

Snapping his jaw up, he held her gaze before he, like an idiot, squawked, "Yeah, hey, I came to see what the hell we're doing."

He was pretty sure there was a better way he could have said that.

Maybe he should have gone with what Vaughn had said to do.

# Chapter SEVEN

"Oh."

"Yeah. I brought food. And flowers."

Wren smiled. She couldn't help it. He was just adorable. Standing there, arms full of food and flowers with a look of pure uncertainty on his face. He was nervous, which was understandable. So was she, but she knew he was doing this for her. Swallowing hard, she nodded as her heart pounded against her ribs, which woke up kiddo, and now he was kicking. But her son's kicks were a little hard to pay attention to when Jensen's eyes were locked with hers. They were such a demanding dark brown that struck her right in the middle of her soul.

Lord, he was pretty.

She had done so well her whole life, ignoring her feelings for him. Yeah, she was attracted to him, but she wasn't going to fling herself on a guy who'd showed no interest in her until now. If that's what he was even doing. She'd thought she was sure, but his terms to their agreement suggested that he was into her, which still blew her ever-loving mind.

"I can see that," she somehow choked out. "Thank you, but—"

"I know you've only got like fifteen minutes, which is why I bought you like, seven dishes because I figured you could snack on them all day when you got time."

"Oh, wow. That's sweet."

"Yeah," he chuckled, his laughter a little laced with nerves as he laid everything down on her desk. "And I know you're not really a flower chick, but I figured these would make you smile." Looking up at her, he gestured toward the vase of marigolds.

Her heart almost came out of her chest at the sight of the beautiful gold flowers. "These are the ones I have outside my bedroom window at home."

He nodded. "I know. I remember when that late winter storm hit that one time and killed them all. You cried for days since you loved them so much, so Dad had us out there replanting brand-new ones."

She beamed, a little flabbergasted. "You remember that?"

"I remember everything."

Her heart fluttered as she gazed at the side of his face. They really had known each other their whole lives. She shouldn't be surprised, but she was. His cheeks were a little red, the hair on his face a little longer than she liked but it was the off-season, so it was expected. His shoulders looked so big in his tank, but all she could stare at was his lips.

Pursing them, he met her gaze. "You look beautiful today."

She blushed. "Thanks, but——"

"Take the compliment, Wren."

She snapped her lips shut and grinned. Her stupid heart was in a frenzy as he held her gaze hostage with his. "I wanted you to see what it was like to have me as your husband."

Her grin grew. "Trying to buy me off with food and flowers? I think I'm supposed to buy you off."

"You don't have to," he said with all seriousness, and her grin stalled.

"Well, then."

He chuckled as he leaned on his arms, his gaze burning into hers. "It would be good."

"Maybe, but it's scary as fuck."

"Of course it is. I'm asking something of you that you don't think you want."

"I don't think. I know."

"So you think." She glared at his total dismissal of what she felt was a valid point, but he just smiled. "But it will be worth it."

She blinked as her lips started to tremble, her heart in her throat. "I don't want——"

"If you say you don't want to hurt me, I'm taking the food back."

Her eyes widened. "But I'm hungry."

He smiled. "Then don't."

"Fine. I won't."

"Because you won't."

She eyed him uncertainly. "You don't know that."

"I do, and if that's what's holding you back, let it go. Because I trust you wouldn't do that to me. We've been very honest with each other, and we'll continue to do so. The great thing is that we were friends before this."

She swallowed hard. His logic was sound, and she should just agree with him. It was what she needed, if maybe not what she wanted, but that was beside the point. She was running out of time, and he was offering her the world. She'd be stupid to turn it down. Even if it did scare her to the depths of her soul and made her want to run the other way.

"So you're fine being the father of a baby that's not yours, lying to my family and yours, mind you, and going into this with no guarantee that we'll work."

"Yes."

"Just like that. No reservations?"

"None."

"Jensen."

"What? It's you. I'd do anything for you."

Her heart skipped as she tore her gaze away, shaking her head. "So you want this?"

"I do."

She scoffed. He was crazy! "Out of all the women in the world, you want to do this with me?"

Looking up, she found him watching her, his eyes trained on hers as the heat gathered all throughout her. Swallowing hard, she watched as he nodded. "All the other women don't matter."

His statement was simple but meant so much. As she got lost in his eyes, she almost didn't know how to respond, but something inside of her was going nuts. Call it her own insecurities, but she just couldn't believe that. He was a great-looking guy, women loved him, and here he was in her office with food and flowers begging to help her. This was bold and completely out of his wheelhouse. He usually stood back, didn't say much. But he was saying more than enough now, and it was hitting her right in her gut, leaving her breathless.

"Jensen—"

But his gaze was off to the side, at her computer. "Jesus, you're still doing these pros and cons lists?"

Her stomach dropped. When she looked to where he was staring with his perfect vision, she saw her computer screen that held her list she had been working on before Tate had come in.

"Well, fuck," she muttered, and he laughed as he started to move toward her computer at the same time she tried to reach for the mouse.

Knocking it out of her hand, he said, "You're doing one on me? I gotta see this."

"Jensen, no," she groaned, trying to stop him, but he blocked her as he read the items out loud. "You'd block a pregnant woman?"

"Yes! I need to see this."

"I can't believe you," she yelled, but she was laughing as he sat in her seat, with his arm across her chest, holding her back. He was so strong and manly, and he smelled like a woodsy lumberjack.

Yum.

"Let's see here, I should take a picture and send it to Vaughn and Wells. They'd get a kick out of this."

"Jensen Monroe, I'll kill you." He laughed as she pushed his arm down, crossing her arms over her belly. "I don't like you right now."

"Ha, this list is so pro heavy. I'm basically amazing."

"Okay, Vaughn Johansson."

He scoffed as he leaned back in the chair, looking up at her. "I love the con of falling in love with me, though. That's what you're supposed to do."

"Says you."

"Exactly, because that's what you do when you marry someone and raise a baby with them."

"I wanted a fake husband, remember?"

"Yeah, nothing fake about me, baby."

She let out a harsh breath. "I'm about to add annoying to the list."

He laughed as he shrugged. "We both know I'm not annoying."

She rolled her eyes at that, and he sent her a grin. "And we've kissed!"

Her face twisted. "When we were younger and it was a stupid dare. You basically just licked me."

"I did not! It was meaningful."

She sputtered with laughter. "It was maybe a second, and you poked your tongue on my lip and then backed away."

"I did not!"

"You did. It was pathetic."

"That's rude." She laughed, and he smiled. "I was like fifteen."

"Yeah. But my first kiss was a dud, for sure."

His grin grew as he gazed up at her. "I was your first kiss?"

"Yeah, and it was horrible."

He gave her a dry look. "Shit, Wren, my ego."

She giggled some more as he shook his head, leaning back in toward the computer again. He sat up then, reaching for the keyboard and mouse. Highlighting the fall in love with him bit, he moved that to the pro side, and he deleted the getting hurt part before he started to type away under the section he had just moved.

**Would love me more than I could ever handle.**

Her skin started to tingle as he hit enter and pushed the keyboard away before rolling back in the chair. She stepped out of his way, and he stood, his big, beautiful body right in front of her as he turned to look at her, his lips turning up in a little bit of a smirk. "Only one thing left."

"Huh?"

Before she knew what was happening, he pushed her against the windows of her office, his knee coming between her legs to spread them for his body, forcing away every single breath she had inside of her. Taking her wrist, he lifted it above her head as his eyes burned into hers, while his other hand moved a strand of hair out of her eyes. "The kiss."

She gasped. "The kiss?"

"Yeah," he said before his tongue came out, wetting his lips while he tipped her chin up. She held her breath as his lips moved at the speed of turtles down to hers, his eyes watching hers intently. Angling her chin up just slightly, she closed her eyes, and he came crashing in. When their lips touched, she swore it was like a huge wrecking ball knocking her out of this universe. His body pressed to hers, her stomach touching his groin as his hand moved from her wrist to take her hand in his, while her other hand grasped his bicep. Time stood still as their lips moved, and when his tongue glided along her bottom lip, she opened her mouth, letting him run his tongue ever so slowly along hers. Fire, that was all she felt. Almost like a good, long shot of brandy. He felt damn good. Tasted like a dream too. Her body was feverish. Between her legs, she was dripping wet, and she swore he could take her right there and she wouldn't mind one damn bit.

Holy mother of God, she was kissing Jensen Monroe.

And she didn't like it.

She loved it.

Already wanted more.

Pulling away, he looked in her eyes, heat and all kinds of naughty things swirling deep inside of his. "Might want to answer that," he whispered, and her eyes widened.

"Answer what?"

"Ms. Lemiere? Wren?"

"Shit," she muttered as she detangled herself from the man who had just kissed her fucking socks off. When the fuck did Jensen find some game? Or kiss like that? What the hell? "Hey, sorry!" she yelled, running her hand down her face as she reached for her phone.

"Your next appointment is here."

"Yes, tell him I'll be five minutes."

"Of course."

Slamming the phone down with more force than she intended, she turned to find Jensen standing beside her, a little smirk on his face as she leaned into the desk, her hands bracing her in an effort to keep her from turning into complete goo. "So."

"So."

"I guess I'll make an appointment down at the courthouse."

She blinked. "Huh?"

"Oh, you still don't know if you want to do this?"

She swallowed hard because, damn it, she did. She wanted to do this so badly, even though it scared her more than she cared for it to. It was the kiss! It had clouded her thoughts, but before she could think more about that, she said, "No, I do."

"Good. So I'll make the appointment."

His eyes were so dark. Full of something she had never seen before. He usually had kind eyes, but at that moment, he had sexy, naughty eyes. "Wow, Vaughn's cockiness is rubbing off, huh?"

He reached out, cupping her face as he took a step toward her. "Guess so."

Leaning in, he pressed his lips softly to the side of her mouth. "I'll call your parents and Wells."

She blinked. "Why?"

"Because it's my place."

"You don't have to. I can do it."

"I want to," he insisted, and she could tell it was a fight she wouldn't win.

She nodded. "Okay."

"How about dinner tonight? Talk things through?"

She nodded. "Okay."

"Pick the place."

"Okay."

"Text me?"

"Okay."

He grinned. "Okay."

When he kissed her once more, this time on her lips, her eyes drifted shut as she leaned into him. She wasn't sure if it was because she hadn't been kissed in six months or if it was because Jensen was just a fucking amazing kisser, but there was no way she was saying no to that. Along with everything else? Yeah, she had no choice. She was in this.

She just hoped he was right and no one would get hurt.

Pulling back, he squeezed her hand and then started for the door. She watched as he reached it, turning to send her one last smile and then a wink before he left. Falling into her seat, she exhaled hard as she shook her head.

"Well, kiddo, that just happened."

Looking toward the computer, she went to shut it down since her next client liked to sit by her desk. But before she could, she saw there was a new addition to the pro column.

**I will kiss you like that anytime you want, and even in the times you're too stubborn to admit you want it.**

**I happened to know I'm a better kisser, by the way.**

**Stop fighting it. Give in.**

**Let me be your first kiss—and your last.**
**Love,**
**Jensen**

Leaning into her hand, she shook her head as her heart went insane in her chest.

She was fucked.

\* \* \*

"So, SHE SAID YES?"

Jensen's lips curved as he looked down at his cell phone lying in the middle of the coffee table. He had three people to call. His mom, Wren's dad, and Wells. Instead, he sat in the living room of Vaughn and Brie's new house with his heart in his throat. He wasn't having second thoughts, not even a little bit, but he hated lying. It wasn't his thing, and he was about to lie to everyone.

For her.

"Yeah."

"So you're going to call everyone."

"Yeah."

"And I get to watch?"

"Yeah. I need your support and Tricksie's," he said as the pup licked his chin, snuggling in his lap. "I'm sort of freaking out."

"Okay, let me pop some popcorn and get a beer first." Vaughn was up before Jensen could stop him.

"Dude, I'm freaking out."

"Okay, well, I can get popcorn and deal with that. What's up? Talk to me."

Jensen leaned back in the couch as he cuddled with Tricksie. "What if everyone hates me?"

"Then you're fucked."

"Vaughn!"

"What? Is she worth it?"

"Yes," he said without reluctance. "But what if she tries to end it?"

"Oh, you know she will."

"How do I stop that?"

"Who knows? You're the one doing this. Not me."

Setting his best friend with a look, Jensen shook his head. "You are absolutely no help at all."

"I know. It's a personality flaw."

"You have a lot of those."

"I do," he agreed, leaning on the bar in his kitchen. "But I think if she sees how to be loved right, she might not try to end it. You're charming. Charm her pants off."

Charm her pants off. Wow, okay. While, yes, he did very much want to get her naked and in his arms, it was more than that. He wanted her heart. He wanted it all. Closing his eyes, he could feel his lips still buzzing, and he could still taste her. Lord. Her kisses were better than he thought they'd be. He'd always known they had chemistry, he just did, but when their lips touched, it was like a cannon going off inside of him. It felt right. Perfect. She was a perfect hot mess he couldn't help but want.

The list… Man, he was still laughing about it. It was so in his favor, but she had still stalled. He got it. She was scared, so was he, but that was okay. They'd be okay. Together. He knew it. He knew it deep down. He just hoped she did too.

Letting his head fall back, he smiled as he looked around the bare house. Brie hadn't had time to do anything with it, but she had apparently hired Lucy Paxton to come in and do the design. Which it needed. Even empty, the little ranch style house was gorgeous. It was obvious Brie had picked it because Vaughn would have picked some big ole mansion that neither of them needed. But this house was perfect for them. Big back patio with a huge yard, and the best thing about it was their backyard butted up against the back fence of NateWay2. Though, word was, Marl, the grounds keeper of NateWay, wouldn't let Vaughn put an entrance in back there. Said he didn't trust it. He was kind of crazy, but they all loved him dearly. Jensen thought it was funny that Marl had said no to Vaughn, the owner of the whole damn place.

When Jensen's phone sounded with a text, he reached for it and saw it was the girl who starred in all his thoughts.

*Wren: Smooth.*

*Jensen: ??*

*Wren: I just got done with my client, and this is the first time I could text you, but I saw your message. First and last kiss, huh? You have some closet game, I see.*

He laughed as he shook his head.

*Jensen: Maybe I've always had game, just had to wait for the moment I could use it on you.*

*Wren: You've had plenty of moments.*

*Jensen: Maybe, but now I've got the next six months to give you all of it.*

*Wren: I'm not sure if I should be scared or excited.*

*Jensen: Both.*

*Wren: Intriguing, Mr. Monroe.*

*Jensen: I thought so, soon-to-be Mrs. Monroe.*

*Wren: …*

*Wren: You sure?*

*Jensen: I am.*

*Wren: I'm a hot fucking mess.*

*Jensen: And you'll be my hot mess.*

*Wren: Confession.*

*Jensen: Yeah?*

*Wren: That is probably the sweetest thing anyone has ever said to me.*

*Jensen: And to think, I'm just getting started.*

*Wren: Crap, well, then I have another confession.*

His heart stopped.

*Jensen: You're on a roll, so let me have it.*

*Wren: I've always associated love and all that crap with pain. So you'll need to be patient.*

*Jensen: You won't anymore, and don't worry, love is patient.*

*Wren: Okay, I'm not touching that. So, dinner tonight? Tacos?*

*Jensen: Send me the address.*

*Wren: Okay.*

*Jensen: Have a good rest of your day.*

*Wren: Thanks. You too.*

*Jensen: I'm about to call your parents and brother.*

*Wren: Oh, thanks for letting me know. I'll make sure to block their numbers for the rest of the night.*

Laughing, he set his phone down as Vaughn sat back down across from him. "Okay, I'm ready."

"We're flirting."

Vaughn's brows went to his hairline. "Shit, I thought you weren't gay."

Rolling his eyes, Jensen sighed. "Not us, dork. Wren and me. We're flirting."

"Oh, good. I mean, you're marrying her."

"I know, but it's nice. Hot."

"And I just puked in my mouth."

Laughing, Jensen shook his head. "I'm excited."

Vaughn shot him a grin. "Good, you deserve that."

They shared a long look before Jensen glanced away, nodding his head before he went to Wells's number. "Wells first."

"Good choice."

But he didn't hit the number. He was freaking out. Looking back up, he asked, "Where is Brie?"

Vaughn gave him an exasperated look. "Shopping with Lucy. Call him."

Jensen paused. "What if he hates me?"

"Well, you should have thought about that before you basically did Wren against the wall to get her to say yes."

"I didn't do her against the wall."

"I'm sure you didn't just peck her lips. You've wanted to kiss that girl your whole life, ever since that poor excuse for a kiss when we were younger."

"It wasn't that bad!"

Laughing hard, Vaughn sputtered, "Her friends called you turtle tongue for, like, months."

"Why didn't I know this?"

Vaughn's laughter subsided as he shook his head. "It doesn't matter now. Call Wells."

Well, shit. Okay. He wanted this.

Hitting Wells's number, Jensen put him on speaker and held the phone out as he waited for his buddy to answer. He didn't have to wait long. "Bro, hey! What's up?"

"Hey, what are you up to?"

"Just lying around as Alex and his parents talk about wedding shit. Being lazy."

"Oh, so you're at his house?"

"No, they're here. Why?"

"I need to talk to you."

"Oh. Well, let me go to my bedroom. Hold on." Jensen chewed on his lip as Vaughn threw handfuls of popcorn into his mouth, a foolish grin on his face. He was such a dork. "Okay, what's up? You okay?"

"Yeah, I'm fine. It's, um, well, it's about Wren."

"What? Is she okay?" Wells panicked, as an older brother would.

"Yeah, no, don't get upset," Jensen said calmly, though he felt like he could puke at any moment. "Listen, um, something happened between her and me back in December. I never told anyone because we both agreed it was silly and just a drunken night of fun."

Vaughn scoffed as he shook his head, which caused Jensen to throw a pillow at him. He glared back, but Jensen ignored him as Wells spoke. "Okay. So you're saying you slept with my sister?"

"Yeah."

"Okay, and when you say you both agreed it was silly, it was really that she didn't want anything more?"

"Yeah."

"She's such a dick. Okay. I mean, whatever, I'm sorry. But why are you telling me this now?"

"Um, she came over the other night and informed me that she's pregnant."

Vaughn leaned in, a grin on his face as Wells was silent while Jensen's heart was going a million miles a second in his chest. "I'm sorry, what?"

"She's six months pregnant…with my child."

"You can't have kids."

Jensen closed his eyes, pinching the bridge of his nose. Man, the lies were adding up. "I thought so too, but apparently, I can."

Closing his eyes, Jensen listened as Wells whispered, "Wow."

"Yeah."

"Are you sure she's not lying? I mean, I love my sister, but she gets around and fucks with assholes who wouldn't want a kid. You're the only good guy she knows, and you'd be a damn good dad. Are you sure, man?"

"Yeah, I asked, and she wouldn't lie to me."

"Yeah, wow. Okay."

"Um, so I want to ask her to marry me, but I want to make sure you're okay with it first."

Once again, Wells was silent as Jensen sat there having a mini panic attack. He hadn't thought this was going to be so hard, but he was finding that he was completely wrong in that sense. This was harder than ever, and he hated it. Every second. But he had to do it. For her.

"Well, she'll say yes because of the stupid inheritance. But, dude, I don't know. I mean, she'll probably blow you off when she gets the money."

Jensen closed his eyes. "That's a good possibility, but I want to try—for the baby."

"Fuck, man, I'm gonna kill her. Jesus."

Jensen cleared his throat. "You know I love her. I won't hurt her."

"Dude, I'm not worried about you hurting her. I'm worried she's gonna fuck with you. Damn it. Are you sure? Like, really sure, dude?"

Jensen's heart ached. Everyone around him, including Wren, thought she'd hurt him. But he was all in. Did that make him a masochist? Maybe it did. Clearing his throat, he said, "Yeah. I love her. I want to be there for her and my child."

"Man. Well, yeah, bro. It's about time she's loved by a good guy, and you'd do right by her. Let's just hope it sticks, and when she gets her money, she doesn't run. You are one of the best guys I know, and it would be an honor to call you my brother-in-law."

"Thanks."

"Of course. Now, if you'll excuse me, I'm going to call my sister."

"She's blocking your number."

"Damn it, she's too smart. I'll email her."

Jensen smiled. "Don't be too hard on her. She's been hiding this for a while."

"Yeah, and I don't like that."

"I didn't either."

"Well, it's in the past. Good luck with my dad."

Jensen laughed. "Thanks. I'll need it."

"No, you won't. Love ya, man."

"You too."

The line went dead, and Jensen looked up. "That went well…"

Vaughn shook his head. "He doesn't believe anything. Wells knows Wren, knows you, and knows it's a sham. He just won't admit it."

Jensen's heart dropped. He'd thought so too, but he was hoping that Vaughn didn't. "I was afraid of that."

"Maybe you'll have better luck with Winston?"

"Maybe."

Realistically, he didn't think he would. "I should have saved Wells for last."

"Yeah, now that I'm thinking about it, probably."

"Thanks a lot."

"No problem, that's what I'm here for. Call Winston."

Jensen went to Winston's number and hit call. His pseudofather answered on the fourth ring. "Jen, sorry, I was in the shop. How you doing, my boy?"

"Hey, Winston, good. What are you building?"

"Nothing, just hiding from the missus. She's always telling me I need to go walking and shit. I'm retired. I wanna eat pie and act like I'm building something."

Jensen laughed as he nodded. "Sounds like something you'd do."

"Exactly. Why can't she get that?" he laughed, a big gruff noise, and Jensen smiled. "So, to what do I owe the pleasure of this call? Usually, you call Lanie, and I get the secondhand conversation."

"I know. I'm sorry."

"Don't be. She can talk to a rock. I hate talking, and I know you do, too."

"I do."

"Ha, so what's up?"

"Um, well, Winston. I was, um—"

"Jesus, you nervous? Forget how to talk? Spit it out, boy."

Jensen laughed, shaking his head. "Yeah, um. I was calling to ask if I could marry Wren."

Vaughn sat on the edge of his seat, taking a long pull of his beer while Jensen glared. It was a bad idea doing this with him here. "Wren? My baby?"

"Yes, sir."

"You want to marry Wren? My daughter, Wren?"

"Yeah, Winston. Uh… I've known her my whole life. I've loved her for just as long, and I'd really like your blessing."

"She's pregnant, isn't she?"

Jensen's eyes widened as he looked at Vaughn, unsure what to say. But Vaughn just shrugged, shaking his head in horror. "Yes."

"She put you up to this? She's making you marry her so she doesn't lose her inheritance?"

"No, sir. I asked her."

"This girl. These kids are gonna put me in an early grave. One's getting knocked up, and my boy is marrying another boy—with glittery doves." Clearing his throat, Winston let out a long breath. "Shit, Jen. Yeah, I'd love to call you my son."

He exhaled hard in relief. "Thank you, sir."

"Good luck getting her to do it, though. That girl doesn't want to be married, and I'm surprised she's keeping the kid. She's a hard one, my Wrenny is."

Swallowing hard, Jensen nodded as he looked down at Tricksie.

The signs were right there, blinking brightly in his face, but Jensen just smiled.

"I love her. We'll be fine."

He just hoped he wouldn't find himself in another situation like he'd been in with Ophelia.

But even with all the signs and everyone, even Wren, saying the same thing, he felt right. He knew what he was getting into, he knew the girl he loved, and he was going to do his best to change her mind.

He'd get his happy ending.

With Wren.

He deserved it.

He just needed her to see that she deserved it too.

# Chapter

# EIGHT

*Dear my amazing sister, whom I love more than anything,*

*I got word today from your male caller that you will be blocking my calls, but I bet you didn't block my emails, so here we are. Male caller, also known as my best fucking friend on the face of the planet, informed me that he somehow developed some magical sperm and knocked you up. Call me surprised to hear this, but then he asked to marry you, which of course, I said yes to because I love him like he is my brother. Though, I couldn't help but know for a fucking fact that he didn't get you pregnant, nor is he marrying you because it's his kid. He's doing it for you. You're using his feelings against him, and that's shitty. Are you fucking kidding me? You asked our best friend to marry you because you got knocked up by God knows who and need a baby daddy because more than likely the dude is worthless?*

*Really!*

*Really, Wren?*

*Jesus, girl, really?*

*I can't believe you, but then I can, because that fucking money is worth it, eh? Hurting our best friend is worth fifty million? I am utterly disgusted, and I hope you're ready to explain yourself because I see through this sham. I see right through it like it's a fucking window. You're using him, and that is pathetic. I swear to God, if you think I'm okay with this, I'm not. So call me. Or I'm flying out there to pinch you since I can't hit you because that's not right and you're pregnant.*

*Which, btw, congratulations. Wells Junior is a wonderful name, works for a girl or boy, and I can't wait to meet my niece or nephew because I already love them.*

*And you. I love you.*

*But I'm fucking pissed because I love Jensen, and I don't want him hurt.*

*Love, your who you've probably diagnosed as, bipolar brother,*

*Wells*

*PS: Don't tell Jensen about this because he told me not to be hard on you, but obviously, I didn't listen to him. He can kick my ass, and since you're his one and only now, I bet he would. So, yeah, keep your pie hole shut.*

*Please & thank you.*

*Call me.*

*Now.*

Clicking off the screen from her brother's email, Wren exhaled loudly. Well, she didn't expect anything less from her brother; he was one for the dramatics. And he was completely right. She could handle her brother; she just didn't like that he saw through them. Not one bit.

Her phone was blinking with the nine thousand calls and texts from him, along with the ten million calls and voice mails from her parents. Sighing once more, she opened her voice mails and hit the first one.

"Baby girl, it's Daddy. Just got off the phone with Jensen. Call me."

"Wren, Dad again. Call me now."

"Wren, I know you aren't this busy, girl. Call me."

"I'm telling your momma, which pisses me off because I gotta leave my woodshed."

"Wren, it's your mother. Call me, please."

"Wren Josephine, I am not playing with you. I can still smack you. On your butt—that ain't pregnant."

"Young lady, why didn't you tell me about this? Lord. Your brother is upset, as is your daddy. We need to talk!"

"Now Wells is claiming you're stealing his thunder! You couldn't wait till after the wedding?"

"Okay, I didn't mean that. Your brother is dramatic. Call me. I love you. I do."

"Wren, I swear if you don't call me by eight p.m., I'm flying out. I swear it."

Glancing at the clock, she saw she had a good three hours before her mom made good on her threat. Rolling her eyes, she deleted everything and all the texts up to the point where Jensen's name was the one at the top of her text screen. A smile pulled at her lips, which calmed her pounding heart a bit.

Licking her lips, she tapped his name and typed out a message.

*Wren: So the family is pretty damn happy.*

*Jensen: Ha. Lies. All lies. Though, your dad did give me his blessing, and my mom cried, said she can't wait to hug you.*

Wren smiled.

*Wren: She did always like me.*

*Jensen: Way more than my ex-wife, so you're starting out well.*

*Wren: Thank god. Wells sees through it.*

*Jensen: I know. How are we handling that?*

*Wren: As planned. What are you doing?*

*Jensen: Nothing at all.*

*Wren: Liar. Watching* Game of Thrones.

*Jensen: Yes. I'm pathetic.*

*Wren: You are. Meet me at the restaurant? I'm starving.*

*Jensen: Leaving now.*

She sent him a kissy face emoji and then stood up. Nerves were running wild through her. Wells would be the last person she'd be calling or writing back, but she wasn't worried about her mom and dad. They would just want facts and to know what was going on. She knew for a fact they adored Jensen, so there was no worry there. But she was worried about Wells. She was also hurt that he accused her of thinking the money was more important than her friendship with Jensen. That wasn't the truth at all.

And now she was getting way more than she expected.

But telling her brother that would ruin everything, and no matter how much she wanted to confide in him, she couldn't. He'd not only blab it to their mother, he'd try to talk her out of it. Hell, he'd probably come at her hard because no one was allowed to hurt Jensen. Everyone had this pathetic notion that Jensen was fragile. She'd admit at one time she thought it too, until he stood in front of her with a list of what would happen if he were to help her. No, Jensen Monroe was not weak or fragile. He was actually pretty damn impressive.

When she glanced at her computer, she noticed in the reflection that she was grinning. She almost didn't recognize herself. For most of the last six months, she'd hardly smiled, not truly. But now, after that soul-shattering kiss, Wren was smiling. Radiantly.

And that worried her.

Damn it. She didn't want this. She didn't want to fall for him or anything like that. She just wanted to get through this because she knew she wasn't worthy of someone like Jensen. Supermodel, sweetheart Jensen Monroe belonged with someone like Taylor Swift or Emma Watson, or even Emma Stone. Pretty girls with banging bodies and shit like that. Not frumpy, fat, and pregnant Wren Lemiere. As much as she hated thinking of herself like that, she couldn't help it.

And that was a problem because she was about to marry Jensen for real, and she was going to have to keep her heart in check the whole time.

It was a very hard road ahead of her, but she didn't have a choice.

As WREN PARKED, she knew she probably should have answered the phone when her mom called four times on her way to the restaurant, but she was hangry and didn't want to yell at her mom. Tucking her phone into her purse, she started to gather all her stuff when her door opened suddenly. Reaching for her pepper spray, she held it up, ready to shoot, but paused when she saw it was Jensen looking down at her.

"Well, that would have put me in a world of suck."

She laughed as she shook her head, throwing it into the cup holder. "I thought you were going to rape and kill me."

"Kill you, no. And rape, I mean, I'm not down with it any other time, but if you wanna do some role-playing, I guess I can get with that if it's your thing."

She sputtered with laughter. "I'm pretty sure you can't role-play as a rapist. You would ask me if it's okay and then ask if you're hurting me as you're supposed to be choking me."

A grin played at his lips as he held his hand out for her. "Probably."

Taking it, she got out as he shut the door, and she put her purse on her arm. "Good try, though," she said, patting his bicep, and he smiled. "I'm not into that stuff anyway. I just like it a little rough. Smack my ass, call me your dirty girl, good stuff like that." His grin grew as his expression turned to delectable. "Why did I admit that?"

"'Cause you're actually letting yourself be you instead of this closed-up Wren who, let me point out, is very frustrating."

She set him with a look. "Or I'm hungry and not thinking clearly."

A smirk pulled at his lips. "Or that. Let's get you and baby fed," he said, placing his hand on the small of her back as they headed toward the restaurant. They were seated quickly and ordered just as fast, both of them knowing what they wanted.

"I really like eating with you," she said, sitting back and exhaling loudly. "Like, for real. No waiting, no chitchat, just order, and get the food."

He smiled back at her. "I know food."

"Right? Me too. I love food."

Folding his hands on the table, he licked his lips, and she found it hard to concentrate when he did that. "So, how was your day?"

Swallowing hard, she looked away as she shrugged. "Busy. So many clients, but it's good. They need it, and I love it."

"Yeah, you're great at it from what I hear."

She smiled with a shrug. "I'm okay."

"Plus, I don't know many pregnant women who can go through a whole day of emotional work and still look at gorgeous as they did when they started."

Her cheeks filled with color as she waved him off. "Stop."

"Never."

He said it as a promise, one she realized he meant to keep as soon as she met his gaze. His lips were tipped at the sides, and for a moment, she almost didn't recognize him. He looked so damn hot, not in the supermodel way, but in a different, explode her world kind of way. She almost couldn't handle it. It was too much, and soon she looked away, shaking her head. "Anyway, did you make the appointment to get married?"

"Yeah, two tomorrow works well for everyone. I called and made sure you didn't have clients."

Her breath caught. "Oh, cool. Did Leah block me out for that time?"

"Yeah."

"So tomorrow?"

Breathless, she watched as he nodded. "Tomorrow. That's okay, right?"

"Yeah, fine. Wow. Okay."

She clapped her hands, and he laughed, shaking his head. "It's gonna be fine."

"Yeah. Totally."

Thankfully, their food arrived, and Wren dug in as soon as the waitress set her plate down, in an effort to hide the fact that she was having a mild panic attack. Since Jensen was the only one without his mouth full, as well as the one with manners, he thanked the waitress before glancing over at Wren. "How many bedrooms does your apartment have?"

"One," she said around a bite. "Yours has two?"

"Yeah. So you wanna move in to mine?"

"Yeah, I guess. I'll pack a bag."

His fork stopped just above his food as he looked over at her. "Or I can get the truck and trailer from Vaughn, come over with some boxes, and pack you up."

She shrugged. "No reason we should bring all my crap."

His expression didn't change, his gaze intent on hers. "Yes, we should. We're moving in together."

"Yeah, but—"

His eyes stopped her words. They were almost challenging, and she didn't get what was going on. Why would she move her whole apartment... But then it dawned on her. "Wait, was this part of your terms?"

"It is."

"So, you want to really do that? Live together?"

"Yeah."

"And make love."

He quirked his lips. "Yes."

She took in a deep breath and let it out through her nose. She could do this. "I'm pregnant."

He smiled. "I'm aware."

"My body—"

"Moving on," he demanded, and she rolled her eyes. While it was kind of sweet that he wouldn't let her bad-mouth herself, it was also quite annoying.

"Then boxes it is. But if this doesn't work out, you're moving me back in to my apartment."

"Well, then it will work even better than expected 'cause I hate moving crap."

"Me too," she agreed as she started to stuff her face once more.

"Also, can you see about taking off the week before the week you're taking off for the wedding?"

She looked up, confused. "Why?"

"I'm going home for the week before to see my family and have my day with the Cup. I want you to be there."

She lit up. "Yeah, of course. I'll— Oh, we'll be a married couple to your parents."

He smiled. "Yeah, just like with your family and at home —our home."

She sucked her teeth. "But that's my family. The point of this."

"No, the point of this is to make something better out of the situation we were given."

She blinked. "You don't have to, though."

"You're right. I want to."

"That makes me nervous."

"Well, it does me too, but it's a part of it."

"Okay, yeah, um… I'll work it out, just get me the dates."

"I'll text them to you tomorrow."

"Great," she said as she took another bite of her meal, her mind going crazy. She knew they were doing this, she was in, but she didn't realize she'd have to do it in front of his family. They were such good, amazing people. Not that her family wasn't, but it would be easier to pretend with them because they were holding her money. With his family, it was different. They were kind. They would love her as their own. They'd love the baby. She would love them even more.

And Jensen.

This was getting complicated.

As she picked at her rice, he cleared his throat. "What's wrong?"

She looked up, shrugging. "A lot to process."

Licking his lips, he reached out, taking her hand in his. "I understand that, Wren, but I'll always be there for you." She swallowed hard as he commanded her gaze. "I won't ever leave you, unless you tell me you don't want me."

Man, she felt stupid for not believing him, but when had anyone ever stood beside her? Other than her family? Yeah, that was it. While, yes, he was family, she just couldn't believe he would. Call it a mental flaw, but she simply couldn't grasp that he would want to. "You know I'm me and you're you, right?"

His brow arched as he laid down his fork. "Yeah, I'm aware, but enlighten me on what you mean."

She glared and he smiled. "Don't get sassy, mister."

"My apologies."

"Anyway, I mean, you're Jensen Monroe, supermodel-hot hockey goalie guy, and you can have anyone. I mean, anyone. Just wear a sign that says 'Looking for a chick who wants to do me,' and they'll line up."

"But I don't want a chick just to do me. I want a wife, I want a family, and guess what? You need a husband and a father for your child, so, hey, here I am. Willing and wanting."

"Jenny, really—"

"I thought this was decided. Why are we circling back around? You're stuck with me," he said, kissing the back of her hand before taking a big bite of his taco. When he glanced up, she was sure he saw that she was gaping at him. "What?"

"I'm me."

He nodded. "I know. So?"

"I'm sort of fat and frumpy, and I've got this mean streak, and it's gonna take me a while to lose the baby fat because I like food—"

"Let me stop you right there, please."

Dropping his fork, he scooted out of the booth. "What are you doing?"

"Coming to you," he said simply before sitting beside her and taking her face in his hands. "Let me tell you something, and we're gonna squash this real quick, okay?"

Her eyes were wide, and man, he smelled so damn good. Swallowing hard, she nodded. "Okay?"

"I don't care about any of that, unless you're deliberately unhealthy. Then together we'll give up the bad foods and enjoy other healthy foods. I'll work out with you if you want. I'll be there for you because that's my job as your husband and because I want to." Her eyes started to water as he held her gaze. "I am not Douche One, Two, Three, Seven, Nine, or Ninety-Nine. Okay? I'm Jensen, your husband, and I will never make you feel less than perfect, because that's what you are in my eyes. Do you understand me?"

She blinked. What else could she do? Who said things like that? Who held someone's face like that while looking into their eyes as if they were the only one in the room? Who, with each word, made it obvious he meant the words like they were his last? No one, and she meant no one, had ever in her life talked to her like that.

But Jensen did.

At that moment, she realized he was way more than just a fake husband. Even though he had implied that from the beginning, she had thought he was just going for an easy lay or something along those lines. But staring into his eyes, she was starting to realize this wasn't a game Jensen Monroe was playing to help her.

He was playing to win her.

She wasn't sure how the hell she was supposed to stay strong against that.

* * *

JENSEN LOVED HOLDING WREN.

She smelled like a mix of pineapples and tacos, or maybe that was just her meal, he wasn't sure, but he loved looking into her beautiful green gaze. Her lips were parted ever so slightly, and her eyes were wide, full of complete wonder. If she thought he was going to be like those other guys she dated, she had another thing coming. He had waited for the moment when he would get to have her, and now that he did, she wasn't going anywhere without a fight.

"Do you understand me, Wren?"

Slowly, she nodded, her eyes holding his. "I do."

He could see the hesitation in her eyes. "But you don't believe me?"

"I'm trying," she admitted, a grimace on her face, and he scoffed.

"You're going to give me a run for my money, aren't you?"

"I told you I'm not easy."

"You did," he said before leaning in and pressing his lips to hers. Her eyes fell shut first, and he loved how perfect she looked when he kissed her. Her lashes were long, her nose fit into the crook beside his, and he could spend the rest of his days kissing her and die a damn happy man. Tasting her was his first mistake, because now he wouldn't be able to let her go. Ever. He'd take a bullet, he'd lay his life down for her in a second.

And while he knew she might not do the same, right now, he didn't care.

He loved her. Passionately.

Pulling back, he dropped his hands from her face as her lips stayed parted and her eyes shut. If he didn't get away, he'd take her right there in the booth; he knew that to be true. Getting up, he headed back to his side, taking his fork in hand as he sat. When he looked across the table, her lips were still parted. "You okay there?"

"You weren't kidding about being a better kisser."

He snickered as he nodded. "Oh, yeah?"

"Yeah," she agreed with a smile before reaching for her fork.

"Well, good to know," he said, resting on his elbows.

Recovering slightly, she leaned against the table. "No one has ever talked to me like that."

"Good. I like being the first." They shared a sweet smile before she went back to inhaling her food. "So, let me ask you something. Are we good with the agreement on the baby?"

She looked up. "What do you mean?"

"Like you won't renege on that, right? You'll let me be the father if for some far-off chance we don't work out?"

"If that is what you want."

"It is."

"Then, of course. I promise."

Swallowing hard, he asked, "And the biological dad, he won't try anything?"

She exhaled, shaking her head. "I called him today, actually."

His heart stopped as he met her gaze. "Oh? I didn't know you still talked to him. Or knew him."

"Wow, thanks," she said dryly, and he smiled an apology. "He's still a big fucking douche, and yes, my child will only know you as his father until he is old enough for us to tell him otherwise."

Jensen nodded. "And you're fine with that?"

She nodded. "In a way. I mean, I would have asked for you, Vaughn, and Wells to be in my son's life anyway. To guide him, y'know? We're all so tight-knit."

"Yeah, but he'll be mine."

"I know," she said, but he still could see the hesitation in her eyes.

"Okay." Jensen looked away, biting his lip. "I heard about what he had said to you."

"Oh?"

"About you not being trophy wife material."

"Brie can't keep her mouth shut, I swear. Yeah, he's a douche."

"Well, I think you're trophy wife material."

She looked up, a grin on her face as she sputtered with laughter. "It seriously is okay. It didn't bother me."

She was lying, and he knew it. "Okay. I'm not saying it to make you feel better. I'm telling you the truth."

"Oh yeah?"

"Yeah, I'd take you over my Cup any day."

Her lips curved more, her whole face rising in the motion of that gorgeous smile. "Liar."

"Nope. Truth."

Shaking her head, she waggled her fork at him. "You'd better stop. You'll have me thinking you really have feelings for me."

He shrugged. "What's wrong with that?"

"Um, because it isn't true."

"Who said it isn't true?"

Her brows touched as she held his gaze. "What are you saying?"

Swallowing hard, Jensen put down his fork and laced his fingers together. "Wren, surely you know?"

She shook her head. "Know what?"

"That—" He stopped himself. He didn't want to tell her over tacos. If she truly didn't know, then he needed to find the perfect time. Not now. He met her gaze once more and was a bit frustrated. It pissed him off that this amazing, beautiful, smart girl didn't know her worth. That she was the light of his life. That he hadn't started living until she'd asked him to be her fake husband. Swallowing hard, he smiled. "That you mean the world to me."

"I know that, but as a friend. Not a wife."

"No, as more."

She held his gaze. "Well, obviously, since you want to marry me."

"So you know."

"I know this is all insane and scary, but I'm in," she rambled. "I don't even know how it's gonna work, but you're convinced."

"And you should be too. We know each other inside and out. We've fought, we've laughed, and everything else——"

"We have never fought."

"Yes, we did. When I got engaged, you told me not to marry her."

She thought that over. "I did call you a dumbass, didn't I?"

"That and some other choice words because you thought it was a horrible idea," he said dryly, but she hadn't been the only one. Everyone didn't like Ophelia and thought he had rushed into it. Maybe he had. To forget the girl across the table.

"It was, and I was obviously right."

They held each other's gaze. "Touché."

"Exactly. I can call them a mile away."

"Is that how it is with your guys? You can call them a mile away?"

She raised an eyebrow. "That's low."

"Hey, just asking. You know they're assholes before you get with them, right?"

"Well, considering I'm only using them for sex at first, I guess so. But then things get a little sideways."

"Is that how little man came along?"

She bit her lip. "I truly thought he loved me. No, it wasn't a relationship, but we had been on and off for over three years, so it sucked."

He didn't like the sound of that, and he was also racking his brain as to who the hell it could be. She hadn't been with anyone, or yet, he hadn't met anyone she was with. She was always solo at events, so he really had no clue. He ran his tongue along the inside of his bottom lip. "Are you over him?"

She rolled her eyes. "If I wasn't before the phone call today, I am now." He nodded, and she held his gaze. "He's not on my radar, I promise."

"Yeah, I'm not worried at all."

He was.

"Good."

"Great."

They shared another smile, and then he clapped his hands together. "You look happy about that," she observed

He held her gaze, nodding his head. "I am. But also, I'm just happy."

She shot him a sneaky grin. "It's a good look on you."

"It looks good on you too, when you let it." She pursed her lips at him, and he chuckled as he started to eat once more. "So a boy, huh?"

She grinned. "Yup."

"Excited? Or did you want a girl?"

Her face lit up a bit. "Well, since I didn't want a kid to start with, at first, it was just a shock. In fact, it was for most of the time until I saw his little face on the ultrasound, and then I decided I just wanted a healthy kid. And he is. Which is awesome."

"It is," he agreed, his heart swelling in his chest. "Has it been an easy pregnancy?"

"No, not at all," she laughed, leaning on her elbow. "Lots of sickness at the beginning, and the cravings are out of this world."

"Good thing you like food, then."

She smiled. "Yeah, but I hate leaving my bed."

"I can understand that." Taking the last bite of his taco, he leaned back in the booth. "Have you thought of names?"

She shrugged. "Not really. Just kiddo."

"Well, Kiddo Monroe won't do."

She laughed, her eyes bright as she nodded. "Agreed."

"You'll have to pick out a name. My mom will want to know."

"Yeah," she agreed, taking a sip of her water. "Any ideas?"

His heart shattered as he stared into her eyes. "I get to help?"

Her face was full of compassion. "I thought he was your kid."

"He is," he said automatically, even though it was hard to breathe. "And thanks."

She gave him a look that was a mixture of fear, but also something more. Almost heat, desire, and soon his body was on fire. More so than it usually was around her. He wanted her. He wanted to pull her into his arms and take her. Make her truly his, but it wasn't time. He had to lay the groundwork, get her full trust before he gave her his body. She already had his heart, but he wanted her everything, and for that to happen, she had to trust him. Believe in him.

As they stared heatedly at each other, her fork pressing into her bottom lip, he was on fire within seconds. He didn't care what anyone said. They had an understanding between them, and he, for one, felt right about it. Good, even. Was he scared? Out of his mind. The people who had problems with this would be people he loved and respected, but he was starting to realize, as he looked across the table at the girl he had loved for so long, that he might love her more than the lot of them.

When her phone started to ring, she broke from his gaze as she let out a long breath. "What time is it?"

He glanced at his watch. "Almost seven."

She exhaled loudly. "I need to take this before the wrath of Elaine Lemiere is upon us." He just laughed as she answered. "Mom. Yes, I'm fine. No, I'm not crazy. Oh, look, Jensen wants to say hi."

As he rolled his eyes, she put her mother on speakerphone. "Hey, Elaine."

"Hello, honey, how are you?"

"Great."

"Well, I'd say so, marrying my daughter after knocking her up. At least he asked your father. Did you know that, Wren?"

"I did, Mom."

"Good, because he's a gentleman."

Jensen beamed as Wren rolled her eyes. "I know, Mom."

"About time you found a good one."

"I've known him forever."

"Well, I always said you two would be perfect together."

Wren made a face. "When did you say that?"

"To your father and Wells. We all thought so." Wren rolled her eyes again, but Jensen just grinned. He might have heard Elaine say that. "Emma is excited. I already spoke to her since you wouldn't answer my calls."

"Cool. I'm excited to see her."

"Okay, so this is for real happening?"

"It is," Jensen said softly. "Are you okay with that?"

"Of course, I am. I love you, honey."

"I love you too."

"And I won't have to worry a bit for her. She'll be taken care of."

"She will—completely," he admitted, and Wren looked at him, a little surprised by his promise.

"I'm going to be a grandma."

"The hottest one in the town," he teased, and she cackled like an old biddy.

"I knew I would love you for the rest of my life when I first met you, Jenny," Elaine admitted, and Wren pursed her lips. "But okay, I'll let you two get back to dinner. Call me later, Wren?"

"So you can yell at me for not telling you anything? No, I'll have Jensen with me every time."

"You are too smart for your own good."

Jensen laughed at that while they said bye, and Wren hung up. "She won't yell at me when you're around."

"Then I guess I'm not going anywhere."

As her cheeks filled with color and she looked away, he didn't care that she didn't believe him. Because, while they were just words, and she was used to words with no promise in them, he was about to show her he meant business.

He'd been waiting a very long time to do just that.

"Ready to get out of here?" he asked, throwing some money on the table with a hefty tip since Wren had made a bit of a mess.

Cleaning up the rice that fell off the plate, she laughed. "Yeah, but man, I'm messy."

"Which is why I left a big tip."

She continued to laugh as she scooted out of the booth to where he waited for her. Once she was beside him, they headed out. "So, two tomorrow? At the courthouse?"

"Yeah, do you want me to pick you up?" he asked as they walked toward her car.

"No, 'cause I'll have to go back to work," she said, obviously immersed in thought. "That's okay, right?"

He nodded. "It's fine. We can have dinner to celebrate. If you want."

"I mean, I love food," she said as they reached her car. Turning to look at him, she shrugged her shoulders. "Did you want to go back to my house?"

He eyed her. "To pack?"

"Ugh, no. I'm too tired for that, but not for other things," she hinted, and he shook his head.

"No, you need to go home and get some rest "

She looked at him skeptically. "Did you just turn me down?"

He smiled. "I did."

"Rude."

"You'll live."

"My ego—"

"Is fine," he answered for her. Though his cock was begging to go home with her, he knew it was a bad idea. He wanted this to mean something, not just be another hookup she'll be able to throw away.

"So, yeah, tomorrow."

He nodded, taking a step toward her, his hands moving to grasp her hips. "Tomorrow," he said, biting his lip as his eyes zoned in on hers.

She swallowed hard, her eyes swirling with desire. "Are you sure?"

"About tomorrow? Or about going home with you?"

"Both."

"Yes," he answered simply before leaning in and capturing her lips with his own. She leaned into him, and his hands slid along her back, holding her in place as she drew the kiss out, her tongue playing hard against his. His whole body wanted her, and he felt like a complete idiot for pulling away and putting space between them, but he knew things would go right where they shouldn't if he didn't.

"Your kisses say something else."

He chuckled, running his hand down his face. "I have no control over my body."

"Obviously, you do," she said as he backed away.

"Goodnight, Wren."

She scoffed as she shook her head. "Night, Jenny."

They shared one last heated grin as he got into his car, letting out a breath he hadn't realized he was holding. His body was shaking and his heart was beating out of control, but he knew he did the right thing. She was reverting to what she knew best. Keeping it to just fucking, and he wasn't going to let her do that. This was real. Yes, he did the right thing by sending her home. Alone.

Didn't he?

# Chapter NINE

Wedding day. *Let's do this.*
       Wren was getting married.
Married.
To Jensen fucking Monroe.
Yeah. Married.
Wren. Married. To. Jensen. Fucking. Monroe.
Fuck, she was getting married today.
To Jensen!
Glaring at her computer screen, Wren saw her face was wrinkled to the max, and she looked like she had to poop. Not very sexy, but she couldn't actually wrap her head around what she was about to do in a matter of hours. She understood that she wanted this, that she had asked him, but when she did that, she'd thought it was going to be easy peasy, lemon squeezy. But now it was fucking hard. It wasn't a simple marriage anymore. No, now it was real.

Well, Jensen wanted it to be real.

Damn it.

Running her hands down her face, she inhaled a harsh breath as she begged her heart to slow down even a little bit. Just a tad so she didn't feel like she was about to pass out. Or worse, have a panic attack. Pushing her shoulders back, she sat up straighter, staring at her screen as she chewed on her lip.

"You're going to be a married woman." The words seemed foreign. "Mrs. Monroe. Or maybe Mrs. Lemiere-Monroe. No, Jensen is old-fashioned. He'd want me to take his name. Yeah. So, okay. Hi, I'm Wren Monroe! Okay, girl, let's be honest, you don't even talk like that. Too cheerful." She swallowed hard, wiggling her nose at her reflection. "Hello, I'm Wren Monroe. My husband is Jensen Monroe, the goalie for the Nashville Assassins. We're having a baby, a little boy."

Well, it didn't sound that bad. Actually believable. Go her.

Who was she kidding? She was a fraud. She didn't believe anything that came out of her mouth. But that wasn't even what was bothering her the most. She still didn't understand why he didn't come home with her. She basically put her vagina on a silver platter, presenting it to him, and he just told her to go home and get rest. What the heck! Did he not want it? He seemed to want it, especially when he kissed the stuffing out of her. Yet, he didn't want to come home with her.

It was weird. This was weird.

She was really doing this.

Dropping her head to her desk, she took in a deep breath before looking at her little belly. "Kiddo, we're getting married today." When he kicked, Wren smiled. "Well, at least one of us is excited."

When her phone sounded, she sat up as Leah said, "Ms. Lemiere, there is a call for you on line one. They said it was about the tube steak you ordered?"

Her face wrinkled. "I didn't order any tube steak."

"That's what I assumed, but he was very persistent in speaking to you before your next client."

"Weird. Okay, thanks," she said, but just when she pressed line one, it hit her.

Wells.

"Crap."

"Yup! Gotcha," her brother cheered, and she closed her eyes, leaning on her hand.

"You suck."

"I rock, and you know it."

"I don't even kinda agree. I'm avoiding you, especially after the douchetastic email you sent me."

He scoffed. "Excuse me for not thinking that through, but I was a bit shocked."

"Still, you were a dick."

"What do you expect, Wren? I can see right through this shit, and what's killing me is you have Jensen believing it's real."

"Who says it isn't?" she snapped back. "I'm pregnant with his child. Yeah, I ran and hid it, but it's real."

"Don't fucking lie to me. You got knocked up by some scumbag, and you're using our best friend. Damn it, Wren, the money isn't worth it."

"You're wrong, and I wouldn't do that."

"Yeah, you would. You've needed this money since college. It's all you've ever talked about, getting it for us. I don't even want it if this is how you have to get it."

Rolling her eyes, she bit out, "I don't even know why I'm talking to you. I've got a big day. We're getting married in a matter of—"

"You're doing that today? Are you serious?"

"Yes, he wants to get married before we go home and see his parents."

"Oh my God, Wren, what are you doing?"

"Trying to give my kid a good life with his father, mind you."

"You've never in your life wanted to get married or have kids. This is all mind-blowing to me."

"Well, I'm sorry, but things change. I'm older—"

"You know I see through you, right? You got knocked up, didn't know how to find a husband since the scumbag wouldn't have you, and you decided to ask the nicest guy on earth because you knew he wouldn't say no."

"That's not true," she tried, but her voice broke, her eyes filling with tears. "I care for him."

Wells scoffed. "You care for him. Wow, Wren, you can't even lie and say you love him? Jesus, you're going to ruin his life."

"I am not!"

"Yes, you are. Because he isn't like you. He does have a soul, and he is a good guy—"

"I mean, fuck, Wells, I'm your sister, and that's what you think of me?"

"Wren, you're the one who always says you don't have a soul because you don't care about anyone but yourself. I see that clearly now."

"Wow, thanks."

"Hey, if the shoe fits."

"Fuck you, Wells, you know nothing."

Her brother laughed. "I know you both, and let me tell you something. I love you. I love you so much, I do——"

"Yeah, like I believe that after what you just said."

He exhaled through the phone as her tears started to fall down her cheeks. "I do, Wren, really. You're my world, my baby sister. But this is low, and if you hurt him, I don't know how I'll ever look at you again."

Her heart fell, her lips trembling as her tears fell faster. "What about me? What happens if he hurts me?"

"He wouldn't do that."

"How do you know? You can't tell the fucking future!"

"Because I know Jensen. I bet when you told him you were pregnant and needed a dad for the baby, he jumped at the chance. Because not only is he a good dude, but he's loved you his whole damn life, but he didn't think he was good enough for you because he couldn't give you kids!"

She snapped her lips shut, almost dropping the phone. "You're lying. He doesn't love me."

"Are you fucking kidding me? Wren, he thinks you fart glitter and make the world turn."

She was speechless. Surely, Wells was lying. This couldn't be. She would have known. Wouldn't she? Did she really not pay attention? It just seemed so foreign to her. It didn't seem right. No, she would have known. "Stop. You're just trying to make me feel bad for something I'm not even doing."

"No, you know it's true. Everyone knows he's had a thing for you."

"I didn't know that!"

"Because you're too consumed with yourself. I'm so mad at you, I could scream. I can't believe you're using his feelings to get ahead, for some money? Money doesn't make you happy, Wren, love does. Jensen knows that, but I know you don't."

Shaking her head, she closed her eyes. "Wow, you're really being an asshole, Wells."

"Someone has to be. Someone has to tell you the truth and protect the people they love. I can't believe you."

"I can't believe you're coming at me like this. You're my brother. Why aren't you being supportive?"

"Because it's all a lie."

"It's not! We're having a baby, he wants to get married, and yeah, maybe I didn't want that, but I need to be. Maybe that's why I agreed, but my intentions aren't malicious, Wells. I care for him."

"Yeah, they may not be malicious, Wren, because you're not a malicious person, but that doesn't mean you won't break his heart when you decide to end it after you have your money. Because you won't need him then."

She shook her head, her tears coming faster down her face. "So that's what you think of me?"

"It's what I know, and as much as it hurts to say it, I have to protect my friend and my niece or nephew because it will cause ill will between you two."

"What about protecting your sister? Did you have this conversation with him?"

"I don't have to."

Silence stretched between them as Wren wiped her face. She understood that Wells was very opinionated and maybe a little harsh sometimes, but usually, he was right. This time was no different, except she didn't feel she was using Jensen in a vicious way. She didn't intend to hurt him; it was the last thing she wanted. She was worried she'd be the one to get hurt. But apparently, everyone had already pegged her for the heartbreaker. What else was new? She was never good enough for anyone.

"I won't hurt him."

"Then don't marry him."

"That's happening."

"Then there is nothing else to say."

"Guess not."

"Whatever."

"Yeah, whatever."

Shaking her head, she slammed the phone down before dropping her face in her hands and letting out a sob that filled her office. "What a fucking jerk."

He had just crossed the line. There were no two ways about it, he did. She didn't care that he was trying to be there for Jensen, or he was protective or whatever, because he was a jerk. God, she hated crying. It made her feel weak, pathetic, but her brother's words stung. They stung so badly she swore she felt the burn on her skin as if it were real. She didn't get it. Why was she always the bad guy? Because she liked to fuck around? Because she wasn't emotionally attached to anyone but Wells and her parents? Why was she like that? The answer was clear. Because she was never good enough.

Growing up, it was always Wells who was the center of attention. He was the next Winston Lemiere on the ice. And at the time, Wells and their dad were best friends. Then Vaughn came along, and everyone loved him. Then Jensen, the golden boy. Wren was always on the back burner. She didn't play hockey, she didn't do sports, and she sure as hell didn't bake, so what did her parents have to talk to her about? They didn't care about the things she did, the books she read, or the movies she watched. No, she was just there. Existing. Even so, she knew they loved her. She did… But she never felt she mattered. She didn't have purpose in their eyes.

They didn't love her for who she was; they loved her because they had to.

Or at least, that's how she felt.

Which was shitty, and the therapist part of her knew she probably needed to investigate it a bit more, but hadn't she done that enough? When she thought about it too much, she'd usually get annoyed and then go find someone to love her for the night. The problem with that method was that, whoever the lucky guy was, he usually turned out to be a Grade A jackass. Nasty cycle. Disgusting. And one that was going to stop.

At least for six months.

Which really meant a year.

Which, really, meant she had to learn to cope.

Right?

Was she grasping at straws?

Hmm. Putting that thought on the back burner, she looked out at her empty office and wiped her face. She couldn't believe the way Wells had acted, and she almost called her mom to tell on him. But knowing her mom, she'd probably question her the same. Who knew? Fucking hell, this was a mess.

When her phone started ringing, she jumped in surprise before she realized it was her cell. Rifling through the papers cluttering her desk since the ringtone indicated it wasn't any of her family, she found her cell beside her pen cup and saw that it was Jensen.

Crap on a cracker.

Clearing her throat, she wiped her face once more and answered, "Hey!"

He paused. "What's wrong?"

She made a face at the complete emptiness of her office that matched her soul, apparently. "Huh? Nothing."

"Liar, you don't answer the phone like that. Are you standing me up?"

Her shoulders fell. "Not at all. Promise."

"Then what's wrong?"

Her lip wobbled, and she let out a small sob. "My brother is a jerk."

He didn't even hesitate. "Do you want me to come to the office?"

"No, it's fine. He's just a douche."

"What did he say?"

"What didn't he say?" she cried, wiping her face as she shook her head. "I'm seriously okay. I'm just overemotional, and he hurt my feelings."

"Want me to kick his ass?"

That made her smile. "Will you?"

"Sure will. Deck him right in the chest."

"You're too sweet."

"Say the word."

She was tempted. "No, it's fine."

"Okay, well, stop crying. Don't let it ruin the day, okay?"

She swallowed hard. Ruin the day, because they were getting married, and that was supposed to be happy. Her tears came faster. "Okay."

"Good, are you sure you're okay?"

She nodded, though he obviously couldn't see her. "Yeah, I'm fine. Promise."

"Okay."

"Okay. Are you okay? Are you standing me up?"

He laughed, and she could just imagine him shaking his head, his mouth turned up in a charming grin. "Never. I was actually calling to see what you were wearing so that I could match you."

She made a face as she looked down. "I'm wearing a yellow tunic and jeans."

"Jeans?"

She paused. "Yes."

"Jeans make sense," he said, but he sounded very annoyed. "We're not getting married or anything."

She bit her lip. "I can see now that the jeans were a bad choice."

"Just a bit, but it's fine. My mom won't care."

"Yes, she will."

"She will, but it's cool. I mean, you're at work, it's fine."

It wasn't fine at all, not even a little bit. God, she was a bitch. A soulless fucking bitch. "I'll stop by… Okay, wait. I can't stop…shit," she said when she pulled up her schedule.

"It's fine, Wren, I'll see you in a bit, okay?"

Yup, she was scum. She heard it in his voice. And then she heard Wells taunting her the way he did when he was right, back when they were younger. Like a dog with its tail between her legs, she muttered, "Okay."

"Oh, did your doorman say if the movers showed up?"

She closed her eyes since that was another thing that had come as a shock. "Yeah, they did, and I told you not to pay for that."

"I want to, okay?"

"Fine. I don't like it, though."

"Noted, see you soon."

"Bye," she said, hanging up and then shaking her head. "I'm complete shit. Wells is right, and I'm dumb. Damn it."

Clicking through her schedule, her heart was in her throat as she got madder and madder with each passing second. She didn't want to be what Wells had said. She wasn't using Jensen; she wouldn't do that. She wasn't that person. She had made it clear what her intentions were at the beginning, Jensen was the one who made it more, but she couldn't tell Wells that. God, Wells made her so angry! But what if she was what he said? She almost turned the movers away that morning. She hadn't even thought to get dressed up for her wedding day. All Jensen wanted was a nice picture for his mom, and he'd even offered to beat up her brother.

Dammit. She was everything Wells had said.

"No, I'm fucking not."

Reaching for her phone, she called Leah. "Hello?"

"Hey, do me a *huge* favor."

"Okay?"

"I need you to go to Macy's and pick me out something I can

get married in. Something pretty, I don't care how much it costs. Put it on the company card—"

"I'm sorry, what? Get married in?"

"Yeah, and make sure it's maternity, size fourteen. Or large. Or maybe extra large, my butt is getting a tad bit bigger than I expected," she said, annoyed. "And then cancel my afternoon. Reschedule for Friday."

"Whoa, whoa, Wren. I'm sorry. I'm completely confused right now."

"With what? What did you miss?"

"Everything! You're pregnant and getting married?"

"Yeah, at two, so I need this all done kind of fast. I'll take the next client, so that gives you an hour to get my dress."

"What in the world?"

"Are we good?"

"I mean, I guess."

"Cool," she said, hanging up and then reaching for her cell phone.

*Wren: Leah is going to go get me a dress. Not sure what the color is, but wear that light gray suit you wore to the gala. It will go with anything she chooses, and I like your eyes in that suit.*

His response was immediate.

*Jensen: Done.*

*Wren: Cool.*

*Jensen: And thanks.*

Sitting back in her chair, she exhaled heavily as she grasped her belly. "Well, kiddo, I'm going to fucking try, okay? But I can't guarantee anything. I'm a fucking mess and I really shouldn't say fucking to my kid, but I am because I'm a mess, and I love you. I don't only love myself, I love you, okay? And you'll always know that. So let's go get married. You'll love Jensen, and he'll definitely love you. Okay?"

When her little kiddo kicked hard, the bump surprising her against her hand, a big grin covered her face.

She was doing this.

She was still scared to the point where she might puke.

But she was doing it.

* * *

Wren looked beautiful.

Jensen thought that of her daily, but staring into her green eyes, a silk flower crown on her head as her long dark hair fell onto her shoulders, he swore she rattled his soul. The dress she wore was completely unlike her, and he knew she hated it, but boy, did he love it. It hugged every single curve on her body, her belly on full display as the top ruffled over, revealing her sexy shoulders. She had redone her makeup softer than usual, and the only reason he knew that was because she had been late. Blamed it on that, but he didn't care.

She looked like a goddess.

Inhaling shakily, he was lost in her eyes as they both repeated what the hired pastor was saying. The room they stood in was so small, he was surprised that they, the pastor, and Vaughn and Brie all fit. But it was nice to be just them, because he couldn't look at anything but her. His body vibrated with his love and need for her. She looked like a deer in headlights, but she repeated every word of the vows. When it was time for her to slide his ring down his finger, she was shaking so badly, but he hid it by holding his hand over hers. The way she looked up at him, almost like he had saved her, took his breath away.

"By the power vested in me, I now pronounce you husband and wife. You may kiss your bride."

Wren looked up at Jensen expectantly, but he hadn't taken his eyes off her since the moment they planted themselves in that spot. Reaching out, he took her face in his hands, his thumbs gliding along her cheeks as he slowly dropped his mouth to hers. Her eyes slowly shut as she leaned into him, and he basked in the look of peace on her face before he closed his own eyes. He wasn't sure how in the hell he was supposed to get used to the feeling of her against his lips, but in a way, he hoped he never did. He loved the fluttering feeling it gave him deep inside. As her fingers dug into his bicep, she clung to him as he deepened the kiss. It felt like a dream.

"Get a room," Vaughn called out.

"For a fake marriage, this sure does seem like a real kiss." Brie must have thought she whispered, but Jensen heard her clearly as he slowly pulled away, opening his eyes to find Wren blinking up at him.

Swallowing hard, she asked, "We did it?"

"We did," he whispered, brushing his thumbs along her cheeks, not wanting to ever move from that moment for the rest of his life.

But then Vaughn was loud and trying to pay the pastor. And Brie was dragging them outside for pictures because the lighting was better. All Jensen wanted was to hold his wife.

Wren. Wren was his wife.

"Are you sure I don't look fat in this dress? I swear, Leah is such a little thing and doesn't think like a big girl—"

"You look gorgeous," he said, cutting her off before he wrapped his arms around her from behind, bringing her against him. Her ass fit perfectly against his groin, and that was bad. Very bad.

"Oh, yes! This is perfect," Brie called out, trying to hold her phone, his phone, Vaughn's, and Wren's. Why they didn't take one picture with one phone and text it to everyone else was beyond him. But whatever, he was holding Wren.

Nothing mattered when he was doing that, he realized.

"Should I push my shoulders back? Do my boobs look good? I feel like they look saggy. I couldn't wear a bra with this dress," Wren admitted, moving against him and driving him absolutely crazy. His cock came alive within seconds, and he wished like hell he'd worn his blue suit. It had thicker pants. "And what about my face? I don't have a double chin, do I?"

Closing his eyes since he was trying to keep it together, Jensen let out a harsh breath before reaching for her chin and tipping it up to him. "You look fucking perfect, okay?"

Her eyes widened before she nodded, his hand still holding her chin before he dropped his mouth to hers. He heard Brie gushing over them, but he didn't care. All he cared about was his mouth on hers. As she held his arm, her lips moving with his, he was bewildered by the fact that, only weeks ago, he'd felt so alone. Now he felt complete. Pulling away, he kissed her nose as his hand dropped to her stomach. She looked down and then up, a small smile on her face as she held his gaze.

"You sure?"

He nodded. "Yes."

"Then this is yours."

"And you're mine," he whispered, and her smile fell as she gazed up at him.

"Wow."

"Yeah," he agreed, kissing her nose once more before taking her hand in his. Glancing back to Brie, he asked, "Get some good ones?"

"Yes!" she gushed, coming over to him and handing him his phone before handing Wren hers. As he swiped through the pictures, he saw they were absolutely perfect, and he knew his mom would love them. He loved them.

"Aw, I don't look fat at all," Wren admitted. "Probably because you're so gorgeous."

He scoffed at that. "Or because you're not fat."

She rolled her eyes as Vaughn came over with his phone held out for a selfie. "Smile for the group chat." They all did as he asked, and then he was on his phone. When the photo came through in the group chat with Wells, Elaine, Wren, Brie, Vaughn, and him, Jensen opened it and smiled at Vaughn's picture and caption.

*Vaughn: Crazy kids did it!*

It was followed by another picture, this time of them kissing with Jensen's hands on her belly.

*Elaine: Oh my goodness, aren't they beautiful! I love it! Congratulations.*

Jensen and then Wren both thanked her, and he glanced over at her. "Do you have to get back?"

She shook her head. "I took the afternoon off, thought we could get moved in. Go to dinner, celebrate." She shot him a smile, not a full one, but a small one as she shrugged. "Or not."

"No, I want to, just surprised," he said before kissing her temple. "Let's go. Are you two coming?"

Brie shook her head. "No, we thought she had to go back to work, so we are going shopping. Go enjoy time alone."

"Yeah, we're gonna go bang too," Vaughn said, and Jensen rolled his eyes.

"Overshare, buddy. Okay, thanks for coming."

"Wouldn't miss it for the world," Brie said as Jensen hugged them both, but he paused when his phone started to ring.

"Okay, I'll see y'all later. It's my mom," he said as he answered. "Mum, just a second. Wren, you wanna ride with me? I'll bring you back to your car later."

She nodded as she hugged Brie. "Yeah."

"Cool. Hey, Mum, did you get the pictures?"

But instead of being answered in English, he was answered in

French, which meant his mom had a lot to say and fast. And boy, was she not happy. As Wren walked beside him, their fingers laced together, he tried to get in a word while they walked toward his car. Opening the door for her, he helped her in as he nodded. He almost didn't want to get in the car, but he didn't want Wren to know that his mom was complaining about her.

Even though she was.

Getting in, he nodded once more and then exhaled. "I understand. I'm sorry you feel that way. I know, Mum. Okay, yes. I love you too. Bye."

Hanging up, he laid his head back before looking over at his wife. Wow, he loved the sound of that. "Well, that was fun."

She met him with a concerned look. "That didn't sound good. I think the last time I heard her like that, she was screaming at you when you guys got caught stealing that car."

Jensen laughed. "We didn't steal the car, we were just sitting in it. Drinking."

"It wasn't yours."

"This is true, but whatever, I was like seventeen. Stupid kid stuff."

"But this sounded like that time."

He nodded. "Yeah, she's upset with me."

"Why? I thought she was good with this."

"She was, until she saw how far along you are. I guess I left that part out."

Her mouth made the shape of an O.

"Yeah," he said, shaking his head. "It's fine."

"So, actually, she's mad at me?"

He bit the inside of his cheek. He didn't want to lie to her, but she had already had it out with her brother. Meeting her gaze, he shrugged. "She feels you should have told me sooner so I could have been there for you. But obviously, she doesn't know the whole story. So, really, it's a moot point." She nodded as she looked down at her belly. "I told her that you were spooked and that it's you. You do that, you keep to yourself, and it's fine. I understand that about you, but now I'm here, and I'll be here for you and the baby." Swallowing hard, she nodded as she picked at her nails. Silence stretched between them as he started the car. "It's really okay," he added when she still hadn't said anything.

She shook her head. "I'm sorry for all this."

His brows pulled together, his hand stalling on the gear shift. "Sorry for what?"

"For asking you."

"Why? I'm glad you did."

Her face scrunched up as if she were thinking about something too hard. "No one wants this, Jensen."

He shrugged. "I'm not no one. I'm me."

She glanced up at him and let out a deep sigh. "Thank you."

"Anytime," he said, leaning over and kissing her lips softly. But before he could pull away, she reached up, taking his face in her hands.

"I don't think I really thanked you."

He smiled, pressing his nose into hers. "You don't have to."

"No, I do. You really saved me with this."

His grin grew. "And you saved me."

He pressed his lips to her nose and then pulled away. Her hands fell into her lap. Her eyes were wanting, needing, and he almost said the words. But he knew in his heart she wasn't ready for them.

And in a way, he wasn't ready to say them.

When he did say them, he wanted them to rattle her the way she rattled him.

Not a moment sooner or a moment later.

So with a contented and utterly blissful smile on his face, he pushed aside his mother's angry rant and asked, "Now, where do you and baby boy wanna eat?"

# Chapter TEN

$\mathcal{L}$ ooking around the apartment at where the movers had put all the boxes from Wren's place, Jensen felt a little over- whelmed. Thankfully, they'd had all the furniture sent to storage since she claimed she didn't need it, but he had no clue what was in these boxes. Her apartment always seemed so damn empty, so he wasn't sure what the hell she could have in there. It didn't matter, though. She was there. Reluctantly...but she was there.

That was the first step to his forever. With her.

"Hey, Wren."

"Hold on, I'm trying to get out of this dress."

He looked over his shoulder toward his room, or better yet, their room. He'd be sharing a bed with her tonight, and that alone had his whole body catching on fire. Though, he knew nothing would happen. "Do you need help?"

"Yes, please," she called, but then she was walking over to him. "I can't get the damn zipper down."

She turned her back to him, and he inhaled as he stepped toward her, reaching out to run his fingers along her shoulder. Taking ahold of the zipper, he leaned down, kissing her shoulder as the parting fabric exposed her back and her hands came up to hold the front of the dress. Turning, she smiled up at him, a little wari- ness in her eyes. "Thanks."

"Of course."

"What did you need?"

Shaking his head to rid himself of the thoughts of stripping her down and taking her against the wall, he pointed to all the boxes. "Why is there only one box for the baby? I told them to bring everything here that was for the baby."

She shrugged. "That's all there is."

He blinked in shock before looking back at her. "One box? Where is his crib? And all that stuff?"

She bit her lip, nervousness filling her features. "I haven't gotten it yet. He doesn't need it yet."

He held his hands out. "Don't you want to get his room ready?"

She seemed a little freaked out by his question. "I mean, yeah, I guess. I've been busy."

"Or you've been in denial that it's happening?"

She gave him a quirky smile. "That too."

Rolling his eyes, he bent down to pick up the only box. "What's in here?"

"A blanket that I saw at Walmart, and a few little onesies."

"That's it?"

Embarrassed, she smiled. "Hey, upside to this, we get to go shopping."

He gave her a dry look. "That isn't an upside. I hate shopping."

"Oh my God, so do I! What are we going to do?"

"Go shopping," he said simply before passing by her to head to the bedroom that used to be his old room. Setting the lone box in the middle of the floor, he rolled his eyes. How the hell had she been pregnant for six months and not bought a single thing? Crazy.

"What's that?"

Looking to the doorway where she was standing, he found she was pointing to the bag beside the box he had just put down. A smile tugged at his mouth as he bent down, picking it up and then opening it. Holding up the little Monroe jersey, he smiled at her. "I got this for him yesterday."

She cooed as she walked over, still holding her dress up but then grasping the jersey. "That is the sweetest thing. It's so small!"

"It is. I'm sort of worried I'll break him."

She gushed, "Me too! Like, it freaks me out, but hopefully he's squishy. I was squishy."

"Yeah, have some girth to him. He'll need it to play hockey."

"Totally." She beamed up at him. "I love it."

"Me too," he breathed as he laid it back down. "Guess we can go shopping tomorrow. When do you get off?"

"I have a full morning, but I can get off after lunch."

"Cool. I have to get a baby gift for Lucy and Benji's baby shower this weekend."

She threw her hands up. "Fuck, I forgot all about that." She bit her lip and then looked up at him. "Will we go together?"

He gave her a level look. "Well, considering we're married, I'd say so."

Panic filled her gaze as she looked away. "So, we'd come out to everyone there."

"Yes."

"To our boss, 'cause you know Elli will be there."

"I guess so."

"Okay, wow, okay," she said before turning and heading back into their room. Shaking his head, he turned the light off. She was skittish as shit, and it only came out when things like that were brought up. When it was just them, it was good. No nerves. Just her and him. It was nice.

After a great dinner, they went to make sure her apartment was completely cleared out. Then they dropped off a payment at the storage facility before getting her car. She had to run back to her office for some things, so he went to the apartment where he waited for her. It was late, though. He was worn out, ready for bed, and he knew she had to get up early to head to the office.

Taking off his coat, he walked toward the closet and undressed since Wren had the bathroom. Once he was in his boxers, he climbed into bed, plugging in his phone as he used his legs to cover himself. Lying back, he cuddled into the pillows as he held his phone up, swiping through Facebook. His mom had posted the pictures of Wren and him on her page, so he started reading all the comments from her friends. Everyone was sweet and it was nice, but when he saw a comment from Ophelia's mom, he glared a bit.

*How nice for him.*

Rolling his eyes, he continued scrolling just as a text came through.

*Wells: SMH*

His brows drew in as he clicked it and saw that it was in the group chat with everyone, right below Winston and Elaine's congratulations.

Before he could write anything, Elaine was on there.

*Elaine: Stop it, Wells.*

*Wells: No, you know what? This is your and Dad's fault.*

*Elaine: How in the world is this our fault? How is anyone at fault here?*

*Wells: If you didn't push that stupid inheritance stipulation on her, she wouldn't have done this.*

Rolling his eyes, Jensen bit his lip just as he heard Wren's phone going off. Great, now she knew about it. All he could hear was her voice when he had called her earlier. He didn't like that voice, the one that had a sob in it. He wanted her happy. That was his job. Annoyed, Jensen hit Wells's name and then his number to call him.

"Hey. What's up?"

Getting out of bed, he walked out of the bedroom. "Cut it out."

"What?"

"You heard me. Stop this. I won't have you treating her like this."

"She's going to fucking hurt you, dude—"

"That's my problem, not yours."

"But it will be mine because she's my sister."

Shaking his head, Jensen leaned into the bar. "And I respect that, but we are good. I can promise you that."

"She's using you."

"She isn't, okay? We made a baby—"

"Dude, I know the baby isn't yours. Stop with that."

Exhaling hard, Jensen counted to ten before he opened his eyes. He thought it would be harder for him emotionally to claim Wren's child, but it wasn't. In his mind, the kid was his, and that's the way it was. He really didn't like how Wells was acting, and he'd be damned if he was going to allow Wren's brother to treat his wife like shit. "Let me ask you something."

"What?"

"Do you truly love and care for me?"

"You know I do. That's why I—"

"Then let it go."

"But—"

"Wells, really, let it go. This is between me and Wren. This isn't your business, and if you want us at your wedding, you'll stop this right now. We'll come, but I swear I'll give you a black eye if you keep going at her like this."

"You have to understand why I'm so upset. She's going to break your heart, man."

"Again, that's my problem, not yours. I know who I married. I know Wren, okay? Let me do this. Let us do this. Okay? It's none of your concern."

"Yes, it is, because I love you both."

"Then, dude, just love us. Don't put stress on her, on us. Just let us be."

Wells exhaled hard as the silence stretched between them. "I can't sit back and let this happen. It's gonna end badly, and then the baby will be lost in the mix."

"Don't you worry about my son in that context, brother. No matter what happens between Wren and me, our son will always be loved by both of us, and we will always get along for him."

"She's spiteful—"

"She's perfect. You're too hard on her, and don't talk about her like that," he said firmly, his heart pounding in his throat. He wasn't sure if he was overstepping. Wren was Wells's sister, but he'd be damned if he was going to allow Wells to stress her out.

"Dude, you're already so far gone, you don't see the end."

"You're right. I only see the rest of my life with her."

"Damn it, Jensen. Come on."

"Wells, really. We're happy."

"It's a sham."

"It's not. We are really doing this, and we'd like your support."

"Damn it," he moaned, and Jensen knew he was pacing around his house. He always paced when he got mad or annoyed. "You're killing me."

"Regardless, will you support us?"

He hesitated, but he blew out a frustrated breath. "Fine."

"Thank you."

"Yeah," was all he said before he hung up, and Jensen wanted to scream. He respected Wells, loved him, but there were enough variables, all a result of Wren Lemiere, that were against them. He didn't need Wells, or anyone else, messing with them. Her hesitation, her insecurities could end them. He knew that, but he was going to do everything to help her through that. He had her now; he couldn't lose her. He loved her too much to allow that to happen. He knew he may very well be out of his mind, but if God had given him this golden opportunity, he did it for a reason.

And that reason was that Jensen had an abundance of love to give.

For Wren and the unnamed child she was carrying.

Even if she didn't want his love.

Pushing off the bar, he headed toward the bedroom, but when he turned the corner, Wren was standing there.

Surprised, he glared playfully. "Stalker."

She smiled. "Guilty as charged."

He moved past her toward the bed, plugging his phone in again before getting in as she slowly approached the bed. She was wearing a pair of sweat pants and a tee that barely covered her belly. He did his best not to drink in her thick thighs or even her thick ass even though they both were covered, but he failed miserably as she got into the bed, exhaling softly.

"Thanks for that. I know it's hard lying to him."

He shrugged. "It's fine. He won't talk to you like that."

Leaning back into the pillows, she looked over at him. "He's usually not that bad. But when it comes to you and Vaughn, I don't matter."

Jensen shook his head as a rebuff. "That's not true. He loves you very much. I know that for a fact."

"But he loves you guys more, and it's fine. Whatever."

But Jensen shook his head. "It isn't whatever, Wren. You shouldn't be talked to like that, and he loves you. More than anyone, I know, he talked about you all the time when we used to go out. You're his world."

"He has a funny way of showing it."

"He's just trying to protect us." She nibbled her lip as she looked down at her hands. "What?"

When she glanced up at him, her eyes were full of tears that he reacted to before he allowed her to speak. Gathering her in his arms, he pressed her body into his as he held her tight against him. She fit against him like a glove, her legs falling right along his, her center pressed into his thighs as her belly laid along his groin.

*Don't get a hard-on, don't get a hard-on.*

And God, she smelled like heaven.

"Don't cry," he whispered through tight lips.

"I hate fighting with him. He's such a tool, thinking he's right and shit."

"I know, I'm sorry. But he'll stop, I promise."

She shook in his arms as her own came around him. "He said I'm using you. You don't think that, do you?"

Shaking his head against her, he dusted her forehead with kisses. "Of course I don't think that, Wren. I would never assume you could do that to anyone."

She nodded against his lips as she held him closer, her tears wetting his chest. "I couldn't, but especially not to you."

"I know that."

"Okay."

"Okay, now, shh. Calm down, it's fine."

She nodded once more as her nose nuzzled his chest, and his eyes fell shut. Her hair was tangled around his fingers, and he swore she wasn't wearing a bra through that thin tee, but it didn't matter. She wasn't ready for him. Though, he was very, very ready for her. It was pure torture to hold her and not strip her bare to taste every single inch of her.

"Jensen?"

"Yeah?"

"Have you been with anyone recently?"

His breath caught. "No."

"How long?"

"Almost a year." He rested his chin on her head as he asked, "You?"

"Seven months."

He swallowed hard. "He was the last guy you slept with? The father, I mean."

"Yeah," she whispered before stillness fell over them. He thought she was asleep, but then she whispered, "He really messed me up, Jenny."

His eyes drifted shut. "Give me a name, and I'll kill him with my bare hands."

She smiled against his chest. "I never took you to be violent."

"For you, I can be."

Tipping her head back, she gazed up at him, her eyes dark and sinful as she whispered, "Were you serious about the making love part?"

She was going to drive him insane. Swallowing hard, he nodded. "Yes."

"So you're sexually attracted to me?"

He almost choked on the word. "Yes."

"Can I tell you something and have you not laugh at me?"

"Of course," he whispered back, his whole body fighting to restrain him from kissing her and taking her to oblivion.

*She's trying to talk. Get it together!*

"He made it to where I didn't even want to be naked in front of anyone."

Well, that was a straight dose of cold water. "What? How?"

"By saying the stupid shit he did. He always made comments about my weight, and that's probably why I haven't been with anyone else. I don't know. It's stupid."

He was flabbergasted. "Wren, that is stupid. Because of that dumb fuck? Just 'cause he doesn't appreciate a beautiful, curvy woman doesn't mean there aren't other guys out there who would."

Her eyes fell shut a bit as she moved her lips up his chin to the spot below his mouth. "Like you?"

Wetting his lips, he swallowed past the lump in his throat. "Yes."

When she took ahold of his lip between her teeth, his fingers bit into her back as he gulped harshly. "Good."

Then her lips were on his, feverishly, and he wanted to laugh.

He really thought he could resist this girl?

The one who starred in all his dreams?

He wasn't sure he was that strong.

\* \* \*

WREN SWORE she had never kissed someone like Jensen.

And she had been through her fair share of men.

But he kissed with a certain kind of something. She couldn't place it, but when he kissed her, it was as if he did it with his whole body. His legs tangled with hers, his hands threaded through her hair as his lips devoured hers. She had been the one to kiss him first, but somehow, he had taken over. It was as if each kiss was his last with her, and his caresses left her utterly breathless.

Sliding her center along his leg, she gasped against his lips, and she knew this was it. The moment when she'd get him naked.

Praise God.

But just as her hand slid down from the small of his back into his boxers, he pulled away, exhaling as he met her gaze. Nothing but heat and lust swirled in his chocolate depths, his whole body almost vibrating against hers. Or maybe that was hers, she wasn't sure. "Well…"

"Yeah, come here," she breathed as she moved against him, but he held his head back, his breath rasping harshly against her lips.

Swallowing hard, he bit out. "You need rest. You have a big day tomorrow."

"A big day? I have work."

"And shopping. We both hate that, so I'm sure it will be just so much fun."

"And I'm good. Promise," she insisted, but he moved away from her, detangled himself as he rolled to his back, running his hands down his face.

"Yeah," he said, blowing out a breath as he stared up at the ceiling. "But I'm tired."

"Too tired to do me?"

"Yup," he said with a simple nod, still not looking at her.

"Jensen, I've seen you play ninety minutes of hockey without batting an eye—"

"This is true, but I'm out of shape."

Lifting the blanket, she took in his hard as ice abs and perfectly toned chest. "Out of shape?"

"It's all a ruse. Don't look at that," he said, putting the blanket back down and holding it tightly against his chest. "Yeah, so goodnight."

He rolled over, and she just stared at the middle of his back. What in the world was happening? Did he just turn her down? Was it the sweat pants? She knew she should have come out in a thong, but she was nervous about her legs. They were so dimply since she had gotten pregnant. At least under the blankets, he wouldn't see them. But he apparently did not want to see anything. Hadn't he said he was attracted to her? What the hell?

"You're serious?" She found herself asking. But she was answered with very exaggerated snoring. "Really?"

"Sleeping," he said then, and she sputtered with laughter "You should too."

"Okay," she drew out, sighing out a breath before she cuddled deeper in the bed. "Not sure why we're not doing it."

When he didn't answer her, her brows pulled in even more as she chewed on her lips. Hadn't he said he wanted to make love, or whatever the hell he called it? If that was the case, why weren't they doing it? Maybe he was having second thoughts. Maybe he was just lying to her. Crap. No, wait, that was good. Right? Shit. Why didn't it feel right? Why did she feel like curling up in a ball and crying? She thought he wanted her. She heard him on the phone with Wells, how he stood up for her when he didn't have to. And the way he kissed her... It felt like he wanted her. Did her breath stink?

Blowing on her hand, she thought it smelled like toothpaste, so she wasn't sure. Looking back over at him, the low-lit lamp the only source of light on his back, she furrowed her brow more. It didn't make sense. But what didn't make sense most of all was the fact that she was annoyed by this. If he didn't want her, good. That meant when the six months were over, they could walk away with no ill feelings. Maybe he was realizing that, and his silly terms were no more.

That should be good.

They'd raise a kid, together, as friends. That was it.

She'd get more than she wanted, and that was good.

But then why did she feel so fucking shitty?

Staring back at his perfectly sculpted back as his shoulders rose and fell, she narrowed her eyes.

Stupid Jensen.

Stupid feelings.

Stupid her for doing what she didn't want to do.

Right?

She didn't want this.

Why didn't that feel right?

Crap.

Why was she such a fucking mess?

\* \* \*

"I WOULD HAVE PICKED YOU UP."

Wren waved Jensen off as she got out of the car and reached for her purse. She knew he would have. But she didn't want him to. She needed the distance. Her feelings were all out of whack, and it was pissing her off. He would say something like he had last night…and then he didn't have sex with her. He was confusing, and she was getting pissed. Or maybe she was sexually frustrated. Or both. Either way, distance was the key. "No reason to drive two cars." He leaned toward her, pressing his lips to the corner of her mouth before he smiled against her lips as her face stayed frozen in stone. "I really like this dress."

She looked down at her little T-shirt dress that used to be big on her, but not any longer, as she held in her not-nice retort. "But you didn't want me naked," she muttered. Well, she'd tried to hold it in. Looking up at him to see if he'd heard her, she saw his brows pulled together.

"What?"

"Nothing, I said thanks," she grumbled, and she hated how annoyed she still was. So he didn't want to have sex with her on their wedding night. It was supposed to be a fake marriage anyway.

Asshole.

When he didn't fall into step with her, she looked back at him. "You coming?"

His eyes narrowed a bit as he shook his head. "Pretty sure that's not what you said."

"Oh, well. Let's go and get this over with."

"Why are you pissy?"

"I'm not. Let's go."

"You are."

"Aren't."

"Are," he said simply, his eyes holding hers. "Quicker you tell me, the quicker I can either fix it or tell you to get over it."

Rolling her eyes, she started for Babies"R"Us as he fell into step with her, his hands tucked into the pockets of his shorts. She couldn't see his eyes behind his dark sunglasses, but he looked annoyed. Which was damn fine with her.

Jerk.

"Or you can just ignore the issue."

"That seems best," she muttered as together they walked through the sliding doors before he reached for a cart. He leaned on it, pushing his glasses up as he rolled beside her. Looking at the cart and then him, she raised a brow as she pushed her own sunglasses up into her hair. "We need a cart?"

He shrugged. "I think so. My mom sent us five hundred bucks to buy stuff for the baby, and then your mom told me to pick out a crib, on her."

Wren glared, more irritation filling her. "She didn't tell me that."

"She said she tried calling you earlier, but you were in sessions all morning. I texted you that too."

Pulling out her phone, she saw his text and then her mom's and dad's texts. Well, then. Tucking her phone back into her purse, her lips pressed together, she rolled her eyes. "Oh. I was in a rush to get here. I didn't want to be late."

"It's okay, no big," he said simply as he headed toward the clothing section, but she was reluctant, as if it were scary or something. But since he was still moving, she trudged ahead. How bad could it be? It was clothing, not a monster house. But as soon as they entered the boys section, Wren's heart jumped into her throat, and panic took over. She liked Walmart, stuff was on an end cap, and not overwhelming at all. But here…yeah, it was different here.

Her eyes widened as she took in her surroundings. Her heart was pounding so hard it hurt in her chest, and she could hear it in her ears. There was so much blue. So much cuteness and…were those little baby Chucks? Babies had Chucks!

"Wren? You okay?"

She couldn't answer him though. Her throat had closed up, her heart was beating out of control, making her eyes vibrate as she gazed around them. Dinosaurs, little ducks, bears, and more stared back at her as she drew in a ragged breath. She wasn't sure what he would like. What if he wanted bears, and she bought dinosaurs! It was all just so adorable, but crap, she was going to be a mom!

And she was a wife!

Jensen's wife.

And he wouldn't even have sex with her.

*Holy. Shit.*

"I should go call your mom and mine, thank them," she blurted out, but before she could even move, Jensen had his arms around her, holding her close to him, his lips by her ear. She tried to get away; she had to get away. She had to breathe.

This was not distance.

"Whoa there, Wren, breathe."

Closing her eyes as his arms came around her a little tighter, she figured she wasn't going anywhere. His hold was like a vise grip, but she didn't want his comfort. She was mad, and she was freaking the fuck out. Her body, though, didn't get that memo because the next thing she knew, she melted against him on an exhale. Kissing her earlobe, he whispered, "Tell me what's wrong. Do you not want to shop? Did I do something wrong?"

Her lips started to itch, as did her eyes as she squeezed them shut to keep her tears in. He didn't realize how loaded his question was, and there was no way she was going to unload on him in the middle of this baby store. Dragging in a breath, she shook her head. "It's just so real. Being here. Looking at this stuff."

He nodded against her cheek, his lips moving along her ear. "I know."

"I'm fucking scared."

"I know," he said once more, kissing the spot below her ear. "But you're not alone. I'm right here. See? I'm not going anywhere. Here, breathe with me."

Soon he was taking in deep breaths and letting them out slowly. She followed suit, though the need to run was great. But she didn't move. She buried her nose into his shoulder, inhaling his woodsy scent before she let it out slowly, breathing with him while getting completely intoxicated by him. She felt safe in his arms. Like nothing could touch her, and while that freaked her out even more than the fact that she was standing in the middle of a baby store buying baby shit for her baby, she didn't move. She stayed in his arms, which was probably a fool move. But then, she was a fool. A fool who didn't know what the hell she wanted. One who got knocked up by a dickhead and had her best guy friend take on all the responsibility. What was she doing? How could she be so selfish? He didn't even want her. It was out of pity.

As he trailed kisses along her temple and ear, she melted even more into him. But yet, if he really wasn't into her, why did his kisses feel so real? "Feel better?"

"A little," she said against his neck. "I feel stupid."

"Does this happen a lot? Not the stupid part, but the freak-out?" He laughed softly, and she shrugged.

"Only when I look at baby stuff. It legit freaks me out."

"I mean, I know I just came on board, but it freaks me out too, Wren."

"But you can drop out at any time."

"But I won't," he said simply. "I'm in this, for him and for you. He's mine as you are mine."

Her heart clenched in her chest, unsure what to believe. Her mind or his words. Words were such shit, though. His actions spoke louder, and he didn't want her. But he was holding her in the middle of the boys clothing section, not letting go.

What did it all mean?

*Just fucking ask him, you idiot!*

"I don't want to be a shit mom."

He pulled back, looking down at her as his hands came up to cup her face. "You are going to be an awesome mom."

Getting lost in his eyes, she couldn't move. "I don't know that I will be."

But he only nodded, his eyes full of the confidence she lacked, as he leaned down, pressing his lips to her nose. "You will be, because I'll be there to help you. To be behind you, one hundred percent. Two are better than one, you know." His lips curved in a goofy way. Loving the playfulness in his eyes, she found herself smiling back at him. "Not so stressful when there is someone there to make you smile. Do it more."

She swallowed hard. "I don't usually have a reason to."

He took that as a challenge. "That will have to change." Gazing into her eyes, he tucked her hair behind her ear. "It's all going to be okay. Having a kid is great, I promise. We're going to do great."

*We're.*

Together?

Or apart?

Wait, that didn't matter.

"I already love him," she said, more to herself.

"You don't have tell me that, Wren, I know you do."

Her heart slowed a bit as she shrugged, looking away. "I just hope I don't suck at it."

"You won't," he promised as he tipped her chin up. "I believe in you."

"You do?"

He kissed her lips. "I do."

And with that, her heart shattered in her chest. He believed in her. No one had ever told her that. Her parents were always proud, she knew that, but they never believed in her. Then, had she given them a chance to believe in her since she had gotten pregnant? No, she'd hidden it right off the bat because she knew they would be disappointed. They'd judge her. But Jensen hadn't done that from the beginning.

He was just there for her.

Which was confusing as hell.

Shaking her head, she moved out of his arms, needing the distance. "Thank you."

"Always."

She gave him a sideways glance as his hand came to the small of her back. She hadn't realized how much that little gesture would mean until she looked around once more. This time she didn't feel like she was drowning in her panic, she actually felt somewhat confident. Excited, sort of. Not much, but a little. It was silly, but she did. Leaning in toward her, he pointed toward the crib area. "So, tell me, you're digging the Disney's Baby Monsters, right?"

When she looked up at him, he was grinning, his eyes so full of eagerness. "You don't want the puppies playing sports?"

"No, there isn't a hockey stick anywhere on there. Which is bullshit, by the way."

"Agreed, but I heard there is a hockey set online I could order, but it's pricey. I bet the Monsters are cheaper."

His smile dropped, all seriousness on his face. "Really?"

Her grin grew. "Yeah."

"Done, we're getting that, and I don't care how much it costs. He needs that."

"I agree. Gotta start him young."

"Agreed," he said, wrapping his arm around her shoulders as he led her toward the cribs and other nursery furniture. There was so much, so many options, and even more things that she didn't even know she needed. Before she could react to it, though, he asked, "Now, big question. Which crib?"

Her shoulders fell as she took in all the options, which were endless and so damn cute. "Crap."

"Yeah," he agreed. "At least it's cute?"

"Yeah, but we're gonna be here forever, aren't we?"

She gazed up at him, and he nodded slowly, a resigned look on his face, though his eyes were full of gusto. "Looks that way."

"But we hate shopping."

"We do, but it's for the little man. Who we really need to name, by the way."

She exhaled once more as she nodded. "This is true."

"And at least we'll be together through it all."

Her lips quirked at the side as she looked up at him. Her anger from the night before was gone, and while she wasn't sure of his intentions, it did feel good to have him by her side. Even if the longevity of his position there wasn't certain. She knew, Lord, she knew, to keep her heart wrapped up tight, but when his lips curved and his eyes brightened as he leaned in, kissing her cheek, the wrapping she had around her heart loosened a bit as he whispered, "That's a good thing, Wren."

She returned the grin as she nodded. "I know."

"So smile."

"I am."

When he poked her side, she laughed out as he wrapped her up from behind, holding her close, his hands coming along her belly. "There you go, now let's do this."

Swallowing hard, Wren felt her heart becoming more and more of a hot-ass mess. But for a moment, she ignored it.

She found herself smiling. Really smiling.

For Jensen.

# Chapter
# ELEVEN

"Maybe we should wait for Jo and Brie?"

Jensen closed Wren's car door as he looked over at her. Of course, he thought she was gorgeous. She blew his mind with her beauty in a pair of simple overalls that stretched across their child and a tank that rode low on her breasts and would be starring in his dreams that night. They were so damn full, so sexy, but he was staying strong. Ish. The last couple days had been hard, but he was doing his best. Though, seeing her change each day that passed, well, it was getting harder.

She brushed a piece of hair out of her face as she looked up at him. Her hair was up in a messy bun, and she wore big glasses that covered her made-up eyes. She had done something to make them brighter, and it had also taken her an extra twenty minutes since she claimed the lines weren't straight on both eyes. He thought they were, but she wouldn't leave until they were perfect. He was pretty sure she thought he was an idiot, but he wasn't. He was completely on to her.

She was stalling.

Ever since her breakdown in the middle of the baby store, he had been worried about her. She used to have small panic attacks when they were younger, especially through college, but the one in the middle of the store was scary. Even for him, who usually handled pressure like that okay. But this time, he had almost been on the brink of tears. Wren wasn't one to cry. She was a strong chick, even through her panic attacks. She'd deal with them and move on, but that one stunned him. He knew it was because it was Wren. Anyone else, he wouldn't have worried, but he worried for her. Completely. Those pregnancy hormones were no joke.

It made him nervous for obvious reasons, but he tried so hard not to think about what could be going through her head. Was she already plotting out her escape when she got her money? Not that he was holding her like a prisoner, but was she ready to go? Sometimes he felt she was, but other times, he felt like she was maybe, sorta falling for him. He wasn't sure, and it was driving him insane. But he couldn't think about it now. All he could do was love her more than he had before and hope for the best. But coming out to the whole team, their boss, and everyone at Lucy and Benji's baby shower wasn't going to be easy. It weighed on her, he could see it in her eyes, and it bothered him. More than he liked. He wanted to be confident in them, but standing beside her as she looked for a way out already, he felt like he was a lamb going to slaughter.

She could ruin him.

Fuck.

"Wren, they're already here. We're late." Reaching into the back seat, he grabbed the little box she had spent another thirty minutes wrapping and tucked it under his arm. "So let's go. We're late."

She bit her lip as she looked up at the Paxton's home. It was something out of a rustic southern magazine, it was so rich with culture. He thought it was gorgeous, but the way Wren's brows pulled in, you would have thought the damn place was on an episode of *Hoarders*. "How late are we? Can we just skip it, you think?"

He rolled his eyes, letting out a sigh. "No, babe. We gotta go." Tucking her hands into her pockets, stretching the fabric so tight across the child he already loved, she nodded as his hand went to the small of her back. "It's fine."

She glanced up at him. "I'm nervous they'll judge us."

He made a face. "Who the fuck cares?" She seemed shocked by that, and maybe he was being a prick, but he was frustrated. He was proud to show her off, and he felt like she didn't feel the same. "I mean, is it that bad to be seen with me?"

Her brows furrowed more as she reached out, holding his bicep. "That's not it at all. I'm lucky as hell to be seen with you, Jenny. I'm worried they'll be like your mom, judge that I waited so long to 'fake' tell you."

His lips pressed together as he nodded. He shouldn't have told her about that conversation with his mom. "My mom didn't judge you. She was just upset it took so long for her to find out."

"She was pissed."

He hissed out a breath. "Either way, it doesn't matter. We don't answer to them. We answer to each other, right?"

She swallowed hard as she nodded. "Yeah. I guess."

"So let's go have a good time with our friends. Celebrate baby Paxton." He urged her forward, but she didn't move, her gaze still on him. "What's wrong now?"

"Are you super sure about this?"

He let out an annoyed breath. "If you're asking if I'm sure that I want to do this and that the child in your belly is mine, then the answer is yes." Pulling down his sunglasses, he bored his eyes into hers as he said, "And please don't ever ask me that again."

Her lips pressed together as he put his glasses back. "I was just asking—"

"And I'm just telling you."

"You're mad."

"I'm annoyed."

"At me?"

"Yes."

"Why?"

"Because you're stalling, Wren."

"I'm stalling because I'm nervous."

"Why are you nervous?"

"I told you why!" she yelled, and he glared. He swore he thought she couldn't piss him off, but lately, he was finding that was a delusional thought. She could irk him like none other.

"And I told you, you don't need to worry or be nervous. Am I here?"

She nodded. "Yes."

"Then you're good. I got you. Remember?"

Even though he couldn't see her eyes clearly, he felt hers on his. "I don't get it."

"Get what?"

"Why you're good to me."

"Because I care for you," he said simply. "Can we go?"

But she still didn't move. As she inhaled deeply, letting it out in a whoosh, she looked up at him and whispered, "You're a really good man, Jensen Monroe."

His shoulders fell on an exhale. Didn't she realize he was this man for her and only her? "And I'm your man, so you have nothing to worry about. Okay?"

Looking at the house, she started toward it, not acknowledging his comment, which annoyed him a bit. But he couldn't push her. He had to be patient. Walking together, they didn't say anything as they followed the signs to the backyard where the party was in full swing. Everyone was there, the whole team, their wives, girlfriends, but to Jensen's surprise, he didn't spot any of the kids. But then, he remembered it was an adult party, which was a nice change.

When Benji stopped in his tracks, his eyes fell on Wren and then on Jensen before he pointed to the both of them. "Hey, guys."

Wren looked like a deer in the headlights as Jensen smiled, handing him the gift. "Hey, man. Congratulations."

"Thanks," he drew out, looking back at Wren as Jensen returned his hand to her back. Benji looked utterly confused, and Jensen wanted to laugh, but before could, Elli Adler appeared beside him, her eyes wider than Benji's when she revealed them from behind her sunglasses.

"Wren? Jensen?"

Before he could answer his boss, Vaughn was waving at him from beside the grill. "Jenny! Wrenny! Over here."

"I see you," he called over to him before he looked back to his boss. "Hey, Elli," he said before leaning over and kissing her cheek.

But her mouth was a little open as she glanced between them. Meanwhile, Wren was shaking against his hand. Guess this was the judgy part she was worried about. As he looked around, all eyes were on them. He could feel it, Wren was about to hightail it out of there. Leaning toward her, he kissed the spot on her temple before whispering, "It's okay."

"Why's everyone staring at you two?" Vaughn asked, coming over and wrapping his arm around Wren's shoulders before looking up at Jensen. He then looked around. "People, really? We are on a team with extremely fertile men who impregnate their wives daily. So, really, this is nothing new. Just our very talented goalie and our therapist who eloped, and guess what, are having a baby! So yeah, let's give them a round of applause."

When he started clapping, some followed suit, but Elli was still staring at them.

"Thank you, Vaughn," Jensen muttered through tight lips.

He nodded with a grin on his face. "Anytime, brother."

"I'm legit going to kill you in your sleep," Wren said for the whole backyard to hear, but Vaughn just laughed it off.

"She threatens me all the time. It's endearing."

Letting her go, Vaughn walked away before Elli stepped up, taking Wren in her arms. "Well, congratulations! I didn't even know you two were dating!"

When they parted, Vaughn appeared again, pointing to their boss. "By the way, Elli, maybe you might have to shred some more paperwork. Hint, hint." When he coughed exaggeratedly, Jensen rolled his eyes. "Dumb-ass non-fraternization rule."

"I'm subcontracted, asshat," Wren supplied, glaring.

Jensen chuckled as Benji shook his hand, along with some of the other guys. Wren explained, "Anyway, it was an on-and-off kind of thing. We've known each other our whole lives, though."

"Oh, I knew that, but I didn't know it was anything romantic," Elli said before taking Jensen in her arms and kissing his cheek. "I'm so happy for y'all."

"Thank you, we're really excited." Jensen beamed since he wasn't lying. But Wren, Jesus, her lips turned up in what he assumed was a smile, and he was convinced people would think she was in pain.

"I usually know everything. You got one by me!"

Jensen laughed as he pulled Wren into the crook of his arm. "She's private."

"I'd say so! So, how far along?"

"Six months."

"Goodness! We'll have to have a baby shower for you!"

But Wren waved her off. "No need. It's fine. Really."

"I insist," Elli said, her drawl coming out as she looked between them. His boss was a smart lady, but she was also very kind and loving. She would give the shoes off her feet to anyone, but she was also a no-holds-barred kind of chick, and she could see through any bullshit.

He was pretty sure she saw right through them.

"I'm just floored that I never noticed."

Wren shrugged. "You always came in when I was sitting behind my desk, and I just didn't tell anyone."

Elli made a noise; he wasn't sure what the noise meant, but she was smiling. "Well, either way, we're excited for a new addition to the Assassins family. Babies everywhere! It makes my heart so happy."

When Wren didn't answer, an awkward silence fell between the three of them while Jensen rocked back on his heels, unsure what to say to make the situation any less awkward. Yeah, this was going awesome.

Not.

When he ran his hand along the small of Wren's back, she looked up at him and he smiled, trying to make it better. When she didn't smile back, his heart sort of stopped. Didn't he say he was there for her? He had her back, so instead of worrying about what to say to his boss, he didn't think, he just leaned in, pressing his lips to Wren's. He watched through her glasses as her eyes drifted shut, and his heart sang while his arm came up and around her neck, holding her to him. Pulling away, his lips only a breath away, he whispered, "Smile. You're beautiful."

Her lips quirked as her hand came to the middle of his back just as Elli said, "Well, I don't know how I didn't suspect it because you two are adorable together."

Jensen nodded. "Eh, she's a little too hot for me, though."

Wren scoffed at that. "Please."

"It's true," he insisted, and for the first time that day, she beamed.

"Stop, I'm getting as big as a house."

"Oh, girl, let me tell you about being as big as a house," Elli said, taking Wren's other hand and pulling her toward the drink table that was covered in pink. Wren glanced back at Jensen, but it wasn't for help. At least, he didn't think so. Instead, her lips were still curved.

Man, she was beautiful.

When an arm came across his shoulders, he looked over to see Dylan Alexander, his backup since Tate was still out. "Dude, I didn't even know!"

Jensen just smiled. "No one did."

"True story, it's like it just happened," Vaughn said from beside Karson King and Jordie Thomas. Markus Reeves and Phillip Anderson stood on the other side of Jordie, all of them with smiles on their faces but curiosity in their eyes. Sending a death stare at his best friend, Jensen shrugged. "Yeah, it was all kind of fast, but we're happy."

"And that's all that matters," Jordie said, gesturing to Jensen. "But congratulations. She's a good girl."

"She is." Jensen looked back to where Wren was standing with Elli and a bunch of the other wives. They were gushing over Karson and Lacey King's new baby girl. Wren wasn't touching her, but the interest was on her face.

When a slap came to his back, he turned to see Shea Adler, a constant presence in the Assassins organization and Elli Adler's husband. "Knocking up the therapist, I'm impressed. I thought she hated everyone."

Vaughn laughed. "She does."

"Obviously not our pretty boy goalie," Shea teased, and Jensen laughed.

"Who isn't attracted to him? He's all hot and shit," Markus joked, and everyone chuckled.

"I'm waiting for them to make us do those calendars again. Thousand bucks says Monroe is the cover model for the whole thing," Anderson teased, while Jensen rolled his eyes.

"Shit, would your wife let you?" Shea asked, glancing back at Wren and the girls. "She looks like the jealous type, also one of those girls who might kill you in your sleep."

Vaughn pointed to Shea. "You have no clue. She tried to smother me when we were teenagers."

Jensen scoffed. "You cut her hair when she was sleeping!"

"What?" Shea laughed, and Vaughn shrugged.

"She kicked me in the balls."

"You popped her bra, breaking the damn thing, and Elaine couldn't get to the school for an hour, so Wren ran around with her boobs floating while everyone teased her."

Vaughn shrugged. "You gave her your hoodie, she was fine."

"But everyone knew," Jensen scolded. "And all you did was laugh."

Vaughn laughed like he had back then. "Her face. She was so pissed."

"Asshole."

"Jesus, how long have you guys known each other?" Phillip asked.

Vaughn and Jensen shared a look before they both said, "Forever."

Everyone laughed at that while Jensen shook his head. They really had known each other forever, and as he gazed over at his now-wife, he smiled. He had really cared for her and wanted to protect her for as long as he could remember. And not a damn thing had changed since them. Even with the need for flight in her eyes, he still wanted to be there for her. Protect her.

He loved her.

"So, do you know what you're having?" Phillip asked, and Jensen looked toward him with a nod, his heart fluttering in his chest.

"A boy."

"Thank God. Everyone is having girls," Jordie mentioned as Jensen looked around the totally pinked-out place.

"Not me. It's a boy. I know it," Vaughn called, crossing his arms over his chest. "I'm a man's man, and I'm having a man child."

They all scoffed, shaking their heads. "I would love to see you with a little girl. She'll shatter your world, just like Brie did," Karson said with a laugh.

"She didn't shatter my world. I shattered hers."

"Yeah, pretty sure she wasn't the one sending you millions of flowers. It was the other way around," Jensen teased, and Vaughn shot him a look.

"Shut up."

"Hey, girls are trouble. All of them. They get you all fucked up, in love with them, and then they give you a daughter who does the same thing all over again," Jordie agreed with a nod as he stared across the yard at his beautiful wife. "In an instant. Just like that, and you're never the same."

"This is true, but so does a boy. I love my boys with everything inside of me," Phillip added with a small grin on his face. "One look at my first main man when he was born, and I was a changed man."

"Every single one of mine took a piece of me with them," Shea said then, his lips curving. "I thought after Elli and Shelli I couldn't love anyone else, but then each one, I loved more and more. It's crazy. Life. Ya know?"

Everyone nodded in agreement, and Jensen's gaze drifted over to where Wren was standing with Elli as she very animatedly told her something. His love for that girl was strong, and he couldn't wait for the moment he'd meet his son.

"Yeah, I have nothing. No kids. And we're not having any for a long time. We just want to enjoy us," Markus said with a nod.

Jordie nodded. "Can't blame you. I wish we would have done that, but when you have a sperm count like I do—and a beard, mind you—it tends to just happen. I spit on her, and she's pregnant."

Karson gagged. "That's my sister, asshole."

"And I love her," Jordie teased back, his face bright as everyone laughed.

When the laughter subsided, Markus slapped Jensen on the back. "You nervous?"

Jensen scoffed, his heart jumping up into his throat. "Nervous? That's only one emotion I have."

They all smiled, most of them knowingly, while Markus nodded. "I couldn't imagine, but I love Wren. She's great. She's a give-it-to-you-straight kind of girl."

"She is." Jensen nodded as he looked back at her. When he saw that Lacey was trying to pass her baby off to Wren, he wanted to laugh at the pure horror on her face. "Excuse me."

Jogging over toward the group of ladies, he intercepted the sweet baby with a smile. "Let me see this bundle of pink. Holy crap, she's beautiful," he said, cuddling her to his chest. "And Jesus, are you sure you had anything to do with this kid?"

Lacey beamed as she nodded. "That's what everyone is saying. She looks just like Karson."

"Like a carbon copy," he laughed, holding the sweet girl to his chest. She sure was pretty and small. Shit, would his be this small?

"Wait until y'all's comes. Wren's eyes with your facial structure? Talk about a pretty little boy," Fallon Brooks said, and Jensen grinned over at her to keep from dying inside. She didn't know the truth, but he did.

And God, he prayed that his son came out looking just like Wren, with no traces of that fucker that left her.

Pushing those feelings to the side, he looked over at Lucas's wife and asked, "Saying I'm pretty, Fallon?"

She blushed as she laughed. "You sure ain't ugly. Hope I'm not offending you, Wren."

Wren smiled as he looked over at her. "Not at all. I know he's hot."

All the ladies agreed, and this time, he was the one blushing. "I feel like a steak between you ladies. Aren't all of you married? Jeez," he teased, and they all laughed some more as Wren peeked over toward the baby, moving the little blanket away from her face.

"She is pretty."

"She sure is. What's her name, Lacey?"

"Rose."

"Aw, how sweet, Mena and Rose. How's Mena taking to her?"

"Perfectly. She loves her."

When he felt Wren's gaze on his, he looked down at her and smiled. "Wanna hold her?"

She shook her head quickly. "I like watching you with her."

"Right? He's amazing with all the kids," Elli said, patting Jensen's back. "And doesn't forget a name."

"I forget your name all the time," he teased, and Elli laughed as she nodded. "No wait, that's a lie. You sign my checks," he said with a wink, and everyone giggled as he looked down at Rose. She was basically covered in pink, but for a moment, he imagined her in blue.

And his.

It felt right.

He glanced back to Wren, and her gaze met his. He wondered what she was thinking. "What?"

"It's nice."

He smiled as Rose stretched her body out, a yawn coming from her small body. "What is? You haven't even held her."

But she shook her head. "I know. But I mean you and her. It's nice."

"Yeah?"

"Yeah."

His heart did a little jig as he nodded slowly. "You sure you don't want to hold her?"

Gone was her smile, and it was replaced by a look of horror. "I could drop her."

"You won't," he insisted as he slowly moved Rose from his arms to a very unwilling Wren. But she took her, cuddling the baby to her with all the fear one could muster in her eyes.

"Is she okay?"

"She fine," he reassured as he moved Wren's hand down a bit to support Rose's bottom. "Have you never held a baby?"

"I was the baby."

"What about Shanna's kids?"

Her lips pressed together as she shook her head. "Nope. I never wanted to."

He knew they weren't talking and he wanted to ask about that, but it wasn't the place. "How does it feel?"

Her lips curved a little on the left as she gazed down at Rose. "Good. She smells like heaven."

"She does," he agreed, wrapping his arm around Wren's middle, holding her against him.

She beamed up at him. "I haven't dropped her."

"Nope, I'd say you're doing well."

"I am," she agreed, looking back down to Rose. "I think I can do this."

"You can, I know it."

Her grin didn't leave her lips as she leaned her head into his shoulder. Her demeanor had changed so much from when they had arrived, and he was thankful for that. He hoped she realized that she was good. Even without him, but she was better with him. He just needed her to realize that because he loved her. He loved the way her lips curved, how the little hairs on her neck flared out, and most of all, how green her eyes were. How they held every secret she was hiding. He wanted to know them all. He wanted her. All of her.

He needed her to give that to him.

As he looked up from Rose, his gaze met Vaughn's. His best friend shook his head as he took a picture of them with his phone. Vaughn didn't have to say anything, though; it was all in his eyes. He was worried for Jensen, and he got that, he did. But as he held his wife, looking down at the first baby she had ever held, he felt good.

Because if he felt anything else, like the fear that could eat him alive, he would drive himself mad. So he would ignore those feelings.

Instead, he would love her.

And hope that she loved him back.

* * *

WREN WAS PRETTY sure she could still smell baby Rose on her.

As she lay back on Brie's couch that was up against the fireplace, not in its usual place since the interior designer was coming over, she cuddled into it as a smile played on her lips. That baby was so sweet, and Wren was glad that Rose was the first that she had held. She was perfect, didn't cry, and let Wren just love on her. It was perfect, but being held by Jensen while she did it was about a billion times better. Exhaling hard, she felt her grin grow as she looked down at the picture that Vaughn had sent in the family thread the previous day.

They looked right. It was sort of nuts. She hadn't noticed how good they looked together. Maybe it was how damn good-looking he was, but they just fit. She looked adorable in her overalls, but then, so did he in his simple shorts and tee. Really, though, when did Jensen not look good? Standing beside him, she came to his shoulder, and his arms fit around her, bringing her against him like she belonged there. His head rested on hers as he looked down at baby Rose, this content, gorgeous smile on his beautiful face. He looked like he was meant to be a husband and father, but when she looked at herself, she was surprised to find she felt she looked the part too.

She didn't look like a fake.

Like an impostor.

She looked like she belonged.

In Jensen Monroe's arms, holding their child.

Holy shit.

Before she could really decipher those feelings, which she felt were a little insane, she was distracted by the thread below the picture.

*Vaughn: Look at them, practicing for when their baby comes! Isn't it sweet? Gaggggggggggg.*

*Mom: Oh my goodness, they are so cute together!*

*Mom: I can't wait to get my hands on her belly!*

*Dad: Why would you want to touch her belly? That's weird.*

*Mom: It's my grandchild, you freak! Come out of the woodshed and spend time with me.*

*Dad: No, I'm hiding from you.*

*Mom: I'm going to kill you.*

*Dad: Bring it.*

*Vaughn: Was that their version of foreplay?*

*Wells: I feel it might have been, and I just threw up.*

*Jensen: I did too.*

*Wells: But hey, you two look cute. Like real and shit.*

*Jensen: Because it is.*

*Vaughn: Ooooooh, he told you.*

*Wren: You guys are losers.*

But even with her addition to the ongoing and annoying thread, she still couldn't stop staring at the picture or Jensen's text to her brother.

*Because it is.*

It was that simple for him.

Too bad she wasn't completely convinced, but then, how could she be? She was realistic, and she knew her track record. Everyone she fell for dumped her like a bad habit. She didn't want to be Jensen's bad habit, the thing he dropped the first chance he got. While the day before had been awesome and they had a great time with their friends, they had gone home and went to bed. Right to bed. No cuddling, no kissing to the point of a boner, nothing. Just sleep. It was boring, and she was losing her ever-loving mind. She wanted him. God, she wanted him. Each little caress, each little look, and those kisses? They were torture! She just didn't get it. Why didn't he want her? Why hadn't he taken her to bed? It was beyond her comprehension.

But then, she felt like a whore. Was she that obsessed with sex? Did she need it that badly to actually feel like he wanted her? Was she pathetic? Because the guy was good to her. Always reassuring her, always there for her, and just all-around great. But the thing holding her back was sex? That was pitiful. She was pathetic. Still, she felt like he didn't want her because he wasn't attracted to her. Yeah, he kissed her, but he kissed her mom. Maybe not like he kissed Wren, but still. It was fucking with her. Yeah, it was her fault she was insecure, she understood that. She was the one with the issues, but she just wanted to know that he thought she was attractive, that he wasn't doing this out of pity. His words weren't enough; she was used to words that usually became lies. She wanted action. More action. She wanted him.

All of him.

"So we go next week to find out what we're having," Brie said then, and Wren set her phone down, looking over at her friend. They were just lying on the couch, playing on their phones. It was completely silly, but they were good. It was nice to have a friend she could just lie around with and not need to talk to fill the silence.

"That's great! It's weird. The baby looks all strange and stuff."

"Yeah, I'm sure it will be," Brie laughed, but her eyes were so full of excitement. "I think we're going to bring Rodney. He wants to come."

Wren lit up. "Aw, he'd love that."

Brie nodded in agreement. "He is excited, told me I had to name the baby Rodney Jr. even if it's a girl."

"That seems legit," Wren teased, and Brie giggled.

"That's what I said." They both laughed as Brie looked over at her. Waggling her brows, she said, "So you two looked supercozy yesterday."

Wren smiled, shrugging her shoulders. "I guess."

"Still holding back?"

Wren scoffed. "Of course I am. I don't believe in this shit. It doesn't happen for girls like me."

"You know, I used to think that."

Wren pulled her brows together. "What? You?"

Brie was gorgeous. Like drop-dead beautiful with the cutest little body and the greatest smile. She was a knockout. "Yes, me! Love didn't come easy, and I tried so hard. So many horrid speed-dating things and shit like that. It took some asshole hockey player, one I never thought I would be interested in, to be there for me. He didn't have to be, but he loved Rodney like I do, and next thing you know, I fell. Even when he didn't fall."

"My situation is so different from yours, Brie. Jensen didn't want this."

Brie made a face, turning so her body was facing Wren's. "Who says he didn't?"

"I do."

"Wren, come on. You're not that oblivious, are you?"

Wren's heart jumped up into her throat, making it hard to breathe. "I don't know what you're talking about."

"He's had a thing for you for as long as I've known him, and according to everyone else, even before."

Wren rolled her eyes. "That's not true. Wells said the same thing, but if that was the case, why hasn't anything happened?" She cleared her throat. "I've known him forever, okay? I flirted with him when we were younger, and he ignored me. Then when we were older, after that whore left him, I put the moves on him again, and nothing. If he had a 'thing' for me, why didn't he try anything?"

Brie shrugged. "I don't know that answer. Maybe that's some-thing you should ask him."

Wren laughed. "Yeah, I'll be like, 'Hey, Jenny, heard you had a thing for me. Is it true? And why didn't you try anything before?'"

"Yes!" Brie laughed, holding her hands out to Wren. "Ask him. He'll be honest."

But she shook her head, not believing any of it. It just didn't make sense. "If that were the case, then he had plenty of chances to get in my pants, and he never did it."

"Maybe because he didn't want to just get in your pants," Brie suggested, holding Wren's gaze. "Maybe he wanted more, and now he's got it."

Wren shook her head once more. "That's stupid. It isn't like that. He's doing this to help me, and he's too honorable and proud to let it fail."

Brie made a face. "I don't think that at all."

When the front door opened, they both looked up to see Vaughn enter with arms full of bags of food. "Why did I go to the store if Lucy isn't even here yet?" he asked as he shut the door. When he turned, seeing Wren, he made a face. "What the hell are you doing here?"

"Vaughn!"

"What? It's weird."

"You're so dumb. We are friends. Like besties," Wren said, leaning into Brie.

"It's true. Look, Jo! I finally have a friend," Brie exclaimed, and her man rolled his eyes.

"Exactly. I don't have to depend on you guys, I have a girlfriend now," Wren said then, and Vaughn was not happy.

"I don't trust you two. At all."

"Don't be jealous, lovebug," Wren called to him, and he rolled his eyes as they both laughed. "He's such a brat."

"He sure is," Brie agreed, leaning back into the couch. "He just doesn't like that we can team up against him."

"Exactly."

"You two have never had a midget and a crazy person come at you," Vaughn called from the kitchen, and they both snickered.

"You're the midget, I assume?" Wren asked.

"Which means you're the crazy person," Brie added. "Should we kill him now or later?"

Wren shrugged. "I'm comfortable."

"Me too," Brie decided, and they both smiled as Vaughn grumbled in the kitchen. "Love slave, bring us snacks."

He laughed. "Kiss my ass. Both of you."

They both smiled. As Brie laid her head against the couch, she looked over at Wren, and she did the same. "Why the hell is my dog put up?" Vaughn hollered.

Looking toward the kitchen as Tricksie barreled out toward them, Brie shook her head. "She doesn't know personal space, and Lucy is gonna be here soon."

He filled the doorway as Tricksie jumped up on the couch, cuddling against both women. "Excuse me. This is Tricksie's house, not Lucy's. She doesn't like my dog, she can leave."

"You're ridiculous."

Vaughn wasn't listening though as he went back to the kitchen, and Tricksie licked Brie's chin when she turned to look at Wren. "I think you're thinking too hard."

"What? No, I'm not."

"Yeah, like your therapist brain is always in therapy mode, and you're always trying to figure everything out. Nothing is ever as it appears. There is always something deeper. Maybe just let it happen."

"Says the person who hasn't been hurt as much as I have."

Brie laughed hard at that. "Wren. Please. The guy I thought I would marry before Vaughn left me because, when my mom died, it was too much to handle. He broke me."

Wren's heart clenched in her chest. "Fuck, I'm sorry."

"Yeah, it sucked. I get that dudes have been shitty to you. That you've had some doozies who have tossed you to the side and threw your confidence in the shitter, but, Wren, you are amazing. You're funny when you let yourself be. You're witty and so smart. Plus, you're gorgeous. I would kill to have your curves and have those lips. And height. I'd love your height."

Wren laughed, her face hurting from smiling so hard. "You're insane."

"You can't even take a compliment! Say, thank you, Brie, for thinking I'm a sexy, curvy goddess."

Wren blushed. "Thanks, bestie."

Brie beamed at that as she leaned into her. "But really, Wren, you've got the real deal. I saw it with my own eyes. He looks at you like you're the queen of his universe."

Swallowing hard, Wren tangled her fingers together as she shook her head. She didn't want to admit it since she was embarrassed, but it was Brie, her newfound best friend. In reality, she should feel bad since her other best friend had no clue why they weren't friends anymore. Jesus, was she a shitty person? Damn it. "Brie."

Her brows came together as she sat up. "What?"

Looking toward the kitchen, Wren inhaled deeply as she looked back to Brie, leaning in. "We haven't had sex."

Brie's face scrunched up. "What? Ever?"

"No."

"Why?"

"I don't know!"

Brie's eyes widened. "Not even on your wedding night?"

"No. He won't touch me. We get to kissing, things are going good, but then he slams on the brakes. It's driving me fucking crazy. Like, I feel like he isn't attracted to me."

Brie shook her head. "He is."

"Then why hasn't he hit it?"

"I have—"

"Because he knows that's all you want."

Wren's lips pressed together as Brie's eyes squeezed shut. At the same time, they both turned back to look at Vaughn, who was standing in the doorway of their kitchen with his shoulder leaning on the wall, a smug smile on his face. "I hear all since this house is empty, and let me just say, Jensen isn't going to just fuck you to get by. He's not that guy. He didn't fuck anyone until he loved them in high school. He's a do-gooder. You know that."

Wren's mouth went dry. "But we're married."

"Doesn't matter. If he doesn't think you have feelings for him, more than lust, then he isn't going to touch you. He's not a douche. Again, you know this."

"Or he isn't attracted to me."

He scoffed. "Wren, really? You're hot. You have a great ass, and he wants it. I know that." He then looked seriously at Brie. "You're way hotter, and I want your ass, twenty-four seven."

Brie smiled, and Wren was jealous of her complete confidence. "I'm fully aware, babe."

He winked at her and then looked back to Wren. "He wants you. He's told me, but he knows how you are. You revert right back to fucking when you start to feel something, to try to protect yourself. It's sad. Stop it."

"Wow, please don't sugarcoat that, Jo."

"Oh, I won't." His eyes held hers. "This is why I didn't want you to ask him to do this. Because he's all in, and you're not. He knows that."

With that, Vaughn turned and left the room, leaving Wren with her heart in her throat and her lips pressed together. She didn't want to accept what Vaughn was saying, but she knew deep down it was the truth. Jensen wasn't that guy. The fuck 'em and leave 'em type. Was that all she wanted? Was that the vibe she was putting off?

"Well."

Brie exhaled hard. "You know how they all are. They're so close."

"I know," Wren said, shaking her head. "I just feel like it's me. That he isn't attracted to me. Though, according to everyone, I'm insane."

"You are."

"And I get that he has his morals, and I appreciate them, but sex is my thing. It works for me. It's how I feel."

"But it's not how he works," Vaughn called from the kitchen. "He doesn't need sex to love you. He just does."

Wren's eyes widened as she met Brie's gaze, but her new bestie just shrugged. "Told you."

But it couldn't be.

Then Vaughn was in the living room again. "And, you don't need sex to love him. You just need to let yourself do it. Didn't you tell me that? Didn't you tell me to stop being caught up in all the shit I had and let myself feel for Brie? I did, and look at us. We're happy, while you're sitting on my couch crying that you aren't getting any from your husband."

She glared at Vaughn, not liking him one bit before she turned to Brie. "I hate your husband."

"He's a special one," she said, looking up at him. "This is an A and B conversation, C your way out."

He scoffed. "You just don't like that I'm speaking the truth."

"We don't," Wren announced, and he grinned.

"Sorry for ya. You hit me with the truth way back when, and now I'm doing the same. Do what I did—don't do what you're used to."

As she held his gaze, they both knew what she was used to.

Running.

Hiding.

Shutting everything out.

"Because unlike everyone and anything else, when it comes to Jensen, he doesn't back down. He won't let you go without a fight, even if it kills him."

Her heart dropped to her stomach as she tore her gaze away and looked at the floor. She didn't want to give Vaughn another thought, but she knew that he was right. She knew her faults, she knew who Jensen was, and even so, she knew that, more than likely, she was going to do what everyone had said.

Hurt him.

If she didn't get it together.

"I have a crazy idea," Brie said, and Wren looked up, seeing that Vaughn was still standing there.

"What?"

"Come out in your sexiest outfit, drive him wild. I bet he won't be able to resist."

Vaughn laughed. Hard. "You don't know Jenny. He'll resist."

"Bet you he won't. She's so hot!"

"No doubt. But when he knows what he wants, he knows what he wants, and he won't do it."

"Yes, he will! Bet you head."

"Shit, bet you butt!"

Wren snorted as Brie's eyes darkened. "Fine."

Vaughn's eyes lit up as he came over, holding his hand out. "Shake on it."

She glared and then did it as Wren laughed. "No pressure, I guess!"

Brie looked over at her, her face red as she sputtered with laughter. "My ass is depending on you."

That had all three of them laughing, but inside Wren's head, Vaughn's words were playing loud and clear.

*He doesn't need sex to love you. He just does.*

And while she sat there as her two friends sparred back and forth, all she could do was wonder if it was true.

And if so, how the hell had she never noticed?

# Chapter TWELVE

*L*eaning against his pillows, Jensen scrolled through his Facebook as he waited for Wren to come to bed. She had been at Brie's house all afternoon, helping with the decoration of the house, and he had missed her. Though, he wasn't sure the feeling was mutual. Which annoyed him. He tried to distract himself by working out with Dylan at the rink and going shopping with Vaughn, but his mind kept going back to her. She hadn't even asked if he wanted to do something that day, she just left. He guessed he should be glad she had a friend, but still, he wanted to spend time with her. They could have set up the nursery or even just hung around. He wanted to be with her.

It was stuff like that that made him worry about their future, and he hated that.

He did, but what could he do?

"What did you do today?" she called from the bathroom, and he laid his phone in his lap, looking up to where he could see only her sweet ass from the bathroom. She was leaned into the sink, her panties basically up her ass as she did something to her face. She had so many lotions and shit. He was pretty sure she didn't know what any of it was, though she did stay in there forever.

"Went and worked out, hung out with Vaughn. Oh. I bought your plane ticket for next week."

"Oh, good, I forgot to ask you about that. We'll fly right out to Colorado at the end of the week?"

"Yeah," he said, looking up at the ceiling. "For the wedding of the summer."

"I'm beyond excited." The sarcasm was so strong in his wife.

"Have you not talked to Wells?"

"Nope."

That bothered him. "Oh."

"Yup, but whatever."

It wasn't whatever, though. He knew it bothered her, but he could sense she didn't want to talk about it. "What did you do over at Brie's?"

"Sat on the couch and then helped her pick out colors for the house. She's so indecisive, and then Vaughn makes it worse. He's ridiculous. He wanted to paint the living room mint because he said she looks good in mint. He's so silly."

Jensen smiled. That was his best friend. "Oh, well, you should have just stayed here. We could have set up the nursery."

Once he said it, he wasn't sure how she would take it. But before he could say something to cover up that his feelings were hurt that she left, she peeked her head out, her face covered in some goop. "I didn't even think about that. You should have said something."

He shrugged. "Didn't want to mess up your plans."

"Oh, well, I'd rather have done that."

That made him smile. "Then we'll do it this week."

She smiled. "Wednesday is my short day."

"I'll be here with a hammer and screwdriver."

Her eyes darkened. "You're good with that hammer, huh?"

When she winked before going back to the mirror, his lips curved. "You're being suggestive again?"

"Always," she called to him, and he laughed, the bed shaking underneath him. She was in a good mood, being herself, and he loved that. He hated the closed-up Wren. She irritated him. But playful Wren, he really enjoyed that girl. Reminded him of the girl she used to be before all those fucking dicks ruined her.

When the water started to run, he exhaled as he reached for his phone once more, scrolling through until he heard the water shut off. He looked up to see her reaching for the light to shut it off, and that's when he promptly dropped his phone. Unlike she had been doing since they had started sharing a bed, gone was the oversized shirt, leaving her in only a very, very skimpy pair of panties and a completely see-through bra. Her nipples were crying for him, screaming at him, and yeah, he was rock hard before he let out another breath.

When she met his gaze, she had nothing but wicked intentions in those green depths. Swallowing hard, he was breathless as she said, "I'm super hot tonight."

"I'd say so," he muttered, and her lips curved in a sneaky grin as she walked around the room, putting away her clothes, and then getting out her outfit for the following day. His eyes were glued to her, his heart pounding in his chest as his whole body shook with want. He wanted to pin her against the wall, slide that bra down over her swollen breasts, and take them in his mouth. He wanted to spread her apart and bury his face between her thick thighs.

He wasn't going to make it.

Forcing himself to move, he reached for his phone, his hands shaking as he begged his throbbing hard-on to just fucking relax. When she came to his side of the bed, his breath caught as he looked up at her while she bent over his thighs to reach for a shirt that was on her side. All he saw was her perky ass as she slowly stood back up in a very suggestive way, muttering, "Sorry."

But he knew damn well she wasn't sorry at all.

Chuckling to keep from reaching out and taking a handful of that sweet ass, he looked at his phone like it was holding all the secrets of the unknown.

Like how not to pounce on his wife and fuck her brains out.

"What's so funny?"

"This meme," he muttered without looking at her.

But then she was beside him, her hands on the edge of the bed, her breasts right fucking there.

*Good Lord above. Take me. Please.*

Closing his eyes, he turned his phone to his Facebook, showing a meme that wasn't that funny, but she laughed nonetheless, the airy sound making his cock throb so much harder he felt it in his chest. "That's funny."

"Yeah," he agreed, looking right at his phone and not at the swells of her perfectly encased breasts.

She was going to kill him.

Exhaling, she stood up and made her way around the bed. "Do you need anything?"

He shook his head. "Nope. I'm good."

She didn't say anything for a moment as he held his phone so tightly, he worried he was going to break it. "Would it bother you if I slept without a bra? I'm so hot."

He closed his eyes as he pressed his lips together. "I can turn the air down."

"Oh. Good idea," she decided, and with that, he watched as she sashayed across the room to the thermostat, turning it down, but all he saw was the curve of that ass and the dimples in her thick thighs. How in the world was he supposed to make it?

"Is that okay?" she asked, turning to look at him, and he just nodded.

"Good," he got out as she headed back to the bed, getting in very slowly, and somehow, very fucking sexily. Pushing the blankets off her, she lay beside him, completely his for the taking, and he knew he was going to die a slow death from lack of blood since it was all in his cock. As her hands slid down her thighs and then up over her belly, his breath caught.

Was she doing this on purpose?

"Oh, he's moving. Wanna feel?"

But before he could beg her not to touch him, she grabbed his hand, placing it on her belly. Within seconds, he felt the baby kicking with all his might. Away went his insane lust as a grin pulled at his lips while he sat up, taking her belly between both hands as the baby moved. It was mind-blowing, and he had always wanted a chance to feel this. For so long he thought he'd never get to, but as he sat there, his hands on her growing belly, he felt tears burning in his eyes.

"That's amazing."

"If I weren't one hundred percent sure he was going to be a hockey player, I'd say the kid was destined for soccer."

Jensen laughed at that. "He can do both. Wow, he's strong."

"He is."

"Is the asshole big?"

When he looked up at her, her lips were pressed together. "Yeah, like you."

"Cool," he said, though he didn't think it was that cool. He hated the guy. "Is he blond?"

"No, brown-haired."

"That's good."

"Yeah," she said simply as his hands moved along her belly.

"Man, he is amazing in there."

"He is," she agreed as her hands covered his. She looked up, and their eyes met. The lust hit him like a puck in the middle of the chest. Her eyes were so dark, her lips so full, and soon she was moving toward him. "I hope he is just like you."

His heart flip-flopped in his chest as she took his face in her hands, her lips coming to his with heated need. His eyes fell shut first, which usually didn't happen, but everything was on fire and he couldn't handle it. Sliding his hands up her body, over her full breasts, he wrapped his arms around her neck, holding her to him as he devoured her naughty little mouth. He was shaking, he wanted her so badly, yet, he pulled back, kissing her lips softly. When she tried to deepen the kiss, he backed away more. "I need to ask you something."

She was breathing hard, her lips parted as she gazed up at him. "Or you can just kiss me, grab my boob or my ass. Whichever."

He chuckled against her lips as he let her go, putting some space between them. "Or, we can talk."

"Talking is overrated."

"I don't think so," he said, sitting back in his place though his cock was basically cussing him out at this point. "Why don't you talk to Shanna anymore?"

When he looked over at her, her face was full of annoyance and a whole lot of sexual frustration. "Really?"

"Yeah. I want to know."

She pursed her lips and then exhaled hard. "It's a long story."

"And we've got all the time in the world."

She glared at the ceiling, and he smiled. She wanted him, he could tell, but he didn't feel it was more than that. Until he did, he wouldn't be giving in. Call him an idiot, but he knew her. He knew how she worked, and he wouldn't be another one of her mistakes.

He wanted to be her forever.

Even if it killed him and gave him the biggest case of blue balls the world had ever seen.

Swallowing hard, she shook her head. "I don't know, Jensen. I don't know how to explain it."

"Try."

She shrugged, chewing on her lip as she chose her words. "I dropped her because I knew if I told her about the baby, she would judge me. She always judged me for my lifestyle because, you know, she's married, kids, the whole nine. She always told me I was too old to be sleeping around. Plus, she'd want to know who the dad is and I don't want to tell anyone and she'd get pissed and, yeah, I just let it go."

"An over twenty-year friendship? Just like that?"

She met his gaze. "Yeah. I knew that she wouldn't support me, so I dropped her before she could drop me."

He held her gaze, knowing it was more than that. "Will you ever tell me who the dad is?"

She shook her head, pressing her lips together. "He isn't important. You're the dad now. So why does he matter?"

In a way, he didn't, Jensen guessed, but he wanted to know. "I just want to know."

Biting on her lip, she dropped her shoulders, and he thought maybe she was going to tell him. Instead, she whispered, "He doesn't matter. Only you matter."

His heart soared in his chest. Reaching out, he took her hand in his and brought it to his mouth, pressing his lips to it. "That's my favorite thing you've said to me thus far, except for the day you told me, yes, you'd marry me."

Her lips quirked as she shook her head. "I don't deserve you."

He scoffed. "Funny, I say that every day."

Her eyes widened as he reached over, kissing the side of her mouth. "Goodnight, babe."

"Goodnight?" she asked as she watched him while he turned over, plugging in his phone and cuddling into the pillows.

While his body was still screaming for hers, he knew he was doing the right thing. Because like his dad had always said, "If you want something you've never had, then you have to do something you've never done."

For her, her default was to fuck her feelings away.

And if he wanted her for the rest of his existence, he couldn't let her do that.

He had to love her.

For her to love herself.

And then, hopefully, him.

* * *

GASPING FOR BREATH, Jensen looked over at Vaughn who was lying on the floor, also fighting for air. "Why do you do this to me?"

Jensen's brows rose. "We are working out."

"I know, but I want to sit on my couch and eat. I'm supposed to be relaxing."

Jensen laughed, though it sounded like he was choking. "We don't want to get flabby."

Vaughn's eyes widened. "What's wrong with being flabby? We can be flabby through the summer and then clean up our act before training camp."

"Or, we can do the two workouts a week that I've set up to keep us good through the summer."

"You're ruining my life," Vaughn decided as he rolled over to his back, struggling for breath. "I hate you."

"I know," Jensen said as he crunched down, running his hands through his hair. He had asked Kacey Thomas for a workout, and she wasn't holding back. He was sweating everywhere, and he knew he was pushing himself to get rid of the crazy lust inside of him. He didn't want to work out. He wanted to veg on the couch, but he had to do something, or he was going to lose his ever-loving mind. Wren was trying to kill him. For the last four days, he had gone to bed with the biggest boner known to man because his wife had decided she wanted to run around in basically nothing before bed.

Those thongs and that bra were becoming his kryptonite.

Watching her as she slathered her face in lotion with her sweet ass hanging out and those thighs... Jesus, those thighs for him to drink in was basically torture. She was killing him slowly, but he was staying strong. And killing Vaughn in the meantime.

As he finished up his burpees, Vaughn fell to the ground once more and lay there, shaking his head. "I'm done."

"We have another round."

"I refuse. Let's go get chicken," he said before sitting up to meet Jensen's gaze, his eyes hopeful. "You love chicken. Hot chicken. I'll buy you all of it. Just for you."

Jensen laughed. "No."

"You're mean."

"It's for your own good."

"You're just taking out your sexual frustration on me," he accused as he stood up, slowly and with a groan. "It isn't my fault you won't put out. That's your own issue."

Jensen laughed. "You know nothing, my friend."

"I know it all, because Wren was at my house bitching."

Jensen's brow quirked. "What?"

Vaughn set him with a look. "Yeah, she was at the house on Sunday, talking to her new BFF—which is very weird to me, by the way—and they were talking about how you won't put out."

"She said that?"

"Well, no, she said you wouldn't do her because you aren't attracted to her."

He scoffed. "That's fucking bullshit."

"I know this, because you've had a boner for her for, like, ever, and I told her that."

Jensen's whole body went cold. "You did? What did she say?"

"She didn't believe me, or Brie."

"I can't believe you told her that."

"Does it matter? She didn't believe me."

"But still."

"Dude, she thinks you're doing this because you're honorable."

Jensen brought his lip between his teeth as he shook his head. "I swear, that girl's confidence is in the tank, and it's fucking annoying."

"It is."

He sat there for a moment, thinking it over, and slowly he moved his head side to side in annoyance. How could she think that? "I don't know what to do. Do I just give in? Or do I keep on? I mean, I seriously tell her daily that she's beautiful. Tell her that I love the little things, her hair, her line thing she does to her eyes, I mean, everything. But because I won't let her use sex as a way to feel something for me, then I'm not attracted to her? That's not fair."

"I hear you, brother," Vaughn added, holding his hand up. "But maybe she needs that."

"No, she wants to rely on it so she doesn't have to feel anything else for me, and that's bullshit."

"But if she thinks you aren't trying to get her naked, how is she supposed to feel sexy?"

"'Cause I tell her!"

"You've said, 'Damn, Wrenny, you're sexy'?"

Jensen snorted a bit. "Not like that, but I tell her she's beautiful."

"Not the same thing."

Jensen grumbled as he thought it over. He understood what Vaughn was saying, but he didn't know if he agreed with him.

"Listen, bro, I got you. I hear what you're saying, and I get it. Really, I do, but you know how she is. She's used to one thing. Maybe that's the way you two can connect, and it won't just be about the sex for her. It will be more."

Jensen bit the inside of his cheek. "Says the person who'd rather fuck than talk."

Vaughn held his hands up. "But let me tell you, Brie and I had a very healthy sex life, and I fell hard for the girl."

"But you never had any intentions of falling for her. How do I know Wren will have feelings for me?"

Vaughn shrugged. "You knew that from the rip, bro. This whole relationship has been like the moment in the crease—where the puck could go in, or you could block it. She's the blocker, and you're the puck trying to go in. It's a gamble. A big one."

Swallowing hard, Jensen admitted he had known that from the beginning. He did, but hearing it once more made it even more real.

And scared the living shit out of him because he didn't know what to do.

Should he stay strong, wait for her to feel something for him?

Or should he just take her to bed and hope for the best?

Fuck, this was complicated.

* * *

WREN'S HEART ached in her chest as she watched Tate struggle in front of her.

He looked so wrung out. His shoulders were down, and his eyes were full of such defeat. She wished this wasn't happening, and she hated her stupid hormones that were making her want to hug him and cry with him. As he looked up, meeting her gaze, she clutched her notepad as he tried to smile.

"You've thought this through?"

He nodded slowly, his eyes filling with tears. "Audrey and I have been talking since our last session. She started crying last night because I was still so unsure, and she just wanted me to be happy. She said that if I want to push myself and try to get back on the ice, she'd support me and she'd love me no matter what, even in a wheelchair. And that hurt me. I don't want to do that to her or my kids. If I retire now, I can give my body the time it needs to heal, and I can be there for them."

"You're right. And good for Audrey. You're lucky to have such a great woman."

His lips turned up in a true smile. "I've loved her since the moment I met her. She's so strong. So beautiful and the best woman I know. She loves me hard, and she loves our children with her whole soul. We've stood beside each other through thick and thin, and I couldn't ask for a better partner for this life." Wren's heart shattered as he inhaled deeply, his lips quivering. "As much as I will miss the ice, miss being between those pipes, I miss playing on the floor with my kids more. Being able to lie with my wife the way she loves…sorry, TMI," he laughed and she smiled. "But I'd rather be able to be there for my family and love them, like they've always loved me. The best thing for me is to retire."

"And that's what you want?"

"Yes."

"Good, I'm glad that we've all worked together to come to this realization. I think it's for the best, but in the end, it's what you want."

He nodded. "I know, and I do. I might not like it fully yet, but I know that if I keep trying to push myself, I'm not only going to hurt myself but my family too, and nothing is more important than family."

Wren's lips started to quiver. She missed Wells. She missed him so much, but she was still so angry with him. It wasn't only that; it was the fact that she knew, like Tate, Jensen would do the same thing for her and her child.

And she wasn't sure she would do the same.

That hurt her.

Pissed her off.

Why couldn't she be like Audrey?

Reaching out, she took Tate's hand and squeezed it. "I'm proud of you, Tate."

"Thank you," he said, squeezing back. "I don't want to stop our sessions, though. I think I still might need them."

Wren smiled, loving that he wanted to keep seeing her. She had been worried he would drop her since he had come to this decision, but she knew he would continue to need her. The pain was still so overwhelming for him, and not playing would take its toll. "I'll always be here for you, Tate. Except for the next three weeks." She laughed. "I'm going back home. But my phone is always on."

He smiled. "That's great. You need a break. Especially with dealing with me."

Wren laughed, shaking her head. "Never. You've been a joy, Tate. I'm so proud of you."

They shared a smile as he slowly got up, reaching for his crutch, before leaning on it. "Thanks, and oh, congratulations. Audrey told me that you and Monroe eloped."

She blushed. "Yeah, we did."

"And that you're having a baby. I hadn't realized."

"Yeah, I just look fat," she teased, waving him off, and he turned bright red.

"Never."

"I was teasing you."

He smiled as she walked with him to her office door. "You know, Wren, he's the greatest guy ever. He texts me at least three times a week to check on me. When everything happened, he brought food for my family so Audrey wouldn't have to worry about it. He babysat for us while I was in the hospital. He's got a great heart, and since I think you're the best, I'm really happy for you two."

Her lips trembled as she placed her hand on the middle of Tate's back and met his gaze. "Thank you. He's wonderful."

"He is. Congratulations again and enjoy your trip."

"Thanks, Tate. Get with Leah for your next session."

"Will do. Thanks."

"Thank you," she called as she watched him walk to Leah's desk.

When her tears started to spill over her, running down her face, she shut the door and leaned her head into it. Everyone had nothing but nice things to say about Jensen. Everyone. She knew the only person who probably didn't like him was his ex-wife, but she was a cunt, so it didn't matter. Wren was married to the best damn guy on earth, and she wasn't one hundred percent committed. She would be home in a matter of days, and she knew in her soul that everyone would see right through them.

She felt like she wasn't doing anything right. She was fighting with Wells. She hadn't talked to Shanna in almost seven months. She missed her friend, she did, but what she had told Jensen was the truth. Shanna would judge her and then push to know the father. Wren knew she would see Shanna when she went home, and she was dreading it. Then on top of all of that, she couldn't allow herself to even entertain the chance that she and Jensen could work. It seemed so foreign to her, and that bothered her. He was such a great guy, and apparently, he adored her. So what was the issue?

Meanwhile, she was in charge of helping men with their mental health?

She was a fucking impostor.

As she wiped away her tears, she shook her head.

"Kiddo, I love you, I do. But man, you are making my hormones turn me into a fucking crybaby who has no clue what to do with her life, and that's not good, man. I gotta figure this out."

Or she was going to be alone.

* * *

LOOKING down at the pile of bills on the counter, Wren closed her eyes as she sucked on the spoon full of ice cream, tears dripping down her face. She'd made the mistake of stopping by her mailbox for her mail. Inside was bill after bill—and the biggest one from their trip to the baby store. She wouldn't let Jensen pay, and because of that, her credit card was maxed out. Her first thought was she'd pay it off with the money from her trust, and that opened up the waterworks.

What if they got home and her dad saw right through them, not giving her their money? What if Jensen was wasting his time? What if she was dumb enough to fall for him, and he decided at the end, when she was flabby from having a baby, that he didn't want her? God, why was she such a fucking mess?

Today sucked.

"Pity party for two. Sorry, kiddo, you're in this because you're inside me."

When the front door opened and Wren saw Jensen coming through it, she turned away quickly, wiping her face as she walked, hoping he didn't see her crying. She hadn't expected him to be home yet since he said he would call. So, of course, she was in the middle of the kitchen with a container of ice cream and tears flowing from the day that had turned her into an emotional mess.

"Whoa, where you going?"

"Nowhere," she said, turning around once she was sure her tears were gone. "I thought I had to pee."

His brows were drawn in, his arms carrying two bags from her favorite taco place. "The bathroom is right here," he said, pointing to the bathroom that was right beside the door and so much closer than the one in the bedroom. "So, want to try that again?" Setting the bags down, he came around the counter as his eyes held hers. "Are you crying?"

"No."

"Yes?"

"Maybe."

"Why?" he asked, leaning his hip to the counter, his eyes never leaving hers. "What's wrong?"

"I had a tough day," she said slowly, shaking her head as she placed her container of ice cream on the counter. "And it sucked and I'm emotional and it's weird because I can't stop crying. I think I've cried more today than I have my whole life."

Coming off the counter, he reached for her. "Come here."

But she held her hands up. "No. I can't think when you hold me."

"More of a reason to come here," he decided, taking her hands and pulling her into his arms. The warmth of him was intoxicating, and she instantly felt safe as his arms went around her completely. How did he do that? "We can dance."

She made a face against his shoulder as her tears started to fall once more. "There's no music."

He paused then, taking out his phone and hitting play before laying it on the counter. Something soft and slow started, she wasn't sure, she hadn't heard the song before as he started to sway with her. Instantly, she was taken back to the New Year's Eve party Elli had thrown, the way Jensen had taken her out to the dance floor and danced with her then. He didn't say much, and he sure as hell didn't try anything, but he never left her side. He was there.

Just like he had been then.

"What song is this?"

"'Sometimes It's Hard' by Jamie Lawson."

"Oh, it's nice."

"It is," he agreed. "I listen to it when I stretch. It's calming."

"Yeah," she agreed, closing her eyes as she leaned on him. The music was beautiful and so very calming. But the words, man, they hit her right in the soul. She hadn't heard of this guy, but she figured he knew her and her situation before deciding to write a song about it. Getting lost in the song, she held on to Jensen as they swayed together in the kitchen. It was silly, but soon her tears dried against her cheeks as her heart gradually slowed in her chest.

Leaning his head to her, he inhaled slowly before whispering, "Now tell me what happened today."

She leaned into him, closing her eyes. He smelled divine, and he felt so damn strong, holding her like she was a feather against him. "You can't ever tell anyone I told you this. Even if you are my husband, it's player confidentiality."

"Of course."

"Tate decided to retire today."

He exhaled hard, shaking his head. "That's a fucking shame."

"Yeah, but he's in so much pain, and seeing him almost in tears as he chose his family over the sport he loved just gutted me."

He nodded against her. "I can imagine. That guts me just thinking about it."

"It sucked."

"It does."

Swallowing hard, she swayed with him, her fingers tucking into the belt loops of his shorts. "What else happened?"

"How do you know that something else happened?"

"While I know you love your job, that's not the only thing to have you crying in the kitchen ignoring the tacos on the counter."

"We're dancing."

"It's tacos, Wren."

She smiled against his shoulder. "You know me so well."

"I do."

"I miss Wells."

His shoulders fell a bit. "I'm sorry."

"And Shanna. But I know Wells and I will work it out before Shanna and me."

"Maybe you can call them both?"

"I don't know."

"Want me to call them?"

She smiled. "No. It's my responsibility."

"I can handle Wells, and you can take Shanna."

She shook her head. "No, it's fine."

"Okay."

"But thank you."

"Always." She let out a long breath and then leaned her head back into his chest. "Is that it?"

She pressed her lips together as his chin rested on top of her head. "I went by my mailbox."

"Oh, good, you've been meaning to do that."

"Yeah, but it was bills galore in that sucker."

"Give them to me, I'll pay them."

"No. They're my bills."

"I don't care. You're my wife."

"Jensen."

"Wren."

"No."

He moved his lips along her temple. "I do what I want."

She smiled against his neck. "I said no. If everything works out, I'll have my money, and I can pay them off."

"There is no if, Wren. Everything will be fine."

But she shook her head. "I'm worried about everyone not believing us when we go home."

"That won't happen."

"You don't know that."

"I do. I'll make sure of that."

She closed her eyes, hoping he was right as she wrapped her arms around him, needing his strength. As they swayed through three more songs, all slow and sweet, Wren couldn't stop thinking about everything. Tate, Wells, Shanna, going home, but most of all, Jensen. She couldn't shake her reservations. Her anxiety over all of it ending in a fiery explosion. She didn't realize it, but she needed this. She needed constant support. She'd never had that, and now that she did, she didn't want to lose it. But she couldn't use Jensen for that. He deserved better than that, but could she truly let herself love him? It would be so easy if she allowed herself to. But what if he didn't love her? What if she was a means to an end?

The baggage for the baby he so desperately wanted.

She opened her eyes as she inhaled harshly. She had to know. Moving her head, she pulled back to look at him as he moved his head. "Jensen."

"Yeah?" he asked, meeting her gaze, and God, he looked so beautiful. So content, so relaxed, while she felt like she was coming out of her skin. But looking into his eyes, she felt herself calming a bit.

Swallowing hard, she almost didn't ask, but then she knew she had to. "I need to ask you something."

His eyes searched hers as his thumbs moved along her back, sending chills up her spine. "What's that?"

Her heart was pounding in her ears and making her head hurt, but if she didn't ask, if she didn't find out the truth, she was going to make herself crazy. "Why won't you sleep with me?"

# Chapter THIRTEEN

*J*ensen's mouth went dry.

His heart rate picked up. It was beating so hard, he was sure she felt it as she held his gaze, slowly moving out of his arms and leaning into the island. "I mean, we've been doing this for two weeks, and we're stalling at first base."

Crossing his arms over his chest, he backed into the counter as she slowly nodded. "I-I want——" He stopped, shaking his head, trying to get his words together. He sensed this wasn't going to go smoothly. "I want to wait."

"Wait? For what?"

"I want it to be right."

Her brows pulled together. "Right?"

"Yeah," he said, his gaze held hostage in hers. "I want it to be for real, as fucking girly as that sounds. I want it to mean something. I don't want it to be because we're both hot for each other and we get carried away. You mean more to me than that, and I refuse to just fuck for nothing."

"It wouldn't be for nothing," she said slowly, bringing her lip between her teeth.

His head fell to the side. "So you love me?"

She scrunched up her face, and his heart dropped to his gut. "People fuck without loving each other all the time."

"Exactly. They fuck, and I don't want to fuck you, Wren. That isn't how I work."

Her eyes darkened. "That's dumb. If we want each other, what's the problem? Do you not want me?"

He swallowed hard, trying to keep his composure. "I want you more than I can even express, but you've been fucked by nothing but assholes. When I finally make love to you, I want you to know that it's for real and that it's forever." When she rolled her eyes before she closed them, shaking her head, his blood started to boil. "When I told you I wanted to show you what it's like to be treated well by a real man, I wasn't kidding." Opening her eyes, she met his heated gaze. "Even if it will require every ounce of restraint I have in my body to keep from taking that sweet ass in my hands and ruining you in a way that no man has ever been able to do."

She gasped slightly as she held his gaze, her eyes dark and annoyed. "I'm sorry, but you're a man. If you wanted me, then you would take me. Men don't have restraint when it comes to fucking. They think with their cocks."

Now he was pissed. "Do you not know me?"

"I didn't say that."

"But by saying that, you don't. Because I'm not like other men, and my cock doesn't run my life. I do. I decide what I want, and while I want you, I know I need to give you time to realize that I can want you without being inside you, before I let that happen."

"That's insane. Take me if you want me, because I don't believe that shit, and I want you. Bad."

Pushing off the counter, he dug his fingers into his palms as he stared down at her. "Wren, I'm not like those other fuckers. I respect you. I care for you. I want you without having to fuck you. I want you for who you are, not how fucking hot I assume your pussy is."

She was breathless as she looked up at him, heat in her eyes. "Or, you just can't do it because you're only doing this as a means to an end."

His eyes narrowed. "Excuse me? What does that mean?"

Emotion flashed in her eyes as she stood in front of him. "It means that I'm your ticket to the kid you want, and you're just staying with me until he comes and I get what I want, my money, before you're out the fucking door."

"Are you fucking kidding me right now?" he roared. "That is the stupidest fucking thing I've ever heard you say. And you know what? That hurts. I can't believe you would think that."

But she was unaffected. "Have you made me think otherwise?"

His mouth dropped open. "Wren, I tell you daily I think you're beautiful. I yearn for you. My cock stays hard around you, but you're trying to revert back to what you know. You know sex, you know how to do that because you don't have to feel anything but good when a cock is deep inside of you. But what I want is you to realize my words are my promise, and everything I say is true. It's hard for you, I get it, but I'm not going anywhere."

"You can't say—"

"I can! I don't care if it pisses you off, but I won't let you fuck your way through your feelings with me. I deserve better than that."

"I'm not trying to do that!"

"You're lying, Wren. I can see right through you."

"Whatever. This is bullshit." She tried to walk away, but he stopped her, standing in front of her.

"No, we're talking this through." She glared back at him as he started to speak. "Let's rewind to that night we went to dinner before we got married. Did you want to sleep with me that night because we were getting married or because you wanted me naked?" She went to answer, but he stopped her. "Honestly. It won't hurt my feelings."

She blinked and then shrugged. "I mean, I guess both. I wanted you naked, but I felt like maybe we should get it on."

"Get it on, not make love."

Her brow rose. "That's dumb. No one makes love anymore, Jensen."

"I do. I make fucking love. I don't fuck. I don't use a girl to get off. I have sex with her because I want to please her. I want to make her yearn for me. Want more because she means something to me. Do I mean anything to you?"

"Yes, of course," she answered quickly. "I care for you."

"Do you like me?"

Her eyes narrowed as annoyance filled her flushed face. "Yeah."

"Do you love me?"

Her eyes widened as she looked away, unsure what to say. "I mean, no... I don't know. Why? Why do words matter?"

Wow, that stung, but before he could wallow in that, he yelled, "Because the words you've been given have been utter shit, and you don't know what it's like to use your words for good. To make someone feel good. To lift them up and make their days better."

"I don't understand why we're having this conversation. If you don't want to fuck me, don't."

"You're right, I don't want to fuck you. I want to make love to you. I want to hold you in my arms and tell you that when I look at you, I see a goddess. I see someone I can spend the rest of my life with—"

Throwing her hands up, she exclaimed, "This was supposed to be fake!" It was as if she'd slapped him. His lips pressed together as her eyes filled with tears. "When I asked you to do this, Jensen, I said it would be fake. You're the one who wanted it to be real."

He swallowed hard as he held her gaze. "You're right, because it's not fake for me. None of it. Everything I feel, everything I say, is fucking real, Wren." Her lips snapped shut as she watched him stare back at her. "This was real the moment I asked you to marry me. And, Wren, I get it, sweetheart, I do. This scares the fuck out of you, but just think how scared I am. I'm investing every single ounce of myself in you with the hope that you don't shatter me. I'm willing to risk a very long friendship with your brother, with your family, shit, even with mine, for you. So yeah, I don't want to fuck you. I want to make love to you, and I refuse to do anything else but that."

Holding his gaze, she shook her head. "That isn't what I wanted, though."

"Still? I mean, shit, Wren, it's been weeks, and you still don't want this? Me?"

The tears started to spill over her sweet cheeks as she shrugged. "I just don't know."

Looking away, he fell back into the cabinets as he covered his face, feeling his heart shatter. He loved this girl, so fucking much, and he felt like he was in a losing battle. Yet, he didn't have it in him to accept defeat. Clearing his throat free of the emotion that wanted to suffocate him, he looked up at her as she cried softly before him. He didn't know what to say, and yet, he just wanted to reach for her. Hold her, calm her. Was he pathetic?

"Do you love me?" she asked then as she slowly looked up at him, her eyes flooded with tears. It left him feeling like he had just taken a puck to the chest with no protection whatsoever, but then, that's how he always felt around her. "Everyone says you do, but surely, if you did, you would have tried something before all this."

Swallowing hard, he nodded. "I do."

A sob escaped her lips. "What? How? Why? You've never said anything."

"Because I couldn't." Her tears fell faster as she shook her head. "I knew you were the most beautiful girl I'd ever seen in my whole entire life the moment I met you. I wanted you. So fucking badly. But I wouldn't disrespect your parents in their house. I just wouldn't, and you never seemed interested in me, so I buried my feelings."

Her eyes widened as her mouth trembled. "What? Since then?"

"Yeah," he said with a nod, his heart clanking against his ribs. "Then I met Ophelia, and I convinced myself I loved her. In reality, I always thought of you. I waited for you to text me, needing me, and I would come because I had this compulsion inside of me to always be there for you. When she left me, I was crushed, but I still thought about you. I knew I wasn't good enough for you. I was sterile, you were fucking gorgeous and amazing, and you needed a man who would give you children. I couldn't do it."

"Jensen," she cried, reaching out, but her hands fell when he backed farther into the counter. If she touched him, he'd lose it.

"But then that time we were out at NateWay, and you were flirting with me about that damn hammer, I thought, this is it, take her in your arms and tell her how you feel. But I didn't. Because my issue held me back, and I knew you weren't into relationships. Then days turned into months. We both were on different tracks in life, and while I never didn't think about you, I knew I wasn't on your radar until that moment you asked for me to be the father of your kid," he said, his voice breaking. "So yeah, this wasn't real for you, but it's been real for me since the moment I met you. And fucking hell, I want you to love me back. I want it so badly because I have loved you and will love you long after you're gone. You're it for me."

She looked away, and her mouth trembled as she ran her hands down her face, catching her tears and wiping them away. He knew he shouldn't have unloaded on her, she hadn't had the best day, but it was bound to happen. In all reality, they should have done this at the beginning, before they were almost three weeks in. But there they were, standing in the kitchen, both in tears. "I don't know what to say."

He let out a harsh breath as he shook his head. "What do you want, Wren?" he asked softly as her body continued to shake with her sobs. Knowing that he meant nothing more than friendship to her really hurt. But had he really expected anything else? He was pretty sure he always knew nothing would come out of this except a good set of parents for the kid she was carrying. Maybe she was using him. "Now that you know how I feel, what I want, what do you want? Do you just want to use me? Do you want to fuck? Get off and keep this simple between us? Fine. Let's fuck, if that's truly what you want."

Now he was being an asshole. He knew that, especially when she looked up at him, her eyes dark as the tears spilled out of them. "No, that's not what I want. That's the last fucking thing I want. I don't want to use you, but you don't have to make it sound so damn vulgar," she said, rolling her eyes as his heart sped up in his chest. "Some people in love fuck too."

"Which I would be completely down for if you had any intention of loving me, but you've made it fully known that's not the case here. So yeah, thanks." Reaching for his keys, he passed by her, going toward the door.

"What are you doing?"

"I need some air."

She sputtered, and the panic was in her voice as she said, "But I thought we were doing the nursery."

"Why? So you can pack it up once he's here? I'll put together the bassinet later."

Reaching for the door, he pulled it open as the tears flooded his eyes. Before he could go out though, she said, "Jensen, please."

He paused, glancing at her. "What?"

Her eyes were wide, her body shaking as she held his gaze, fear in her expression. "I don't know."

"Well, when you know, it'd be great if you could let me know."

With that, he left.

Without his heart.

Wren had owned that for as long as he could remember.

And the problem was, he didn't know how to get it back.

Or if he wanted it back.

It was hers.

Even when she disintegrated it.

* * *

STARING at the back of the door, Wren's lips trembled as her tears fell in droves down her cheeks.

Well, that was awesome.

Not.

Sliding down the back of the island, she sat on the ground and tried to lean on her legs, but her belly was in the way. She let her arms drop as she looked up at the lip of the counter and the ceiling, her tears continuing to roll down her face as she cried. She hadn't expected for this to happen. She hadn't wanted to fight with him; she'd just wanted an answer. That was all. But instead, she ended up with way more than she thought she would have gotten, and now, she didn't know what to do.

Every single one of his words hit her in ways she didn't expect them to. She didn't believe anyone else when they'd said almost the same thing that Jensen had said, but hearing it from his lips, watching as his eyes bored into hers, she knew she couldn't deny his words. He meant them, and they rattled her soul like a pothole did a car. How in the world had she been so oblivious to how he felt? Years, he had felt like that, and he'd thought he wasn't good enough for her?

She let out a sob as she shook her head. "He's too good for me."

Would things have been different? Would she have changed her ways for him? Or would she have fucked him and left him? She didn't know, and that made her feel worthless. What was wrong with her? As she sat there, her tears nearly drowning her, she kept asking herself the same question he had asked.

What did she want?

But she couldn't answer what should be such a simple question.

At first, she had only wanted to get her money. But now…now, she felt different.

She wanted more.

The last couple weeks had been a whirlwind for her. She went from being completely alone, facing everything by herself, to having this gorgeous, amazing man stand beside her through a storm that wasn't his, but one he welcomed. Brie was right; he did look at her like a goddess. He loved her.

Fuck. He loved her.

And she just told him she didn't know how she felt.

What the hell?

She probably hurt him. Well, no, she knew she did, and that hurt her most of all. She didn't want to do that. Even from the beginning of this, she'd never wanted that. Promised everyone she wouldn't do it, but she had. What in the hell was she doing?

Was she using him?

Damn it.

Reaching for her phone, she hit her brother's number, and as the phone rang, she begged for him to answer. She wasn't sure why she was calling the one person who was completely against this, but she was. Thankfully, he answered in his low voice, "Wow, never thought you'd call me first."

"Wells," she cried, her voice breaking all over the place.

"Whoa, Wren, are you okay?"

"No," she admitted, her heart aching. "We got into a fight."

"We're brother and sister, it happens. I still love you."

"No, not us," she said, shaking her head. "Though I love you too, even if you're a dick. I mean Jensen and me."

"Oh," he said softly, and then she heard a door shut. "What happened?"

She swallowed hard. "I can't tell you."

He inhaled harshly. "Okay, do you want me to come kick his ass?"

She scoffed at that. "No. Just tell me what I want."

"What do you mean?"

"I don't know. Like, what do I want in all this? What am I doing?"

He laughed. "Hell, I can't tell you that. I sure as shit don't know. You're a complex one."

She closed her eyes. "He's going to leave me."

His laughter stopped abruptly. "Never. Jenny wouldn't do that."

"I'm going to push him away." When Wells didn't say anything, Wren knew she was right. "And I don't want to do that. I care for him. A lot," she admitted, and her words startled her.

Clearing his throat, he said, "I don't know what happened since you won't tell me, but if I know one thing, Jensen doesn't hold a grudge. If you apologize, he'll forgive you."

"I don't deserve his forgiveness. I might be using him." She cringed, her heart sinking in her chest.

Wells muttered something along the lines of "I knew it" before he clucked his tongue at her. "Wren."

"I know, I know you said I was, and I denied it. But I've gone two fucking weeks more worried about when we're going to fuck than seeing all the signs that he truly loves me."

He exhaled into the phone. "He does. For as long as I can remember."

"And that's not fair."

"It isn't."

"Because he's a good man."

"The best."

Her sobs racked her body as she slowly shook her head. "I don't want to hurt him."

"Wren, you don't have to. Don't you know that?"

"But it's scary. Like the whole opening up thing. But I feel like if I don't try, then I'm letting him down. I'm lying, and he doesn't deserve that."

"He doesn't."

Running her hands down her face, she leaned into it as she took in a deep breath. "I'm sorry, Wells."

Breathing into the phone, Wells chuckled. "No, I'm sorry, Wrenny. I love you."

"I love you too."

"I was gonna call you tomorrow and apologize, but I figured one more day of being a prick would be good, even if Jensen threatened to kill me."

Her brows pulled together. "What?"

"I just got off the phone with him. Like seconds before you called."

"Jensen?"

"Yeah, he called to tell me to get my head out of my ass because I'm hurting you. That you love me and feel like I don't love you, which is completely untrue. I love you, Wren, so damn much, you know that. Don't ever question that."

But she wasn't worried about that, only Jensen. "He called you?" she asked, her heart skipping in her chest. "Even after we just fought?"

"I could tell he was upset, but he was direct and to the point before he let me go—without giving me a chance to speak."

She couldn't wrap her brain around it. Why would Jensen do that? "I don't understand."

"That's Jenny. He loves you, Wren, and even when he's mad at us, he will always do what's best for everyone. He's loyal to a fucking fault."

Her lips trembled as she slowly shook her head. "Can I tell you something?"

"Anything," he said simply. "You know that."

She almost couldn't breathe as she whispered, "I don't want to lose him." A sob broke free. "Like, now that I have him, I don't want to think about not having him. I don't know if it's for selfish reasons or for, like, real, ya know?"

Wells chuckled. "Let me tell you something, okay?"

"Okay?"

"You remember that summer—I think we were seventeen, so you would have been fifteen—and we were at Richard Oberlin's pool party?"

She paused for a second and shrugged. "What does this have to do—"

"Yes or no."

"Yes, jeez."

"Okay, I remember I saw Jensen staring at you—you were in some stupid purple bathing suit that had a rainbow across your ass—and I started teasing him for staring at you. He ignored me, like always, even when Jo gave him shit, but he didn't care. He kept staring at you, this dumb grin on his face. But then Richard came over, and he was talking shit, that the rainbow on your ass was so big that the pot of gold on the other side was probably massive... Well, before I could kill him, Jensen plowed his fist into Richard's mouth in a way that was straight out of some damn ninja movie. Jo started laughing so hard, while I stood there in shock before Jensen very calmly told Richard if he ever said anything about you again, he'd kill him."

Wren's face broke into a grin. "I remember his nose bleeding, but I didn't realize that's what had happened."

"Yeah, and I knew from that moment that one day he would get you, that you would notice he felt way more than just a friendship for you, and I knew you wouldn't have a chance. Did I think it would be like this? No, but I always knew. Wren, really, don't destroy this. Don't let the past ruin your future. Because Jensen is one of a kind, and you'll never find anyone like him."

"I know—"

"Listen, I get it. You've been through your fair share of assholes, everyone knows, and we all understand. You've been scorned. But maybe this one time you can let something good happen for you."

Swallowing hard, Wren's eyes fell shut as she leaned back into the island.

*Don't let the past ruin your future.*

She repeated her brother's words a million times in her head, over and over again.

The problem was, it was easier said than done.

But damn it, she didn't want to fail.

This was supposed to be fake, a means to an end so she could get her money. Now, things were different. It wasn't about the money anymore. It was about the woman and the mother she could be with Jensen by her side.

Holy fuck, that was one terrifying thought.

But it didn't just come out of nowhere.

Which meant something.

Right?

# Chapter FOURTEEN

"I thought you said you were poor when we were younger?"

Jensen looked over at Wren as they drove down the long driveway that led to his parents' house. "I was."

She looked back at the house that was in the distance before scoffing. "We have two very different views on being poor."

He laughed. "When I was drafted, I used my bonus to rebuild my parents' house."

"Oh," she drawled, and he looked back out the window, taking in the beauty that was his parents' home. It used to be a two-bedroom cabin, but now it was three bedrooms with bigger rooms and much more space for his parents. With his father's diabetes and his immobility, it was good to have the room for his wheelchair and then the pool in the back for exercise. Jensen loved his parents' home, and thankfully, they did too. "It's big."

"Yeah, my dad is in his wheelchair more than he isn't."

"That sucks."

"It does," he agreed as they pulled in beside his mom's van. "But he doesn't let it get him down. You ready?"

She looked over at him and let out a shaky breath. "Nervous."

"So am I," he admitted as he reached for the door. "But they're excited to see us."

She didn't look sure of that as she got out and he did the same, going to the back for their luggage. Meeting him by the trunk, she ran her hands down her belly, fixing her shirt as she looked around. "What if she's still mad? Your mom?"

He looked over at her as he lifted up one of her bags. "She wasn't ever mad. She was just annoyed."

She gave him a dry look. "Same damn thing."

"I beg to differ, but either way, she won't say anything. She isn't one for confrontation."

"When it comes to her son, she is just fine with confrontation. I've heard her go at it with your coach plenty of times. Remember how my mom would put her on speaker? Man, she would go off."

Jensen's mouth quirked. His mom was a firecracker when she needed to be. "That's different. It wasn't my wife."

She pressed her lips together as she looked toward the house. "Still. Makes me nervous."

Reaching out, he cupped her by the back of her neck before pulling her toward him. "We're good, okay?"

Before she could answer, he pressed his lips into hers, and she stepped toward him willingly. She wrapped her arms around his waist, and his heart skipped a beat. At first, he wasn't convinced by the list he had found. He knew how she was. She made lists, and most of the time, if she didn't like the outcome, she would ignore it. But that was the second list that had to do with him, and he didn't think she was ignoring it. It felt a little like a dream, but he really did think she was trying. That she was letting go and trusting him. It had only been a few days, but he swore he felt closer to her in that time than he had in the three weeks they had been together.

It was either that, or he was making it something it wasn't.

He wasn't sure, but he wouldn't deny that he enjoyed the way she clung to him or leaned into him as she kissed him.

Pulling away, he kissed the side of her mouth and then her nose. "Everything is going to be fine."

She nodded as her eyes met his, and damn it, she was beautiful. Her eyes were so green, that pretty makeup on her eyes that made his insides feel all crazy. Her lips were glossed up, and her hair was down in big curls along her shoulders. She was wearing a pair of shorts and a long, very thin long-sleeved shirt that hugged her belly in the most delectable way. As much as he wanted to wait out the sexual connection between them, he had to admit he was struggling more and more lately.

He wanted her.

Every single part of her.

Exhaling hard when she turned out of his arms and looked back at the house, he closed his eyes and prayed that his mom didn't say anything. Surely, she wouldn't, but his mom was a mama bear to the extreme. Shutting the trunk, he carried the bags while Wren walked beside him toward the house. Before they could even step onto the walkway, his mother was yelling out, *"Mon chou!"*

His mom was wearing one of her trusty house dresses, and her dark hair that had a wide silver streak through the middle was up in a big bun. She had aged since he had seen her last, but he still thought his mother was beautiful. Wren looked up and plastered a grin on her face as his mom made her way down the stairs to them, wrapping Wren up first. "Look at you! Ah! My grandbaby!" Taking Wren's belly in her hands, she cried out as she started speaking very quickly in French. Wren's eyes widened as she looked back at Jensen, and he smiled, "She said he'll be as big as I was. I was eleven pounds."

Wren's mouth dropped. "No wonder you had only one."

His mom laughed as she nodded. "You have no clue."

"You're a strong woman, Mrs. Monroe."

His mom waved her off quickly. "Mum." She took Wren's face in her hands. "I'm so happy to see you. So beautiful," she gushed, kissing Wren's cheeks before hugging her tightly.

"You too," Wren somehow muttered between kisses before his mother was on him, knocking the bags out of his hands. But his grin was unstoppable. As he held his mother, his eyes fell shut as she cried into his shoulder. It has been so long since he had seen her, at least eight months. She felt the same, crying in French as she held him, kissing him over and over again.

"You're too skinny." He scoffed as she lifted his shirt. "You don't feed him, Wrenya?"

"Wren," he corrected and she nodded.

"That's what I said," she said with a look before shaking her head, and he knew not to correct her. "You're hungry, let's go eat."

He laughed as she turned, wrapping her arm around Wren before leading her toward the house. They didn't get far before his father was hollering at them. "Who is that? Is that my son? His wife?" Jensen's stomach dropped as he picked up the bags again.

Surely, his father hadn't forgotten what he looked like. "Come closer, my sight is going."

Wren looked back, surprised since they both thought it was only his legs that were failing, and Jensen found himself unable to breathe before his mother shook her head. "Stop it, Ant."

His father laughed loudly as he waved them off. "I kid. Come here, son. I really can't walk, and I've missed you."

Rolling his eyes, Jensen made it up the stairs swiftly before dropping his bags and wrapping his arms around his father. He was in his wheelchair, his legs bandaged up as he clung to Jensen. "My boy," he muttered into his shoulder, hugging him tightly. Jensen's eyes burned as he held his father. It had been so long, longer than seeing his mother, and he regretted that. He should have come sooner. After smacking Jensen's back, his father pulled away and grinned up at him. His face was sunken in from the massive amount of weight he had been losing, but his dark brown eyes shone like he wasn't a day over sixteen. "Too long, you know."

"I know," Jensen agreed before he gave him a smacking kiss on the cheek.

"Now move. Let me see this wife of yours, Lord!" After he pushed Jensen out of the way playfully, his father widened his eyes as he shook his head. "Man, you married up, didn't ya?"

Jensen chuckled as he looked back at Wren, who flushed deeply. With a wink, he said, "I sure the hell think so."

"Yeah, the last one, Wren, was skinny as all hell and not that pretty. But you, you're gorgeous."

Wren smiled. "And not a skinny bone on me," she teased before coming up the stairs and holding out her hand. "It's wonderful—" But before she could finish, his father pulled her into a big hug.

"Family doesn't shake hands, girl."

Wren's lips were still curved as she hugged his father. Pulling back, he held her hands, looking her up and down. "I don't remember you being this pretty. Em, was she always this pretty?"

"I was thinking the same. She's gorgeous now. Looks just like Elaine."

"She sure is. Goodness. Here, have a seat right here beside me. Son, go put everything up. Let your mum fuss over you a bit."

Looking to Wren, Jensen smiled. "You good?"

"Why you asking that? Of course she is. Go," his father scolded, his hands still holding Wren's. She sent him a nervous smile, but she didn't look panicked, which he took as a win. He knew she was nervous about his parents liking her, and he was glad they were making a fuss over her. Not that they wouldn't have, but he had been nervous too.

Leaning over, he pressed his lips to her temple. "I'll be back."

"Okay," she said as his dad took her attention.

"Now, hit me with some names. He needs a strong name. Antoine is a good one."

Jensen's mom laughed. "Please don't do that to my grandbaby."

As his mom led him inside, Wren's laughter ran down his spine. His mom directed him to their room, which used to be his old bedroom until it was completely redone with an added bathroom. She had decorated it with all the memorabilia from Jensen's youth in hockey. All kinds of pictures of him growing up with his stick in his hands adorned the walls, along with photos of all the major moments. When he had won the cup when he was a junior, which was awesome since he had beaten out Wells and Vaughn on the US team. They had talked so much shit, but Canada wasn't one to mess with. A big picture of the day he was drafted made him smile because it wasn't just him, it was his parents along with Vaughn and Wells. Then one of them and Wren too. She looked so small next to all of them as they all cheesed for Elaine. That was a good day, and he couldn't help but grin ruefully as he took in Wren and him.

How the hell hadn't she known?

His hand lay on her hip, and she was basically clinging to him, her face so bright, her grin so big.

They were so young.

With a smile as he set the bags on the end of the bed, his mother asked, "Good trip in?"

He nodded. "Great. I'm glad to be home."

"We're glad to have you two here," she said, coming to him and taking his biceps in her hands. "You look happy."

His lips quirked as he nodded. "I am."

"And seeing you with her. The way she looks at you. My goodness, it's breathtaking."

He rolled his eyes gently at that. "Mum, we've been here ten minutes."

"And you two haven't taken your eyes off each other at all."

Patting his face, she turned, demanding in French that he follow, but he didn't move. A stupid grin came over his face as he shook his head. He wanted to believe his mom, he wanted to believe what was in his heart, but he could still hear Wren's words of uncertainty in his head. Man, he hated them, but he knew they were just words. Things were changing.

He could feel it.

\* \* \*

"I FEEL, in my heart, that this can count as my exercise."

Looking down at his wife as she swam in a circle in his parents' pool, Jensen laughed, shaking his head. "We'll walk when the sun goes down."

She let her head fall back. "You're ruining my life."

His father laughed beside him. "Why do you have to exercise?"

She held her hand out to him. "Exactly."

Laughing, Jensen shook his head as he took a long pull of his beer. "Her doctor is advising her to since he thinks she's putting on too much weight with the pregnancy."

Antoine scoffed. "Please, she's perfect."

"That's what I said," Jensen said when he looked back to her, and her lips pulled up a bit. "But I want to make sure she's healthy."

"Ah, well, ya gotta stay healthy, Wrenya, or you'll end up like me," Antoine pointed out, shaking his head. "And this hurts. I refuse to have you ever be like me, you hear me?"

Her lips pressed together. "Yeah, I'll go walking later."

"Good girl."

Jensen shared a grin with her before leaning back, his feet in the water as she swam around, letting the sun kiss her face. She looked carefree, happy, her hair spread out in the water as her belly peeked out. She was wearing a black bikini that hardly covered her ass, but he wasn't complaining. Her breasts were swollen and delectable and were the main reason he had a towel over his lap. "How're your parents, Wrenya? I haven't talked to your dad in months."

Wren laughed. "Because he's hiding. He hardly talks to me."

"Me either," Jensen added. "But he's doing well. Try texting him."

"Ah, I hate texting," his dad said, waving him off. "But I'll try. And your mum is good?"

Wren smiled. "She is."

With a nod, he asked, "Wells won't be upset that we can't make it to the wedding, will he?"

"No, not all at. He understands, honest."

"Okay, good. We were worried, but he said the same. Such a good boy." Letting out a pained sigh, he shook his head. "Damn legs."

"Just get healthy, Dad, that's all we want. Vaughn said the same."

"Ah, my Jo. I love that kid. He's so damn cocky."

"Beyond. You know his girlfriend is pregnant too."

"Yeah, he called and told us. I hear she's a good girl."

"She is, really good," Jensen agreed. "They're completely into each other."

Antoine chuckled loudly, filling the backyard with his laughter as he leaned back in his chair. "Funny, I remember when all you boys were here that summer, and no one could even talk to a girl. Wells was the worst—we all know why now—but still, I remember just laughing at you guys. I tried so hard to help, pushing girls at you, but all of you would just shut down. Even Vaughn." Antoine shook his head as Jensen laughed while Wren smiled.

"Were they awful?"

"Yes, so bad. Elaine told me they were just as bad at home."

"They were," Wren teased, smiling. "Jensen was my first kiss, and he was so awkward about it."

Antoine laughed hard, from the gut. "I don't doubt it. But now, I don't think he's awkward at all when he kisses ya."

Wren's face deepened with color as she met his gaze. "He's all right."

He scoffed at that as she swam backward. "Either way, look at all of you. Getting married, married, and engaged. Babies coming, it's nice. I'm a proud papa." Reaching out, he squeezed Jensen's arm. "The happiest for you though, after that awful divorce."

Jensen shrugged. "It wasn't that bad."

"It wasn't that good either. Her mum is always asking about you when we see her at the market. Mum's chest puffed up the last time we saw her. She goes, 'Jensen got married to a beauty, and they're having a baby. Plus, he's bringing the Cup home.'" He laughed, shaking his head. "We're damn proud of you."

"Thanks, Dad."

"And you're a shoo-in for the Vezina."

Jensen made a face. "Not sure yet."

Wren laughed at that. "You broke records this year, and you're the best. So yeah, it's yours."

He looked over at her and smiled. "Yeah?"

"Yup. I know it."

"So I guess I gotta dedicate it to you two, then? Since you both know?"

His father looked over at Wren, and they both nodded. "Seems legit," she said as his father said, "I agree completely."

Shaking his head, Jensen laughed along with them as the sliding door opened and his mum's voice filled the back. "Ant, love, time to change your bandages."

His father's shoulders drooped as he waved her off. "Em, later."

"No, honey, we can't mess up the schedule because the kids are here. Come on now," she said, coming to his chair and taking the handles in her hands.

Covering her hand, Jensen asked, "Mum, you need help?"

She shook her head, reaching out to cup his face. "No, honey, stay out here with your bride. We'll be out in a jiffy."

Grumbling, Ant shook his head. "Make sure you exercise, Wrenya, you hear?"

"Yes, sir," she called as she leaned on the side of the pool, her chin on her hands.

"Dad, you know her name is Wren, right?"

He shrugged. "That's what I said."

His mom clucked her tongue. "He said that to me yesterday. Probably needs his ears checked. Puck probably shattered his eardrum or something."

Wren snickered as they made their way inside, and he shook his head. "They're calling you Wrenya, right?"

She smiled as she shrugged. "They are. But it's nice. Leave it."

He glared. "Make me crazy, those two."

"They're amazing."

He smiled as she came close, leaning her chin on his shin. "They are."

"Your mom is a cooking machine. Vaughn and Wells weren't kidding."

Leaning back on his elbows, he nodded. "Yeah, that's all she does when I'm here, cook and feed me. I had to tell her last night to take it easy on you."

Wren glared. "Why would you do that?"

"Because I care about your health. I gain an easy ten pounds when I'm home."

"That's rude," she decided, and he scoffed. "I love food."

"I'm aware."

She glared, and he sent her a wink as she shook her head. "So, you haven't been home in a while?"

"Nope, almost ten months. But I saw my mom about eight months ago. She came to see me before I left Colorado."

"Wow, why?"

"Busy. I knew I wanted to be traded, and when it went down, I knew I had to put in a crazy amount of work to get noticed by the Assassins."

"If they hadn't noticed you, they wouldn't have brought you to the team."

He shrugged. "Maybe, but I knew I had to work harder."

Moving her finger along his calf, she smiled. "You've always been the hardest worker."

"I have. I don't give up easily," he said, and she looked up at him.

"Well, I know that firsthand," she teased, and his lips curved wide.

"Damn right, you do."

Holding his gaze, she pressed her lips together. "Wanna get in?"

He shook his head. "Rather just watch you."

She pursed her lips at him, her eyes flashing with mischief. "Like watching me? All wet and slippery."

"You're evil."

She giggled as she kicked off the side, going under the water before coming up, running her hands down her face. "It's super nice in here."

"It's even better from right here. Every once in a while, I get a nice peek of that ass."

She rolled her eyes as she held his gaze. "But if you're in here, then you get a closer look."

He thought that over. "You could be right about that."

"I am right, always right."

He laughed hard. "We both know that's a lie."

She glared. "I am!"

"Sure," he said before he moved the towel that was on his lap and slowly slid into the pool. "Man, it does feel good in here." It was a hot day, hotter than he expected, but the water was nice and cool. He had put the pool in for his father, for his therapy, but since his legs were so messed up, he hadn't gotten to use it that summer. But he would. His dad was a fighter and didn't give up, which Jensen guessed was where he got it from.

"Told ya," she said, swimming toward him. "Oh, I have to tell you something."

His brow furrowed since she looked so distraught at that moment. "What?"

Stopping in front of him, she said, "We might have to go shopping if my dress doesn't fit for the party."

He laughed. "I thought it was something bad."

She gave him a dry look. "Shopping is bad."

"Eh, not too bad when I'm with you," he answered, and her face broke into a grin before she reached out, wrapping her arms around his neck and then her legs around his waist, like a koala. Her belly pressed into his as his arms came out, holding her close. But then she paused.

"Is this okay?"

His face wrinkled. "Why wouldn't it be okay?"

She shrugged, her fingers dancing along the top of his back. "I don't know."

Leaning his nose into hers, he closed his eyes. "It's perfect."

When she pressed her lips to his, his heart slammed into his chest as he kissed her back, holding her as close as he could. She felt damn good in his arms, and soon he was harder than the steel pipes he stood between most of his life. As her mouth moved with his, his body shook with need, but there was no way he was taking her right there in his parents' pool. Even if he had paid for it, that was disrespectful. But man, he wanted her. Sliding his hands down her back, he cupped her butt as she pulled back, her dark eyes meeting his. "Well, great hand placement, Jenny."

His lips quirked against hers. "I mean, you said I can get a closer look at this fine ass."

She was trying not to smile as she ran her fingers up the back of his neck. "Are you saying I have a great ass?"

"The best I've ever seen, and that's no damn lie."

He fully expected her to ignore his comment. But instead, her grin grew as she pressed her lips into his top one. "Well, thank you."

"You are very welcome," he muttered against her lips, his hands sliding lower on her thick ass, squeezing her as his body shook. "You're entirely too sexy in this bikini, by the way."

Closing her eyes, her face broke as she giggled loudly. "Stop."

"Never."

"You're making me blush!"

"Good, I love the color," he said as their eyes stayed locked. "I love it all."

Her lips pursed as she leaned into him, holding his neck tight, and just as she was going to kiss him, they heard his mother say, "I love newlyweds."

But then his father added, "No hanky-panky in my pool!"

And with that, they were both falling over each other laughing.

He hadn't felt more alive in his entire life.

* * *

"I can't get over how beautiful you are, Wrenya."

Wren looked up from where she was cutting up carrots and smiled. Jensen's mom, Emma, couldn't say her name right at all, but Wren wasn't correcting her, and she wasn't letting Jensen either. She found it endearing. But even she had to admit that everyone calling her beautiful, at every turn, was making her feel all kinds of ways. She wasn't used to it. It wasn't like her family told her she was beautiful all the time, but the Monroes never stopped reminding her. "Thanks, Emma."

"*Ma chou*, Mum," she said, patting Wren's back as she walked behind her, getting some water. Wren had no clue what *ma chou* meant, but she was going with it. Since they had arrived in Jensen's home country and then traveled the two hours from the airport to a rural part of Canada, Wren found Vaughn and Wells hadn't been joking when they said Jensen was from the backwoods of Canada.

The sheer number of moose she had seen in the matter of hours of being there was a little outstanding. And awesome. She loved every second. But she loved Emma Monroe and adored Jensen's dad, Antoine, or Ant, as he insisted she call him, more than ever. When she had met them so long ago at Jensen, Vaughn, and Wells's draft day, they hadn't paid her much attention. But from the moment she'd stepped into the house, they'd both showered her with love, and she realized why Jensen was the way he was.

Because he was his parents' world.

"Mum," she repeated, and Emma beamed at her. "I'm done."

"Good, good," she said, taking the carrots and throwing them in the pot. "Potatoes next."

Wren got to work, a little unsure of herself since she wasn't much of a chef, not that she would tell Emma that. She'd already complained that Wren wasn't feeding Jensen enough, and Wren wouldn't dare tell her that Jensen was the one who usually got the food. Apparently, it was her job, and she would try to do that. Though, Jensen had already joked that he didn't trust her cooking. A grin pulled at her lips as she looked back to where Jensen sat in the living room with his father, hanging out while the ladies worked in the kitchen.

He was lounging on the sofa as his father sat in the recliner, his legs up since Emma had just changed his bandages. The men looked like two peas in a pod, and Wren knew Jensen was beyond happy to be home. And so was she. Especially with Ant, he was funny, and she could see so much of Jensen in him. While she enjoyed and loved Emma—she was a good woman, very sweet— Wren couldn't help but feel there was a little animosity toward her. She couldn't blame Emma. Her son got married and was having a kid, and she only found out about it a month ago. She hadn't mentioned it, nor brought it up, but Wren felt it coming.

"I bet you're excited to see your mom next week. It's been a while, yes?"

"Yeah, I am. It was before I got pregnant, and she keeps saying she's ready to get her hands on my belly, whatever that means."

Emma laughed. "I should tease her, tell her I got to go first."

Wren met her with a smile. "Yeah, she wasn't too pleased we came here first. She wants to see us. But this was planned first, and we'll be there for almost two weeks with the wedding and all."

"Yeah, she told me the same." Emma looked up, a smile tugging at her weathered face. "It's all a surprise, I'm sure. Especially with my Jensen. She probably didn't expect that."

Wren shrugged. "I don't think anyone did, really." She laughed then. "Especially us."

She shouldn't have said that. Emma's brows pulled together. "So you didn't have a crush on him before? He's always had one for you, *ma chou*."

Wren chewed on her top lip as she slid the knife along the potatoes. "I mean, I've always thought he was a very attractive man, but I never thought he had a crush on me. I didn't find that out until after we—"

When she paused, Emma waggled her eyebrows. "Got it on? That's what you call it, right?"

Wren sputtered with laughter as she choked on an inhale. "That."

Emma nodded. "He is so damn quiet and shy, at least around you, he was. But he used to tell me that he was going to marry you."

Wren's mouth dropped open as a nervous laugh left her lips. "No!"

"Yes! He came home one summer and said 'When Wrenya is old enough, I'm going to tell her how I feel.' I waited and waited, and nothing. Then that other girl comes home, and he's marrying her. I was very confused."

Wren's heart was in her throat. "Wow."

"Very upset. I didn't like her."

"You didn't?" Wren asked with a grin.

"No, not like I like you. But then, what did I expect? If he weren't going to go after you, someone would snatch him up. He's so handsome, obviously from my side of the family."

Wren giggled as Ant called from the living room, "Lies, Wrenya. Don't listen to her. He's my boy, and that baby will take after my side."

Wren smiled as she looked down, praying to God that the baby came out looking just like her and nothing like Bradley. Just thinking of him made her gut hurt. It worried her to no end, but there was really nothing she could do about it. Though, the more she thought about leaving the safety and comfort of the Monroe home, the more she realized she'd probably see him when they went back home. She wasn't sure if Wells had invited him to the wedding, and she couldn't ask, but more than likely, he'd show up for the party for the Cup. It was huge for Vaughn and Jensen, and the whole town would all be there. Maybe she could skip?

That was an idea.

"Obviously, he's delusional, and we know Jensen takes after me." Wren winked at her. "Of course."

"You're my favorite." Wren beamed but then instantly felt bad. Was she Emma's favorite under false pretenses? Or was it real? Shit, this wasn't supposed to be this hard, but it was. She loved Emma and Ant. The last three days had been a blast. Once they got there, the two of them spoiled them, laughing and eating, just being together. Ant couldn't walk much, but he tried. Though Emma wouldn't let him go on the stupid walks Jensen was forcing on her. While it was sweet that he was taking her doctor's orders, and she knew she should have felt bad for sneaking candy when he fell asleep at night, she didn't.

Maybe she should reevaluate.

Bad life choices. She did that a lot.

Other than that, her time with the Monroes was going great. Every morning, they enjoyed the beautiful summer weather in the backwoods of Canada before spending the afternoon in the pool, and she felt like she was at home. Ever since getting there, she had been herself. Things were good between her and Jensen. Great, even. She felt herself letting him in somehow. Though, maybe she wasn't. She wasn't sure, but she was trying. She was. She knew that, but she had an inkling that he was still upset about their fight. Maybe she was overthinking it because when they were close, or even in the same room, he looked at her like she was the sexiest piece of cake he had ever seen. It was mind-blowing, and she loved it. His quick smiles, his sweet looks, and his caresses… God, she yearned for them and more, but she wasn't thinking too much about that. Just him. And her. And his family.

"So, how far along are you now? Almost seven months? Yes?"

"Yes," Wren answered, slowly chopping as she chewed on her lip. "I'm due in September."

"Oh, good month. Maybe Ant will be better by then, and I can come to America for the birth. I want to see my grandbaby when he makes his debut."

"We'd love that, and if not, once everything is settled because preseason will be starting, we'll come here," she promised, and she meant it. They had been so good to her, accepting her from the moment she stepped on their land. She was thankful for that because once they got home next week, it wouldn't be as easy as it was here. She knew her family would be full of doubts and questions once they arrived.

"That would make my day, but I understand, which is why I'll try to come there. Hopefully, Ant can come," Emma said as she stirred the pot of meatballs she was cooking.

"We'll work it out."

They shared a smile before Emma reached out, squeezing her hand. "You're a good girl, Wrenya."

Guilt flushed through Wren as she looked back down, cutting the potatoes and feeling like anything but a good girl. She felt like a fraud, like she should tell them the truth, but she couldn't. The baby was Jensen's, and that was that. She wasn't lying. This was their normal, and they were good with it.

Everything else was a bit up in the air, but that was certain.

The kid was Jensen's.

"You two have been married almost a month?"

Running her tongue along her lips, she nodded. She had been waiting the last three days for this conversation. They hadn't been alone, she and Emma, they were almost always with Ant or Jensen. So she knew it was coming, that Emma was upset about it, and that worried her. "Yup. A month tomorrow, actually."

Emma nodded as she reached for the bag of pigs' feet out of the sink, and Wren quickly covered her mouth as she watched her mother-in-law begin to clean them. "Well, at least you two are married before he comes. Though, nowadays, things are so different. No one cares about having babies out of wedlock."

Dropping her hand, Wren shrugged. "Jensen does."

Emma looked up and smiled. "Because he's a good man. A gentleman."

"My mom said the same thing."

"'Cause she knows. We did well with him."

That made Wren's smile grow. If her mom were there, she would have gushed all over Emma. There wasn't a moment when Elaine didn't worry that she was doing right by Jensen, but Emma always said that Elaine Lemiere was the best thing to happen to their family. "You guys did."

Emma looked up, meeting her gaze, and then she looked away. "I need to admit something."

Wren watched her as she looked out of the kitchen toward the living room where Ant and Jensen were. "Okay?"

She looked back to Wren. "Yeah, I was very upset with you, with how my Jensen didn't find out until much later. I felt you lied to him, and I didn't like that."

Laying the knife down, Wren leaned into the counter. "I completely understand, and you're right. I did, and I'm so sorry for that. I didn't mean to hurt him or you——"

But Emma held her hands up, and Wren's mouth slammed shut. "But I was wrong. And the reason I say that is because Jensen knows you best of all, and he told me you do things in your time. While I didn't like that one bit, I have to say, it doesn't matter that it took you so long to tell him, because you did, and my baby hasn't ever looked happier, Wrenya. Ever. Even when he was with that awful girl before, I have never seen him look at someone the way he looks at you." Breathless, Wren looked away as a smile tugged at her lips, her heart jumping up into her throat. "I always knew he cared for you, that he even loved you, but seeing it, seeing you two together… Goodness me, your love for him and his love for you, I swear it's deeper than an ocean. I'm amazed, truly amazed."

Her love?

His love, yeah. But hers?

Had she been lying the whole time she had been there? No, she had been herself. But she didn't love Jensen. She cared for him, a lot, and maybe she'd fall. But what was Emma talking about? She didn't look at him like she loved him.

Did she?

Wait, did she love him?

No.

*You don't fall for someone in a month. That was dumb.*

Biting her lip, Wren looked up and smiled. "He's amazing."

"Damn right, I am."

She looked over her shoulder as Jensen came into the room toward her, wrapping his arms around her waist and holding her belly in his hands. Before she knew it, she was leaning into him, and he kissed her beneath her ear. Then he said, "I'm sure you're talking about me."

Wren scoffed as Emma shook her knife at her. "*Mon chou*, I tell her, you two are adorable together."

"Of course we are," he said, kissing Wren's jaw before he leaned his hip on the counter beside her.

"Everyone has been telling me that," Emma said.

"They have?" Wren looked puzzled.

"Yes, everyone in town says you two should never stop having babies."

Wren laughed as Jensen looked down at the ground, kicking it with his toe as he shook his head. "I don't know, Mum. Wren doesn't like being pregnant much."

She nodded. "I don't."

"Why? It agrees with you," Emma said, dumping the pigs' feet in the pot, causing Wren to gag.

When Emma turned to the sink, Wren looked at Jensen with wide eyes, and in a very low voice, said, "I'm not eating that."

His face lit up, the biggest grin coming across his mouth. "What? It's the best part!"

"I swear, I'm not."

"Fine, I'll eat yours."

She made a face. "I'm not kissing you, then."

He laughed at that before taking her in his arms and nibbling on her jaw. "Like you'd deny me kisses," he whispered in her ear before biting her lobe. "I'll kiss you with my pigs' feet breath."

She gagged, and he laughed as she pushed him away. "You're disgusting."

He stuck his tongue out as his mother turned, shaking her head. "Jensen, don't do that. It's rude. She's your *chou*."

He shot her a cheesy grin as Emma left the kitchen. "She keeps calling me that. What is that?"

"My cabbage."

Her face wrinkled. "What! She's calling me a cabbage?"

He laughed. "It's her favorite food."

Wren shook her head. "I don't know how I feel about that."

"Feel good. She never called my ex-wife that. Ever."

Wren grinned at that. "So I guess that means she doesn't hate me?"

He shook his head. "She can't."

"Yes, she can."

"Nope."

"Jensen!"

"Really, she can't."

"And why is that?" she asked, holding his gaze, and she loved the smile on his face. Being home opened him up. He was so much happier, so full of life, and it was beautiful to see.

As he leaned toward her, his eyes sparkled as he said, "Because I love you, and she loves what I love ten times over."

Kissing her jaw, he left the kitchen, and all she could do was watch him in complete awe. In that instant, she was jealous. She wanted to feel that. To be so confident in them.

She wanted it.

She did, but she didn't know how to get it.

Inside, she wondered if she already had it, but she was too stubborn to see it.

Why was being an adult so hard?

\* \* \*

THE WINDOWS WERE OPEN, the curtains drifting with the cool night breeze, and the moon was the only light in the room. Watching as the curtains floated, Wren held her stomach as her son moved around like he was trying to rip out of her. It was insane how much he had grown and how hard he could kick. She loved it.

God, she loved him.

Beside her, Jensen lay on his back, on his phone as she watched the night sky, the silence so peaceful and perfect. She loved sleeping there. It was still and serene. Letting out a sigh, she whispered, "It's beautiful here."

Jensen chuckled beside her. "I used to hate it until I came to Colorado and it was loud as hell there. Now, I swear, I sleep the best when I'm home."

She smiled into her pillow, her hand moving up and down her belly. Her back was to him, but his body warmed her in more ways than one. "I bet."

"Are you enjoying yourself?"

"I am," she admitted. "It's amazingly beautiful, and your parents are so hospitable."

His hand came to rest on her ass, his thumb moving along her skin, causing her to break out in gooseflesh, before he said, "Good."

Silence fell between them once more, and she felt calm. Even if in one second she felt her life was falling the fuck apart, being in that room, the window open with Jensen's deep breath filling the air, his thumb moving along her, she felt tranquil. It was an insane feeling, something she didn't feel a lot, but God, she welcomed it. She ached for it. She'd move here in a second, a nice little cabin, just her, Jensen, and kiddo.

"I love it here."

"I can tell."

"Yeah?"

"Yeah. You don't think. You're just enjoying. Except when I make you walk or when you're trying to sneak those Kit Kats."

Shit, he saw that? Her laughter shook the bed. "I don't know what you're talking about."

When she heard a wrapper opening, she glared. "Yeah, and this isn't one of your Kit Kats either," he said to her, and she laughed.

"You're a pain in my ass."

"You're the epitome of a pain in my ass, Wrenya."

Her face broke into a grin as her eyes fell shut and the summer breeze kissed her face. "Are you going to start calling me that too?"

"I think so. I like it."

Her smile didn't falter as he squeezed her hip. "We should move here."

He chuckled beside her. "Considering we both have really great careers, that would be a waste."

She smiled. "True. Can we vacation here?"

"If you want."

"I do."

He leaned over, kissing her shoulder. "I love the sound of that."

"Me too," she answered as he rolled back over, her heart picking up in speed. Things were going really well. She loved the flirty and sweet side of them. Yeah, he had always been charming and polite, but she felt like maybe she was being the same. Well, in her own way, but it was meshing. They were meshing. Even if his mother's earlier observation sort of freaked her out, she felt good.

She couldn't help but think maybe being in love with him wasn't such a crazy thought.

She rolled over slowly, and his phone went into his lap as he looked over at her, a smile on his face. "Can I ask you something?"

"Of course," he said, his eyes on hers.

"Are you still mad at me?"

His brows drew in. "About what?"

"Our fight."

"Oh," he said, thoughtfully. "I wasn't ever mad, Wren. I was hurt. Big difference."

She looked away, moving her hair out of her eyes. "So, are you still hurt?"

He chuckled. "I mean, not like I was a few days ago, but it still stings."

She nodded as she chewed on the inside of her lip. "I feel like things are still a bit tense between us."

"I don't think so."

"I do," she said, looking at him. "And that's me and my many issues."

He shrugged. "I'm not tense. I promise. I think things are going great. We aired out what we felt, and we're moving on. I just want this to work, and I know you're trying. I do, and I feel it. It's nice. We're good."

Holding his gaze, she felt her lips started to tremble. "We are?"

"We are," he whispered before going up on his elbow and reaching out, taking her face in his. "The fight had to happen, you had to know how I was feeling. That I wasn't fucking around with you. That, to me, this," he said, running his thumb along her bottom lip, "is real. That we're real, and I'm not giving up on it."

Leaning into his hand, she held his gaze as she bit down softly on his thumb, his eyes widening in surprise. Letting him go, she whispered, "I don't want to, either."

"Then don't," he said, dropping his face to hers. "Don't give up."

With her heart beating so hard her ears ached, she nodded. "I don't want to."

"Then there is nothing else I can ask for."

But she was pretty sure there was more. Swallowing hard, she held his gaze. "Does it hurt when you tell me you love me and I don't say it back?"

Licking his lips, he shrugged. "I mean, it doesn't feel good, but I wouldn't say it hurts. It just sucks."

Her face turned serious. "I'm sorry."

"Sorry for what? Not loving me when you had no clue I've loved you for over fifteen years? That's not your fault. I should have said something."

"Yeah, you should have," she answered, holding his gaze. "Because then maybe I wouldn't have gotten knocked up by some asshole because I would have been with you."

His lips quirked at that. "Because you would have wanted to be with me? Come on, Wren, don't tease me."

But she shrugged. "I don't know, maybe."

His smile dropped off as he held her gaze. "Everything happens for a reason."

"It does."

"And we're here, in this moment, for a reason. For him," he said, taking her belly in his hands, running his thumb along her belly button. "So yeah, maybe we didn't get to do this earlier, but we have forever now, and I like that a lot better."

Her breath caught as she held his gaze. "So you still want forever?"

He nodded. "With my whole soul."

Breathless, she leaned her nose into his, but before she could say anything, his lips were on hers in a heated, tantalizing way. Her fingers tangled in his hair, and his mouth moved with hers. His body pressed against her side, and shit, she could feel every inch of him as his leg hooked over hers. Her hands fell to his shoulders for a better grip as his hands held her tightly in place. He was so strong, so fucking sexy, and when his tongue swept into her mouth, she swore she came right then. Arching against his leg, she gasped into his mouth, and she could feel his body vibrating against hers.

Was this about to happen?

Holy shit.

Pulling away, he closed his eyes, his nose pressing into hers as she gasped for breath. She held on to his shoulders, her body shaking with want. "I can't handle you," he muttered, trailing kisses down her jaw. "I can't."

Speechless for a moment, she nodded. "I get that you want to wait, and yeah, cool, but those kisses are going to be the death of me."

His lips broke into a grin against hers. "You're already the death of me, Wren. Completely, and it's killing me. Honestly."

Her lips parted as she held his gaze. "I'm basically Little Caesars. Hot and ready, big boy. Take me."

His eyes lit up, and then he was laughing, hard. Soon, she couldn't hold it in, she was laughing too. Falling off her, he cuddled her into him, and he was thick and hard against her, taking her breath entirely. Placing a kiss to her shoulder and then her neck, he inhaled deeply as his nose tucked against her ear. "Well, Caesars, I pride myself on my restraint."

She laughed out loud. "I'm mean, you could basically pass as a priest at this point."

He chuckled against her neck before placing a kiss against it softly, his hand sprawling over her belly. "Well, just so you know, I want you. Badly."

Her eyes fell shut as she leaned into him, her hand coming over his. Turning her head, she took his mouth with hers in a hot embrace that made her insides tremble. As their tongues played, her heart was pounding in her chest. She knew she shouldn't, but she found herself guiding his hand down her belly to where she wanted him most. When his hand covered her right where she was throbbing, he hissed out a breath against her lips. "Wren."

Just her name. A simple word, but she swore it shattered her. "Jensen," she whispered, her lips moving with his. "I'm right here."

Moving his nose along hers, he found her lips with his once more before his hand slowly slid her panties to the side, taking her whole pussy in his hands. She arched into him, her center throbbing as her body shook under his touch. When his finger ran up her swollen lips, she cried out against his mouth before she held her breath, unable to handle his touch. When his tongue entered her mouth, his finger entered her too, just one, slowly finding her bundle of nerves. She squeezed her eyes shut, unsure what was happening. Never in her life had she been that wet, had she wanted someone as much as she wanted him. She gasped against his mouth, and he moved only a little bit before she shattered against his hand.

Pathetically.

Crying out, she squeezed his wrist as her orgasm took over her whole being, her body clenching as he continued to kiss her. Pulling away so she could breathe, she sucked in a deep breath as she slowly shook her head, fully shocked at herself for coming apart so quickly. She had been waiting months for him to touch her, and she couldn't even handle it.

And she wanted to have full-on sex with this sexy guy?

God help her.

"Well," she muttered as his teeth raked over her jaw. "Pretty sure you got the fastest time for making a girl come."

His lips quirked before he kissed the side of her mouth. "And you got the fastest time for a guy," he answered back before kissing her again and getting out of the bed. Her brows rose as she sat up on her elbows, watching as he went to the bathroom.

"Really?"

He laughed as he shimmied out of his boxers. The moon kissed his sweet ass, his huge cock only a silhouette as he washed his hands. "Really."

She laughed. "You know that's pathetic."

He nodded. "I've dreamed about touching you like that for years. And yeah, it was better than I thought." Her face flushed as he pulled up another pair of boxers before coming back to the bed, crawling in, and cuddling up beside her. "I think the last time I came in my boxers, I was seventeen."

"I've never done that."

"Good to know."

She met his gaze with a grin as she shook her head. "I'm disappointed in us. I wanted hot, crazy, sexy times."

He shrugged. "Instead you got us coming for each other like teenagers."

When he met her look with a grin, she smiled back. "Yeah. Might be better, though. The anticipation."

"Agreed. I think it's a good addition to our little story."

Leaning into him, she kissed his jaw. "It is."

As he wrapped his arm around her neck the way she truly loved, his lips pressing into hers, she realized their story was a story she didn't want to end.

And she thought, maybe, just maybe, she could get a happily ever after.

# Chapter

# FIFTEEN

"*E*lli! What in the world are you doing here?"

Elli Adler flashed a wide smile over at Wren as she reached out, hugging her tightly. "I wanted to come to all the boys' days with the Cup, and let me tell you, I didn't realize how much I'd be traveling," she laughed, and Wren beamed back at her. "I'll be in Sweden for the rest of the week until I come to Colorado for Johansson and then off to Chicago, New York, and then home for a week. The kids are pissed, but Shea is amazing. No one knows, but this is like a mini vacation for me."

Wren giggled as she nodded. "You're probably one of the best owners in the league, Elli."

Elli shrugged. "I try."

"It shows."

Squeezing Wren's arm, Elli looked out to where Jensen was in the middle of a huge street hockey match. "This is amazing."

"His dad did it all. He planned everything for this day, and then his mom planned the party for tonight."

Elli snapped her fingers. "I'll miss the party, but seeing all the kids, Lord, look at them all," she gushed, and Wren couldn't stop grinning as she looked around at where the whole town had gathered for Jensen's street party. The town was very small, only about nineteen hundred people, and Wren was sure they were all there. Which made closing the street even easier, she guessed.

The Cup was set up to the side, with two big dudes guarding it, as the match happened in the middle of the street. The children looked at Jensen like he was a god. It was beautiful to watch him with all of them. He was having a blast, for sure. "This is awesome. Best party so far."

Wren scoffed. "Wait till you see what Vaughn has planned at his hockey rink. It's going to be ridiculous."

"I'm sure, in true Vaughn form."

"Very true."

Elli looked back over at her. "You look great. Like, really."

Wren looked away bashfully as her hands came up to hold her belly. It was a warm day, so she was wearing a pair of shorts and an Assassins tee with Jensen's number on the back. It was his and was massive on her shoulders, but her belly fit perfectly. "Thanks. I feel huge, but Jensen has made me go walking every day we've been here, and he won't let his mom stuff me full of her amazing French cuisine."

Elli scowled. "That's rude."

"That's what I said!"

"I'll fire him for you."

Wren laughed out loud at that. "We both know you won't."

She exhaled hard. "Not after my poor Tate."

"I know. I talked to him last night and then Audrey too for over two hours," Wren added, shaking her head. "I'm still torn up over it."

"It's for the best, I know that, but I love that guy."

"I do too, he's a good man."

"He is, but I think he's going to be on the goalie team, which will be excellent. I just need him to get better."

"He'll do awesome."

"He will," Elli agreed, squeezing Wren's hand. "Thank you for everything you do for my boys."

"That's what you hired me for."

Elli waved her off, though. "But you go above and beyond, like I do. You care, and it means the world to me."

"Well, thank you," Wren said, her lips curving. She leaned into Elli. "I have a great boss."

"Damn right, you do," she teased and then laughed before shaking her head. "But really, Wren, I can't get over how good you look! At Lucy's party, you looked like a deer in the headlights. But today? So damn happy."

Wren looked away, a grin pulling at her lips as her gaze fell on Jensen. He tackled a little kid, carrying him over his head, laughing loudly with all the kids that were around him. He was a natural out there, and she hadn't seen him smile so much in one hour as he did when he was out there with those kids. Wren's heart sped up as her hands ran along her own child growing inside of her. She admitted, "I have a damn good reason to be happy."

"Yeah, you do," Elli agreed as she leaned into her. "He's a damn fine man."

"Wrenya!"

Looking over to where Antoine was calling her, Wren held up a finger. "Jensen's dad needs me. I'll catch up with you later."

"Give me a hug in case I miss you before I leave," Elli said before they embraced.

"Thanks so much for coming."

"Of course, see you soon."

Sending her one last smile, Wren headed toward where Antoine was manning the scoreboard in a huge tent since he didn't do well in the sun. "Hey, what's wrong?"

"Wrenya, sorry for calling for you like that, but can you get me a water? Emma is off running her mouth with all these people and forgot that I need to be watered."

Patting her father-in-law's arm, she nodded. "Of course. I'll be back."

"You're the best," he called, though it was hard to hear over all the laughter and joyful activity around them. Heading toward the concession stand, Wren went in the back and grabbed two bottles of water before sending a grin to the girl that was running it for Antoine and Emma. Wren hadn't realized everyone knew everyone in this town. Being back at the Monroes' house, where no one was around for at least twenty miles, she'd thought there wasn't anyone else in the area, but coming into town, she realized she was very wrong.

The town was small, but its residents loved each other dearly. The whole morning all she heard was people asking about Antoine's health and then how Wren's pregnancy was going. They accepted Wren as one of their own, acting as if they had known her her whole life. It was insane. Everyone was just so kind, and they treated

Jensen with such beautiful respect. It was obvious he was the golden boy in the town. It was lovely to watch, and she was having a blast.

All while trying really hard not to think about the fact that she'd be heading home in two days.

Being with the Monroes was almost like a fairy tale. Or maybe that was Jensen. He just made her feel so good. She wasn't sure, but she didn't want to leave. She wanted to stay there, in the security and strength she'd found in the Monroes' home. No wonder how Jensen was so damn confident and strong; he had two wonderful people to model himself after. She also understood why he strived for a love-filled marriage. His parents had that, and it was something she had never been able to observe. Her parents loved each other, sure, but it was different with Antoine and Emma. It was more than love, it was… She wasn't sure, but it was beautiful to witness.

Heading toward where Antoine was waiting for her, she found herself stopped by Emma, who was standing with a few women Wren had seen more than once that day. "Wrenya, come here, love."

Wren did as she was asked, and Emma wrapped her arms around her, kissing her cheek. "This is my gorgeous daughter-in-law, Wrenya."

Wren smiled awkwardly as everyone wished her well. "You look like Jensen's best friend. The thicker one," one of the ladies said.

"Wells, yes, that's her brother," Emma pointed out before turning to Wren. "This is Jensen's ex-mother-in-law."

Looking back to the thin woman, Wren tried to smile. Though, she pretty much hated his ex-wife and anyone associated with her. "Oh. Nice to meet you."

"You as well. My lovely Ophelia is on her fifth pregnancy, you hear, Emma? Though, I'm still sad that she and Jensen never could work it out."

"It was all her fault," one of the other ladies said.

"Who lets go of someone like Jensen Monroe?" another asked, and Wren grinned.

"Yeah, her loss, my gain," she said, which caused the lady's face to wrinkle a bit before she flashed them all a smile. "If you'll excuse me, Ant needs me." Kissing Emma's cheek, Wren headed toward where Ant was waiting under his tent, and when he saw her, he lit up.

"Thank God, I'm dying here."

Wren giggled as she handed him the water bottle and sat down beside him. "How's it going?"

"Wrapping up, then they'll do the shootout."

"The shootout?"

"Yeah, all the kids will get a chance to score on Jensen, and whoever does will get to hold the Cup first."

Wren's lips curved. "That's cute."

"Yeah, it will be fun," he said as he added a point from where someone had scored. "Have you seen my woman?"

"She's over there talking to Jensen's ex-wife's mom," she said, her face twisting as if she had something nasty in her mouth.

"She's jealous. She loved Jensen, but her daughter was a whore."

Sputtering with laughter, Wren nodded. "Got that right."

Shaking his head, he leaned into Wren. "See, the problem with Ophelia was she didn't love Jensen with her soul. You know what I mean?"

Wren pressed her lips together. "I don't, sorry."

"Okay, see, I love my Emma with my soul. Not my heart, because a heart can stop. And not with my mind, because a mind forgets. But a soul, Wrenya, a soul never stops, nor does it forget. It just loves. Same thing with you and Jensen—you love with your soul."

She met his gaze, and his infectious grin had her smiling back. "That's beautiful."

"That's love. Always love with your soul, you hear me, Wrenya?"

"I do," she said, patting his hand, and he captured her hand before bringing it to his mouth.

"Good girl," he said, kissing her hand before he rang the bell. Everyone stopped, and then Jensen started speaking very rapidly in French before the kids all let out a variety of ecstatic cries. It was sexy. People started wrangling the kids as Jensen came to the table with a grin on his face. "It's going great, son."

He nodded. "It's awesome, Dad, thanks." Looking to Wren, he asked, "*Ma chou*, you see Elli?"

She glared at the nickname as he fought back his laughter. She loved when he did that. His eyes were bright while he tried to keep his lips from forming a grin. Man, he was cute. "I did. I thought it was sweet."

He nodded as he started to put on his goalie equipment. "It was. She's heading out."

"Aww, too bad."

"Yeah," he said before standing up and putting on his chest shield. "Hopefully I don't get hurt."

Wren smiled. "They're some big kids out there."

"I know, that's what I'm saying," he laughed before leaning over the table and kissing her lips. "See ya."

"Good luck," she called as he went back out into the street, the kids all cheering loudly for him. When he dropped down, stretching and then doing a few drills that she had seen him do on the ice numerous times, her brow furrowed. "Wait, he's serious out there?"

Ant laughed. "Of course he is. We play to win, Wrenya."

"They're kids!"

"So?" he laughed, and she shook her head. Sure as shit, once the shootout started, Jensen was in full goalie mode.

She had to admit, it was fucking hot.

He batted everything away, poke checked more kids than she'd care to admit since it probably made him an asshole, and taunted the bigger kids while trying to lift up the younger ones. She was completely amazed by him, so much so that she missed the little girl who was standing at the table, speaking very sweetly in French.

Looking up at the girl and then her mom before glancing at Ant, Wren asked, "What's going on?"

"She's late and wants to play, but they cut the lines off," he said to her quickly before holding his hands out and saying something to the mom. When the little girl's shoulders fell, so did Wren's heart.

"Oh no, she's getting her shot," Wren said, standing up and grabbing a stick. "Do you know English?"

"Yes, ma'am."

Thank God. "Good, what's your name?"

"Maude."

"Awesome. Maude, I'm Wren. Come on, we'll go together."

She took the hand of the little girl, who couldn't have been over six, and they walked out toward the street where everyone was, cheering on their friends. One of the volunteers went to stop Wren, but she held her hand up. "Married to the guy in goal."

"But the lines are closed."

"And I don't care," she said simply, heading toward Jensen as the little girl giggled happily. Standing beside the person who was controlling who went next, she tapped him on the shoulder. "We'd like a try."

His brows pulled together. "But the line is closed."

"Wren, what are you doing?"

She smiled before looking past him to Jensen. "She didn't get here in time and wants her chance. I'm using my wife card to get us a shot."

Pushing up his helmet, he had the widest and most gorgeous grin on his face as he nodded. "Bring it."

"Hear that?" she asked Maude. "We get our shot." But the little girl didn't move. Bending down, Wren grasped her arm. "What's wrong?"

"What if I miss?"

Wren's heart cracked as she held the sweet girl's gaze in hers. "You know, you miss every single shot you don't take."

Her face broke into a grin. "Wayne Gretzky."

"Yup. So if you don't try, how do you know if you'll miss?"

And as the child slowly nodded, Wren realized that her words meant more than she intended them to. Not for Maude, but for herself. But before she could really dissect what she was feeling, Maude put her stick down and nodded toward the guy running the line, who threw a puck down to her. Stick handling it like a pro, she gazed up at Wren. "Will you come with me?"

Wren beamed down at the little girl. "Of course."

Wren grabbed a stick and put it down, and Maude passed the puck to her. Wren passed it back as the crowd lost their ever-loving mind. Looking back at Jensen, she could see him grinning, but he was ready. When Wren got the puck, she acted as if she was going to shoot—of course, she was way slower, and Jensen saw the whole thing—but she passed it to Maude nonetheless, and she shot it through his legs with ease. Maude threw her arms up, and everyone went nuts as Maude came over, hugging Wren tightly.

Tears flooded her eyes as she held the girl who was shaking with excitement. Wren felt like a baby, but she didn't care. It was a damn good day. When she looked up, Jensen was standing there, handing Maude the puck. "You got me."

She beamed up at him. "You started out as a forward. I know this because you're my favorite player ever, and I want to be just like you."

He bent down, cupping her face. "You'll be better, don't ever forget that," he said before squeezing her shoulder. "Great job."

"Can I have my picture with you and the Cup?"

"Of course, you'll get it first!"

She almost came out of her skin before looking up to Wren. "Thank you, Mrs. Monroe. You made my whole life."

As the little girl ran off toward her mother, who was crying, Wren fought back her own tears. "Cutest damn kid ever."

When Jensen's hands came around her waist, she turned into him, wrapping her arms around his neck. "I was convinced you weren't going to let her score."

He scoffed, his lips curving. "I wasn't going to, but I thought you were taking the shot, and you're the only person I'll let score on me."

Before she could smile or say anything else, his lips were on hers in a downright sinful way. Their night together, only a few nights ago, still shook her to the core. They hadn't had a moment like that again, mostly because when they got to bed, they passed out from the day, but she yearned for him like no other. Running her fingers through the coarse hair on his jaw, she leaned into him and didn't care at all that he was sweaty and sort of stinky.

All she cared about was kissing him.

And that didn't scare her one bit.

Which was a win in her book.

\* \* \*

"I swear, I have never seen a more dashing man in a suit."

Jensen rolled his eyes as his father boasted up at Wren from his wheelchair. It wasn't often that Jensen saw his father in anything but his sports shorts and tees, but even he had to admit he looked great. Not that he was telling him that. "Hey."

Wren grinned over at him as Antoine laughed. "Hey, son, can't help how sexy I am. Right, Emma?"

"Right," she agreed before pressing her lips to Antoine's cheek. Jensen smiled as his father kissed her back, rubbing her shoulders, not the least bit concerned that he was in a wheelchair. But that's how it always was.

When Wren threaded her fingers through Jensen's, he looked over at her as she whispered, "Don't worry, I think you're hotter."

Leaning his head to hers, he kissed her nose as Emma gushed over the food. "Damn right, you do."

She sent him a grin as he looked around the party his mother had thrown. It was too damn lavish for the little town, but she didn't hold back. The food was divine, and the decorations, which included lots of the number 1, along with purple and black for the Assassins colors, were everywhere. There was even an ice sculpture of his face.

Yes, his face.

Wells and Vaughn were geeking out.

Looking down at his phone, he scoffed as Vaughn and Wells went back and forth about the picture Wren had sent them.

*Wells: What the shit? I should have come! My stupid wedding is holding me back!*

*Vaughn: Right? I'm pissed. I wanna lick your nose.*

*Wells: Or stick carrots in his eyes.*

*Wells: Too bad it isn't your body, I'd stick a carrot up your ass.*

*Vaughn: Whoa, man, too gay. You jumped over the line with your straight best friends. Go back, abort!*

*Wells: My bad, stepping back over.*

*Wells: But really, I need more pictures. I'm texting Wren.*

"Did my brother say he wants to stick a carrot up your ass?"

Laughing, he shut his phone off and tucked it into his suit pocket. "Yes."

"Wow, he went really gay on you."

"Doesn't happen often," he laughed, shaking his head. "He's silly."

"Yeah," she said as she took a long pull of her not-wine, as she kept calling it. "This is a beautiful party, Emma."

His mother waved her off. "Please, I bet your mom puts on better shows."

Wren smiled. "Not as pretty as this. It's gorgeous."

"Well, thank you. I swear, I love you more and more as the days pass."

"Me too," Jensen found himself saying, which caused his father, mother, and Wren to look over at him with smiles pulling at their lips.

Wren's face deepened with color as she pressed her shoulder to his. "He knows how to make a girl swoon."

"Gets it from me," his father said, and Emma rolled her eyes.

"Don't listen to him. I did that," Emma demanded, and Antoine laughed as Jensen smiled. Little did they know, they'd both shaped him into the man he was. Along with the Lemieres. To say he was honored by the party his mum had put on was an understatement. He almost felt like he didn't deserve it, but then, he had worked really fucking hard. In the middle of the dance floor was the Cup, shining in all its beautiful glory, and he wanted to hug it. It had been a great day. The kids were awesome, the town was astounding, and now, he was at a party with his woman on his arm.

And boy, what a sight she was.

She was wearing the dress from their wedding, and it did hug her a little tighter than before, but he found it sexy as hell. Her hair was down, big curls with that flower crown she'd had on at their wedding. Unlike that day, her makeup was dramatic, and her lips were as pink as the gown. She looked fucking fantastic, and he wanted nothing more than to bury his face in her neck and live out the rest of his days there.

She blew his mind.

Holding her hand, he drew circles on her palm as she talked to his parents like she had belonged there since day one. In a way, he knew she did. There wasn't a moment in his life that he hadn't looked around and wished she were there. But this moment, one of the biggest in his life, his homecoming with the Cup was one day he was more than glad she was a part of.

Wren walked around his town like she owned it. She was beautiful, regal, and fearless when she brought Maude up for her chance to shoot on him. Jensen had been so engrossed with the beauty that was his wife, he couldn't even focus on the sweet girl who was coming at him. But he didn't care. All he cared about was watching Wren's face light up when Maude scored. And the way she kissed him. Yeah, he cared a lot about that.

He almost couldn't believe that it was happening.

That she could be falling for him.

But in a way, he felt it. Deep in his soul.

And he prayed that he was right and not just grasping at straws. Because when he looked at her, he didn't see anything but their future. Moving his hand up her arm, he placed it on her growing belly and found himself sighing happily. He couldn't wait to meet his little guy, his son, his boy. He hoped to be a father like his dad because Antoine Monroe was one hell of a dad. So supportive, as was Winston Lemiere, his other dad for all intents and purposes. He had such great male role models, and he couldn't wait to be that for his kid.

When Wren's hand covered his, his lips curved as she moved it over to where the kiddo was kicking like mad. He beamed as his eyes closed, a euphoric and beautiful feeling engulfing him as his son moved. When the baby's activity subsided, Jensen opened his eyes to find Wren watching him.

"It's pretty damn cool."

"It is," he answered, and then he leaned over, kissing the side of her mouth. "So are you."

"Me? No."

"Yeah, you're right, you're not cool. It's all me," he teased, and she laughed as his mother tapped his hand.

"*Mon chou*, if you're done eating, I need you to go socialize."

Jensen groaned inwardly. "Of course, Mum. Excuse me."

"No, take Wren. She's so gorgeous, show her off."

This time it was Wren groaning as she stuffed a few bites into her mouth. No one said no to Emma Monroe, and Wren had learned that quickly. Getting up, she chewed as he threaded his fingers with hers. "You could have said no."

She scoffed. "Please."

He laughed softly as they moved from table to table, greeting everyone. From all stages of his life were people who had been there with him. His teachers, coaches, his friends, their parents, and more. It was like a reunion of sorts, and everyone was so kind to him and Wren. They gushed over how gorgeous she was and how beautiful she was pregnant. All Jensen could do was completely agree.

She was the most gorgeous pregnant woman he had ever seen.

And it gutted him that he wasn't the one to do that to her.

But he wouldn't dwell.

He couldn't, or he'd drive himself mad.

"Man, if I ever feel insecure, I'm moving here," she teased as they walked away from the table that held all his high school teachers. "I'm apparently Miss USA around these parts."

He pressed his lips to her jaw. "You are, everywhere. At least to me."

She rolled her eyes, leaning into him as her face lit up. "Stop."

"Nope. Never."

Setting him with an annoyed but playful look, she shook her head. "Why can you make me blush, but no one else?"

He wrapped his arm around her neck, probably messing up her hair, not that she cared. "Because when I say it, you know I mean it, and it's true."

Kissing his nose, she nodded. "Maybe."

"Actually."

"Possibly."

"Truthfully."

She glared and he smiled. "A chance."

"Honestly," he asserted back, and she found herself grinning.

"You're lucky I'm drunk on my not-wine and can't think of another word."

He laughed. "So what you're saying is that I'm in luck because I'm a bit tipsy and yet I can find a word?"

She nodded, pleased with that assessment. "That's exactly what I'm saying."

"That's—"

"Jensen."

Stopping in his tracks, he looked up to find the last person he thought he'd see.

His ex-wife.

Ophelia stood in all her glory, tall and wearing even taller heels, her bone-straight brown hair down along her shoulders as her dress hugged every single inch of her. She didn't look pregnant, but he had heard she was. By the dick who stood beside her.

"Ophelia."

He could feel Wren tense up beside him as he let her go to lean over and press his lips to Ophelia's cheek in a chaste way he didn't want to, except out of politeness. Holding his hand out to the guy she married after she had left him, he said, "I'm Jensen. Nice to meet you."

"Colton, nice to meet you."

Well, that name was off the list now.

"This is my wife, Wren. *Ma chou*, Ophelia and her husband, Colton."

Wren gave him a sideways look as she smiled curtly. "Hey."

Colton moved to her, but he paused when Wren shot him a look that clearly stated not to touch her. When Wren glanced back at Ophelia, her eyes were wide as she looked at Jensen. Smacking her hands together, Ophelia said, "Who would have guessed! Wren, Wren Lemiere. The girl from your billet house?"

Jensen looked to her and smiled. "Yeah. Wells's little sister."

She scoffed, shaking her head, anger floating in the depths of her blue eyes. "Wow, I could have sworn I was told that you didn't have any feelings for her. You made that clear to me. Funny how things change, huh?"

Jensen cleared his throat as he nodded, feeling Wren's gaze on him. "Yeah—"

"Or maybe it wasn't the right time, right place? Now it is." Wren smiled smugly.

"Obviously," Ophelia said curtly, her eyes falling to Wren. "Guess, congratulations are in order."

Jensen could feel her animosity and see the irritation in her eyes, but he wouldn't let it bother him. She meant nothing to him. With a smile, he nodded as he reached out, holding Wren's belly. "Thank you, we're very excited."

Ophelia gave him a stern look that he knew meant she was pissed before she added, "Well, I'm sure—since we were told you couldn't have children."

Jensen swallowed hard as he looked around, hoping no one heard her, but thankfully, the music was loud. Before he could say anything, though, Wren covered his hand with hers as she said, "Well, maybe it's because he wasn't with the right person."

"Excuse me?" Ophelia asked, her eyes narrowing to slits.

"I didn't stutter, for one. And for two, all this doesn't matter because you left him for this guy you cheated with. So surely you don't care about what or whom Jensen is doing."

"I didn't—"

"Oh, please, don't worry. You don't have to convince us of anything because we aren't worried about you. We're good. Great, even. We're having a baby, we are married, and one thing is for certain, I'm sure as hell not going to leave him high and dry the way you did," Wren stated simply, her face darkening with color. "So yeah, go fuck off. And watch your back, Colton."

As Wren pulled Jensen away, he was a bit stunned while she led him out onto the dance floor. She was trying to cut through, but he had another idea. He tugged back, and she turned into his arms as he wrapped his arms around her. "Can I have this dance?"

With a grin cresting her sweet lips, she moved her hands up his chest and around his neck before she nodded. "Always."

Moving his hands along her hips, he wanted to be closer, but their son was in his way. "You didn't have to do that."

She rolled her eyes. "I don't like her."

"Totally aware of that."

"She's lucky we're both pregnant. I would have decked her."

"I would have paid to see that."

She scoffed, looking up at him. "She's awful. Why'd you even go for her? She's the complete opposite of me. I'm pretty sure my big toe weighs more than she does, and she's pregnant! With her fifth kid! Ugh, it makes no sense to me."

"Exactly," he said simply, his hands sliding to the small of her back. "She was nothing like you, no reminder of what I couldn't have. With her, I didn't have the constant reminder that I didn't have you. But I tried. I tried so hard to love her and be the man she needed, but in the back of my mind, my heart was always with you."

He got lost in her eyes, and she was breathless as her fingers moved along the back of his neck. "You know what kills me?"

"What?"

"That you felt all that for me, and I never knew it."

But Jensen shook his head. "You knew, Wren, you just ignored it."

Her eyes dilated as she leaned her head into his chin. "You think so?"

"I know so," he said, moving his lips along her forehead, the flower crown on her head tickling his nose. "And the sooner you realize that you've felt something for me all along and you feel more, the better off we'll both be."

As the song changed to Hannah Miller's "We Can Always Come Back to This," Wren's head fell back when his mouth dropped to

234 | TONI ALEO

hers. Waiting for her eyes to fall shut, he felt his heart pound before he allowed himself to do the same. There was nothing like kissing her. Winning all those games for the Cup couldn't even compare. Nothing. He would never get used to it, and he never wanted to. He wanted each moment his lips touched hers to blow his world to smithereens. He needed it to, just so that he would never feel anything but alive.

He pulled back, and they moved together, her lips lightly brushing his as she clung to him. Moving her chin to his shoulder, she turned her face, pressing her lips into his neck, while he leaned his head to hers, holding her to him. As the song transitioned into another one, he continued to sway with her, unable to move and not even wanting to.

"Jensen."

"Yeah, Wrenya, *ma chou?*"

She snickered against his neck before she kissed it softly. "I'm getting used to this."

His eyes fell shut as he asked, "What do you mean?"

"You. Us. This. I'm getting used to it, and I don't know if I can let it go."

His heart skipped a beat before he pulled away to look down at her. "You don't have to." Her eyes searched his before he dropped his head to hers, pressing their foreheads together. "You never have to."

She pushed her nose into his, and her eyes stayed wide as she nodded. "I'm holding you to that."

"Please do. Because my word is my promise."

"I know."

"Then you have nothing to worry about."

She smiled. "But I will."

"Annoying, I know."

Her face lit up before she closed her eyes. "How do you know how to make me happy?"

Taking her in his hands, he ran his thumbs along her cheeks as she slowly opened her eyes back up, meeting his heated gaze. "Because for fifteen years, I watched you. Anything that made you smile, I banked in my brain, so that when I got you, that smile would be permanently in place. Then the whole world would be graced with the beauty that is you, because I love you. So very much." As her eyes filled with tears, her mouth moving but no words coming out, he knew she was panicking. He could see it in her eyes. Slowly, he shook his head as a smile spread across his lips. "It's fine. Just kiss me."

She exhaled harshly before capturing his lips with hers, and yeah, she couldn't say it, that she loved him.

But he was truly starting to believe she did.

# Chapter SIXTEEN

"*I*'m so blaming you for leaving early."

Wren looked over at Jensen and gave him a look. A playful look, but he had a determined expression. She wasn't sure what the hurry was to leave right away, but she'd be damned if she was getting in trouble with Emma. "Like, all you."

He didn't look at her, nor did he smile as he turned down the driveway to his parents' home. "I'll take it all."

She eyed him. "You good?"

"Great," he muttered as he pulled into the spot he had been parking in the whole time they had been there. Shutting off the car, he got out, and she slowly did the same. Was he mad at her? He didn't seem mad when he was kissing her on the dance floor, but she saw in his eyes he didn't like that she didn't respond to his profession of love. And what a profession. She was still swooning and felt all these fluttery feelings deep in her gut. She wasn't sure how someone could feel all that, but to be on the receiving end of such emotions, yeah, she was feeling pretty damn good.

Freaked out.

But good.

As she stepped out, he took her hand in his, helping her with a gentle pull before slamming the door shut behind her. Her eyes widened, but then his body was covering hers, pressing her into the car before his mouth captured hers in a heated fury. Surprised, she held on to his biceps as his hands slid down her ribs to her ass, squeezing her hard. Gasping against his mouth as he pressed his very large and hard length against her soft spot, she opened her eyes, meeting his gaze. His very dark and passionate gaze. "Oh."

He was breathless as he held her gaze, his lips moving against hers as he whispered, "I want you."

"Oh."

"Yeah."

"Here?"

He shook his head. "Might not be sanitary, with the baby and all."

"This is true. I'm very pleased you can be practical at a moment like this."

His lips quirked. "Believe me, I'm impressed with myself at this moment."

Reaching between them, she took ahold of his length as he groaned against her lips. "As am I."

Swallowing hard, he took her mouth once more, and her heart was flying. Clinging to him, she moved her hand up and down his cock through his suit as his body vibrated against hers. But when he pulled away, she pouted. "Hey."

He just sent her a grin before taking her hand and walking backward toward the house. "Are you still going to blame me for getting us out of there before my parents?"

Her face broke into a grin as she held his hand. "I guess I'll take the blame. I am so tired, you know?"

"The pregnancy takes a lot out of you."

"And you, being the most amazing husband, had to bring me home."

"Exactly, they raised me to please you."

Her lips curved. "Oh, is that right?"

"Yeah, but I'm pretty sure their definition of pleasing isn't what is about to happen."

"Oh, no?"

"Nope, I'm about to worship the shit out of you."

Breathless, she shut the front door behind her. "What's the holdup?"

Still leading her, his eyes playful, he shrugged. "I respect my parents, and you, too much to make love to you on the living room floor."

She sputtered with laughter. "That's so sweet."

He sent her a grin as he led her into their room, shutting the door and pressing her against it. Covering her body with his, he trailed kisses along her jaw and her neck as his hand reached out, flipping the light on. Her head fell back, her flower crown hitting the ground as he gathered her dress in his hands. "There is a zipper."

"I don't care," he muttered before lifting it up and over her head with more force than he should have needed, but it was a tad bit tight. Cupping her breasts in his hands, he dropped his face between them, tucking his tongue between the swell of her breasts as she clutched at his head, gasping out as she arched into him. As he licked up her chest to her neck, she pushed off his jacket and started on the buttons of his shirt. But he stopped her, taking her wrists in his hands and lifting them over her head. He met her gaze, and a smile tugged at his lips before he pulled the front clasp of her bra and her breasts spilled out. The lingerie fell behind her, getting caught on her ass. Running his tongue along his lips, he slowly shook his head. "I swear, you are the most gorgeous woman I've ever laid my eyes on."

Arching off the door, she pressed herself into him. "Jensen."

But he didn't take her nipple in his mouth like she wanted; instead, he took her mouth once more, his hands sliding down her arms, cupping her breasts and molding them together, his tongue sweeping along hers. When she tried to put her arms down, he pulled away, shaking his head. "Stay put."

"And if I don't?" she challenged, and he grinned at her.

"I'll bend you over my knee and smack that sweet ass of yours."

Her eyes sparkled. "Promise?"

Hissing out a breath, he lifted his head from where he was devouring her breasts. "Evil."

She giggled, an airy, sweet sound that didn't leave her often as he kissed down her breasts to her belly. Falling to his knees, he trailed kisses over her swollen stomach, his eyes meeting hers, and she wanted to hold him. He was so beautiful, his eyes so dark as he held her gaze, such love and admiration swimming in his fathomless depths. Sliding his hands along her stomach to her hips, he took her panties in his fingers, and she came off the door as he slowly slid them down her legs, helping her step out of them before he started to kiss down her hip to her thighs.

Feeling insecure, she wiggled underneath his lips. "Stop."

"Never," he demanded, running his tongue along the dips and disgusting cellulite along her thighs.

"Jensen, really, I hate my legs."

He paused, looking up at her. "I love them," he said, his heart in his eyes. "Like this spot right here," he said, running his tongue along one of the bigger dips in her legs. "It begs me to kiss it every time I get a peek of it. And this one," he added, the spot right above her knee. "It taunts me. Fuck, Wren, your body is a blessing. My blessing."

When he ran his tongue back up the inside of her thighs, her eyes fell shut as her heart went crazy in her chest. She felt as if she was coming out of her skin with each kiss and touch of his tongue to her burning hot skin. As he nibbled on the inside of her thighs, she cried out as her hands came down and she threaded her fingers through his hair.

"Wren."

"I can't! It's too much."

"You don't want me to get ahold of that ass," he warned, and slowly she moved her hands back up, not sure if she did or did not, in fact, want to let him get ahold of her ass. The naughty part of her craved it, but the practical part, the part that knew how big his hands were, was shaking in her nonexistent boots.

"Maybe I want you to," she tried, and his grin turned sinister as he slowly stood to his full height, towering over her. She had never seen him as huge, but at that moment, he was a gorgeous giant. "Or not."

"Oh no, you want it," he said roughly, grasping her hip. "I can see it in your eyes. You evil thing, you."

Her eyes were hooded before he turned her around quickly, her hands coming out against the door as her chest pressed into it. Coming up behind her, he ran his hands down the sides of her body before pressing his long, hard cock against her ass. "Fucking hell, you're so sexy."

Wrapping his arm around her neck, he brought his hand up under her chin before he turned her head so her lips were by his. She was breathless, her mind going wild as her heart was stalled in her chest. When his hand came crashing hard onto her ass, she cried out against his mouth, and he smiled against her lips. "I could live off that sound," he muttered against them, his hand landing once more against her ass, taking her breath away. Gazing into his eyes, she was lost in her lust as his hand came again, his eyes dark and never leaving hers. Kissing her nose, he rubbed her ass as he moved across her shoulder before trailing kisses down her spine. Her breath burst out in spurts as she moaned slightly, his tongue doing just the naughtiest things to her.

When he stopped at her ass, kissing one cheek before the other, he ran his tongue along the spot he had smacked before arching her hips back so her ass was on full display. Sliding his fingers over her ass, he moved them inside of her dripping wet pussy before he groaned against her. Her own cry mixed with his in the most beautiful sound she had ever heard in her life while her body squeezed his fingers. Moving them in and out of her, he bit her ass softly as she clung to the door, her body shaking.

She was going to come hard, she could feel it, but then he removed his fingers from deep inside of her, replacing them with his mouth, and she about came off the door. "Oh, fuck," she muttered, and he chuckled against her pussy, running his tongue up and down her pussy lips, licking every single inch of her as she cried out, arching into him but trying to escape at the same time. She couldn't handle it. It was too much, and soon she was shattering against his mouth, his name coming out in a cry that was so loud, she was damn glad his parents weren't there.

Sucking her clit into his mouth, he squeezed her ass cheeks as she screamed, her body thrashing forward as she tried to get away. Shaking, her legs gave out. But he was there, catching her in his arms, kissing her back as he steadied her to her feet. Turning her around, he had a wicked grin on his lips as he bent down, taking her by the back of her legs and lifting her up in one sweeping motion. Crying out, she wrapped her legs and arms around him in complete shock, until he tipped his head back and demanded, "Kiss me."

"Jensen! Put me down. I weigh a ton."

But he wasn't even struggling. "You weigh nothing. Kiss me."

And she swore the wall around her heart cracked even more. Dropping her mouth to his, she could taste herself on his lips and feel the slick wetness from her pussy all over his face. And that was fucking hot. As he carried her to the bed like she, in fact, weighed nothing, her heart was singing in her chest. He slowly laid her down, kissing her body before he stood up to undress. As she watched him, her eyes hooded only for him, she asked, "You planned on doing this all night?"

He shook his head. "Nope, not until we were dancing did I know I was going to take you home and make love to you."

Desire danced in his eyes as he stripped down to his beautifully naked body. His toned chest, his abs, his thick quads, good Lord, he was gorgeous. Coming onto the bed, he went between her legs, kissing her thighs and then her knee, while all she could do was watch him, praying that her next breath came.

Because Jensen Monroe was stealing them all.

As he covered her body with his, his cock lying against her pussy, throbbing, Wren couldn't even form a thought, let alone think of anything but Jensen. He was beautiful—his eyes, his lips, and Jesus, she wanted this so bad. He moved his finger along her lips as his other hand braced him up over her belly, and his eyes bored into hers as a grin pulled at his lips.

"What?" she found herself asking, cupping his face, her thumb moving along the coarse hair she was finding she loved a lot.

"I was just thinking."

Her brow quirked. "Do I want to know?"

He scoffed. "Probably not."

"No?"

"No, but I'm gonna tell ya anyway," he muttered, his lips caressing hers as his eyes fell shut. She swore she had never seen a more beautiful man than the one who was hovering above her. "I swear that meeting you so long ago, coming to your home as a billet kid, was my fate. It was. But becoming your friend was my choice because it was easy. This, though, falling for you, madly and completely the way I have, was beyond my control." She took in a quick breath as his eyes met hers once more. "And I wouldn't change a fucking thing."

And with that, he moved into her, taking her breath away once more as he filled her completely, their moans mingling together as her nails bit into his biceps. He was so big, and fucking hell, she wanted to blame that another orgasm was building on the fact that she hadn't been with someone for so long, but she knew it wasn't the case.

It was Jensen.

All Jensen.

Sitting up on his haunches, he took her hips in his hands and thrust into her, hard and with meaning, his eyes never leaving hers. Holding on to his wrist, she bit her lip as he continued to move into her. Each thrust, she swore, was like a hammer to every wall she had built up around her soul. He was so honest, so fearless when it came to how he felt, what she meant to him. It was downright mind-blowing. Never in her life had she been fuck— No, he wasn't fucking her. He was making love, which was why this was so different.

Why she felt so much special.

As his speed picked up, she arched up against him, her body tensing up as he muttered her name, his fingers digging into her hips. As another orgasm racked her body, surprising her but also shattering her core, she couldn't help the smile that pulled at her lips. Not long after that, a guttural yell came from him as he stilled, jerking ever so slowly into her as she gasped for breath, her body shaking under his.

When her eyes opened, Jensen's eyes were closed, his lashes kissing his skin as he sucked in a deep breath, letting it out in a hiss before he did it once more, his body covered in a sheen of sweat that drove her wild. Using his arms to pull himself up, he fell out of her before her lips met his, and she wrapped her arms around his chest. His arms came around her neck as their kiss deepened. Pulling back ever so slowly, he cupped her face, his eyes burning into hers.

"You are it."

Her eyes widened as she held his gaze. "I am?"

"You are, and I swear, I'll never be the same."

As his lips curved, he fell next to her, pulling her with him so she was tucked up against him. Wrapping his arms around her, he kissed her temple and then her forehead as her heart clanked hard against her ribs. While he was probably enjoying the afterglow of their amazing sex, Wren's mind was running a million miles an hour.

They had done it.

Which meant he felt that she felt something for him.

That it wasn't just a fuck.

And it wasn't.

Even she knew that.

Biting her lip, she angled her head up to look at him. His profile was stunning, his lips parted as he took in a breath and let it out slowly. His lashes kissed his cheeks, and his nose was so perfect, unlike Wells's and Vaughn's since they had both broken their noses before. Jensen could have been a model, he was so beautiful, yet he was lying in the bed with her.

Making love to her.

He must have felt her looking at him because he turned, his eyes meeting hers as a grin pulled at his lips. Moving up his body, she pressed her lips into his, her eyes falling shut as her heart jumped up into her throat, her whole body shaking with fear. But when she pulled away, her eyes held hostage by his, she whispered, "Me either."

His eyes widened as his lips parted, turning up in a grin, and she was thankful he knew what she was talking about since she didn't trust herself to be able to say the words that came so easily to him. "Yeah?"

She nodded. "Yeah."

Taking a chunk of her ass in his hand, he kissed the side of her mouth. "Damn right."

Her laughter came quickly, as did the euphoric feeling.

A feeling that worried her since it could only mean one thing…

She was falling hard for Jensen Monroe.

Quickly.

Which usually meant one other thing.

It was going to end just as quickly.

\* \* \*

"I DIDN'T HURT YOU, did I?"

Jensen's heart was beating out of his chest, he swore it, but yet, he held Wren close to him, trailing kisses along her jaw. Never in his life had he felt so emotionally in sync with a woman until he got inside of Wren. The way she moved, the way she whispered his name, her lips… God, he was still shaking from his lust for her.

His love for her.

God, he loved her.

Kissing the side of her mouth, he looked down at her. "I think I got carried away."

A sneaky grinned pulled at her lips. Her hair was everywhere around her, her eyes bright as her face was flushed, her lips swollen from his kisses. "Not at all. It was more than I wanted."

"Good thing, right?"

She nodded, arching into him. "Very, very good thing."

His eyes fell shut as he kissed her some more, his hand holding her belly as she cuddled into him. "I've wanted that for a long time."

She nibbled at his neck. "I never would have guessed."

"No?"

"Nope, not even kinda. Maybe you should do it again, convince me. I don't feel at all special," she teased, and he pulled away, looking down at her blissful face, her bright eyes, and her lips that were curved in the most sinfully gorgeous grin.

"Are you saying you want more?"

"Want and need are two very different things."

"Oh?"

"Yes, like I want to be able to eat what I want and not get fat. But I need to have you inside of me, feel your lips on me, and look into your eyes." Her words hit him right in the gut as he got lost in her eyes. "You know what I mean?"

"I think I got the basics."

Her lips curved. "Oh, Jenny, there is nothing basic about the way you just worked me."

"Same here, baby."

"We should have done that sooner."

But he shook his head. "Nah, I love the slow burn and the big explosion."

Her eyes sparkled, her lips parting. "I think I do too."

"You do."

Her eyes were challenging as she ran her fingers along his hip, sending chills up his spine. "So, you think we got time before your parents come home?"

Leaning down, he pressed his nose into hers. "We have all the time in the world. I locked the door."

"That won't keep your mother out."

He nodded. "You're right, but it gives me time to cover us up."

Giggling, she shut her eyes. He swore he thought she couldn't gct any more beautiful, but he was wrong. Each time, her beauty stunned him in place. "Good plan."

"I thought so," he said, sliding his hands between her legs, cupping her softly, his breath stopping. She felt like heaven. Being inside her was better than anything he had ever experienced, and she was his. All his.

"Mmm," she muttered, her lips dusting his. "Can I admit something?"

Moving his fingers inside of her swollen lips, he nodded. "Can you make it quick?" She gasped against his mouth as his finger found her clit. "Because I can't control myself around you."

"That's a damn lie," she said with a dry look. "You've been torturing me for a month."

Pressing into her clit, her back arching as her eyes darkened with lust, he scoffed. "Ha, me? You mean you've been torturing me with those naughty panties and these delicious thighs?" Her lips curved as his lips met hers. "And I've loved every moment."

Smiling against his mouth, she cupped his face as his finger swirled around her bundle of nerves. Breathless, she asked, "Can I make a confession?"

"Do you need to?" he asked, licking her bottom lip.

"You're killing me," she gasped as he slid his finger inside of her.

"I was thinking the same thing."

She chuckled, and her face was bright and flushed as she said, "Really, this is important."

Letting his head fall to her chest, he nibbled on the swell of her breasts before he said, "Fine."

He met her gaze as his fingers continued to move in and out of her slick center. "Are you listening?" she rasped out.

"Somewhat," he admitted, and she glared. Stalling his hand, he held her gaze, but his heart was beating so hard, it was messing with his vision. "Fine."

As her lips tilted and a wicked gleam sparkled in her eyes, she whispered, "At least our first time was a hell of a lot better than our first kiss."

His laughter bubbled in his chest. "Really?"

"Really. I was worried. You failed me once."

"Oh yeah?" he asked, his fingers going deeper inside of her. "I'll make you forget all that."

With her eyes on his, her laughter running down his spine, she said, "Please do."

With that, he did.

Because he loved her.

Only her.

And he knew she loved him too.

* * *

"DO WE HAVE TO LEAVE?"

Looking over at Wren, who was very slow to pack, he smiled. He swore he could still see her naked, feel her skin against his tongue, and taste her. She was beyond sexy, even when she was pouting. "Pretty sure your mother will kill us if we don't show up, Oh, and Wells. He'll kill us for not showing up for his wedding. Which we are both in, by the way."

She pouted as she threw in her dress that was now a wrinkled mess since neither of them had picked it up off the floor after it was left there. They hadn't stopped since then. Every free moment, he was tasting her or inside her. They had a lot of time to make up for. But his wife must have forgotten that as she grumbled, throwing a shirt in her bag before she looked up. "What if we don't answer the phone when they call?"

"Then we would be assholes," he said, coming to her side to help fold her clothes since he had finished packing. She looked a bit like she had in the baby store, and that worried him. "Why don't you want to leave?"

She shrugged as she threw another shirt in, which he, in turn, grabbed and folded. "Because I love it here. Here, we're good. There, it's going to be a fucking clusterfuck."

"Tell me how you really feel," he teased, and she exhaled hard before leaning into him.

"I don't like it there."

"Wrenya, come on, it's your home."

"This could be my home," she suggested, and he smiled, his heart soaring in his chest. He loved that she loved his home. It made his body ache with happiness. Though, they couldn't stay there. As much as he wished they'd never have to leave his bed, he knew her family wanted to see them. And with Wells's wedding, there was no way they could skip out. "I feel good here, and I don't want to lose that yet."

Kissing her temple, he said, "Then don't. Take it with you."

"Jensen," she complained, shaking her head before she fell on the bed, her hair going everywhere as she covered her face with her hands. "You just don't get it."

Not liking how that sounded, he picked up her bag, setting it on the ground before falling beside her, on his stomach so that he could see her face. "What don't I get?"

"They always make such a huge deal about Wells. And with the wedding, and then with your and Vaughn's Cup day, I'll just be in the shadows. So why do I need to go? It's pointless, and I hate how much I want to be noticed. I feel so pathetic."

Reaching up, he pulled her hands off her face before he moved toward her, resting his chin on hers. "Well, I can guarantee you that you'll never be in the shadows where I'm concerned. I only see you."

Her shoulders fell into the bed as a grin pulled at her lips. "And that means the world to me, it does, but here, we're good. Like, no one is questioning us, or me, and I don't have to deal with anything hard. Here, it's easy. Just me and you, that's it."

"It can be that way there too, if you let it."

She gave him a dry look. "So, I'm doing this?"

"Yeah," he said simply. "I mean, I feel like you're making the excuse of them ignoring you because you know that, while they might do that, they'll also be questioning your every move. I get that. I understand that stress, But, baby, if we're good here, we'll be good there, because we're great. That's all that matters, right?"

Reaching up, she cupped his face, her eyes a hopeful light green color. Yet he could see she was holding something back. "I'm just scared," she whispered.

"Why? You'll never be alone when I'm right there. I promise, it will go off without a hitch. If they ignore you, fine, means I get all of you, and we both know I won't be complaining."

A grin pulled at her lips. "Yeah, you're right."

"And if they're in our face, then we'll be together. If that's what you still want."

She nodded as she ran her thumb along the coarse hair of his face. "It is."

"Then we're solid. Get through the next two weeks, you'll get the money, split it with Wells, and we'll pay off all that debt that is freaking you the fuck out, buy us a pretty house, a vacation house, and a college fund for our little no-name kid."

Her grin grew as she chuckled. "He does need a name."

"Badly," he decided with a shake of his head. "But it's fine. No one will ever suspect anything, okay? The money is yours."

But she shook her head. "I don't care about the money," she whispered, and he wanted to be elated. He wanted to throw his hands up in the air and fucking know he had won, but then her eyes started to cloud with tears, and his heart stopped.

"Whoa, Wrenya, what's wrong?"

Looking away, she sucked in a breath while she shook her head. "It's nothing. I'm just nervous."

But he knew she was lying. "Wren. Don't lie to me."

As her lips trembled, she sat up, wiping her face. "It's nothing. Just insecurities."

Before she could get away, he pulled her down into his lap, wrapping his arms around her middle as his lips pressed into her neck. "Baby, look at me." She hesitated, but then she did as he asked, her green eyes floating in her tears. "Tell me about these insecurities. How can I ease them?"

But she shook her head once more. "It's nothing."

"Tell me."

Swallowing hard, she bit her lip before she blew out a breath. "I don't know what to say."

"The truth."

"The truth is…" She paused, laughing soullessly. "I'm a fucking hot mess, and going home and seeing… Fucking fuck, Jensen, it's… Fuck." She came undone, clinging to him, and he held her tightly, his lips by her ear as she cried into his neck. "I just don't want you to leave me, and that place brings out the bad in me."

"Oh, Wren, no, it doesn't. Baby, it's okay," he whispered, rubbing her back. "That won't happen. I promise."

Before he could say more, though, her mouth was on his, moving feverishly as she clung to him, her belly pressed into him. Her need for him was apparent as she shook against him, holding him as tightly as he held her. Pulling away, she whispered against his lips, "Just kiss me, Jensen, please."

Meeting her gaze, he knew she was holding back so fucking much, but he did as she asked.

He kissed her.

Because he loved her.

And he didn't question her anymore. Not after they packed or even after they said goodbye to his parents where she cried like they were dying. She didn't want to leave, he got that, he didn't want to either, and it was obvious she had fallen in love with his parents. It was beautiful, and he was so thankful for that. But her silence to the airport, and even on the plane, made his body hurt. He didn't understand it, but he didn't want to question her about it. He didn't want to push, but deep inside, he was worried.

It concerned him, though, because pushing could lead to her shutting down completely, and she was finally opening up to him. He couldn't mess that up because it could turn into a slippery slope with her. Though the anxiety she had caused with her earlier concerns was eating him alive, he was patient, he was kind, and he just loved her. Even when she tried not to let him, he did it anyway. It had been working thus far, and he wasn't one to mess with something that worked.

He just needed her to shut off her damn brain.

Reaching for the bags and putting them in the back of the rental once they landed in Colorado, he glanced over at his wife as she was busy on her phone. Her silence was killing him, and he worried she had already shut down. Shaking that thought from his brain, he reached for her door. "Baby."

She looked up. "Thanks, told my mom that we just landed."

"Oh, good," he said as she got in and before he shut the door. Walking around the car, he exhaled harshly. He wished he'd never left home. He liked his wife way better in Canada.

As he got in the car, she said, "I texted your mom too, and she says she misses us, that the house is quiet."

He smiled. "Yes, the guilt-tripping is strong with my mother."

When he looked over at her, she smiled, a true smile that took up her whole face. "I told her we'd be back sooner rather than later, and she sent me a kissy-face emoji."

"Good," he answered, moving to start the car as his heart pounded in his chest. He knew he shouldn't, but he couldn't hold it back. Unable to bring himself to start the car, he shook his head. "Stop it."

When he looked up, she was staring back at him oddly. "Stop what? Texting your mom?"

"No, please don't ever stop that. I mean this. You're being weird."

"I am?" she asked, her eyes narrowing. "No, I'm not."

"Yes, you are. You haven't spoken more than yes or no to me the whole way here, and I can tell your whole demeanor is off. Please don't do this, Wren. I can't, okay? You've fucking spoiled me with the girl I had in Canada. And I get it, you're nervous to be here, but believe me, I'm here with you. Nothing will happen."

Her lips pressed together as she reached out, lacing her fingers with his. "You're right, I'm sorry. I just don't want to be here."

He nodded. "I understand that, but don't take it out on me."

Her eyes softened as she pursed her lips at him. "I'm sorry, I didn't mean to."

He swallowed hard. "I just want you to be happy, and I know being here isn't doing that. But we have to be, and we are. So, let's make the best of it."

Bringing his hand up to her lips, she placed a soft kiss to his palm. "Okay."

His mouth quirked up at the side as he leaned over, and she met him halfway, their lips joining. He wanted to believe that she was okay. That she was letting it go, but he knew her better than that. Her mind was going a billion miles a second, and there was nothing he could do. But he'd made her aware of her actions, and he just prayed maybe she'd be more conscious of them.

But he wasn't naïve. There was a reason she didn't want to be home, and he didn't believe for a second that it was only her family. They were good people. They loved her, and he understood she wasn't the center of attention—that was all Wells, and sometimes, Jensen—but they loved her. So he knew it was something else.

He just wasn't sure what.

Or if it was a who.

# Chapter SEVENTEEN

"They're here!"

Jensen's face broke into a grin when he pushed the door open to the home that was his home away from home, and Wren walked in before him. "Winston! They're here!" Elaine Lemiere came running down the hall toward them in a trusty pantsuit and her hair in perfect curls along her shoulders. Always the picture of perfection, Elaine Lemiere. "Oh my God! Look at you, come here!"

Wren looked back at Jensen, but only for a moment before her mother wrapped her arms around her tightly. Wren hugged her mother back as she kissed her hard on the cheek, and Jensen sighed. She needed this. "Wren Josephine! I can't! Look at you! I never thought I'd say this, but pregnancy agrees with you. Your eyes, your face... My God, you're glowing, sweetheart!"

Wren's face burned as she laughed. "Mom, come on, I'm fat."

Before Jensen could get on to her, Elaine was shaking her head. "No, you're pregnant, big difference."

"I told her that," Jensen added. "She doesn't listen."

"Does she ever? Stubborn as a mule, this one is, but let me just say, I have a feeling this glow isn't just about being pregnant and has everything to do with this stud. Come here, you," Elaine demanded before taking Jensen in her arms and squeezing him hard. He could feel Wren's gaze on them but only for a second before another voice joined them in the hallway.

"Aw, my darling." Jensen opened his eyes to see Winston take

Wren in his arms and hold her tightly as he kissed her head. Unlike Jensen's dad, Winston was younger, not at all gray, and a lot chunkier than his father. He didn't skip a meal, that was for sure, but he also wasn't sick. "Look at you."

Wren looked unsure as she kissed his cheek. "Hey, Daddy."

"Jesus, have you lost weight? Jensen, are you not feeding my baby?"

Jensen beamed as Wren rolled her eyes. "Funny, my mum claimed Wren wasn't feeding me."

Winston laughed. "You both are skinny! Goodness!"

"Daddy, I'm as big as a house."

"You're skin and bones with a bump. I'll kick your ass, boy. Feed her," he demanded, and Jensen laughed as Winston wrapped him up in a hug. "You hear me?"

"Loud and clear, sir," Jensen answered, and Winston grinned over at him, squeezing him.

Pulling away, Winston smacked Jensen's arms once more in a fatherly way before he reached for their bags and looked to Elaine. "Where am I going with these?"

"Wren's room. Come on, kids. We've got all kinds of wedding stuff to talk about!"

Elaine walked ahead of them with Winston, and Jensen stopped Wren by wrapping his arms around her waist, kissing her jaw. "See?"

"See, what? The only good thing that came out of that is that maybe you can't stop them from feeding me."

He scoffed. "That will happen. And they were good, all about you."

"Because it was expected. Why haven't they hit us with questions?"

"Maybe 'cause they're excited to see us?"

"No, that's not them," she added suspiciously. "Whatever, let's go talk about Wells."

"Wren," he said, and she pressed her lips together.

"I'm being a bitch?"

He shrugged. "I was gonna say difficult."

She gave him a teasing grin. "And you claim to love me."

He continued to hold her. "I do, all of you."

She exhaled, leaning into him. "Well, at least someone does."

Placing a kiss to his cheek, she moved out of his arms, leaving him in the hall shaking his head. He wasn't sure why she felt that way, but he still believed it had nothing to do with her family.

And everything to do with something else.

Or maybe some*one*.

\* \* \*

"WELLS THIS, Wells that. Did you know that Wells needs to have his ass bleached before the wedding? No? Well, he does." Jensen scoffed as he scrubbed his head, listening to Wren complain. "Honestly, Jenny, did you hear anything about us? Did they ask once how our marriage was going? Or even how your parents are? It was all about us at your house. But here, it's about every fucking thing but us. Ugh!"

"Babe, it's nothing to get worked up about."

"But it is. Doesn't it bother you?"

"I mean, it was annoying, but I'm not going to let it bother me."

"Well, I am."

"Obviously."

"And I think it's rude! Not once did my mom ask anything about my pregnancy. All my dad did was bitch about the money for the wedding. I swear, I don't get it. Like, where are the questions? Why hasn't anyone brought up the fucking inheritance? Nothing!"

"Maybe because they believe us?"

"No, they're up to something."

"Wren, that's a little ridiculous. Just be happy."

"No, I don't trust them. I hate it here."

"I sort of got that."

"Well, just in case you're wondering. Why aren't you done?"

He smiled at the shower door, the same shower door he had used when he was growing up. His bedroom with Wells connected to one side of the bathroom, while Wren's connected the other way. Even when they were younger, they would do this. He'd be in the shower while she did her makeup or hair or whatever. It had been normal for them. But now...it was different.

Because he wanted her in the shower with him.

Well, he probably wanted that when he was younger too, but he hadn't seen enough porn then to realize it could definitely happen.

"I'm talking to you."

"Well, hurry up. I wanna get in so I don't have to go back out there."

"You don't want dessert?"

"No. I want to shower and go to bed."

"Someone is grumpy, and probably needs dessert."

He could just imagine her face all scrunched up, and it brought a grin to his own face. "Someone needs their family not to care about only one kid when there are two."

Shaking his head, he pushed the door open, popping his head out and around the enclosure to see her leaning on the counter, messing with her nails. Her eyes were flooded with tears as she looked up to find him watching her. "Baby."

"No, I'm fine."

"You're not."

"I am, and I'm just being a child. I don't need their love. I don't need their attention."

"Wrenya."

She shook her head as a tear ran down her cheek. "It's just annoying, and I hate that I think I need it. I'm a fucking amazing woman, I have a great job, I'm married to you, and we're having a kid. I'm obviously good, so I don't know why I fucking care."

*"Ma chou."*

She looked up. "What?"

"Take your clothes off."

Her brows pulled together. "What? Why?"

"I mean, I can pull you in here, clothes and all, and still make love to you, but I'd rather not ruin the shirt you just bought."

Her lips quirked as she watched him, her eyes widening a bit. She then pushed her shorts down her legs with her panties, leaving her deliciously naked from the waist down. "So thoughtful."

"I thought so. Now come on." Before he went back into the shower, he caught a glimpse of her pulling her shirt off, and then she was entering the shower, so damn beautiful, his breath caught. "Come here," he said, pulling her under the hot water and wrapping his arms around her as their lips met. Clinging to him, she slid her hands down his wet back to his ass, holding him as he devoured her mouth. Moving her against the wall, he kissed down her neck to her breasts before nibbling on her nipple.

"Trying to distract me, I see."

"Is it working?" he asked before moving to her other nipple.

"I'd say so," she said, her head falling back as she moved her fingers through his hair. "Jesus."

His body went rock hard as a chill ran down his spine, while he gave nothing but love to her swollen, beautiful tits. As he cupped her center, she arched into his hand, and he shook with want. He still couldn't believe he was doing this. With her. Making love to the woman he had loved for as long as he could remember. He had dreamed of this, and the reality was better than any of his dreams. She was perfect. Kissing down her stomach, he dipped his tongue into her belly button as the water moved down his back and over his ass.

"Jensen," she breathed as he ran his tongue along her lower lips, kissing her inner thighs. She tasted like heaven. "Jensen, I want you inside me."

She didn't have to ask twice. Sliding up her body, he went to pick up her leg, but she moved him around, pressing her body into his as his back hit the cold tile. "Got ya," she teased, her eyes wickedly evil as she kissed down his chest.

"I think this is the only time I want to be gotten."

Chuckling softly, she raked her teeth down his chest, her fingers following her mouth. He was in awe of how sexy she looked, the water flowing down her beautiful body, her sweet ass perked out as she dropped to her knees, running her nose along him with her fingers following and taking away his breath. He gasped out when she took his hard length in her hands, and she sent him a kittenish grin before running her tongue along his tip. His toes curled against the tile, his heart freezing in his chest as she took him into her beautiful mouth. His cock disappeared inch by inch until his eyes fell shut and his muttered groans filled what felt like a suddenly tiny shower.

Threading his hand in her hair, he arched into her mouth as his body shook. Her mouth, her teeth, drove him downright insane. She took him in and out of her mouth, her eyes never leaving his, and he wasn't sure what was better. The torture her sweet mouth was inflicting, or the destruction those green depths were causing to his soul.

"I fucking love you," he muttered, his hand gripping a handful of her hair as she moved up and down him, sucking him so deep

256 | TONI ALEO

and with so much force, he was sure he was coming out of his skin. As she sucked him hard, her mouth moving off with a loud popping noise, she gazed up at him. "Ever imagine this when we were younger?"

He couldn't breathe, but he somehow got out, "I don't think I saw enough porn to ever imagine this."

She giggled, running her tongue along his head. "Remember that one summer? I think you were eighteen, and you had come for that camp. I don't remember what—"

"Junior training." He then paused. "Why are we talking?"

She giggled. "I need to tell you this." Her eyes were playful, her tongue coming out to wrap around his swollen, throbbing cock. "We had gone to that bridge over off Old Man Knocker's hill."

"Yeah," he gasped as her hand cupped his balls. "I remember."

She smiled, moving her hands up and down his length. "Well, we were gross, and Wells decided to shower in Mom's room. So we raced for this bathroom, and you beat me. I remember you had started getting naked in the living room, and the only reason you beat me was because I saw your dick, and it stunned me. Dead in my tracks. All I wanted was to know how it felt in my hands. To touch you, to watch you squirm. It was insane what I was feeling."

His brows drew in. "You must have been watching porn way before me." Her face broke into a grin as her laughter filled the bathroom, and he reached down, pulling her up and into his arms as he turned them, covering her body with his. "I can't take that torture."

"Aw, but it's fun," she whispered against his lips. "Your squirm is sexy."

"You're damned evil, woman."

"Only for you," she answered as he picked her up under her knee, opening her and entering with one thrust that had their mouths mingling in a moan as his fingers bit into her leg. Picking up speed, he gripped her, his own orgasm building even more as he thrust up into her. His whole body was tingling, his heart was pounding, and he knew damn well it would never feel like this with anyone else but her.

Only her.

And as he came, he came hard, lights going off behind his lids before he braced himself to keep from squishing her, and he stilled inside of her. Gripping her leg, he moaned loudly against her mouth, but she caught it in hers, kissing him hard as her fingers threaded through his hair. Dropping her leg, he wrapped his arms around her neck, kissing her as he tried to breathe, his heart nearly coming out of his chest as he opened his eyes, meeting her gaze.

Pulling away only slightly, she whispered, "Thanks, Jenny."

"For what? I think I'm the one who should be thanking you."

She smiled against his lips, nibbling on them as she whispered, "But you made me forget that my family sucks."

While he didn't feel the same, he understood she did. "It is my job as your husband to make all the bullshit go away."

Her lips pressed lightly against his. "Yeah, but I think you go above and beyond."

"I do. For you."

Her face flushed as she moved her hands along his jaw. "Can I take advantage of that?"

He scoffed. "'Cause you don't already?" he teased, and she beamed up at him.

"I don't!"

"I'm kidding," he said, kissing her nose. "What do you want from me, *ma chou*?"

She giggled, her fingers moving along the hair of his jaw. "Your French is sexy."

His lips dusted along hers, "Tell me what you want, *ma chou*."

Her eyes glittered with happiness, and he felt good. He felt alive, and he fucking felt loved. By her. And that was enough to have him doing anything she wished. But he knew her, and she wouldn't ask for much. As she moved her lips along his, his gut swirled with desire and love as she whispered, "Will you wash my hair?"

His grin broke as he kissed the side of her mouth. "Yes, I will."

"And then go get my dessert? Bring it to bed? Eat it off me, maybe? Or let me eat it off you."

"Slave driver, huh?"

"Please," she begged, her arms squeezing around him. "For me?"

"You know my weakness," he decided, falling out of her before turning her around into the water, taking in every single curve of her gorgeous body. "And you're lucky I want to eat pie off that sweet ass of yours."

She giggled happily as he reached for the shampoo. "You made my day."

"That's all I want," he said as her eyes met his.

When she smiled, he felt it in his gut, and at that moment, nothing else mattered but her.

He found it was always like that when he had the chance to love her.

* * *

WREN WANTED to slam her face into the counter until she was bleeding profusely and she died.

Dramatic? Yes.

Did she care? Not even kinda.

"Where the hell is Wells? Shouldn't he be here? Dealing with this?" she finally yelled, and her mother glared back at her.

"Don't yell, Wren. It doesn't fix anything."

When Jensen's hand came to her thigh, she let out a sigh as she met his gaze. "Early grave."

He tried to smile as he shook his head. "But, really, when is Wells coming over?"

"He and Alex went away with Alex's family for the weekend. They'll be back tonight. So I gotta make sure this is all well and done before he comes."

"Fuck. My. Life," Wren muttered as she held her face in her hands. "I feel the flower issues should fall on him. Let him deal with it."

"No, he doesn't need that stress!"

"Neither do you," Wren yelled back as her mother glared at her.

"I don't know why we're spending all this money. He probably won't be gay much longer," Winston called from the counter, and Elaine exhaled hard, shaking her head.

"Anyway, you'll both have fittings tomorrow."

"For a wedding that is a complete waste of time," Winston added, shaking his head.

"Dad, you aren't helping," Wren called out, sending a look to her father. "At all."

He ignored her like always before looking to Jensen. "Tell her, Jenny. Wells isn't really gay."

Looking up, Jensen held Winston's gaze. "He's been gay since we were kids, Winston. I think it's who he is."

Winston rolled his eyes. "I swear, the boy doesn't think. He could be getting millions. Instead, he's letting his sister get it."

With that, he left the kitchen as Wren glared at his back. That was the first he had mentioned of the inheritance. Yet it wasn't directed at her, more at Wells, but she felt it coming. She didn't trust that guy. Yeah, he was her dad, and she loved him, but damn it, something was up. It had to be. "I see he is still being difficult."

"Difficult is the nice way of putting it," Elaine said, shaking her head. "He's stressing me out, Wells is doing the same, and they won't stop fighting. It's killing me slowly."

Wren swallowed hard. "I told you to hire someone, Mom. You don't have to do all this."

"It doesn't help that your father refuses to accept Wells is gay. Plus, your brother feels better if I do it."

"Well then, tell him to stop fighting with Dad and help at least," Wren announced, and Elaine tapped her hand.

"Easier said than done." When her phone started ringing, she held up a finger. "It's the florist. Be right back."

Getting up, Wren rolled her eyes as she grabbed an apple, sitting back down beside Jensen. "Can we leave yet?"

Shaking his head, Jensen leaned on his elbows. "Yeah, I agree. This is dumb."

"See and, like always, I'm just a sounding board. Or the ringleader for the stupidity around here. My brother can't even be here. Let's escape, go to a hotel."

"Wren."

"What?"

"Come on, you love being home."

She shook her head. "No, I don't. It's always about Wells and Dad, or whatever party my mom is throwing. I don't matter around these parts."

"Well, you matter to me, and I'm in these parts at the moment, so you matter," he said, leaning into her and nipping at her nose. "Now, smile so I can smile."

He was so sweet. So amazing and she hated that, no matter what, he could make her smile. It scared her. Down in her soul.

Because she was falling fucking hard.

Like, face first in concrete hard for Jensen.

She knew there was no way it would last.

But yet, her lips quirked a bit, and so did his. "Come on. Bigger."

"Leave me alone."

"Never," he said, capturing her mouth as her hands came up to hold his face. His kisses hit her in the gut, and she wanted nothing more than to escape to their bedroom and undress him slowly, before taking him with the need that was bubbling inside of her. It was insane how badly she wanted him. She had always been attracted to him, but being with him in that way… Yeah, nothing could touch that. He was magnificent, and she swore her soul felt him.

All of him.

Pulling away, she met his gaze as a smile pulled at her lips, and he said, "There's my baby."

Her grin grew as she leaned her head on his shoulder, exhaling hard because no matter how happy he made her, nothing about being in Colorado was good. Not only did she have to deal with her shitty parents and her dramatic brother, she knew she would see Bradley. That alone had her heart aching in her chest. She really needed to tell Jensen before it happened, but she couldn't bring herself to. Closing her eyes, she pushed that thought aside before she whispered, "When Wells comes, it will be worse."

"Then we'll escape to the bedroom."

Her hand slid down the inside of his thigh. "Or, we can go now?" He gasped as she moved her hand up the lump in his shorts. "I can take you against the door this time." When he chuckled sexily, she sat up and grinned back at him. "All of you."

"Evil woman," he muttered as she giggled. Then her mother came back into the room.

Unfortunately.

When it was just them, Wren was happiest.

"Well, that was almost a disaster. They ordered yellow instead of blue. Wells wants blue flowers."

"Oh, darn."

"Wren."

Wren exhaled loudly. "Jesus, Mom, hire someone. Please."

"No, it's fine," she said, waving her off, but even Jensen could see this was stressing her out.

"She won't, Wren. She likes the stress. Gives her something to do," Winston said, coming into the room and shaking his head. "You know how she is, always needs something to plan and do. She's never happy with what she has."

"That's not true," Elaine called back to him. "I love you, and I haven't killed you yet. I love my children, I just like planning stuff."

Wren looked away, her shoulders falling against her wishes. She didn't want to have her feelings hurt, but if her mom loved her and cared about her, why hadn't she even thought to ask Wren how she was? Moms were supposed to be there for their daughters, especially when they were pregnant, but Wren didn't have that. Elaine Lemiere was always too busy.

"Oh, crap, Wren. Shanna wanted to come by tomorrow. What time is good for you? She said she texted you."

Wren's heart dropped. "I changed my number, remember? I haven't gotten anything."

Her mother tsked. "Well, I'll need you to talk with her. She's doing the decorations for me, and I don't want any bad blood between you two. I don't know what happened, but I need you to fix that."

Not because they'd been friends their whole lives, but because of Wells's wedding.

Exhaling hard, Wren shook her head. "We're busy."

Elaine's face scrunched up. "Busy? You stayed in bed till one today!"

"'Cause we're tired. I don't want to entertain anyone right now. Maybe later."

"Wren, that's pathetic."

"I think it's pathetic that you don't care if I'm friends with her, only that I smooth things over so that Wells's wedding goes off without a hitch!"

Jensen held up his hands. "Whoa, why don't we change the subject?" he suggested, and Elaine looked up, her brows pulling together as Winston looked over at him too.

"To what? Honey, I have so much to do here, especially when your wife is being her difficult self," Elaine said, moving her hands over all the books and calendars around her. "Planning a wedding isn't easy, not that Wren cares about that."

Wren's blood was boiling, and her face was burning as she went to tell her mother where she could stuff Wells's wedding, but before she could get a word out, Jensen was talking. "Neither is having a baby, but we are. We would love some advice, or hell, we can talk about my family since they made sure to ask about you two while we were there. Also, we can't figure out a name for the kiddo we're having, and you haven't asked how Wren's pregnancy is going. So, I feel there's a lot we can talk about."

With each word that left his mouth, Wren's eyes widened more. He had never spoken to her parents like that, and when she looked back at them, they were both wide-eyed and shocked.

Holy. Fuck.

"I... Well... I guess we can talk about that," her mother drew out, and gone was Wren's shock, replaced by pure hurt.

*She guessed.*

Wow.

"I just didn't realize—"

But Wren was already moving, sliding out of the breakfast nook as she fought back her tears. Walking past her mom, she called out, "It's fine, Mom, plan your wedding."

"Wren," Jensen called, but she waved him off.

"Wren, honey," Winston called, but she shook her head. "Wait a minute."

"No, I *guess* I fucking need a goddamn moment," she said, walking away and heading for her room. She fully expected Jensen to follow, but he didn't.

Instead, she heard him back in the kitchen. Pausing at the door, she looked toward the kitchen as he said, "I don't think it's dramatic for her to want her parents to ask how her life is going."

"We know she's fine. She hasn't told us any different," her father bit out, and her heart sped up in her chest as she walked back toward the kitchen, leaning on the wall that held all of Wells's and Jensen's awards.

"Have you asked?"

"I don't have to. She'd tell me."

"Or she wouldn't."

"Jensen, honey, really, we know our daughter. If something is wrong, the whole world knows. Plus, Wren is just so independent. She doesn't need anyone, and if anyone tries to be there, she pushes them away. I know you've been with her for the last month, but honestly, we know her."

She heard Jensen moving before his voice came out cold and hard, "That's the furthest from the truth because in that month, I think I now know her better than both of you, and that's sad. I hate that for you because that woman is the most amazing girl I've ever met. Yeah, she's independent and she pushes people away, but if you don't let her, you get the real Wren. And that girl..." He paused, shaking his head as a grin pulled at his lips. "She's vulnerable and needs love."

Her father huffed out a sound as he yelled, "Now, son, don't come into my house, saying we don't love our daughter!"

"I never implied that at all. I know for a fact that you love her, but does she know that?"

"Yes," her mother yelled, her chair moving out and her hands coming down on the table. "Yes, she knows that, and I don't know why you are questioning us."

"I'm not," he said simply. "I'm just saying, I get Wells's wedding is important and it needs to be planned. But maybe take ten minutes to find out how Wren is doing. She didn't even want to come here because she knew you guys would be like this, and I didn't believe her. But she was right and, guys, she is fucking amazing. Beautiful and we're so excited for our future. Be excited for us, her too. Not just Wells. Lots of things are happening, and I want to be able to come here with my son for you two to see, and not to have my wife crying because she doesn't want to be here."

Wren's eyes filled with tears as she covered her mouth, holding in her sob. "I love you two. I love you like I love my own folks, and you both know that. I don't know how I never noticed that you guys did this, but looking back, it was always Wells and me. Always. But now that she is my wife, my heart and soul, I won't let you guys hurt her. I don't care about anything but her happiness and my son's health. Please, God, please, don't ruin an already fragile relationship with that woman. Please."

Silence stretched through the kitchen, and all Wren could hear was her own heartbeat as she waited for someone to say something. Never in her whole life would she have expected this from Jensen.

He didn't talk to anyone like that. Maybe on the ice, but not to the people who helped raise him! He wasn't ever that bold, but apparently, she was very wrong.

Then her father said, "I don't have any clue what you're talking about. We love that girl. Our relationship is fine."

"And that's part of the problem. You don't even know you're hurting her, you just call her dramatic. Given the fact that I'm basically a part of this family, more so than as just her husband, I hope you understand that I'm saying this because I love her and I love you two. So please do the right thing and fix this with her."

When she heard Jensen start to move, she took off through the living room, then the den, and entered the bedroom after he did. When he turned from looking in the bathroom, he jumped in surprise as she shut the door and said, "Holy fuck."

"Where the hell were you?"

But she shook her head. "You just went off on my parents!"

He shrugged. "I don't think I went off on them, but something had to be said. You were listening?" he asked, his brows pulling together. "You are a stalker."

But she didn't care. Reaching out, she took him by the biceps, her eyes searching his. "Jensen, no one has ever done anything like that for me."

His eyes were full of worry, but then she saw love too. Love for her, and just like that, he said, "I love you, Wren. I'd do anything for you. You know that."

The wall around her heart, deep down in her cold, dead soul, crumbled to pieces. She wrapped her arms around his neck, pressing her face into the middle of his chest. "I can't believe you did that."

Gathering her in his arms, he kissed the top of her head. "I'm surprised you can't believe that. When have I not been there for you?"

The answer was *never*, but her heart was in her throat as she clung to him, scared to death of the overwhelming feelings that were shaking her core. As her lip wobbled, her eyes clouded with tears before she looked up at him. He ran his thumb along his bottom lip. "I-I just—"

Before she could say whatever the hell she was going to say, the door opened and Wells was looking at them with a big grin on his face as he laughed. Her brother was tall, like Jensen, with dark green eyes and darker hair. Unlike her, he was thick but nowhere near overweight. He was strong. Massive. His face was full of sharp angles, and hair dusted his jaw where his grin grew. "So I heard some dude with a huge sac just went off on our parents? Surely it wasn't your husband?"

She looked up at Jensen, while he scoffed as he rolled his eyes, but her heart soared. "Yeah, it sure was."

# Chapter
## EIGHTEEN

"I hardly told them off."

Jensen's heart was in his throat. He hadn't meant to get carried away, but he'd felt he was still respectful. Maybe he hadn't been. But sitting there, watching his wife's shoulders fall and her face look so defeated, he couldn't handle it. Something inside him caught on fire, and he had to fix the situation. Not only for Wren, but for her parents too since he knew they loved her. They did, they were just too consumed with everything else to realize their mistake.

"Not what I heard. But Jesus, what did you do to my sister?" Wells asked, coming toward them and pulling her into his arms, hugging her tightly. "She's huge. Did you put a monster baby in her?"

Wells shared a look with Jensen, and Jensen's face warmed as he shrugged. "When we were home, Mum told her I was eleven pounds."

"Monster, I tell you. But look at you. All pretty and shit. I can't with how beautiful you are, and I have to stand beside you when I'm getting married? You're going to upstage me!" he teased, and Wren beamed up at him as she hugged him tightly.

"Everyone keeps saying that. I don't see it."

"Don't know how," her brother said before kissing her hard on the head and then reaching for Jensen. "I feel like it's been years, you big asshole. How are you?"

Hugging his best friend who was more like a brother, Jensen smiled. "I'm great."

"I can tell. Look at you two, all cute and cozy. Who would have thought it?"

Wren smirked as Jensen smiled over at her. "I always did."

"Ugh, even that's too gooey sweet for me, dude. Tuck it in." Wells flashed him a grin before winking. "So I guess I'll go out there and do damage control. I left Alex out there. Dad is probably trying to make sure he's really gay. Or that I am. Who knows? But one thing is for sure, don't come out until I fix things."

With that, Wells left. Jensen watched him go out the door and shut it. His stomach was in a knot, and while he didn't think he'd done anything wrong, he didn't like that his parents away from his parents felt he had gone off on them. Looking back at Wren, he found her watching him. "You want to go apologize?" she asked.

"No, but maybe I should just talk to them?"

She shrugged. "I mean, I think everything you said was truthful and real. I wish I would have said it, but then, I think I'm a glutton for punishment." She held up her hand. "Actually, from my years of psychoanalyzing myself, I felt that was the only way I got attention. So instead of pointing out what they're doing wrong, I got angry. I closed myself off."

His face scrunched up. "Do you do that a lot?"

"The angry part?"

He laughed. "No, the analyzing part. I know you get angry a lot."

She pursed her lips at him. "I feel that was a dig."

"One I made with love," he added, and she rolled her eyes.

"But yes, you have no clue how much I have to do it. I'm probably the only therapist in the world who probably needs therapy."

He laughed. "Haven't you said everyone needs therapy?"

"They do, me included."

He chewed on his lip as he shook his head. "Either way, it had to be said. I don't regret it, I just don't like the way they received it. But if it makes me the bad guy, oh well. Since they are aware, maybe they'll fix it."

Lying down on the bed, she cuddled into the pillows. "They won't."

"Wren, come on. Give them the benefit of the doubt. They love you. I know they do."

She shrugged. "I mean, I know they do, but it will always be everything else before me. I'm easy, according to them, as long as they don't piss me off and I get 'dramatic.'"

Jensen looked back at the door, hearing Wells out there with his parents. "I don't know."

"I don't think you should apologize."

He looked back at her. "Because you're enjoying this."

"Oh, I am," she teased, her lips curving. "Never has anyone stood up for me like that. I'm so hot, I'm on fire."

"Okay, Corny Christina, relax."

Her sputtering laughter made him smile as he looked back at the door, unsure what to do. Should he apologize?

"I've got an idea."

He looked back at her. "Yeah?"

"Why don't we take a nap?" she suggested. "We all know I'm always tired, so a nap is good, and we can cuddle."

"That's unfair. You know I love naps, and I love cuddling with you."

"I know, I'm evil."

"You are," he decided, crawling into the bed and wrapping his arms around her. "Maybe it's good to give them a minute. Give Wells time. I'll wait."

"Yeah, give them a minute. Let Wells tell them the same thing, and let it work itself out. Because you aren't wrong, Jensen. You weren't rude, you were stern. And I, for one, really appreciate it." Cupping his face, she kissed his top lip. "A lot. It means a lot to me that you did that."

Holding her gaze, he ran his finger along her collarbone. "It was nothing. You did it for me with Ophelia."

Her face changed, her eyes darkening as they narrowed with a sinister gleam. "I hate that bitch."

He chuckled. "Yeah, I think that's pretty much established."

"She's a cunt."

"She is."

"All fucking high and mighty. Man, she's the one who missed out on a great guy."

Jensen's lips quirked at the side. "Oh yeah?"

"Yeah, and like I told her mama, 'Her loss, my gain.'"

"Oh," he asked, his ears perking up. "I'm a gain for you? When did this happen?"

She rolled her eyes. "You know you are."

His face broke into a grin as he kissed her chin. "Still nice to hear you say it."

"Okay, Needy Nelly." He laughed as she smiled, leaning into him. "Hey."

His laughter subsided, and he closed his eyes as she cuddled into him. "Yeah?"

"Something was bothering me when we were at home with your parents."

Surprised by that since he'd assumed she would tell him something else sweet about him being a gain, he opened his eyes as he leaned his lips into her temple. "What's that?"

"Did they not know that you couldn't have kids?"

His heart stopped as his mouth went dry. He completely hadn't seen the conversation going this way. Swallowing hard, he shook his head. "No, they didn't. No one knew but Ophelia and me, and then Vaughn and Wells."

"They never suspected? Because you said you two were trying for a while."

"Nope, it was never brought up on either side of the family, and when she cheated on me, getting pregnant, everyone was so mad she did that to me that no one asked why. Her mom didn't talk to her for a year, neither did her dad. People were devastated."

"Not you, though?"

He chuckled a bit. "I was embarrassed more than anything. But everyone acted as if she had cheated on them and not me, so I just ignored it. Did me. Thankfully, it happened during NateWay going up, so I focused on that. Oh, and those shorts you always wore."

Laughing, she shook her head before cuddling into him and nibbling on his chin. "Can I ask something else?"

"Do you still have those shorts?"

"Jensen!" she laughed, and he smiled. "I don't, and I doubt they'd fit even if I did."

"Still like to see ya try," he said, and she bit him softly as he laughed.

"Anyway," she singsonged as he cuddled deeper beside her. She was so warm, so soft, and smelled so damn good. "I know you don't like talking about this, but I've wanted to know this for a while."

Without opening his eyes, he said, "Then ask."

"Have you been back? To check and see if you still can't have kids?"

That made him open his eyes. He stared at the wall above her head, and his heart stopped dead cold in his chest as his eyes started to blur. "No, I haven't."

"Why?"

"I don't want to know. I sort of gave up on it."

She looked up at him, her brows pulled together. "You? Give up?"

He shrugged, his heart hurting. "I figured that if it were meant to be, it would happen. Plus, I already felt like a loser, not even a man, so I didn't want to make that any worse."

Her eyes softened as she cupped his face with one hand. "Oh, Jenny."

"It's fine. Really."

"It's not, though. I can see that," she whispered, her lips brushing his chin. "But that doesn't make you a man, Jensen. I mean, it does because that's how babies come. But when I look at you, I don't see that you're a man by your ability to father children. I see that you're a man by your ability to give love."

He met her gaze, and his heart picked up in speed. "Yeah?"

"Yeah, and you love hard."

"Eh, that's only for you."

She gave him a look. "No, you love everyone, you care for everyone, and you'd do anything for anyone."

He inhaled deeply. "While that's true, the only person who truly matters, and whom I care so much for in the hopes of making them fall in love with me, is you. Only you, Wren."

Her eyes dilated a bit as she leaned into him. "It's working."

His eyebrows rose. "It is?"

"Yeah, all of it. It's working."

His heart jumped up in his throat from the tone of her voice and the fear in it. "That's a good thing, Wren."

"It would be if I could stop being an asshole and let it happen and not worry about it all coming down like a decaying sack of crap."

He blinked. "That is a vivid image."

"My mind is something insane."

"I know," he answered, kissing her cheek. "And I love it. All of it."

She shook her head. "You shouldn't. You should run."

"Never," he answered, kissing her once more. "You're mine, Wren Monroe."

Her lips curved as she pressed her nose to him, her eyes playful but still full of concern. Concern he wished like hell he could ease. Wasn't he doing that, though? He did everything he thought she needed. What more could he do? Pressing her lips to his, she whispered, "Which means you're mine, Jensen Monroe."

He nodded. "Completely."

They shared a sweet smile as she glided her nose along his. "I want to be like you. Completely in."

"You aren't?"

She bit her lip, unsure of herself. "I don't know." While it hurt, he was thankful she was honest. "I don't want you to leave me. Every time I fall for someone, they're gone before I can say it."

"Well," he said, capturing her mouth with his for a long, drawn-out kiss he knew they both wanted and needed. As she melted into him, he held her close before pulling away only slightly. "I know for a fact that if you told me you loved me right now, I wouldn't run. I'd be right here, telling you right back that I loved you too. You can try it. Like a test run."

Her face broke into a grin as her cheeks flushed deep with color. "I can't. Not yet."

He didn't like that. It should come easy. But while some things were easy for him, he understood they weren't the same for her. Even if it did frustrate the living fuck out of him, he understood. He knew it going in. He cleared his throat, and she looked up at him. "Why?"

Her brows pulled together. "What? Why I can't say that?"

"No," he said, shaking his head. "Sorry, no. Though, I'd love an answer for that if you have one."

Her smile faltered a bit as she held his gaze, and his breath completely stopped as he got lost in her. Her mouth moved, but nothing came out before she pressed her lips together, swallowing hard. "I mean... I feel... I feel the same."

272 | TONI ALEO

He glared. "You feel…you feel the same? Seriously?"

She smiled. "I know, it's pathetic."

Shaking his head in complete amazement, and not the good kind, he muttered, "Yeah."

"Jensen, I've told you from the beginning, I'm the epitome of a perfect disaster."

He couldn't help it, he smiled, pressing his nose to hers. "And like I've said from the beginning, that is everything I want. You. I want you."

Her eyes were wide as she shook her head. "All of me? Even the really annoying, unsure part of me?"

"Every single part."

She inhaled with her whole body before exhaling just as hard. "I do really feel something for you, Jensen. I promise. I do. It's just scary, and my track—"

He smiled. "I know, baby."

"I suck, I know."

"You don't suck, you're just frustrating." She swallowed hard, her shoulders drooping before he added, "But that's not what I wanted to know. Since I knew the answer to all that."

"Oh?"

"Why'd you ask me that? About me having kids?"

She blinked once and then twice, holding his gaze as she shrugged. "I just wanted to know."

"Why?"

"Because."

"Because, why? Do you want more kids?" She bit her lip as she shrugged, and just like that, his heart was in his throat. "Wren?"

"I don't know," she answered quickly. "I just hate the thought that you think you can't have kids when maybe you can."

Pulling back a bit, he held her gaze. "I mean, if I can, then awesome. But by the grace of God, in the meantime, I have my boy," he said, his hand coming down and resting on her belly. "Right?"

"Yes, please. Don't think I meant anything by this. I was just asking."

"It seems like more than that, and you've never asked."

"You don't like talking about it," she said simply, looking down at where his hand was on her stomach, rubbing softly. "If I don't like talking about shit that bothers me, I don't want to ask you to."

Silence stretched between them as voices from the kitchen leaked through the door. He didn't pay them any mind, though. His eyes were on Wren. "While I appreciate that, you can ask me anything, Wren. I'll tell you anything you want."

She worked her lip as her hands came up, resting on his chest. "Still. I deal with people opening up all the time, and I know how much it can suck. I don't feel you should have to too."

"But we're married. We're supposed to be open books to each other."

She scoffed at that. "Please, you don't want me opening *The Fucked-Up Book of Wren* to you."

"You mean like the part that involves the douche who knocked you up?"

Her eyes widened. "I guess."

"Because I pretty much know everything else."

She seemed uneasy as she exhaled. "Yeah, I guess you do."

She held his gaze, her eyes burning into his as he spoke. "Let me ask you something, Wren." Her eyes filled with something—fear, anxiety, he wasn't sure—but she didn't move as he asked, "Does he live here?"

Looking away, she chewed on the inside of her lip. "Don't make me answer that, please." He watched her profile as tears filled her eyes. "He doesn't matter. You're our no-named son's father, so why does he matter?"

"Because I want to know. I want to know what man disrespected you and left you high and dry. And after I beat his ever-loving ass, I want to thank him for giving me the greatest gift in the world." She looked back at him, her lip trembling as tears leaked out the sides of her eyes. "A woman I will love until my dying day and a son I will not only love the same, but be the best father to."

Breathless, she shook her head. "Jensen, please, he doesn't matter. What you just said is all that matters."

"True, but obviously he does. To me, at least."

"He doesn't. Not even a bit. Don't think of him. I don't."

"You don't?"

"No," she answered, her face scrunched up in disgust. "The only man I'm currently thinking of is you, and that's all I care about. So just let it go."

"Wren, I think it would be best if you told—"

"I'm done talking about this," she said, turning over and giving him her back. "And I know that makes me a fucking child, but I refuse to give that motherfucker any fucking power over us."

Confused, Jensen threw his hands up. "How the hell would that give him any power by my knowing who he is?"

"Because it will," she answered, pulling the blankets up and by her face. "Goodnight."

"It's three p.m."

"Good fucking afternoon, then," she spat back at him, and he shook his head, falling to his back as he stared up at the ceiling. He wasn't sure what the hell was the issue, why she didn't want to talk about it, but he was getting really fucking annoyed. It was frustrating. Fucking frustrating. But then, she was right. The dude didn't matter. Or, did he? Jensen wasn't sure, but one thing was for sure, between her not admitting her damn feelings and the douche who knocked her up, he was sure to lose his fucking mind.

Especially when he couldn't shake his thoughts that centered around the guy. Or the dread that filled him every time his mind wandered that way because that trepidation was born of true fear. He wasn't sure if it was because he knew the dude mattered, or if it was related to her earlier statement, that she thought Jensen was going to leave her. There had to be a reason for it, because he was doing everything he could to ease her concern.

That alone worried him more than her unsure feelings.

Her feelings, he could handle, but a wayward deadbeat daddy was something Jensen wasn't ready for.

Because the baby in her belly was his.

Plain and simple.

No one would ever take that away from him.

\* \* \*

NOT LOOKING AT JENSEN, Wren cuddled deeper into the bed with a moan. "Vaughn won't care."

Jensen looked back at her as he buckled his belt. "Probably not, but I want you there."

"I know, and I'm sorry, but I didn't sleep well. I'm so tired, and my head hurts like mad. I just want to sleep. I'll be grumpy. You don't want to hang with me when I'm grumpy."

He looked away toward the mirror as he fixed the top of his shirt. It was a button-up, plaid with purple and black that apparently Vaughn would be wearing too. His off-season beard was growing in really nice and thick, almost making him unrecognizable. She was finding it turned her on more than she liked. But then, maybe it was him. All of him that had her trembling in her skin at the mere sight of him. "Your grumpiness doesn't bother me."

"I just don't want to ruin your time, or even anyone else's. I'm so tired."

He looked back at her in the mirror, and she could see it in his eyes. He didn't believe a damn word she was saying. "You were fine to go the other day."

"I know. I'm just not up to it."

"You sure it isn't more?"

Hell yeah, it was more than that! She was scared. Everything was happening so quickly. Her feelings were overwhelming for her, and Jensen was just... He was just...him. Jensen. Perfection in the form of a huge-ass goalie who somehow loved her insane ass. And watching him go at her parents? Yeah, that annihilated any walls around her heart and freaked her out. Because as much as she wanted to look into his dark brown eyes and tell him she loved him, she knew she had to tell him about Bradley.

She just couldn't.

Between being embarrassed and her general hate for the guy, she couldn't. How would Jensen react? They had all grown up together. Bradley lived right down the road, five houses down, her whole life. He used to play hockey with the boys. He was the fourth amigo sometimes, but he was so much younger than everyone, so he was often treated that way and left behind a lot. But still, everyone knew Bradley, loved him, and for him to do this—to Wren—it would be ugly.

Shit, was she protecting him?

No, no, she was protecting herself because she couldn't help but feel like everyone would think it was her fault.

He was allegedly a stand-up guy. Loved his momma, his sister, great with his nephews, and was very successful. The guy Wren was dealing with wasn't the guy everyone knew. But Wren was Wren. She had slept around, she had fun, she was stubborn, and as her mother put it, dramatic. They'd all assume he would have wanted Wren and the baby, but she blew him off. Or something along those lines. No one would believe her.

Well, Jensen would.

Wouldn't he?

"You've been quiet, babe."

She shook her head. "I've been very vocal with you."

"You haven't spoken to your parents."

"'Cause I need time to think."

When she met his gaze, his eyes were dark. "How's that going?"

"Awful. I basically called myself a dumbass at least twenty times and decided the sooner we go home, the better."

"Why?"

"Because I want to go home. Our home. I hate it here."

"See, I don't think you've been like this before. Yeah, you and your parents have your issues, but last time I checked, you loved coming home. You used to come all the time. So what happened to change that?"

Bradley.

Glancing at the clock, she exhaled hard. "You're going to be late."

"Wren—"

"Jenny, please. I'm exhausted. Go have loads of fun."

A silence fell between them as he walked to her side of the bed, sitting on the edge as his hand came to rest behind her back, his other cupping her face. "I can't have loads of fun without you. Maybe a little fun, but not loads."

Her lips curved up as she leaned into his hand. "Then go have some fun."

"I wish you'd come."

She shook her head. "I'm tired and not even the least bit ready. I would make you late, and I just don't want to go."

He nodded slowly. "Okay."

Looking up at him, she could see the wariness in his eyes as he leaned down, pressing his lips to hers. Closing her eyes, she covered his hand with hers as she deepened the kiss, twining her tongue along his. She felt horrible. Guilty. And she knew she should tell him the real reason she didn't want to go to the Cup day, but as he pulled back, a smile faint on his lips, she said nothing.

"Call me if you decide to come."

"I will," she answered as he kissed her once more. "Have a tiny bit of fun."

He smiled as he got up, squeezing her hip. "You enjoy your nap."

"Oh, I will."

He laughed as he gathered his wallet and keys before leaving the room, shutting the door softly behind him. As she let out a long breath, her shoulders fell, and she leaned back into the pillows. Without her even realizing it, a lone tear rolled down her cheek, down her jaw and onto her chest as she bit her lip.

Closing her eyes to keep the rest of the tears in, she couldn't help but think she was playing with fire. Coming home, bringing Jensen as her husband, and him claiming the baby as his was bound to produce flames. She wasn't sure when or how, but she was sure it would blow up in her face. That alone should give her reason to tell him, but when did she ever listen to reason?

CRAWLING OUT OF BED, Wren slid up a pair of cloth shorts and then tugged down her big Assassins tee before pulling her hair up. She had slept for a couple of hours and felt somewhat refreshed, but her earlier thoughts were weighing heavily on her. She wasn't sure what to do, but she was pretty sure if she didn't figure it out, she could lose Jensen in the process. Something that she did not want —at all.

Huh. Funny how things had changed.

Wren pulled open the door to her old childhood room that, praise God, her mother had ordered a bigger bed for since trying to get her pregnant ass and Jensen's long ass in her old bed would have been a feat. She headed out into the hall, on her way to the kitchen. Her mother had ordered a new living room suite earlier that year, trading in the trusty yellow love seat for matching brown recliners and a nice, cream-colored couch. Pictures of everyone growing up were everywhere, and they brought a grin to her face. This was her home. But lately, she hadn't wanted to be there, and she didn't like that. This was supposed to be her safe haven.

Now, she was finding that her safe haven was Jensen's arms.

She expected the house to be quiet, but the radio was playing in the kitchen. Her mother must have left it on when she left. Or, so Wren thought, but when she entered the kitchen, her mom was sitting at the bar, all the wedding planning stuff in front of her. Wren hadn't spoken to either of her parents since Jensen had had it out with them, but the last she had checked, they were both supposed to go to the Cup day.

As Elaine looked up at Wren, her smile was very unsure. "Hey, honey, how are you feeling?"

Wren cleared her throat as she came into the kitchen, heading for the fridge. "Better. I was just really tired."

"Oh, good. Jensen was worried, and since he couldn't skip, I told him I'd stay."

Wren's brow rose as she reached for the OJ. "Miss gushing over Vaughn and Jensen to all your old biddies? I'm surprised. Plus, didn't you throw the party for them?"

Elaine waved her off. "I did, but there are people there running it. Vaughn wouldn't let me do it all myself."

"Oh, good, you don't need any more stress." Reaching for an apple, Wren grabbed a knife to cut it. "But you don't need to stay, Mom. Go. I'm fine."

"No, I want to stay." Wren chewed on the inside of her cheek as she cut the apple slowly, unsure what her mother was doing. "Do you want me to make you something? Emma told me this morning that all she did was cook for you and sneak you food when Jensen wasn't looking."

Wren beamed as she nodded. "Yeah, it was funny. Between her and Ant, I was well fed, despite Jenny's efforts at enforcing portion control."

Elaine smiled back as she nodded. "I see he makes you walk."

"Yeah, I bitch the whole time."

"He's sweet."

"He is."

"And Emma is the best cook I know."

"She is. It was great. We had a blast."

Elaine's smile faltered a bit as she looked down. "And then you come here, and you're not having fun."

"I didn't say that."

"You don't have to. I mean, you only come out of your room for food. I've known Jensen for fifteen years, and never once has he raised his voice to me. But he did, and that hurts, Wren."

Wren shook her head. "I didn't tell him to say that to you—"

"I didn't say you did, and neither his tone nor his words hurt, Wren. It was that everything he said might be true."

Wren looked up suddenly and her brows touched. "What?"

Holding up her hands, Elaine reached over, taking Wren's hand in hers. "Do you truly feel that way? That we ignore you?"

Blinking, unsure of herself, she shrugged. "I mean, yeah, sometimes. It's real Wells-heavy around here. Sprinkle in some Jensen and Vaughn, and yeah, no room for me."

Elaine looked stricken. "I don't mean for it to be. He's just so needy. I always knew he was gay. I also knew that your father wouldn't take it well, so I think I baby him because of it." She held her hands up. "Which isn't right at all, I know this, but you've always been so independent. Always reading, always watching those murder shows and crazy-people movies. You always kept to yourself."

Swallowing hard past the lump in her throat, Wren held her mother's gaze. "Because no one had time for me."

"Wren, no. That's not true. We just thought you didn't need us."

"A girl always needs her mom and dad. But I guess Wells needed you two more. Oh, and then there was Jensen."

Tears flooded Elaine's eyes as she squeezed Wren's hand. "I never meant for you to feel that way. Why didn't you say something?"

"Because there was no point, and if I tried, you guys said I was being dramatic and ignored me."

Letting Wren's hand go, Elaine shook her head as her tears fell. "Because it was so out of left field. You'd just start screaming and yelling for no damn reason, or so I thought."

"I just wanted to be heard," Wren whispered, her own eyes clouding with tears. Watching her mother wipe her eyes, Wren ached as her tears started to fall while the silence stretched between them.

"I'm not mad at you, or even Daddy. I just hate being here because of it. Because I'm so pathetic that I want to be noticed, that I want you guys to care about me. I feel like you both just brush me to the side because, yes, I am independent and, yes, I can take care of myself. But sometimes, it's nice just to know that you guys want to be there for me. That you worry for me. Because I don't know that. I mean, Mom, I am seven months pregnant, and you never had a clue."

"Because you hid it! You never said anything."

"You should have been able to tell something was up."

"I did, and I asked. You ignored me!"

"You didn't try hard enough. Listen, I know you both love me, I do, I know that. But you have to because I'm your kid."

"No, Wren, we love you because of the person you are. Because you are independent and strong and beautiful. Lord, you're so damn smart, my love. I never meant for you to feel like that. I don't call to check up because you wouldn't tell me if I asked anyway. You're very private, and I respect that. Maybe, as your mother, I should push, but I'm always worried you'll shut me out."

"I'd try. Ask Jensen, I'm really good at it. It's a character flaw I'm working on. But, Mom, when you call me, it's usually about Wells or even what needs to be done for Wells. You don't call to see how I'm doing unless you get a call from Jensen saying he's gonna marry me."

Elaine laughed, her eyes full of remorse and tears. "That was one hell of a call." Shaking her head, she wiped her tears, her makeup smearing as she let out a long breath. "I hate that this has happened. That a wedge has been put between us. Your father is stricken and wants to fix it, but you know how he is. He just grumbles and bitches about money. He doesn't do feelings well."

Wren smiled. "I probably get it from him, then."

She laughed. "Oh, my love, you are your daddy made over— with my beauty, of course," she teased since Wren looked nothing like her mother and everything like her father. "But still, honey, I'm extremely sorry. Truly. I am."

Meeting her mother's gaze, Wren wiped her own tears away. "I know, Mom. You don't do it to hurt me. I just don't think you notice."

"I didn't. And that's my fault. But I know now, okay?"

"Okay," Wren said slowly, hoping like hell that her mother meant her words.

"I love you. A lot."

"I love you too, Mom."

"Good," she said, kissing Wren's palm before reaching for a sheet of paper. "Now, names. Because my grandson will have a damn good one if I have anything to do with it."

Popping an apple slice in her mouth, Wren smiled as she chewed, and her mother spat off names left and right, marking them off and then bolding others. Wren knew darn well things with her parents weren't fixed completely, but they were heading that way, and at least that had her smiling. She loved her parents, she loved her brother, she did. But most of all, she loved Jensen.

A lot. And he deserved to know that since he went above and beyond to tell her how he felt.

Problem was, she wasn't sure how to say those three words that taunted her.

She also had the issue of Bradley.

Yeah, life wasn't easy, and that was probably her fault.

Which wasn't anything new.

# Chapter NINETEEN

*Wren: You didn't tell me my mom was home.*

*Jensen: I didn't know she was staying until I was walking out the door. At that point, I figured, surprise!*

*Wren: Well, actually, it has been.*

*Jensen: Yeah?*

*Wren: Yes, while I'm sure you're having TONS of fun, Mom and I talked, and now we're picking out baby names.*

Jensen's face broke into a grin as he stared down at his phone. The party for the Cup was going great. Like Jensen had done, Vaughn was doing a town tournament. But since the town was so much bigger than Jensen's back home, they actually had teams of five instead of just throwing all the kids out there. Way bigger and loads of fun. The Vaughn Johansson Rink was done up with so much purple and black, there was no denying Vaughn was an Assassin. The Cup sat in a glass box in the middle of the score box, while little kids pressed their faces against the glass to get a look. People were everywhere, trying to see their children and then catch a glimpse of Jensen and Vaughn. It was one hell of a shindig.

He stood against the boards with Vaughn and Wells, and they watched as the final two battled it out for a chance at a picture with the Cup and also to hold it.

*Jensen: Picking out names without me, rude.*

*Wren: Hehe. What do you think of Gunner? Or Alec?*

He thought that over, tapping his finger against the phone.

"Gunner Monroe? Alec Monroe? Both are good, solid hockey names."

Glancing over to his best friend, who was also horribly nosy when it came to looking at Jensen's phone, Jensen nodded. "Yeah. I like Gunner."

Vaughn nodded. "I like Alec better."

Wells looked over. "But it's too close to Alex, my fiancé."

They all agreed. "Yeah, so Alec is out."

*Jensen: Alec is too close to Alex. The dude your brother is marrying.*

*Wren: Ew, right, okay. So, Gunner is a front-runner, then? Dad picked it out. Told Mom last night. I asked Emma and Ant, they like it.*

*Jensen: Yeah. Put it on the list.*

*Wren: Cool. Have no fun.*

Jensen laughed. Thank God she was in a better mood.

*Jensen: Done. No fun is being had. I'm miserable.*

*Wren: Good.*

A playful grin pulled at his lips as he tucked his phone into his pocket before he leaned on the boards. But then something occurred to him. "Wouldn't you like to have your nephew named after your soon-to-be husband?"

Wells looked over at him, shaking his head. "No. Not at all. That's weird."

Vaughn scoffed at that, while Jensen held Wells's gaze. "Really?"

"Really. It's weird."

"Oh, okay," Jensen answered as Vaughn laughed.

"Trouble in paradise, bro?"

Thankfully, Vaughn said it because Jensen was thinking it. "No," Wells spat back, rolling his eyes. "We're fine."

"Yeah, we totally believe that," Vaughn teased, and Jensen chuckled.

"Yeah, no." When Wells glared over at Jensen, he shrugged. "We know you, dude. Spill."

"I'm not spilling to you two dweebs."

Vaughn held his hand up. "My woman says I'm a dork, not a dweeb, so you can tell me."

"My wife would agree," Jensen added with a grin, and Wells let out a sigh, annoyance all over his face.

"It's nothing. Just a tiff."

"Dude, the wedding is in like a week. Tiffs aren't allowed at this point," Vaughn said, leaning his elbows on the wall to look over at Wells. "Tiffs turn into full-on blowouts."

Wells shook his head, but Jensen added, "Unless you're both stressed. The wedding seems like a production."

"It is," Wells agreed, swallowing hard. "But he's being impossible, and it's pissing me off. We'll be fine, though. This isn't the first time."

Jensen's brows touched as the horn went off for a goal. Turning his attention to the ice in the middle of the rink, they all cheered as if they'd seen the goal, when really, none of them had. As the boy who scored high-fived his team members, he skated to them, tapping their hands too before going to the middle of the rink for the drop of the puck.

"Attaboy!" Vaughn called out as Jensen smiled, Wells doing the same.

When the puck dropped, Jensen looked back to Wells. "What? What's going on?"

Rolling his eyes, Wells exhaled hard as he tucked his hands into his pockets. "He thinks I'm still in love with Matty."

"You are," Vaughn said simply, and Jensen threw him a dirty look. "What? He is."

"You're not helping," Jensen scolded before looking back to Wells. "I mean, are you?"

Wells shrugged. "I don't know. I mean, I guess I'll always love him, and I hate how we ended things, but I do love Alex. I do." When he looked to Vaughn, he glared. "I do, asshat."

Vaughn held his hands up. "I didn't say anything!"

"You don't have to. Your fucking face says it all. Asshole," Wells grumbled, leaning into the boards as he watched the game. "He's being difficult and demanding shit. Like deleting Matty from my Instagram and my phone and shit. I told Alex he had nothing to worry about, and he doesn't. But he wants to know why I won't do what he asks."

Jensen whistled nervously. "Yeah, man, that's something you need to figure out. 'Cause if Wren wanted me to delete someone from my phone or social media, I'd do it."

Wells glared. "Because you'd walk through fire for that girl."

"Damn right, I would," Jensen laughed, a grin pulling at his lips. "'Cause that's how it is when you love someone. Right, Vaughn?"

"I mean, maybe not fire, but I'd walk through some glass for Brie."

When a jab came to his back, they all laughed, turning to find Brie standing behind him with a huge plate of nachos in her hand. "I'll kill you dead."

Taking a nacho, Vaughn nodded to her. "I mean, I'd walk through a volcano for my love."

"That's better," she said, cuddling into his side as she munched on her nachos. "Where is my bestie?"

Vaughn moaned as Jensen laughed. "She wasn't feeling well."

"I should have said that."

"Hey!"

She beamed up at Vaughn. "Even."

"Even."

Jensen laughed as he leaned into Wells. "Don't worry about it, man, it will work out. But if, for some reason, you wanna call off the wedding, please let me know first so Wren and I can leave before your mom finds out."

Wells laughed at that as he nodded, holding his fist out. "Deal."

Jensen tapped his fist to Wells's and they shared a smile, but Jensen knew Wells would be okay. Wells loved Alex, Jensen knew that. Though he didn't care for the guy much, Alex was Wells's dude, so Jensen would treat him like he did Wells, with nothing but love. But Jensen wouldn't be naïve to the situation. Wells had loved Matty like Jensen loved Wren, and that kind of thing didn't quit. He knew that firsthand, and Jensen wasn't sure what that meant for Wells and Alex.

Either way, he prayed he and Wren weren't there for the aftermath of whatever the hell happened.

"Where is Alex?" Vaughn asked them, and Jensen glared.

Shrugging, Wells was looking at the ice. "He didn't want to come."

Vaughn made a disgruntled face. "Well, that's not good. We are family, and you gotta celebrate with us. What, he doesn't like us?"

Jensen jabbed him with his elbow when he noticed Wells getting upset. "Let it go."

Vaughn glared. "But, really—"

Before he could finish, though, someone said, "There they are! The Turbulent Three."

Holy shit, he hadn't heard that in years. As he turned around, a grin covered his face when he saw who had said it.

"Bradley Washington! Man, how are you?" Jensen said, taking his hand and being drawn into a man-slapping hug. He hadn't seen Bradley in years. Every time Jensen was home, Bradley was usually up in Colorado Springs where his law firm was, so they kept missing each other. "It's great to see you."

"You too, man. I was worried I'd miss everything. I was hauling ass back. How are you?"

"Great, thanks," he said as Vaughn hugged him tightly and then Wells.

"I just saw you, like, last week," Wells laughed, and Bradley nodded as Vaughn brought Brie out, wrapping his arms around her.

"This is my girl, Brie, and, yes, I knocked her up."

"I wouldn't expect anything less," Bradley teased as he shook her hand. "And I have to say, you did good, Jo."

"Damn right, I did," he said, kissing Brie's cheek as she rolled her eyes.

"Nice to meet you."

"You too," he said, clapping his hands together. "So you guys are going to have to let me buy you a beer, celebrate this big win!"

"Yeah, we'd love that. Because I love beer, especially free beer," Vaughn said, and everyone laughed.

"Yeah, 'cause I'm sure you're hurting for money."

Vaughn pressed his lips together. "Yes, help me, I'm poor."

"Stop! Don't listen to him," Brie laughed, smacking Vaughn's chest. "He's insane."

"Hey, Shanna! Over here!"

Everyone looked to where Wells was yelling as Shanna grinned, coming over toward them, a baby on her hip and one holding her hand. "Hey, everyone!"

"Hey," they all greeted as she handed off one of the kids to Bradley.

"I was worried I wouldn't be able to find you guys. This is some crowd. Congratulations, guys!" She leaned over, kissing Jensen's and then Vaughn's cheek before she waved Wells off. "I just saw you."

"You did, but I think you're more gorgeous than yesterday."

She laughed. "I combed my hair." Everyone laughed as Jensen looked Shanna over. She hadn't changed since they were kids. Still with the big, dewy eyes and thin as all get-out. He wasn't sure he believed what Wren had said about Shanna judging her because it seemed to him she was exactly the same, and still kind. But then, he had only been around her for like five seconds, so what did he know? Her brother, though, was bigger, goofier-looking. Jensen never thought Bradley would do much with his life, but he had been wrong. Big-time lawyer, but still put out a douchey vibe.

When Shanna met his gaze, Jensen smiled as she beamed before saying, "I hear I need to send you an even bigger congratulations."

His grin grew. "Thanks. We're really excited."

"Where is Wren?"

"She wasn't feeling well. She's always so tired, so she's back at the house."

Her shoulders fell. "Well, hell, I wanted to see her. I haven't spoken to her in forever," she said sadly, and Jensen nodded, unsure what to say.

But then Bradley asked, "Wait, what?"

Shanna looked back at him. "You know, Wren and Jensen got married, are having a baby! Isn't that awesome? I always knew you guys would end up together. She had such a crush on you when we were growing up. Even after that horrible kiss you two had."

Vaughn and Wells sputtered with laughter as Jensen glared. "It wasn't that bad!"

"That's not what I heard," she laughed, and even Brie was laughing. Everyone was, except for Bradley.

"Wait, what? You married Wren? Wells's baby sister?"

Jensen eyed him as he nodded slowly. "Yeah, about a month ago. I mean, I don't see her as a baby," he laughed, waggling his eyebrows at Wells, to which he gagged.

"Please. Don't."

The laughter surrounded Jensen, and he missed Wren. He wished she were there.

"You married Wren Lemiere."

Looking back at Bradley, Jensen furrowed his brow. "Yeah, why?"

Bradley protested, shaking his head. "Dude, it's weird. I never saw that coming."

Shanna scoffed. "What? They were totally hot for each other! For, like, ever."

That made Jensen smile, but he didn't know how he felt about Bradley's confused gaze or the way his mouth was still hanging open. "I didn't realize."

"Yeah, Jenny here has been sticky-sweet for Wrenny-boo his whole life. Now he's got her, got himself a son coming along, and yeah, we're proud of the man he is becoming," Vaughn teased, and Jensen rolled his eyes. "He finally lost his virginity."

"Stuff it, asshat," Jensen shot back as they laughed at his expense. "You're doing the same thing. Shit, so are you."

Wells shrugged. "Hey, I'm happy for you."

"So am I, I just like teasing you," Vaughn said, smacking him on the back.

"So, it's a boy?"

Confused, Jensen looked back at Bradley as Vaughn said, "What?"

"Wren is having a boy?"

Jensen's face scrunched up, and he couldn't help but notice that Bradley looked as if he was having a coronary. "Yeah, she's due in September. We haven't named him yet. We are kind of sucking at that," he laughed, trying to ignore Bradley, though it wasn't working. Something didn't seem right about his reaction to all this.

"I told you, Vaughn is a solid name."

"So is Wells."

"No and no," Jensen said simply as Brie and Shanna beamed up at him.

"I really wanna see her. Maybe we can all do lunch? I know Jay would love to see you again. He's at home with my oldest, he's got strep."

"Oh, that's too bad. Let me talk to her, and she'll get ahold of you. I'll make sure of it," Jensen said sweetly, though Shanna didn't seem convinced.

"Wow," Bradley said again, and now Jensen was glaring. "I can't believe it."

He wasn't sure how to take that. Staring his old friend down, Jensen almost told him to shove it, but Shanna beat him to it.

"Believe what, Brad? People have babies and get married all the time. You just did it, so why is it weird for Wren and Jensen? You're being stupid, stop." Shanna scowled, shaking her head. "He isn't too bright."

But Jensen wasn't sure that was the issue.

No, he was pretty sure it was more than that.

* * *

"Dad is pretty set on Gunner. He said it again when you guys got home."

Looking over at Jensen from the list she and her mom had made that afternoon, Wren pursed her lips. "But I don't have a middle name to go with it."

Jensen was leaned back in the seat, his hand hanging loosely on the wheel as he drove up to Colorado Springs. Since their little town didn't have a trendy club, as Alex had put it, for everyone to gather at, they were making the trek up to the nearest one, which was about thirty minutes away. Plus, Alex wanted everyone to get dressed up and be ritzy for the night. And boy, did her husband come sporting. He wore a nice, fresh blue suit that hugged his thighs perfectly, and Wren was getting hot staring at him from the seat beside him. His hair was brushed to the side, his face freshly shaven since apparently Wells said he wouldn't have Jensen looking like a lumberjack in his wedding pictures. She sort of missed it, and soon, she found herself reaching out, cupping his chin.

"I miss your beard." He smiled before nipping at her hand as she giggled, letting her hand fall to his thigh. "So what do you think?"

He had been quiet since he'd gotten home. She was pretty sure he was pussyfooting around her parents. Though, they both hugged him tightly and told him they loved him dearly, she knew he was nervous about upsetting them. Even when they were getting ready, he seemed to be in his own world. "I miss my beard too."

She smacked his thigh. "I mean the name, dork."

"Oh, yeah," he said, flashing her a grin. "Gunner...Gunner, yup, I got nothing."

She laughed. "Gunner Antoine?"

"No."

"Gunner Winston?"

"Ew, no."

"Gunner Wells?"

"Wren, no."

She giggled. "Gunner Vau—"

"You say it, and I swear on everything holy, I'll never put my mouth between your legs again."

That had her laughing from her gut, shaking her head. "Fine, Gunner... What's your middle name?"

His lips quirked. "You don't know my middle name?"

"No."

"Jesus, what kind of wife are you?"

She scoffed. "'Cause you know mine?"

"Yeah, it's Josephine."

She shrugged. "That's cause my mom yelled it all the time. What's yours?"

He laughed. "Cade."

A grin came over her lips. "Cade? I love that. Jensen Cade Monroe. That's hot."

"I'll tell my mom you think so," he teased, and she beamed over at him.

Saying the name over and over again in her head, she finally said it out loud. "Gunner Cade Monroe?"

He nodded, obviously thinking it over. "I think I love it."

"I do too!" she gushed, circling Gunner on her list and then writing Cade beside it. "Did we finally name our kiddo?"

Covering her hand with his, he nodded. "I think we did."

"Hear that, kiddo? You got a name now, it's Gunner Cade. What do you think?"

She waited for something, a kick or movement, but her little guy must have been sleeping.

"What did he say?" Jensen asked.

"Nothing, he's probably sleeping."

"Well, if he's anything like you, that's definitely a possibility."

She shot him a look as she said, "Har, har, har."

Kissing her palm, he held her hand at his lips as he pulled into the trendy nightclub that Alex had picked out for them. It was large and made of brick, but she knew the inside would be insane. Lots of techno music and lights. Parking the car, he kissed her hand once more before looking over at her. "You seem to be in a good mood."

She smiled with a shrug. "It was good to have that talk with my mom."

"I'm sure, and I'm glad you did."

"Me too," she agreed, her eyes meeting his. He looked so damn good, so handsome that she found herself moving without even realizing it, and she pressed her lips to his. "You look really good tonight."

"I have to say, I was thinking the same about you," he whispered against her lips. "I wanna slide that naughty skirt of yours up, take ahold of that gorgeous ass of yours."

"Mmm," she murmured against his lips, kissing him once more. "Who's stopping you?"

A devilish grin came across his lips as he slid his hand to her thigh, taking the hem of her skirt in his hand. But before he could lift it up, pounding came to both sides of the car. Jumping in surprise, they bumped heads before groaning. "What the hell?" he snapped before looking over to see her idiot brother grinning at them through the window like a ten-year-old. On the other side was Vaughn.

"Fucking children," she muttered as her door opened, and Vaughn was there to take her hand.

"Did we interrupt something?"

"Shove it, Jo," she spat at him as he helped her out before he scoffed.

"God, you're getting big."

"Thanks," she bit out as Brie smacked him.

"Don't say that! You aren't, Wren. You look gorgeous. I wish I looked like you."

"Shove it, Brie," she teased, and Brie laughed as they hugged tightly.

"But, really, can I borrow this dress? You look smoking in it."

Wren looked down at the dress that held to her curves like a second skin. Jensen had picked it out for her when they had gone shopping after her suit fitting. Yes, she was wearing a suit to her brother's wedding, despite her mother's protests. Wells was adamant about it. Even if it was annoying and Wren looked dumb in a suit, she did it for him. It was his wedding. Though, her mother was trying her best to change it even after Wren said she'd wear a dress to the reception.

Either way, it was a bunch of pointless drama, but that was her brother.

But her dress was pretty. It was a wrap dress with a long slit in the front and was strapless, which was becoming an issue with her huge tits, but Jensen had loved it. He had been basically drooling in the shop, so of course, she'd bought it. Paired it with high, sparkly pumps that made the purple of the dress pop. She'd admit it, she looked damn good.

"I mean, if it can fit your itty-bitty body, then sure."

Brie waved her off. "We're the same size."

Wren scoffed. "On Mars."

That had both women laughing as they locked arms and walked toward the building, and the boys followed behind them. "So you missed one hell of a Cup party."

"I know. I'm bummed, but I was so tired. I haven't been sleeping well."

"Yeah, and at least you came out tonight since I'm pretty sure this Alex guy doesn't like me."

Wren scoffed. "I don't think he likes any of us, except for Wells."

They giggled together as Jensen held open the door, and soon they were seated in the VIP spot Wells had secured for them. The club was rocking, lights and bodies moving as one as Wren sat down on the couch. Jensen sat beside her, his body pressed against hers in such a natural way. Drinks were ordered, along with Wren's not-wine, which was water, and it wasn't long before the conversation was flowing just as the music was. Things were going great, everyone was having a good time, the appetizers were great, and Wren couldn't take her eyes off Jensen.

He was gorgeous.

Leaning into him, she pressed her lips to his ear. "I want to do you, right here."

He smiled so hard as he covered her hand with his, stopping her from feeling him up in front of everyone. "Are you sure you're only drinking your not-wine?"

She giggled. "Yeah, I'm not intoxicated by anything but you."

Turning his face, he met her hot gaze, and she swore she had never seen him smile so brightly. "I can't with you. Stop it before I carry you out of this place."

Testing him, she moved her hand up, coming right to the bulge in his pants. "Promise?"

"Fucking evil," he muttered, shaking his head before he captured her mouth and everything just stopped. His lips were magical, his hands were sinful, and she couldn't handle it. She really couldn't. She was two seconds from climbing in his lap, when he pulled back, once more shaking his head. "Stop."

"What?" she asked innocently.

"You've got those damn sex eyes blazing at me. Quit."

She giggled softly as she pursed her lips. "Kiss me."

He did as she asked, cupping her face as he did. When he pulled away, his eyes were soft as he whispered, "I love you like this."

She exhaled dreamily. "Me too."

He gave her a wink just as Wells called for their attention. Kissing her once more, Jensen turned back to the conversation he was in before Wren interrupted him. Not that she cared. She could if she wanted.

He was hers.

The thought made her fucking giddy.

When Alex reached over, taking Wren's hands in his, she was shocked since he had never touched her before, but she smiled nonetheless. Alex, on the other hand, was drunk, but still, this was her future brother-in-law. "Wren, I need you to teach me to do makeup. You're amazing!"

Brie nodded, holding her water up. "I tell her that all the time. She's so gorgeous."

"She is. You have to teach me your ways."

But Wren laughed. "For what?"

Alex grinned. "Because I'm going to start competing in drag shows. Wells didn't tell you?"

Wren's face scrunched up because she hadn't heard that at all, and that was well beyond what she thought her brother was into. He liked his men low-key gay, but manly. He wasn't into flamboyant types. She knew that for a fact since she'd tried hooking him up with a lot of her ex-coworkers. "Oh. No. Okay. Yeah," she was sputtering since she was confused, but who was she to judge?

Whatever made her brother happy.

But when Alex went to the bathroom with Brie, Wren leaned toward Wells, across Jensen, but before she could say anything, Jensen was in her ear. "Let's dance."

"Hold that thought," she muttered. Though she wasn't much of a dancer, she'd take every chance to dance with Jensen.

Every. Single. One.

"Wells."

Her brother looked over at her. "What?"

"Dude, Alex is going to be a drag queen?"

Rolling his eyes, he leaned back in his chair. "So he says. I think it's dumb, and I had no clue he was into that kind of thing."

"Wait? What? Like dressing up like a girl, right?" Vaughn asked. "That's weird. If you want a girl, go get one."

"Thank you, my straight best friend, but I don't want a girl."

"That's crazy. Did you tell him you aren't down for that kind of thing?"

Wells shrugged. "I mean, I've mentioned it, but he's pretty set on it. He's been training for it for a couple years, and I just found out."

"Which is why you date for a while before you marry someone," Jensen added, and Wells scoffed.

"Says the dude who married my sister with no dating at all."

Jensen shrugged. "I've known her my whole life."

"Yup, and I don't have any hidden shit like that," she said, but even as the words came out of her mouth, she knew that was a lie. Especially when Jensen's gaze fell on her in disbelief.

Thankfully, Wells didn't catch on as he shrugged. "It's whatever. I love the guy."

"Okay, whatever makes you happy." But Wells didn't seem happy as he leaned back, nursing his beer. "This is what you want, right?"

He nodded. "Yeah."

She wasn't convinced but left it alone. Then Wells leaned on his legs, his gaze on Wren. "Guess who we saw today?"

Her stomach dropped because she had a pretty good guess as to who that was. "Who?"

"Shanna and Bradley."

"Oh?" she asked, feeling Jensen lean forward against her, his hand sliding down her back, resting on the outside of her hip.

"Yeah, Shanna was asking for you, of course. She wants Jensen and you to have lunch with her and Jay."

She nodded. "Eh, maybe. We'll see."

"You know you're gonna see her at the wedding," he asked, but that wasn't who Wren was worried about. Yeah, she needed to talk to Shanna, apologize, even if she had no clue how she was going to do that.

"Yeah. I'll text her."

Thankfully, he seemed to believe her as he said, "Good."

She wanted to ask if Bradley would be there, but she couldn't, nor would she have. Then Vaughn asked, "Did anyone else think Bradley was being weird?"

She looked toward him, wide-eyed as Wells nodded. Luckily, she couldn't see Jensen's face. "What do you mean?" she asked, and Wells shook his head.

"I don't know. It was like he couldn't comprehend that you and Jenny were together and shit. It was strange. He kept asking about it, and then he was all...weird. Shanna had to shut him up. Dude has always been a dud."

Wren's heart was dead in her chest. Shit. Had Jensen noticed?

Vaughn scoffed. "That's 'cause you hit on him, and he turned you down."

Wells held his hands out. "Come on, doesn't he give off the vibe?"

"No, not at all."

But all Wren could do was balk at him as Jensen asked, "You hit on Bradley?"

Wells shrugged. "Yeah, like five years ago. Before Matty."

"That's funny."

"Right?" Vaughn agreed, shaking his head. "Either way, dude is a weirdo. I don't know what his issue was."

"Yeah, that's odd," Wren found herself saying, and she wished she hadn't. She wished she would have just ignored it.

"Because, really, it was like he was jealous. Or was that just me?" Vaughn asked, and she wanted to smack him. *Shut it, Jo!*

"No, I got that vibe too, but it was almost like he didn't believe it," Wells added, and Vaughn smacked his arm in agreement.

"Yeah, as if it was so crazy for them to be together. Let's all be honest, we knew it was coming as soon as Jensen got his head out of his ass."

"And Wren stopped being a cunt when it came to love," Wells added, and Wren glared.

"Wow, really? A cunt?"

"What? You were."

"Watch it, Wells," Jensen warned, and Wells grinned.

"It's bizarre you having backup," he winked, and Jensen

laughed. "Anyway, if Shanna hadn't have stepped in when she did, I would have told him off. Because, come on, you and that douche? Please. That's disgusting. He used to whack off in the bathroom at school, you remember that?"

Vaughn laughed out loud. "Yeah, and that teacher caught him with his pants down, cock in hand, and walked him to the office."

"Didn't he get fired for it?" Jensen asked, but Wren had stopped thinking.

What in the living hell was going on?

"Yeah, I think he did. But still, shit was funny," Wells laughed, shaking his head.

"For real, he needs to get it together because I'll whoop his ass. Wren is Jensen's, that's it, and he needs to move on. Right, bro?" Vaughn said, holding his beer to Jensen, which Jensen tapped eagerly with his own.

"Right."

"Come on, that wouldn't happen. Right, sis?"

Wren swallowed hard as she nodded feverishly. "Right, duh."

Leaning back against the booth, she glanced over to find Jensen looking at her.

"Yeah?"

His lips curved. "You're beautiful."

The tension in her shoulders dropped as she went to lean into him, but he was getting up, holding his hand out to her. "What are you doing?"

"We're dancing," he said, pulling her up and into his arms. With his arm around her waist, he led her out to the private dance floor that was beside the VIP area. It was awesome, and soon they were moving together as Justin Bieber sang about whatever girl he had done wrong. When Brie and Vaughn joined them out there, Wren was in knots laughing as Brie was doing her signature dance, her pelvic thrust. Poor Vaughn was embarrassed, trying to stop her, but she was owning it, and Wren couldn't love her any more. When Vaughn wrapped Brie up in his arms, basically picking her up off the ground as his mouth pressed to hers, Wren's heart soared for them.

Jesus, they were made for each other.

Which sort of made Wren laugh. For so long, she didn't believe in that kind of thing. Didn't think it could happen, but then, it did. Not only for the people around her, but for her.

Jensen happened.

Wow. It was sort of overwhelming.

It made her feel like she was flying.

When Zayn's newest filled the little space around her, her fingers danced along his shoulders as his lips came across her chin and then her earlobe before resting there. Her eyes fell shut as she held him, never wanting to let go. She felt safe in his arms. "So that was weird."

Still with her eyes shut, she asked, "What was?"

"Bradley."

Her eyes shot open as her blood went cold. Her voice was shaky as she muttered, "Yeah, it sounds like it."

"I thought for a second he was the douche who knocked you up." There it was. Swallowing hard, she squeezed her eyes shut as she clung to him. "But then, the more I thought about it, the more that would be crazy. He's like five years younger than you, and he's married."

"Yeah," she agreed, and damn it, why did she do that?

Because it was the easy fucking way out! God, she was pathetic.

As they danced together, Wren looked over to see Brie and Vaughn doing the same, and she smiled. But inside, she was dying. She should tell him the truth. It was the perfect opening, but she couldn't. Not only was he a little drunk, but it wasn't the time or place.

Shit, was she lying to him?

Crap.

As the music changed, Ed Sheeran's "Perfect" blasting through the speakers, Wren found herself pushing her insane thoughts aside and focusing only on Jensen. On what they had. She felt good. Great, even. When she did that, when she stopped thinking about all the outside shit, only focused on them, things were great. She was who she wanted to be. Her arms went up and around Jensen's neck as he held her as close as he could, her belly the only thing keeping them apart. As Ed sang about his perfect girl, Wren couldn't help but feel like she was Jensen's perfect girl. Especially with the way he was gazing into her eyes. She couldn't ruin that. She couldn't ruin this moment.

Fuck Bradley. He didn't matter, and if he hadn't said anything to them there, he wouldn't say anything anywhere because he was a fucking coward. So, fuck him. Why was she even worried about him when she had a man who was looking at her the way Jensen was at that moment? No one had ever looked at her like he was. No one had ever stood up for her the way Jensen always did. No one had ever told her they loved her like Jensen did, continually, over and over again.

As she listened to the lyrics to the song she had heard a ton of times, the words meant way more than she realized. Jensen's head fell to hers, his nose along hers as his lips whispered the words, taking away every single breath she had in her body. She clung to him, and his hands slid down her back onto her ass. Her heart pounded in her chest, shaking her to her core as his eyes never left hers. He wasn't singing, because that wasn't Jensen. He did not sing, but he was speaking the words, and she hadn't known how much that could rattle her. How the simple movement of his lips to hers, speaking the words ever so softly, could make her want to wrap her arms around him and never let go. How she wanted to scream those three words at him and never stop screaming them.

What was happening to her?

As the tears started to well up in her eyes, Jensen's lips curved. "Great song."

She nodded, a lone tear rolling down her cheek. "It is."

"Written just for us."

Her face broke into a grin, her tears stalling in her eyes from grinning so hard. "Says every couple in the world."

"Well, forget them. It's true for us." Closing his eyes, he pressed his lips to hers as she fell into the kiss. She molded her body with his as she held on, never wanting to leave that moment for the rest of her existence.

They were solid.

Her and Jensen.

There was no other option.

Just the two of them.

And the baby.

Gunner.

Their baby.

"I love you," she whispered, and his eyes widened, gazing into hers.

"Shut up," he said, and her face broke as laughter escaped her lips.

"Wow! See if I say that ever again!"

Laughing, he slid his hands under her ass, lifting her off the ground, and for the first time, she towered over him. There wasn't an ounce of fear in her because Jensen had her. He always had her. "Say it again. Right now."

Her face flushed, but she knew deep down in her soul the words were true. "I love you, Jensen Cade Monroe."

His eyes fell shut as the most beautiful grin came across his lips. "Again."

She laughed as she bent down as far as she could, pressing her lips to his. As he kissed her, he slowly put her down, carefully, before wrapping his arms around her neck like he always did. Like she loved, and when he pulled back, he pressed his nose into hers as she whispered, "I love you."

She knew he probably couldn't hear her, but that didn't stop him from saying, "I love you more."

Elation filled her soul, but just as quickly as it came, it vanished, that nagging fear scratching at her happiness. Because she was pretty sure she had lied to Jensen, to her brother, and to Vaughn.

And she wasn't sure what to do about that.

# Chapter TWENTY

"You amaze me."

Between kisses, Wren held on to Jensen's neck as he carried her into the hotel room he had booked for them. "I thought we'd go home."

"Nope. In that dress, I needed somewhere where I could make you scream all night long," he gasped, his kisses sloppy as he slammed the door behind them.

Breathless, she whispered, "You even packed a bag for me?"

"I did. I brought that black stuff for your eyes."

Her heart sang. "And my lotions?"

"Yup, and even the cocoa butter for your belly."

"My hero."

Throwing the bags on the ground, he moved his other hand to join its mate on her ass before he carried her across the room to what she assumed was the bed. But when he placed her down, she saw it was the bench in front of the bed.

"That fucking dress is going to be the death of me," he said, his words tight and strained. Feeling sexy, Wren stretched her legs out before slowly crossing them as he threw off his jacket and started unbuttoning his shirt.

"This one?" she asked, parting the slit even more so he could see between her legs.

"Is that the lace thong I bought you?"

Her eyes sparkled with lust. "It is."

He groaned, pushing his shirt off his shoulders and letting it fall behind him. His chest was thick and wide, and she wanted to lick him all over, he looked so damn delectable. "And I'm not wearing a bra."

His eyes drifted closed as he squeezed his cock through his slacks. "Yeah, hard as a rock."

"That was my goal," she teased as he came for her, his shoulders pushing her legs up as his mouth met hers in a zealous embrace. He was squishing her, but she didn't care. She only wanted to kiss him. But when he pulled back, his brows drawn together, he asked, "You okay?"

"I mean, it's tight but hot, so please continue."

But he didn't, dropping instead to his knees, which removed the pressure, before he let her legs fall over his shoulders. He reached up her dress, pulling down her thong before pushing her skirt up to her waist. He met her gaze for a second, and she leaned back against the bed, a grin on her lips as he exhaled hard, his eyes so full of love. When he dropped his mouth to her, she arched into him, crying out as he found her clit, torturing to it. He didn't let up; he loved her pussy like it was the only purpose in his life. She was convinced she could feel his mouth everywhere, her body going completely taut as he destroyed her. When he slid his fingers into her, slowly fucking her as his mouth kept at it, licking around her clit and then along her lips, she came off the bench, crying out his name as her body shook.

She couldn't handle it.

Everything was intensified; at least, that's how it felt. Her heart was beating ridiculously fast in her chest, her pussy was clenching around his fingers, and she felt nothing but heat all over her body. When she came undone, she knew she had never cried out so loud in her life. His name fell from her lips as she came down from her beautiful little orgasm cloud before he slowly kissed her thighs, her pussy, and then up her belly.

Gasping for breath, she said, "Good plan on bringing me here if that's a bit of the preview of the night." He scoffed against her chest as his tongue moved along her breasts. She could hear him undoing his pants, the belt falling before she felt him enter her with one thrust. "Fudging hell," she gasped, and he smiled against her lips.

"I can't handle you," he murmured against her lips. "I need you."

"Me too," she murmured back as he went deeper, his fingers biting into the bedding behind her. As her fingers ran along his ribs, his back, and then his ass, she was breathless, and she pressed her nose to his chest, his body so hot and tempting. When he stopped, she cried out in protest, but then he was pulling her up with him, pressing his lips to hers with so much need she felt it in her soul. As she got lost in his kisses, his cock pressed into her thighs, hard and throbbing, and fuck, she wanted him.

But he pulled away, kissing her nose before he turned her around. "Hold on to the bench."

A grin pulled at her lips as she slowly, seductively bent down, wiggling her ass at him. "Just like this?"

He looked pained as he licked his lips, kicking out of his pants as he ran his hand down his cock. "Fuck yes."

Biting her lip, she held his gaze until he came up behind her, entering her as he gently rubbed both her ass cheeks. He filled her completely, to the hilt, and Lord, he was so big and so fucking hot. Her pussy wrapped around him like a vise grip, and she couldn't find her breath as he started to pound into her. The sounds of their lovemaking filled the room along with his grunts and her cries. The sounds were beautiful, like the hottest love song she had ever heard in her life.

When his hand wrapped around her hair, she cried out as he pulled it back, the sting only intensifying her pleasure before his mouth met hers. His body pressed into her back as he stilled inside of her, drawing the kiss out of her. As his tongue swept over hers, she squeezed him, her body crying for him, and she guessed that's what did him in. Because then he tore his mouth from hers, took ahold of her hips, and started to pound into her, bringing her to her toes as her fingers dug into the bench.

As he came with a shout that sent chills down her spine, her eyes closed while his hands moved up her body, taking ahold of her breasts. Gasping for breath, he lay against her back as she tried to catch her breath, her body vibrating in the most heavenly way. Kissing along her shoulders, he brought her up against him, his cock still deep inside of her as their lips met with so much passion her soul cried out with glee.

She'd never love anyone like him.

The realization scared the living shit out of her, but as he turned her in his arms, kissing her more, his fingers biting into her skin, she knew it was true. But then, would anyone ever love her like Jensen did?

He basically worshiped her.

Something she had never experienced in her life.

Man, did it feel good.

Right.

Perfect.

It felt fucking perfect.

As he moved his lips along hers, nibbling on her bottom lip, his eyes opened just a bit in a hooded, hot way before he whispered, "I love you, *ma chou*."

And for once, she didn't pause, she didn't hesitate, she didn't even try to stop herself. She whispered back, "I love you too."

With that, a grin came across Jensen's lips before he lifted her up and carried her to the bed for round two, three, and even four. While she enjoyed every freaking moment of it, after she had washed her face and found herself lying awake beside him, for once, it wasn't because of her fucked-up feelings or the constant movement of her little guy, Gunner.

But because of Bradley.

She had no clue what the hell she was going to do.

\* \* \*

"OH MY GOD! I NEED THIS."

Wren looked over the racks of clothes where Brie was holding up a little tutu onesie that read "My Uncle's Princess." "Rod would flip his shit."

"It's supercute, he would for sure," Wren gushed as she picked up almost the same thing, but in blue with no tutu. "Aww, look, they have a boy one. Wells will love it."

Brie squeaked happily as she threw it in her cart that was overloaded with stuff. How Brie was going to get all that home was beyond Wren, but she wasn't going to say anything.

Her cart was just as full.

"I'm having a blast! Thanks for asking me to come."

"Of course. We're besties, remember?" Brie shot her a grin as Wren sorted through all the puppy- and dinosaur-decorated stuff.

She remembered back to a month ago when standing in the middle of a baby store would bring her to her knees in fear, but not any longer. No, now she was excited. "I figured since the boys were all going out to play some pickup, we would need something to do. My mom is currently still planning her brains out, and my dad went with the boys, so I had to hightail it out of there."

Plus, she wanted to talk to Brie about Bradley.

It had been three days since she'd found out about Jensen, Vaughn, and Wells seeing Bradley at the rink, and she still had no clue what to do about it.

"I thought you and your mom were getting along."

Wren made a face. "Oh, we're fine, but now she's smothering me. Whenever I'm in the room, she's basically on her hands and knees trying to please me. I had to tell her to go away last night, and then my dad hollered at me. Of course, then he apologized because he doesn't want me hating him." She paused, rolling her eyes. "It's basically normal behavior in the Lemiere household. Everyone is dramatic."

Brie giggled as she moved toward where Wren stood. "You guys are funny."

"We're all insane."

Brie nodded in agreement as she laughed. "Did Alex stay back with your mom?"

Wren shrugged. "Not that I know. I heard he went with the guys."

"No, he hates hockey."

Wren's face scrunched up. "He's marrying a hockey player!"

"Exactly. Vaughn doesn't think they'll get married."

Wren laughed. "They'd better. The damn thing is in four days, and my mom is set on there being a wedding. I think even my dad is being better about it. He hasn't been fighting with Wells as much."

"That's good," Brie said, and Wren shrugged. "But yeah, Vaughn says it's gonna be a clusterfuck."

"Oh, I'm sure," Wren laughed, shaking her head. "But whatever, it's my brother's life. I'm there to support him—and for the food I can smuggle without my husband seeing me."

Brie smiled wide as she nodded. "Jensen is so adorable."

"He is," Wren agreed as her heart fluttered. She had thought they were only spending one night in Colorado Springs, but Jensen had other plans. They stayed for two nights and one of the days, and he had the day full of pampering. They had a couple's massage, a mud bath, and she even got her hair done while he sat by, watching her. It was amazing, and she couldn't stop thinking about it.

When they passed a belly-casting set, Wren scoffed. "My mom is making Jensen and me do this."

Brie's eyes lit up. "No way! When?"

"Who knows? Probably tomorrow or today. Knowing her, she'll probably torture me today," she laughed since she thought it was stupid, but Brie looked all too excited as she reached for it, throwing it in her cart. "But apparently, you think it's cool."

"It is. I can have Rodney draw on it!"

"Oh, that is cool."

"Right?" she gushed as they started toward the shoe aisle.

Scrunching up her face, Wren declared, "They never have cute boy shoes."

"I know, but they have so much girls stuff. Vaughn is gonna be broke."

"He won't care."

"I know," she giggled as she grabbed a few pairs of all kinds of pink shoes. Looking around the aisle as Brie for real drove Vaughn to bankruptcy, Wren noticed no one was around them, so she leaned toward Brie.

"I need to ask you something."

Brie looked back at her, seven pairs of shoes in her arms, before blowing a piece of hair out of her eyes. "That sounds juicy," she said, dropping the shoes into her cart. "What's going on?"

"So, say you got pregnant by someone else, and he's a douche, told you to get an abortion, said he didn't want you, whole nine—"

"I think I've heard this scenario."

Wren glared. "Shh, listen," she demanded while Brie just stared at her, her eyes wide as she fought back a grin. "Well, new guy comes in, loves you, loves your kid, he's ready for the future, and now you are—"

"Aww! You love him!"

Wren's eyes narrowed. "Focus, Brie."

"Tell me! You do!"

"Yes," Wren snapped, throwing her hands up, and Brie just

grinned. "I do. A lot. And now, the baby's father could be a problem, and I don't trust him—"

"I don't think you trust anyone, though," she supplied, and Wren thought that over.

"This is true, but he's up to something. And now, I don't know if I should tell Jensen about him, when I've been tight-lipped this whole time, or if I should just hope it doesn't blow up in my face."

Brie just blinked. "Okay, yes, this is a predicament because Jensen will be upset."

"Yeah, and the problem is, I think I lied to him."

"Wren."

"I know, I know," she protested, shaking her head. "But not really, because he implied he thought he knew who it was, and I didn't deny it. But I didn't confirm it, and I'm worried that if he finds out, he'll get upset because I had the chance to tell him."

Shaking her head, Brie held her gaze. "It's that Bradley guy, isn't it?" Wren's face must have given her away before Brie smacked her hand to her thigh. "Vaughn said it was. He was convinced, and I told him no. I mean, fuck, Wren, that dude looks like a douche!"

Closing her eyes, Wren let her head fall back. "I know. I've known him forever, hot passion, he's hung, and yeah, it was stupid. Please don't tell anyone."

"Oh, you suck."

"Please, I'm pulling out the bestie card. You can't tell anyone."

"Fucking hell. I mean, I really can't 'cause if I tell Vaughn, he's going to jail."

Wren itched her brow in distress. "I know. They're all gonna be pissed and go after him, and I'm worried he's gonna try to play it the other way. Try to make me out to be the bad guy. Some would even believe him because everyone knows I wasn't one to keep my legs shut."

"No, they won't."

"You don't know that. You don't know Bradley and his family."

Brie thought that over, and then her mouth dropped open. "Holy shit, that's your ex-best friend's brother. Jesus, Wren, what did you do?"

"I know," Wren groaned. "I was distracted by a big cock, and I wasn't thinking. It went on for years, and then he happened," she said, pointing to her belly. "But I don't know if I want to tell Jensen because what if he looks at the baby and only sees Bradley? I don't want to ruin this for him."

Brie made a face. "Ew, yeah. But I don't know, I think you need to tell him. Just to be safe. Fuck."

"Exactly."

"Wow," she drew out, looking at the floor as she shook her head. "Is Bradley coming to the wedding?"

"I don't know."

"And we can't find out without being suspicious," Brie said, more to herself, and when she looked up, Wren could see she had no answer either. "He was really weird. Do you think he's gonna try something?"

"I don't know, that's the problem. I thought about calling him again because he doesn't have my new number, but I don't even want to look at him."

"Gosh, this sucks."

"It does. I told you, hot fucking mess express, right here."

"Like, legit," Brie agreed, shaking her head. "Man, Wren, if it were me, I'd tell Jensen. But I get why you don't want to. You've made it pretty clear the dude doesn't matter, but I think Jenny would rather find out from you than in some shitty way since we don't know this dude's game. Maybe you should call him, see what he is thinking?"

Wren shook her head at that, though. "I don't want anything to do with him, and yeah, you're right."

"So you're going to tell Jensen?"

Wren looked away, shrugging. "I guess. I don't know when."

"Before the wedding."

"Yeah," she said, but she was pretty sure that was another lie.

She had no clue how to look into the eyes of the man she loved and tell him the darkest secret she had in her book.

She was pretty sure that would send him running for the hills.

Especially if Bradley was up to something.

"I DON'T like you right now."

Laughing, Jensen gazed over at his wife who was huffing and puffing up the hill they were climbing. They had been graced by a cool, beautiful, early morning on the day Jensen had planned for a hike. "I mean, really, you wake me up at butt-crack o'clock, you give me a granola bar when you know darn well I want pancakes and sausage—"

"I got some sausage right here for you, baby," he teased, and she glared.

"I don't want your sweaty dick that has no protein in it!"

He waggled his brows at her. "The protein comes after you get me off."

She gagged at that. "You're disgusting."

"And you're beautiful."

She glared as she shook her head. "Don't try to flirt with me! I'm angry. I want my bed, pancakes, and sleep."

He laughed as they turned the corner. "You need exercise since we skipped yesterday, and also, I thought inviting Brie and Vaughn would make you happy."

She flashed him the driest look he had ever seen. "Yes, watching as my petite, fit best friend, who has the cutest little baby belly, run with her equally fit boyfriend up a hill in only shorts and a bra was going to make me ecstatic. I'm enjoying this so much."

"Well, I think you're fit."

"Jensen, the only thing fit about me is if I'm lucky to fit in my jeans on a good day."

"Well, I think otherwise. Plus, you're way hotter than Brie."

She rolled her eyes. "Stop sucking up to me, you're still not getting laid today after all this torture."

He scoffed. "I can bribe you with a Snickers."

She didn't even bat an eye at that. "Probably."

Laughing, he reached out, taking her hand with his as they trekked up the hill that Vaughn and Brie were more than likely at the top of. "We used to come out here and run when we were kids."

"I know. I stayed home." When he looked over at her, she smiled. "Lazy."

His heart was full as he nodded. "But still hot."

"Yeah, that was back when I had a decent metabolism that allowed me to eat pizza and only gain three pounds instead of the ten I gain now."

"You're ridiculous."

"I hear that a lot from you." He flashed her a grin as he brought her palm to his mouth, kissing it softly.

"Because it's true."

"Says you."

He laughed as she rolled her eyes before she changed to subject. "So you think Wells and Alex are gonna get married this weekend?"

His brows pulled together. "Why wouldn't they?"

"Jenny, you didn't see the look on Wells's face when Alex brought his makeup box into the house. I thought Wells was going to scream, especially when my dad saw it all."

Jensen shrugged, shaking his head. "You know that's their problem. When I asked him, he said he loved the guy and they were doing it."

She clucked her tongue. "Brie and Vaughn don't think they will. Watch them call it off Friday."

Jensen's face filled with horror. "He'd better warn us, so we can leave before your mom goes crazy on everyone. I'm pretty sure that will be the moment she kills him."

"Right?" she agreed, laughing as she swung their hands back and forth. "Like, dead. To the ground."

"Exactly, and I can't watch that."

Wren grinned. "I could, with popcorn. Wells does no wrong, so that would be awesome."

"You're an asshole."

"Aww, I love you too," she gushed, and he laughed, bringing her in and kissing her temple.

"Why couldn't you be like this from the beginning? You're so sweet and cuddly."

She glared up at him, sweat dripping down her forehead as she pursed her lips. "What in the world are you talking about? I've been a joy and a delight this whole fucking time." She couldn't even keep a straight face; she sputtered with laughter as he shook his head, kissing the side of her mouth.

"You've been a pain in my ass, but I love you, so it's okay."

She beamed up at him, leaning her head on his shoulder as they walked leisurely along the beautiful wooded trail. He had so many memories on this trail. He kissed a girl on this trail. He got drunk on this trail. He was pretty sure he stole Wells's and Vaughn's clothes one time, and they had to run down it naked. It was a good trail, but it was better when he had Wren up under his arm.

God, he loved her.

Things had been so great between them. Picking the baby's name. Being together. They were vibing, things were good, and fucking hell, he was happy. She seriously brightened up his day. Even with her complaining about everything he was doing for her with the health and fitness, he loved it because he knew she knew she needed it. Plus, he knew she wouldn't do it for anyone else other than him. But above all, he was on cloud nine because she loved him.

Wren fucking loved him.

Jensen had thought that moment would never happen. He'd thought he was going to get hurt and she was going to ruin him, but no, she loved him. They were planning things, they were doing things that a family did, and he had wanted that for so long that he almost couldn't believe it. He was sure he pinched himself daily, yet it hurt and she was still looking up at him with that devilish little grin of hers. He had loved her his whole life, and finally, he had everything he wanted. A great job, a beautiful wife, and soon, a son he could love just as much, if not more than the woman who had his whole heart.

Jensen Monroe was one happy fucking guy.

Bringing her hand up to his lips, he kissed her softly as she said, "Do we have to do that plaster thing when we get home?"

He chuckled. "Elaine is pretty set on it."

"Ugh," she groaned. "It's so weird, and I'm so fat!"

"Shut it, woman."

She rolled her eyes as she moved away from him, making a face but still holding his hand. "You're hot."

"So are you," he said with a wink, and her face flushed as she looked away.

He swore—and he knew he thought this a lot—she was honestly the most beautiful woman in the world. With her hair up in a tight bun, she wore a sports bra with a light workout tank over it. She was wearing a pair of shorts that showed those juicy thighs he loved. But what he couldn't get over was how much their son was growing. She was bigger, her stomach stretching, and he was convinced she was due tomorrow rather than September.

He couldn't get enough of her.

He wanted her, constantly.

She was just fucking luscious.

As his heart sped up in his chest, he bit his lip, unsure how he was going to say what he had to say. He had actually brought her up there to talk to her about his issue, but now, he was getting cold feet. He just hated it; he felt weak. But when Wren looked at him, he didn't feel weak, he felt like the Hulk. As if nothing could touch him. Or them, for that matter.

"Hey, babe—"

"I need to talk to you—" she said at the same time, and they shared a smile. "Go first."

"No, you," he demanded, but she shook her head.

"Mine is dumb, you go," she said before looking away, and he noticed that she seemed nervous. He wasn't sure what that was about, but if he didn't get this out, he wasn't ever going to.

"Okay, so, I was wondering, if, um, maybe—"

"Wow, is this a struggle?" He glared, and she smiled. "Sorry."

"Actually, it is," he answered, moving his free hand down his face.

"Oh, my bad. Sorry," she said, guilt flashing in her eyes. "I'm a jerk."

He laughed, shaking his head. "No, it's fine. I'm nervous."

"Oh. Okay?"

Inhaling hard, he didn't look at her as he said, "I was actually wondering if maybe, when we get home, you'd go to the doctor's appointment with me that I had made."

She scrunched up her face. "For what?"

His mouth went dry as he exhaled through his nose. "To see if I'm still sterile, and maybe working on getting that fixed."

Her eyes widened, and he bit down hard on the inside of his cheek. He knew she hadn't asked him to do it, nor had she implied for him to. Also, he didn't even know if she wanted any more kids after this one. But if she did, he wanted to give them to her.

He wanted to give her the world.

"Really?" she asked, her eyes locking with his as she stopped, which stopped him.

Unsure of himself, he nodded. "Yeah."

"Jensen, wow this is out of the blue."

"I've been thinking about it a lot since our conversation, and I want to go back, really look into it."

"Are you sure this is what you want? You aren't doing this because of what I asked?"

"No, I want this. Because if one day you look at me and tell me you want another kid, I want to be able to give you one."

"So, it is for me. I would never ask you do something you aren't comfortable with."

"I understand that, and yeah, it is for you. But it's for me too, Wren. So, um, will you go?"

She didn't move, her eyes searching his as his heart went nuts in his chest. Her lips curved up in a smile as she stepped into his arms, her eyes sparkling with the possibility of their future as her chin dug into his chest. "Of course, I will."

He exhaled hard, moving her stray hair out of her face. "It freaks me out."

"Don't let it, because I'll be there with you."

His grin matched hers as he pressed his nose into hers. "Which is all I need."

"I know, I'm pretty stinking amazing," she said, kissing his chin.

"You are," he agreed, and then he smiled as he touched his lips to hers. When he pulled back, he remembered that she'd had something to ask too. "What did you have to say?"

"Oh, I forgot. It wasn't important, I guess." Waving him off, she pressed her lips together as she shook her head. But from the look in her eyes, he could see she was holding something back. "Really, it was nothing." She tried once more before threading her fingers through his hair. "All I care about is our future."

"Me too."

"So stop stalling and kiss me."

She didn't need to ask twice. He dropped his mouth to hers and fell into the kiss. Her arms wrapped around his waist as she met him with the same demand he felt deep in his soul.

A soul that belonged to her.

* * *

"AM I SQUISHING YOU?"

"No, I'm fine."

"Mom, this is awkward. My ass is squishing him."

"It's not."

"Wren, he said it isn't."

"He's too nice to say so!"

"I'll say it. Your ass is huge," Wells called to her from the bar, and Jensen glared. "I mean, you are a beautiful butterfly."

"I hate you," she hollered at him as her mother laid another strip of plaster onto her belly and over their hands that were making a heart. As Brie laid one after Elaine, Jensen smiled, leaning his head into the back of hers. She didn't want to do this, she wanted to go to bed, but he had convinced to do it for Elaine. Her mom had been so excited when she'd found the set to plaster Wren's belly. And since he still felt bad about the argument the day he had gotten there, he was all about getting Wren to do something she hated. When she groaned loudly, he chuckled against her neck as his son moved inside of her. "Are we done yet? Even Gunner hates this, he's hungry."

"Jesus, Wren! We just got started. Someone feed her, please," Elaine called back to Vaughn, Wells, and Alex, who were sitting at the bar.

"I'm not. I saw her tits, and it freaked me out," Vaughn said, shaking his head.

"Right? Like big, sand-dollar titties. Is that normal with pregnancy?" Wells asked, and Jensen decided he didn't need Wells to call off the wedding because he was going to kill him.

"Mom! I told you I should have worn a bra!"

"I didn't want lines on the plaster," her mother yelled back, and Jensen just laughed.

"Yeah, I would have gone with lines instead of seeing those big ole titties," Vaughn teased.

"I swear, if I wouldn't have to start over with this, I'd kill you both!" Wren yelled at them.

"But seriously, are your nipples supposed to be that big?" her brother asked, sputtering with laughter. Before she could answer, Jensen set him with a look. "I'm not too good with boobs, but in porn, they're always so much smaller."

"Wells!"

"Sorry, Mom, but really. Big titties on that girl."

"Watch it," Jensen warned.

Silence fell upon all them, and he realized he might have yelled that.

"Yes, sir," Wells said, saluting to him as Vaughn shook his head.

"I don't know why you mess with her. Jenny will kill you. He'll kill anyone for Wrenny-boooooo," Vaughn sang, and Wren rolled her eyes. "He luvvvvvvsss herrrrrr."

"Yup, that whip is in full force between those two," Wells teased.

"So? I'm proud to love my wife and make her happy. I see nothing wrong with that."

"You gave up hot chicken for her. That's whipped!"

"He did not," Wren asserted.

"Yes, he did!"

"I didn't. I just didn't eat it around her because it made her sick," Jensen answered matter-of-factly, and Wren looked back at him the best she could.

"Really?"

"Yeah, you always got queasy when I brought it home, so I stopped."

As a grin spread over her lips, Vaughn and Wells yelled, "Whipped!"

Winston scoffed from the doorway. "Like the whip isn't in full force with you two. That boy right there tells you to jump, you do, Wells. And Vaughn, all this gorgeous girl has to do is give you a look, and you come running," he threw back at them.

"She's really great in bed," Vaughn laughed, and Brie's eyes widened.

"Vaughn!"

"What? It's true!"

"Well, don't tell your other parents that!"

As Vaughn and Wells shared a look before giggling like children, Elaine took Jensen's face in her hands, rubbing the plaster all over him, but he didn't care. He was getting in the shower after this anyway. Hopefully with Wren, if he didn't have to kill Wells and Vaughn first. "You are the best thing ever, Jensen Monroe, and I love you. So damn much."

Jensen grinned as Wren turned, kissing his cheek. "He is pretty great and not whipped at all because he doesn't need to be whipped to love me."

"Ha! Please," Wells called back, shaking his head. But Jensen wasn't listening because beside Wells, Alex was turning red. When Alex leaned toward Wells, whispering something in his ear, Jensen watched as Wells rolled his eyes.

"Babe, she doesn't know you like she knows Jenny."

"It doesn't matter, my parents love you."

Jensen looked to Elaine, but she was talking to Wren and Brie about placement while Winston was watching, giving his own directions. No one was paying attention to the hissy fit Alex was throwing.

"They probably don't want us to get married."

"That's not true. They're happy for us."

"Whatever, your dad hates this."

"I know, but he's still coming."

"This is bullshit," Alex decided, getting up and leaving the room, walking out the back door.

When the door slammed, Elaine turned, her brows up in her hairline. "There is no slamming doors in my house—"

"This isn't a damn barn," Wren, Jensen, Vaughn, and Wells all finished for her since they had been hearing that since the dawn of time.

She just nodded. "Exactly."

"That was creepy," Brie laughed, shaking her head while everyone else just shrugged. But Jensen was watching Wells, who slowly came off his chair.

"Sorry, Mom."

"Was that Alex? What is his problem?"

Wells just shook his head, and Vaughn, being the pain in the ass that he was, said, "He's pissed because he thinks you don't love him like you love Jenny."

Her face scrunched up as Wren asked, "Why does it matter? Plus, Mom helped raise Jensen."

"Which is what I tried telling him, that you guys don't know him as well as Jensen. Yeah, he's being a brat. He's nervous about the wedding. It's fine," Wells said, holding up his hands in a calming motion. "Let me make sure he didn't leave me."

As he walked through the kitchen, going out the back door, Vaughn laughed from his seat. "Hundred bucks says they don't get married."

"Vaughn Johansson, you shut that mouth of yours right now!"

316 | TONI ALEO

Elaine yelled, and he did as she asked, looking down at the food in front of him.

"I mean, I don't like that he's gay, my boy, but even I think that guy's a little bit of a sissy for him."

"He is," Wren and Vaughn said together.

Elaine just made a face, looking out the back window. "Well, I don't care. Wells told me he loved that boy and he wants to marry him, so I'm throwing a damn wedding, and they better get married."

"Or else we'll all need to get alternate housing since you'll probably blow this one up with him inside," Winston supplied, and Elaine glared.

"That's a little dramatic, don't you think?"

Winston scoffed as Jensen said, "Not for you."

She pinned him with a look, and Jensen hid behind Wren as she laughed. "I used to love you, boy."

"Sorry," he muttered against Wren's neck, and she leaned into him.

"I'm the favorite now," Vaughn laughed.

"No, you're not. Brie is."

"Yes!" Brie said, fist-pumping as Wren just laughed.

"You're the one who put the damn thought in my head," Elaine said worriedly as she looked out the window and then back to everyone in the room. "Do all of you think it's not gonna happen?"

"I do," Brie said slowly, holding her hand up.

"I totally do," Vaughn added with both hands up.

"We can't hold our hands up, but we do," Wren announced, and Jensen glared at the back of her head.

"I don't!"

"Yes, you do," she said, and he scoffed but didn't protest.

Maybe he was whipped.

When a car door slammed outside, with someone calling someone a drama queen, they all looked to Winston as he nodded. "Pretty sure we just wasted half a million, love."

Sputtering with anger, she threw a plaster strip down and muttered, "I swear to God, I'll kill him."

When Wren looked over at Jensen, he smiled before she leaned into him, pressing her nose into his. "I told you I didn't want to do this."

He just kept grinning. "I did. I get your ass on me for a solid hour."

"I mean, if you wanted me to sit on you, I would have done it without this!"

"Yeah, but this way, we make your mom happy."

She glared as Elaine said, "And this is why he's my favorite again."

"Hey!" Brie complained, and Elaine flashed her a grin.

"You're my second favorite."

"Hey!" Wren and Vaughn complained, and then everyone was laughing.

And at that moment, Jensen didn't want to be anywhere else but with his arms around his wife in the middle of his second family's kitchen, with his loved ones.

He went from having no one to having so much love it was overwhelming, and he wouldn't change a damn thing.

# Chapter
# TWENTY-ONE

*B*rie: *Did you tell him?*
    *Wren: No, I chickened out. Twice.*
*Brie: Wren! It's the day before the wedding, you need to tell him.*
*Wren: I know, but I have bigger things to deal with at this time.*
*Brie: What?*
*Wren: I'm meeting Shanna for lunch.*
*Brie: Oh. Shit.*
*Wren: Exactly.*
*Wren: Fucking Jensen.*
*Brie: How the hell did he manage to get you to go?*
*Wren: He was going down on me, and he asked right when I was screaming yes, so he took that to heart.*
*Brie: Wow. Smooth. And smart.*
*Wren: Yeah, gotta give it to him, he knows how to work me.*
*Brie: That's so cute.*
*Wren: I hate you.*
*Brie: Aw! We're like Vaughn and Jensen.*
*Wren: I don't think that's a good comparison.*
*Brie: Maybe you're right.*
*Brie: Well, Godspeed. Let me know how that goes.*
*Wren: Will do.*

Glaring at her phone, she tucked it into her purse as the warm air of the summer breeze hit her in the face. It was a gorgeous, hot day in Colorado, and she'd rather be in the air conditioning than trekking to the little restaurant Shanna and her husband were waiting at. When she squeezed Jensen's hand, he looked over at her as they walked down the little street of the town. "Do we have to go?"

He nodded. "Yes. I told them we'd meet them."

"Can we blow it off?"

"Wren, come on, she misses you."

"I'll go down on you in the car," she suggested, and he scoffed, his face beaming with a grin.

"That's unfair."

"But I will."

"No, I think you need this."

"How in the hell do I need this?"

"I think you need the closure. If you don't want to talk to her after this, that's cool, because at least you'll give her a reason and explain your reasoning."

"Or, I can keep ignoring it."

"Or, you can get out those lady balls I know you have and tell her the truth."

The truth. God, she hated the fucking truth at that moment.

Clearing her throat, she grumbled as they made their way to the little burger joint that had been in the town since the dawn of time. She didn't want to do this. She knew it made her an asshole to cut Shanna out of her life the way she had, but she seriously couldn't help it. She felt Shanna wouldn't have been there for her, and she couldn't deal with any more rejection at the time. Bradley had done enough, and she couldn't take it from her best friend. So she did what she did best, she shut everyone out.

When he reached for the door, she looked up at him. "Don't leave me alone."

"Wren, be real."

"Jensen Monroe, promise me right now."

He shook his head. "Fine. I'll piss my pants to keep from leaving you alone."

"Solid plan," she said as he opened the door, and he laughed, letting her in before him. When her gaze fell right on Shanna in a booth, alone, her stomach dropped.

Where the fuck was her husband?

Unsure of herself, Shanna got up slowly, a grin pulling at her lips. "Oh my goodness! Look at you!" Wren plastered the fakest smile she could muster and met her halfway in a tight hug. "I can't believe it. You're pregnant."

"Yup, I couldn't believe it either."

"Right? You never wanted kids."

"And now I couldn't imagine not getting ready to have one," she said nervously before Shanna hugged Jensen.

"I was telling Jensen at the rink how excited I am for you guys. This is awesome. I always knew you guys would get together."

Wren smiled up at Jensen as he pressed his hand to her back, helping her into the booth. "You and him, both. I was late to the game."

Jensen smiled. "Better late than never."

He kissed her temple before she looked around nervously. "So, where's Jay?"

"So now, the other two boys have strep, and I was worried if I told y'all he wasn't coming, you wouldn't."

Wren wouldn't have.

"Oh, no, of course, we would have come. I might have let Jensen stay home, though," she joked. "I doubt he wants to hear about girl shit."

"I can leave," he suggested, and Wren's eyes widened.

"Really? That wouldn't hurt your feelings? I would love to catch up! Just us girls," Shanna all but screamed, and Wren slowly turned her head, her eyes burning into his.

*Don't you leave me, don't you leave me.*

"I mean, it's up to you, babe," he said, his eyes widening with hers.

Oh, she was going to kill him dead.

She could feel Shanna staring at her, pleading with her eyes. Damn it, she owed it to her. Jensen was right. She needed some sort of closure. So, reluctantly, Wren nodded her head. "Yeah, go. I'll call you when we're done."

"You sure?"

"Yes! I'll take care of her, promise," Shanna gushed, patting his hand, and he sent her a grin.

"Yeah, go help Vaughn with NateWay."

"Okay, I will. Call me, okay?" he asked, and she nodded as he kissed her temple before getting out of the booth, saying bye to both of them. Before he could get out the door, though, she was already texting him.

*Wren: I'm gonna kill you.*

*Jensen: Not if I can find the biggest Snickers and chuck it at you.*

Keeping in her laughter, she looked across the table at her ex-best friend. Shanna looked so much like Bradley with her light brown hair and big blue eyes. She wasn't as tall as Bradley, but then, no one really was. Except for every other man she knew. God, she was nervous.

"So!" Wren gushed, and she never gushed, so she pressed her lips together to cover up the fact that she was freaking the fuck out. This was the last thing she wanted. Damn it. "How's life?"

She saw something flash in Shanna's eyes before she shrugged. "You know, just raising kids and being a wife. I don't do anything special."

Wren could hear the hostility in her voice. It was expected, but then, Wren sort of thought Shanna would have hit her with it a little later in their stupid lunch date. "That's not true. Mom said you are decorating for her."

She nodded. "That's for your mom because, for the longest time, she was my second mom. But then, that just changed."

Wren slowly looked down at the table. She couldn't do this. She couldn't sit and deal with the borderline hostility in Shanna's tone. Yeah, she was good at ignoring shit, but she wasn't afraid to get her hands dirty, especially when it was her fault they were a mess. "So, we're doing this now?"

"Doing what?"

Wren looked back up. "It's obvious that you don't want to talk about life. You want to know why I dropped you like a bad habit, and that's understandable," she said as strong as she could as she met Wren's gaze. "And the answer is I got pregnant, and I knew you'd judge me for my floozy-ish lifestyle."

Shanna's eyes narrowed as she held Wren's gaze. "How are you a floozy if you're married to the guy?"

Swallowing hard, Wren didn't want to lie, but she couldn't tell Shanna about Bradley. There was no way in hell. If she was having a hard time telling Jensen, who she knew would love her no matter what, there was no way she could tell Shanna. "We hooked up, and

I got pregnant. I didn't tell him until about a month and a half ago. He asked me to marry him, and I said yes."

Shanna nodded slowly. "So you kept it from everyone? No one knew?"

Wren licked her lips. "Yeah, no one knew until I told Jensen."

"And so you stopped talking to me because you assumed I would judge you?"

"I didn't assume anything, I knew you would. You wanted me to be like you, settle down, have kids, and get married, but that wasn't what I wanted—"

"But look at you now," she pointed out. "And you seem happy."

Wren's eyes narrowed. "I said it wasn't what I wanted. Things are different now. I love Jensen, I love my son, and I'm happy. But I knew you wouldn't support me, and you would get pissy with me because I wouldn't know what I wanted to do."

"Because you never know what you want to do. You let your need for attention take over, and you fuck whatever you see. It's sad because you're a beautiful girl, a good girl, smart, but you treat yourself like a slab of meat and get fucked by assholes."

Too bad the main asshole was Shanna's brother, but Wren didn't say that. "You need to put all that in past tense."

Shanna's brows pulled together. "What?"

"All of that isn't true anymore. You're right, I did do all that. But I haven't since I got pregnant, and the reason why it took me so long to tell Jensen is because I knew I would officially be done with that life, and I wasn't ready to accept that. That's all changed now. I'll be the first to tell you that not everyone changes, but I feel I have. Or maybe Jensen just loves me the way I need to make myself better. But I'm proud of that because, you're right, I didn't think highly of myself. Due to my need to be loved, I was pathetic. But now, after knowing what real love is, I'm good. I love who I am because of the man who loves me."

Inhaling deeply, Shanna held her hands out. "That's all I wanted for you."

"Well, at the time, I didn't want to hear that. I wanted to figure it out on my own, but I couldn't. I needed Jensen." Wren's heart sang in her chest, saying the words she had been thinking for so long. She wished Jensen were there so he could hear her because she was sure he wouldn't believe her when she told him later. "I'm sorry.

I'm so fucking sorry, Shanna, for more than I can ever tell you. But I had to do what I did, for me. And call it selfish, but I couldn't take what I knew you'd give me."

Shanna looked down, running her tongue along her teeth as she shook her head. "I wouldn't have been that bad. I would have said that you needed to settle down—"

"But I didn't want to hear that."

"Jensen is a wonderful guy, and I would have pushed—"

With her heart throbbing in her throat, Wren couldn't take it anymore. The guilt was overpowering.

"I lied." When Wren said it, her own eyes widened, not expecting herself to say that.

What the hell was she doing?

"What?"

"I lied about Jensen, and there is a chance you could tell everyone, but I'll deny it."

Shanna's face scrunched up. "What the hell are you talking about?"

"Jensen isn't my baby's biological father. I know who the father is, but he told me to get an abortion after throwing a check at me. And when I refused, he told me I was stupid and he was done with me."

"Wren," Shanna gasped, reaching out to take her hands. "What in the world? Who is it?"

*Your brother.*

"It doesn't matter. He didn't want my child or me, and that's the biggest reason I didn't tell you or my mom or anyone. I was trying to figure out what the hell I was going to do because of my inheritance and all that—"

"Jesus, I forgot about that inheritance of yours. Such a stupid stipulation."

"Yeah, so, no, I shouldn't have cut you out. I shouldn't have cut anyone out, really, but I was embarrassed, I was scared, and I didn't know what the hell I was going to do." When her eyes started to well up with tears, she looked down at the table as her mouth twitched, trying to hold back the sob that wanted to escape. "It took Jensen coming into my life, steamrolling me into a marriage I asked for, even though I didn't want it. He changed everything and made me realize I was worth a man like him, a love like he could give me, and a chance for my son to have a father who would love him as his own. It took Jensen. Only Jensen to make me finally love myself, and he's the reason I'm here. He knew I owed it to you to explain myself and to apologize because, Shanna, I'm sorry. I am. Really sorry."

When Wren looked up, tears rolling down her cheeks, she found that Shanna was in tears herself. Holding her gaze, Wren saw the girl who had been her constant companion growing up. Her best friend and not the hostile girl Wren had done wrong.

"Wren, you know I've loved you as my sister since I was four. So we hit a snag. Oh, well. I love you and I'm sorry you felt that way, but I know you, and I know you do things your way with no second thoughts. So I forgive you, I do. I just wish you'd have done this a long time ago."

"Me too."

"But all in all, this is all I ever wanted for you, Wren. Jensen is amazing, and I know he'll love you and your son for the rest of his life. He's a damn good dude, and fuck the dude that did you dirty."

Wren's heart tightened. "Thanks."

"Of course," Shanna said, squeezing Wren's hands. "Now tell me everything. Pregnancy, everything. I want it all."

A grin pulling at her lips, Shanna picked up a napkin and wiped Wren's cheeks, which made them both laugh before Wren found herself having one of the best afternoons with a friend who was supposed to be her lifelong friend. Wren had shut everyone out in the past, and that was her fault. But she knew she had found someone who would never allow her to do that to him.

And when Jensen came to pick her up, she wrapped her arms around his waist and looked up at him with nothing but the love and praise she had just spent the afternoon gushing about. But he was looking back into the diner, his brows up. "I don't see blood, and it took three hours for you to call me, so I'm assuming there was no one injured?"

Wren scoffed. "It was nice. We talked everything out."

He seemed surprised. "So, you two are good?"

She shrugged. "Do I think we'll be as close as we were? Never, I ruined that, and I own it. But I'll check in, and we'll text. But this needed to happen."

"It did," he agreed, kissing her forehead. "I'm very proud of you."

She laughed. "For being an adult?"

He grinned. "Hey, adulting is hard for you."

Nodding very fervently, she agreed. He loved her, even her faults. All of her. How in the world did she get that fucking lucky? To keep from crying, she beamed as she joked, "Right? Pants, wearing pants is the hardest part. I hate them."

"This is very true. We should all be able to walk around pants-less," he teased, holding her close as they headed toward his car.

"Yes! And everyone would be okay with it. But no, people are worried about indecency. Pathetic, I tell you."

"We should start a no-pants uprising."

"Yes," she laughed. "We can be the ambassadors!"

"We'd be the best."

"We would!" she agreed as they reached the car, and he opened the door for her. But when she didn't get in, he looked down, confused.

"You ready to go?"

Exhaling hard, she reached up, taking his face in her hands as her eyes started to well up. She wanted to tell him. Right there. Tell him the truth and hope he would be okay with it. But she found she didn't have it in her. She loved the way he looked at her. Loved the way he loved her, and she couldn't fuck with that.

She couldn't.

"Can I tell you something?"

His eyes softened as he nodded, his hands coming to her hips. "Of course, what's up?"

Biting her lip, she struggled with her words. But then, a grin pulled at her lips as she whispered, "Thank you."

His face twisted in confusion. "For what? I thought you were gonna kill me for leaving." She laughed, and he smiled, the kind of smile that made her belly flutter funny. "I actually have your Snickers in the car."

Shaking her head as her laughter subsided, she leaned into him. "No, Jenny, not that."

"Then what?"

Holding his gaze, she curved her lips into what she felt was the biggest smile she could possibly muster. "For loving me enough to force me to love myself."

His lips quirked as he dropped his head to hers. "Well, that just made my day."

"Good, because you've made all my days since the moment back home at the restaurant when I asked you to be my husband."

"That was a damn good day," he said, squeezing her ass in his hands as she giggled against his lips. "Because, of course, I'm the most awesome ever."

"I'm awesomer."

"I beg to differ."

"Shut up."

"Don't tell me to shut up. I am your man," he teased.

"That's right, so shut up," she challenged as she beamed up at him, her heart in her throat. "And kiss me."

When he dropped his lips to her neck, she giggled as he kissed her over and over again, up her jaw, to her chin before finally smashing his mouth to hers. Coming to her toes, she fell into the kiss, knowing that everything she had said that day was completely the truth. She never thought this would be her life, but now, she wouldn't want it any other way.

With anyone else.

Only Jensen.

* * *

HE LAY ON HIS STOMACH, Wren's naked body pressed to his side, her belly in his hip as her hand moved lazily along his back. His son was moving like mad, and her nose glided along his shoulder. She looked like a goddess. Her hair was falling over her shoulder, a mess, but a beautiful mess. Her face was flushed, as was her body, showing marks from his mouth and hands.

God, he loved her.

"I didn't hurt you, did I?"

She scoffed, biting his shoulder and causing him to hiss out a breath. "Did I hurt you?"

He laughed, shaking his head. "No."

"Same here, then. I swear you think I'm made of glass."

Closing his eyes, he nodded. "To me, you are, and especially with my boy in you."

Silence fell between them as his body still vibrated from their lovemaking. It was early in the morning; the sun was starting to come up, but when she got up to use the bathroom, coming back in just her panties since she was burning up, he had to have her. He knew they'd fall back asleep and probably not wake up until twelve, which would, of course, piss Elaine off.

Wells's wedding was at six, so there was no way they could sleep in. No way Wren could get her hair and makeup done in time. Even he knew that.

But sleep, at that moment, sounded like heaven to him.

"Go to sleep," he muttered, reaching for his phone. "We gotta get up soon."

"What time is it?"

He opened one eye to set his alarm for three hours later. "Five."

"Ew."

"Yeah, shh."

She snickered beside him as she cuddled closer. He threw his phone back onto the nightstand before turning his head so that his nose was smothered in her hair. Taking in a deep breath, he smiled as he let it out, kissing her head before closing his eyes once more. Her fingers were so relaxing against his back, and soon he was drifting off to sleep. Well, until she whispered his name.

"Jensen."

He groaned. "What? Are you hot? Scoot over, you're the one holding me."

"No, it isn't that."

Still with his eyes shut, he asked, "Then what?"

"I told Shanna the truth."

He opened one eye. "What truth?"

"That the baby wasn't yours by blood."

He opened his other eye, surprised by that. "Why?"

"I didn't want to lie to her anymore. I wanted to be honest about why I didn't tell her, that I had shut everyone out and even tried with you, but there was no shutting you out."

He shrugged. "This is true."

"And so, I've been thinking about it all day."

He groaned. "The shutting me out part? Ugh, Wren, you gonna try that again?"

She glared, her little nose wrinkling as she shook her head. "No, dork, not that."

"Then what?"

"About the douche that knocked me up."

He didn't know what to say, so he got on his elbows, looking at her, fully awake at that point. "Okay?"

"I don't want to tell you. I was going to. I had every intention to, but the more I thought about it, the more I worried that when you looked at our son, you'd think of him. I'm worried I'll do the same, but that's my cross to bear, and I don't want that to be on you. I want you to look at our son and see only me, to see only your love in his eyes. That may be selfish, or even stupid of me, but I don't want to do that to you."

His heart stilled in his chest. "So I know him?"

She looked down at his shoulder and shook her head. "I don't want to answer that, Jensen, I really don't. Please don't ask me that again."

His eyes searched hers, and when they started to well, he tried so damn hard to get past his jealousy of that fucker, to understand what she was saying, what she wanted for him because it was kind. It was sweet, and he appreciated that, but could he let it go? "I love you, Jensen, and you're it for me. So, really, he doesn't matter. Only us and Gunner."

Holding her gaze, he didn't know what to say. He wanted to be a good man, a great man for her, but could he get past this and be that man? Or would he be a jealous bastard? Even though she didn't admit that he did know the guy, he couldn't help but feel he did. Just like that, again, Bradley's face came to mind, and he swore the anger that coursed through his body was worse than anything he had ever experienced.

And he had lived and grown up with Vaughn Johansson.

Gazing into Wren's eyes, he knew that he loved her, and that he had to trust her wishes for them if he expected her to do the same. Things were moving, things were good. Could he really let this hold them back? Clearing his throat, he said, "Wren—"

But before he could go on, his phone was ringing. "What in the world? Who would call you this early? Or late?"

His heart sped up as he said, "Only Vaughn, Wells, or my mom."

She sat up as he did the same, reaching for his phone as her heart dropped. "Mum?"

His mother spoke fast in French as his heart slowly but surely fell out of his chest. Looking up to Wren, he saw her eyes were full of worry as he spoke back just as quickly, trying to find out information about his father. Wren's face mirrored exactly what he felt, completely terrified. The conversation was brief and to the point, but usually it was when his father found himself in the hospital. As he told his mom he loved her, he hung up and ran his hands down his face, fighting back the tears.

"Babe, what's wrong? Is it your dad?"

He nodded, blinking back his tears as his heart jumped into his throat. "He spiked a fever this morning, Mum rushed him to the hospital, and they found a spot on the back of his leg that she must have been missing, and it's terribly infected. She's freaking out because she doesn't know how she could have missed it, but Dad is saying it wasn't her fault. That it's where his leg was up against the chair or something."

"But I saw her. She'd hold his whole leg and clean it. I helped, I never saw anything but what we cleaned. I don't understand."

"I don't either. She said it's right above the back of his knee," he said, feeling the tears welling up in his eyes. He was just sick of his dad being sick. He wanted him to be healthy; he wanted the man he had grown up with. He felt like he didn't get enough time with him since he was always in America with the Lemieres. A tear fell, and Wren made a sound of distress before wrapping her arms around his neck. Smothering his face in her neck, he inhaled deeply, getting lost in her intoxicating scent.

"What are they saying?"

Moving his face as she held him, he sniffed as he squeezed his eyes shut. "They're pretty sure they're gonna have to amputate his leg."

"What?" she gasped, pulling back to look at him. "Is he healthy enough for that?"

"They say so. Mum won't know more for a few hours. They're waiting for some tests to come back."

Wren let him go and scooted out of the bed, struggling to get up. But when she did, she went to turn on the light. "What are you doing?"

"Packing. Find us a flight."

"Wren."

"No, he needs us."

"Wren, Wells's wedding is in a matter of hours."

She made a face. "I don't care. This is your dad. He needs us, and damn it, Wells will understand that. Find us a flight."

His heart, man, he couldn't take the love that was suffocating him at the moment. "Baby."

"Jensen, you heard me. Don't fight me on this," she said as she reached for her suitcase from under the bed, her ass perking up and doing crazy things to his heart.

"I asked Mum if I should come home since I wouldn't ask you to miss your brother's—"

"They are my family too," she said simply, looking up at him as she stood. "Wells will understand. If you go, I go."

His eyes welled up. "And miss your brother's wedding? Your only brother?"

"Yes," she said, her eyes burning into his, and he could see she was holding back tears. "You are my husband. Where you go, I go," she asserted once more.

Silenced stretched between them as he threw the blankets off, getting out of bed and taking the suitcase from her before throwing it on the bed. Reaching for her, he pulled her into his arms before he wrapped an arm around her neck. "Mum said not to miss Wells's wedding, that she has everything under control. But if that changes, she'll call us."

She blinked, a tear rolling down her face. "What do you think?"

He shrugged. "I want to go, but my mum knows what she is doing. I also know I'll feel like shit if I rush out there, miss my best friend's wedding, and everything is fine. But then, what if I don't go, and he di—" His words fell off. Closing his eyes, he bent his head to hers as he drew in a deep breath. "I have to trust my mum. This isn't the first time, and we knew there would be a chance he'd lose limbs with his diabetes."

Holding on to him, she kissed his jaw. "I'm sorry, Jensen."

He nodded against her head. "He'll be fine. I know it."

"Yeah, but maybe we should pack, just in case."

"Or let's sleep. We have a big day today," he suggested.

"Like you'll sleep," she countered, and he shrugged.

"I am mostly worried about you sleeping."

"Don't. I'm fine. Let me worry about you."

A smile pulled at his lips as he cuddled her in tight, feeling completely and utterly secure. He was worried, and it ran deep, but he trusted his mum. He knew if it was serious and he needed to come, she would tell him. Plus, Wren had him.

He trusted that entirely.

"I don't know how I ever made it without you."

She scoffed. "Please, you were fine. I was the hot mess express going straight into a wall," she joked, kissing his jaw before taking his hand in hers, hitting the light, and dragging him to the bed. They cuddled together, their legs tangled, their hands all over each other. He kissed her temple before she reached over him, taking his phone and laying it on the pillow above them. "Just in case."

He nodded. "She said she'll call me in a couple hours."

"So we'll hear it."

"Yeah," he agreed, moving a piece of hair out of her eyes.

"I'm worried," Wren whispered, and Jensen nodded.

"Me too."

"Maybe we should call?"

"You can, get the wrath of Emma Monroe."

"That's not fair," she complained, and he smiled against her hair.

"She'll call."

But Wren was already moving. Reaching for his phone, she was pushing buttons, and then he heard his mom's voice. "Hey, no, it's Wren. Is everything okay? Oh, okay. Yeah, no Jensen said. Oh, okay, well, do you want us to come up there? Oh. Okay. No, I understand. I know, I love you too. But we should…or not. Yeah, you're right. Wells would understand, though. Yeah, okay, so call us as soon as you hear something? I know you told Jensen that, but I just want you to know it doesn't matter what's going on. Call us. Okay. All right. Love you too." Hanging up, she gave him a grim smile. "She told me I was distracting her."

"Yeah, I figured she would."

"She said she's got it under control, and she'll give us updates."

"That's what she told me."

Wren seemed annoyed as she set his phone back in the spot by the bedpost before lying back in her spot. "Does she always do that to you?"

He laughed. "Every single time."

332 | TONI ALEO

Still annoyed, she lay down. "Fine, I'm going to try to sleep,"

"Good plan," he said as she kissed his cheek, his eyes falling shut before she wrapped her body around his.

As she lay there, her heart was pounding in her chest, and the rhythm was mind-altering. He wanted to say he was about to fall asleep, but that wasn't going to happen. His mind was moving a million miles a second, and he was worried for his dad. He wanted to call his mum again, but like she had done with Wren, she would do to him, but worse. He sort of wished he had let Wren take him away.

But that wouldn't be fair to Wells, or even to his father.

Antoine would get so mad if they made their way up there and missed Wells's wedding. His father was untouchable in Jensen's eyes. The diabetes was just a setback, he would be fine, but Jensen wasn't naïve. His father was aging, and he wished he had listened to Wren, bought a house up there and never left. But then his dad would have really had killed him for giving up his dreams. Antoine was Jensen's biggest cheerleader when it came to him living his dreams. Because of that, Jensen knew he was going to be there for his son the way his dad had been there for him.

His son.

Man, his heart ached.

Opening his eyes, he watched as she stared at the wall, and a grin pulled at his lips. "Hey, babe."

She looked up at him, her eyes wide and ready to go. "Yeah? You wanna go?"

He shook his head, his throat closing up as his mouth went dry. "I won't ask again." Her face twisted in confusion, and he figured he'd given her nothing there. "About the douche that knocked you up. This baby," he said, pressing his hand on her belly, "is mine."

"He is."

"So I won't ask, and I appreciate your reasoning because I think you're right."

"You do?"

"Yeah, I don't want that either. I like the thought that I'll only see you, and maybe me, in him."

"I love you too much to allow you to do anything else when I know you love Gunner so much."

"I do, but, Wren?"

"Yeah?"

"I love you just as much."

Her lips curved as she ran her finger along his jaw. "I love you too."

"And thank you for wanting to run off to be with my dad."

"Of course."

As their lips met, Jensen knew they were going to be better than okay.

They were going to be great.

# Chapter
# TWENTY-TWO

*J*ensen exhaled hard, letting the phone fall to the bar as he looked up at Wells and Vaughn, who were sitting across from him in the kitchen. "They aren't going to have to amputate Dad's leg."

"Oh, thank God," Wells said as Elaine came over, wrapping her arms around him.

"So he's good?" she asked, and he shrugged, hugging her back.

"They are getting the infection under control, and it seems that way. Things are still up in the air, though. Dad claims he's fine. But Mum said she'll send me updates as she gets them. She wished you a beautiful wedding," he said to Wells, and his best friend smiled.

Getting his phone out, Wells said, "I'll text her."

"I'm so glad. I was very worried," Elaine said, and Winston nodded from the breakfast nook.

"So was I. I'm texting him now, and he says he's fine," Winston said with a laugh, and Jensen smiled.

Man, what a weight off his chest. He felt a lot better, yet he was still very tired since he didn't catch a wink the rest of the morning. He felt like shit that Wren hadn't slept at all either. She'd stayed wide awake beside him, holding him before they both decided there was no point and got up for the day. She even made it to her hair and makeup appointment, which was surprising to all, especially Elaine since Wren had thrown a fit that she didn't want to leave Jensen.

Reaching back for his phone, he dialed her number. "Hey, you good?" she asked.

"Yeah, my dad just called."

"Oh! Did he? What did he say?"

"Things are good. They don't have to amputate, and they think they've got it under control."

"Oh, thank God! I'm so happy. I'm gonna call them."

"Okay, love you."

"Love you," she said before hanging up, and he set his phone down, shaking his head.

"What?" Wells asked, and Jensen grinned up at him.

"She was really worried, and I like hearing her peppy after being pretty down this morning."

"Yeah, she loves your parents. We all do. I would have understood if you had to miss it, dude. Plus, I would have been pissed if you hadn't gone and something went wrong."

Jensen nodded. "I know, and I appreciate that."

"We all would have understood. Antoine is family."

Drawing in a breath, he exhaled it hard before saying, "I'm just glad he's okay."

"We all are," Elaine added, rubbing his arm softly. "Very much so."

While he was happy his father was okay, he still felt a bit of guilt as he stared down at his phone. Maybe he should have been there. Stayed in Canada a bit longer, but he knew that couldn't happen with the plans in Colorado. "I feel like I need to visit more. I don't because I'm always so busy, and man, it's about to get harder with Gunner coming."

Wells looked up, nodding his head. "Yup, life is about to get busy as hell for all of us, and that's cool. That's life, but you'll make the time to go see your mom and dad. I know you will."

Vaughn agreed, "Yeah, maybe we can all go up at the end of the summer. He'll love having all of us, and Brie has been wanting to check out Canada."

Jensen loved the sound of that. "We'll have to see if Wren will be allowed. She's getting big."

"Yeah, she is. My nephew is gonna be huge," Wells added, shaking his head.

"He'll be perfect, just like our Jensen," Elaine cooed from the sink, and Jensen chuckled as Wells and Vaughn made faces at her.

"Gag, Mom," Wells teased, and Vaughn scoffed.

"Yeah, Mom, we all know who your favorite is. You don't have to keep reminding us."

She glared. "I love all three of you the same."

"Lies, all lies, Jensen's her favorite," Winston called from the table, and she glared back at him while all three men laughed. There wasn't a moment growing up that this hadn't already happened. Everyone was always fighting for the love of Elaine Lemiere.

No wonder Wren felt so left out.

But she'd never feel left out again.

Not with him around.

"Oh, look, I gotta get to the salon."

"Why didn't you go with Wren and Brie?" Wells asked, and she waved him off.

"I don't have as much hair as they do, so my appointment was later," she answered, reaching for her purse. "Now listen, all of you need to be at the venue by three, get ready, and be ready to go by five. There are drinks and food there."

"Like beer? Right?" Vaughn asked, and she shot him a look.

"No, I'm not giving you three beer so that you can't act right at this wedding." She paused and then shook her head. "Who am I kidding? You three can't act right together sober. Alcohol wouldn't have mattered."

"This is true," Wells said as she rolled her eyes, going out the back door as Vaughn laughed.

"Are we really that bad?" he asked and Jensen nodded.

"We weren't good, that's for sure."

"For damn sure," Winston added.

"My dad was telling Wren about that summer we went up there and all those girls were next door—"

"Maxie, Trinity, Layla, and Selena," Vaughn said with the stupidest grin on his face. Jensen and Wells both looked at him with such perplexed gazes.

"How the hell do you remember their names?" Jensen asked, completely flabbergasted since he couldn't remember them to save his ass.

"You always remember the girls who gave you blow jobs and who you had sex with."

"You had sex with all of them?" Wells asked, his eyes wide.

Vaughn shrugged. "I mean, you weren't hollering at them. Poor Layla was in love with you, and I told her I could give her more, so I did. And then Selena and Trinity were all about Jenny, but I told them my dick was bigger. And that's how that happened. But Maxie, that was my sweetie, and man, she rocked my young little heart."

"I'm disgusted," Wells said, shaking his head while Jensen laughed.

"I can't believe you."

"Hey, some of us love sex."

"Yeah, all of us, just not with multiple women—or men, in Wells's case."

"Thank you," Wells said with a nod, and they all laughed as Winston just shook his head.

"Man, it's like old times with you three home."

They all nodded, sharing a familiar moment as Winston got up, heading out of the room toward the bathroom. Watching as his father left, Wells shook his head. "How'd he not know?"

Jensen shrugged. "Denial, probably."

"Yeah, because you never brought home a girl. Oh! But remember, man, what was his name?" Vaughn said, snapping his fingers, and Wells scoffed.

"So you can remember all the girls you were with, but not my first boyfriend?"

Jensen laughed at that as Vaughn shrugged innocently. "Yeah, sorry."

"Nicolas," Wells said, shaking his head with a grin pulling at his lips. "Man, I loved him."

"Yeah, and I'll never forget your dad catching you guys kissing. I heard him down the road," Vaughn laughed.

"I wouldn't leave my room. Neither would Wren," Jensen chuckled. "We sat on the bathroom counter and just listened to the screaming."

Wells's face didn't change, a grin on his face as he shrugged. "That's when I came out to him. It was nasty." Exhaling hard, he looked out the door and shook his head. "At least he stopped screaming at me about it, and he's coming to the wedding."

Jensen and Vaughn both agreed, but only with a nod as a silence fell over them. Jensen wasn't sure what everyone else was thinking about as they ate the pie that Elaine had made for them, but Jensen's mind went back to his dad. He couldn't imagine not being able to talk to his dad without raised voices. But that was Wells's life since his dad had found out. They used to be best friends, but that all changed when Wells came out. To that day, Jensen still felt bad for them. While it wasn't Jensen's cup of tea, Wells was his best friend, and he loved him for him, not for who he loved. Jensen just wished Winston could see that.

"So you're still gonna marry him?" Vaughn asked, and Jensen closed his eyes.

"Really, Jo?"

Vaughn looked over at Jensen. "What? I mean, I'm just making sure."

Wells scoffed. "Yeah, man, I'm marrying him."

"You sure? We can head out, no questions asked."

Reaching out, Wells wrapped his arm around Vaughn's shoulder. "I love him."

But Vaughn wasn't convinced. "You sure?"

"Jo! Stop."

"Hey, this is our best friend. We have to make sure, and you know damn well he doesn't look at Alex the way he looked at Matty."

Jensen pressed his lips together, looking away. "It doesn't matter. It matters what he feels. He loves the guy, leave him be."

When Jensen glanced up, Vaughn and Wells were sharing a look. "I only ask because I love you, man. I don't want you to make a mistake."

Wells sighed heavily as he shook his head. "The only mistake I made was giving Matty my whole heart when he didn't even give me a piece of his."

Vaughn looked to Jensen with his eyes wide, and of course, he was telling him clearly that he was right. But Jensen shook his head before looking over to his friend. "Do you want to marry him? Alex?"

"Yeah, because I have to."

"You don't have to do shit, son." They all three looked to the door, where Winston stood, his brows pulled together as he glared at Wells. "If you don't want to marry this boy, don't. I don't care how much money we've spent. I want you to be happy."

A little taken aback, Wells's hand came to his chest. "No, Dad, it's not that. I do love Alex, I do. Which is why I have to. It's the right time."

Winston slowly nodded. "Then that's that."

With that, he turned and headed out the back door, and Jensen assumed he was going to his woodshed. Looking back to Wells, he found his best friend with his mouth hanging open as he watched his father cross the backyard to his shed. "What just happened?"

"No clue," Vaughn said, his mouth hanging open too.

Pointing to his father's woodshed, Wells asked, "Did my dad just accept my lifestyle?"

"I think so," Jensen said, a little shocked too.

"Or we all blacked out, and this is a dream," Vaughn supplied, but all three of them nodded.

"That seems more believable," Wells muttered before the three them found themselves laughing from the gut.

Leaning on the counter, Jensen looked over at the two men who had been his constant buddies. Two men he knew he couldn't do life without. His best friends. As Wells's laughter subsided, he looked between them and grinned. "I'm thankful to have you two. Honestly. You've never stopped loving me in a non-gay way, and I truly love both of you, in a non-gay way, for that."

"I mean, we are all pretty much the coolest dudes ever. It's only natural we flock together," Vaughn said in his own cocky manner.

Snorting, Jensen reached out, squeezing Wells's shoulder. "Right back at you. I was just thinking the same thing, that this life would be boring without you two."

Rolling his eyes, Vaughn scoffed. "Whatever, you've replaced us with Wren."

"Oh yeah, she's your life now," Wells teased, and Jensen flipped them off.

"While, yes, she is my everything and so is my son, I know I need you two assholes, too," he admitted, looking down at the counter. "So I hope you two are ready to raise my son with me."

Wells let out a sigh as Vaughn laughed. "And my daughter with me."

"I can get a dog for you guys to help raise if I need to since Alex doesn't want kids yet, but I'm so down for raising some babies!"

Wells announced, and Jensen's face started to hurt, he was grinning so hard.

"In due time. But in the meantime, let's go get you married."

"Or drunk so you can get married," Vaughn supplied, and Jensen shot him another dirty look. "What? I still don't think it's gonna happen."

"I hate you," Wells groaned, but then he squeezed Vaughn. "But I love you too."

"It's complicated with me."

"Everyone knows that," Jensen informed him. "Like everyone."

"Poor Brie," Wells teased and Jensen chuckled.

"Right?" Vaughn added.

Again, the kitchen was filled with laughter from three guys who grew up together and who had continued to be brothers for the last fifteen years. There was never a dull moment with them. If they weren't laughing, they were fighting, or they were crying. They were brothers. And while, now, all of them were older, probably not a bit wiser, they were still the best of friends.

All Jensen could think was that he was living a dream.

The same best friends?

And the girl he had loved just as long as he had known them, and a kid on the way?

Yeah. It was all just too good to be true.

* * *

"Mom, I want to go hang in the room with the guys." Her mother rolled her eyes, taking a big gold bow from the stack of bows Wren was holding and tying it to the pew. "Isn't there someone else who can do this?"

Elaine shot her an evil look. "You think if that were the case, I would have asked you? Everyone is getting the reception ready since everything was late getting here. Wren, please, just help me."

"Fine," she groaned, but her feet were killing her. There was no way she was going to make it in these insanely high heels Wells had insisted she wear with her suit. Which was all a little tighter that morning. She probably should have skipped that packet of Snickers she snuck when Jensen was hanging with the guys this morning. Maybe she should listen and take better care of her body before she turned into a whale. "Mom, these shoes suck," she complained, kicking them off.

"I told Wells they weren't gonna work. You're damn well pregnant!"

"This is true," Wren agreed as she moved with her mom, putting bows everywhere.

"Just go barefoot, and if he complains, I'll throw them at him."

Wren's lips quirked as she giggled. "Ah, you'll inflict pain on your favorite for me?"

Elaine glared back at her. "I'm not doing that with you, Wren. You're my favorite."

"I know, Mom," she said sweetly as they continued to hang the bows.

"Did you talk to Emma?"

"I did," Wren said with a grin tugging at her mouth. "Antoine is doing much better today. No fever thus far, but they're keeping a close eye on him."

"Good, that's what she told me, and Dad texted Ant too, heard the same thing. I know Jensen was worried."

Wren nodded. "Worried is one word. I don't see him freak out often, but when he does, it's scary."

"Oh, I'm sure. He is his daddy's boy."

"And his mom's."

"Right? And mine, hell," she laughed, and Wren chuckled. "He's a good boy, really good boy."

"The best," Wren decided.

"I walked in right on time, eh?"

Turning, she found Jensen coming toward her dressed in a slick black suit that was tailored to his body and made him completely scrumptious. His hair was smoothed to the side, his face free of stubble while his brown eyes sparkled as he drank her in. She wasn't sure she was sold on the whole pregnant woman in a suit idea, but she had to admit, she was cute. It didn't fit her the way it fit Jensen, but she did love that she didn't have to wear a bow tie, leaving the first couple buttons open to show off her chest. Her hair was in big, beautiful curls down to her shoulders, while her makeup was dramatic and beautiful, capped off by dark red lips.

She was feeling herself.

She was feeling Jensen more, but then, he was a hundred shades of gorgeous.

"What right time? We aren't talking about you," she teased as he wrapped her up, smiling down at her belly.

"Sure, you aren't."

"Nope, we were talking about these bows."

He laughed as he kissed the side of her mouth, sending hot waves of lust through her whole body with just the simple motion. "Well, that's disappointing. I needed an ego boost. Wells said my ass looks big in these pants, and I blame it on you and all the Snickers I eat to keep you from eating them."

Laughing out loud, she shook her head. "Your ass is beautiful."

"It is," Elaine added, and Wren sputtered with laughter.

"Ew! Creepy cougar!"

Elaine scoffed with laughter. "Please."

But Jensen was beet red. "Is your mom hitting on me?"

Still laughing, Wren shook her head as she handed her mom a bow. "She's losing her mind."

"I am," Elaine decided. "And aren't you supposed to be helping Wells, Winston, and Vaughn with taking all the boxes into the reception area? Oh, and did someone make sure they grabbed the Céline Dion CD from the counter? Alex wanted it to be authentic from his childhood."

"This wedding is so damn cliché," Wren muttered, and Jensen laughed.

"Yes, I grabbed it and got it to the DJ. I was doing that, but then I saw my beautiful wife and obviously needed a kiss."

"Obviously," she gushed before pressing her mouth to his. "Take me with you," she mouthed as they parted, and he smirked back at her.

"Nope, enjoy the bows," he teased before kissing her once more and heading back down the aisle and out of the room.

"That man is smitten with you, Wren. You are a lucky lady."

"I know," she said as an exhale, her lips turning up. "Mom, I'm hungry."

"You're always hungry. We're done, but listen. Before you run off in the search for whatever you'll go find to eat, please fill the vases with that gold glitter for the becoming one ceremony."

A blank look came over her face. "Do you know how insane this is getting?"

Elaine just looked at her. "You have no clue, but since you didn't give me a wedding to plan, here we are."

Wren scoffed as Elaine took the empty bow box from her and pointed to the other box with glitter inside before disappearing out the back. Curling her toes into the carpet of the venue, Wren looked up and smiled. The altar was completely insane with big white flowers and glitter adorning it, while a huge W and A—made of glitter, of course—were hung in the middle. It was beautiful, but she didn't get why her brother wanted so much glitter. He usually wasn't this sparkly. Or maybe it was Alex? Who knew.

Nevertheless, her mother had done a beautiful job, and Wren sort of wished she had given her mom a chance to plan her wedding. But the thought made her laugh. She didn't even want a wedding six months ago. She had just wanted a husband, but she got more than that.

She got her future.

Pulling out her phone from her handy pocket, probably the best thing about the suit, she clicked Jensen's name.

*Wren: We should plan a wedding when Gunner gets here.*

*Jensen: I'm sorry, who is this? It says this text is from my hot-ass wife, but my hot-ass wife doesn't do weddings.*

She laughed, the room filling with the sound, and she almost didn't believe it.

*Wren: Right? I must be drunk.*

*Jensen: Or you have a sugar high since I found your empty bag of miniature Snickers.*

*Wren: Those were my mom's.*

*Jensen: That you ate, in the bath.*

*Wren: I have no clue what you're talking about.*

*Jensen: Sure you don't.*

When she sent him the wacky emoji, he sent back a peach with a hand beside it, which meant he was going to get her ass. Within seconds, she was hot as she giggled and texted him back.

*Wren: Promise?*

*Jensen: Name the place and time.*

*Wren: Here, now*

*Jensen: Not fair. I'm unloading packs of glitter with your dad, while your mom yells at us because Vaughn decided to throw some on me and Wells. It's in my nose and my mouth, Wren. I might kill him today.*

Sputtering with laughter, she shook her head.

*Wren: Fine, rain check?*

*Jensen: Yup, like tonight, me and you.*

*Wren: Sounds like a plan.*

*Jensen: Agreed.*

With a smile that took up most of her face, she tucked her phone into her pocket before opening the box and getting out the three bags of glitter that she needed for the tall vases that were under the W&A. When she dropped one of the bags, she complained to herself, bending down and struggling to get back up, but her grin stayed in place.

Jensen drove her absolutely wild.

Before she could get to the center table, she heard, "Well, well, there you are."

She froze, his voice crawling down her spine as she looked down the aisle before Bradley started up it. He hadn't changed. Still so big, taking up the room, but she did notice he had put on some weight. His face was a little thicker than she recalled. Once upon a time, she remembered getting that fluttery feeling for him, but she felt nothing now. Not even anger. She just didn't want to see him. He was nothing to her.

"You're a hard one to get ahold of Wren."

She was holding her breath, clinging to the packs of glitter as her eyes widened but never left his. "Maybe 'cause I don't want to be gotten ahold of."

His eyes narrowed to slits. "I figured that. But then, surely that wasn't the case for the father of that baby inside of you. A boy, I hear."

"Bradley," she breathed because she didn't want him to know that. She didn't want anything from him.

"Wren, gorgeous as ever." Coming up to her, he reached for her, but she moved out of his reach. "How's my guy doing?"

She swallowed hard. "He's not yours."

"Oh, he is," he said, looking up at her. She was disgusted. She'd cared for this fucker at one point, but why? He did look like a douche, an unhappy one. "At least that was the claim before. Were you wrong?"

She stepped back from him. "What do you want?"

"To talk."

"You said we have nothing to talk about, multiple times, and I think you were right."

"I think I was wrong."

Her brows shot up to the damn ceiling. "Excuse me?"

"I was wrong," he admitted. "We obviously have a lot to talk about since I talked to your husband, Jensen Monroe, and found out a whole bunch of fun stuff."

Her eyes narrowed. She didn't like the way he said Jensen's name. "I don't know what you're talking about. Nothing has changed."

"Oh, sweetheart, a lot has changed," he said, his voice deep and sinister. She used to be turned on by his dark parts of his voice, but that wasn't the case any longer. Now, fear built up inside of her. "I shouldn't have done what I did."

"While that is true, it doesn't matter anymore."

"Sure, it does. Because I want to make this work."

Her brows came together as her face twisted in repulsion. "Now? Out of the blue? Aren't you married?" she spat back, not believing a single word he was saying.

"I mean seeing you, being near you, is doing things to me, something that Misty doesn't do."

She felt filthy, and when he tried to touch her, she moved out of his reach once more. "Don't touch me. I'm married, and Jensen is way more of a man than you'll ever be."

He snorted, his eyes narrowing in a way that had fear settling deep inside of her. "So you have him thinking he's the father. Jesus, Wren, that is dirty."

She was shaking. "Jensen knows the truth. He didn't run, he stood by my side."

Bradley rolled his eyes. "Ha, no, baby girl, he heard you needed someone to be your baby daddy. And he knows darn well around that inheritance you'll get for being married and with child. So of course, he's in. For the money. Don't be dumb."

"Oh, fuck off, that's not true," she said sternly, shaking her head. She wouldn't let him get in her head. Try to put that fucking doubt that liked to peek its ugly head into hers. Because even though she didn't realize it from the beginning, she knew it now. The truth was that Jensen loved her. "He loves me, and I know that."

"No one loves you, Wren, be real. You know that. You've always complained that your family doesn't pay you any mind. Why do you think that? They use you. Everyone does—for a damn good time. Because they don't care. But, sweetheart, I care."

She glared, her chest hurting as she shook her head. "No. The hell you don't."

"Yes, and you know it. Look at me. You know I love you, sweetheart."

As he took another step toward her, she held her hands up. He made the term *sweetheart* disgusting, and she found herself hating the word. Her stomach hurt, not where her son was, but behind him. It hurt; Bradley was making her ill. "You're delusional. So I'm going to ask you one more time. What the fuck do you want?"

Giving her a hard look, he pointed to her belly. "I want to be the father I need to be for my son. Jensen isn't the father. I am."

"No. Not even no, but fuck no. Jensen is the father. More so than you. Even if he has your fucking blood, it's all he'll ever get from you."

"Wren, be real. Jensen is nothing, except someone trying to get some money. He doesn't care about you or our—"

"He is *our* son, mine and Jensen's. Not yours. You were just the sperm donor," she reiterated firmly. "You walked out on us, you didn't want us, and by the grace of God, he gave me a man who wants us—"

"I'm not listening to that because we can both get quick divorces and then be together. I want you back."

When he reached for her, she smacked his hand away as her heart pounded in her chest. "Again, not even no could cover my answer here. It's fuck no again."

His face filled with anger as he glared down at her, reaching for her once more, taking ahold of her waist. "I'm his father."

Pushing into his chest, she yelled, "I don't—"

"Get the fuck away from her."

Wren froze.

She knew that voice. It was Vaughn's. And as she turned slowly,

Bradley finally letting her go, to look to the end of the room, she prayed Jensen wasn't there with his best friend.

*Please, God, please.*

But God must have been saving someone else at that moment because not only was Jensen standing beside Vaughn, but so was her brother.

And her mom.

And her dad.

Fucking. Awesome.

# Chapter
# TWENTY-THREE

Wren found it hard to breathe as her eyes met Jensen's, and all she could see was the pure betrayal on his beautiful, stony face.

"This isn't what it looks like," she tried to say as she held up her hands. "Jensen, I didn't—"

But Jensen wasn't talking, he was moving, with Vaughn and Wells flanking him while her parents looked on with their eyes wide and their mouths hanging open. As they came down the aisle, Bradley took a step back, holding his hands up. "Now, guys, this wasn't something new. I've been fucking her for years."

"Watch your mouth," Jensen said very slowly and very softly. "Not only am I married to her, but her parents are in the room. So have some respect, you low-life piece of shit."

"Yeah, douche," Wells added, shaking his head. "You were like family. Really, guy?"

"Who leaves her high and dry like that? Douches, that's who. You," Vaughn quipped, glaring, his fists bunched up as his face matched those of Wells and Jensen.

Pure and utter fury.

"You don't know the circumstances. I thought I didn't want this—"

"So you tell her to get an abortion? Throw her out on her ass, stressing her to the point that she shuts down and doesn't reach out to any of us? She has a family who loves her, you piece of shit. We don't need you, so at least let her go with some decency and respect. I mean, really? Your mom didn't raise you like that, I know that for sure," Wells said, his eyes filling with tears. "And who are you to say we don't love her and don't care about her? That's you, you bastard, and if I weren't getting married in this spot in a matter of hours, I would pound your fucking face in."

"I'm not getting married, and I'd love the chance, you fucking pathetic loser."

When Jensen's hand came to his chest, and then Vaughn's, Wells looked down at it before meeting Jensen's gaze. "He isn't worth it."

"I beg to differ. He needs his ass whooped, and I don't mind catching a charge for it," Vaughn announced, rolling up his sleeves. But Jensen stopped him once more.

"Guys, relax. He's gonna piss his pants."

"I am not, Monroe. You think you're so fucking high and mighty. You're nothing but a bottom dweller who lived off their family," Bradley spat at him, and Wren glared.

"He is more of a man than you'll ever be, you son of a bitch."

"Shut up, you know nothing other than what your pussy tells you you like," he shot back at her. When Wells made a noise, she knew Bradley was dead, but before her brother could swing on him, Jensen gripped Bradley's neck, his face coming so close his nose touched the other man's.

"I am two seconds from killing you. Watch it."

"Hey, asshole, watch your mouth because if they get ahold of you, I won't stop them. And when they're done, I'll kick your ass too," Winston called from the back of the hall as Jensen let Bradley go, his body shaking with fierceness.

"And then I'll kick you too, in the shin," her mother added, and Wren wanted to laugh, but her eyes were trained on Jensen. He wouldn't even look at her. "You're a bastard, Bradley, and I'll be sure never to donate to your firm again."

When Bradley rolled his eyes, Wren couldn't believe she had ever wanted to be with someone like him. But that didn't matter now. Her eyes went back to Jensen, who appeared calm, but she could see his shoulders, taut as all hell, and his eyes wide with anger. She was fucked. Like really fucked and she knew that damn well. She should have told him, she knew that, but her reasoning for not doing so, she had felt was right. Obviously, she was wrong. She could see the hurt in his eyes.

Damn it.

"Let me handle this," Wren heard Jensen say in a hushed tone, and her heart couldn't take it.

"I'm going to kill him."

"He isn't fucking worth it."

Pulling in a deep breath, Jensen looked past Bradley to Wren, and she froze, her heart jumping up into her throat. "So you want him back, I assume?"

Wren's eyes widened. "What? Him?"

"Yes. He's the father, so I assume—"

"Well, you assume wrong. I don't know when you guys decided to walk into this clusterfuck, but as I was telling this asshole, I don't want anything to do with him. I only want you," she said, stepping toward Jensen, but he held his hand up.

"And you think you want her back?"

Bradley looked at Jensen as his eyes narrowed. "I'm the father, and I sure as hell don't want you being with her and my child."

"You've always been jealous of Jensen, dude. We all know you don't want her, you're just trying to hurt him," Vaughn snapped, and Bradley scoffed.

"I don't give a shit about any of you. I just want to be with my kid."

"Whoa, what?"

Everyone turned at the same time to see Shanna standing by the side door, looking beautiful in a black dress that hugged her body. Wren's eyes closed as tears gathered in them.

Could this get any worse?

Where were the cameras? There had to be cameras for this damn clusterfuck.

When Shanna's eyes cut to Wren's, her heart sank. Well, there went the friendship she was trying to fix.

Shanna's eyes dragged from Wren's to Bradley before she said, very firmly, "Bradley, what did you say?"

Bradley's eyes widened as he looked at his sister before looking to Wren and then back to Shanna. Before he could speak, Wren said, "I couldn't tell you—"

"I'm not talking to you, Wren. I'm talking to him," Shanna demanded, and Wren snapped her mouth shut as she looked down to the ground, her heart hurting in her chest. She wasn't sure what the hell was going to happen, but this wasn't good. None of it was.

Lifting her head since Bradley was still sputtering, she looked to Jensen, who was staring at her, his eyes dark and full of so much hurt.

"Jensen—"

"Bradley, I asked you a question!" Shanna yelled, and when Wren looked over at her, her eyes were full of tears. Soon Wren's own tears were falling down her cheeks.

"I used to screw around with her, and she got pregnant."

The words hurt. Like knives going into her chest one by one. Why. Why him? But then she found herself thinking, *If it hadn't happened, you wouldn't have Jensen.*

But was she about to lose him?

"So explain to me why, just the other day, Wren was telling me that the guy who got her pregnant decided he didn't want her or the baby and wanted her to get an abortion. Is that true?"

There it was.

He'd lie, and everyone would believe him.

She just knew it.

Tears gushed from her eyes, falling down her cheeks as she stared at the floor.

"It wasn't completely like that. I got scared. I never told her to get an abortion," he lied, and she could only shake her head. It was her word against his. This fucker.

But to her surprise, Vaughn yelled, "Yes, you did, you fucking asshole. She wouldn't lie about that! Wren doesn't cry much, and when she does, it's for a good reason." When she looked up again, everyone was glaring at Bradley.

"Our baby wouldn't lie!" Elaine yelled, shaking her head.

"Be a man. Own up to what you did," Wells added, his eyes falling on Wren's. "You at least owe her that."

Wren's lips trembled as she sucked in a deep breath.

"He doesn't know how to be a man," Shanna said, and Wren's head whipped around to her, her mouth hanging open. "Wren wouldn't lie about that, so don't you dare lie to me."

Holy crap.

Bradley looked down, tucking his hands into his pockets. "Why does it matter? She didn't do it, and now I want to be the dad."

Shanna laughed, but there wasn't a trace of humor in it. "You? Want to be a dad? Are you serious? And you're ready to leave your meal ticket? Because you won't have a firm if you leave Misty. Also, do you know how much child support Wren can get out of you? How about taking care of the kid? Would you be able to handle that by yourself? Because if our parents find out, you're screwed."

Bradley shook his head. "I never said I was leaving Misty——"

"You told me to get a divorce and be with you not five minutes ago," Wren snapped, her tears rolling down her face. "Why do you lie? Why are you doing this? You don't fucking care about me."

Bradley went to speak, but Shanna stopped him, walking toward them as her eyes were trained on her brother. "You don't," she said sternly, her eyes so full of tears Wren couldn't believe they hadn't spilled over yet. "You aren't ready to be a father because you're not even a man. And the thing is, Bradley, you aren't the father of this child. Jensen is, and you need to leave that alone."

"Shanna——"

"Leave it alone," she said once more. "And get the fuck out of here."

Wren's eyes widened at the curse word, surprised that Shanna had said it to her baby brother, who had always apparently hung the moon. Shaking her head, Shanna covered her mouth, turning to leave, but Wren went to stop her. "Shanna, I'm so——"

"Don't touch me. Don't you ever talk to me again. You were with my brother? And you never told me? Don't. We are done," she said sternly, moving away from her and going out the door as Wren's shoulders drooped, her eyes falling shut as the silence fell over the lot of them.

"Your move, fucker," Wells said, and Wren shook her head.

"Just let him go," she added, wiping her face. "He doesn't matter."

"No——" Vaughn tried, but Jensen interrupted him.

"What do you want Wren?"

She opened her eyes, looking at her husband, but he wouldn't look at her. "I want you. I want us. I don't want this asshole. At all."

He nodded slowly, swallowing as he looked to Bradley. "So, your move, Brad. Want to take her to court?" Wren didn't miss that Jensen hadn't said *us*, and when she opened her eyes, he was glaring at Bradley. "Because I don't think she's letting you near the kid."

The kid. Not *our* kid.

Fuck.

Looking around, Bradley shook his head as he was breathing heavily, sweat gathering at his brow. And if three huge, angry hockey players were looking at her like they were about to kill her, she'd be sweating too. Turning to her, Bradley held her gaze. "You don't want me in the kid's life?"

"Not even kinda. But when he turns eighteen, I'll tell him who you are. If he wants you, he can find you, but Jensen will be his father."

Bradley chewed on his lip but not for long before shaking his head. "Fine, fuck it. I'm out," he said, holding his hands up, and she let out the breath she was holding as her gaze fell back to Jensen. He still wasn't looking at her.

"Best decision you've made today," Winston called up to him before shaking his head. "By the way, you aren't welcome around my family ever again."

Wells nodded. "Exactly, and if you don't want your mama finding out, I suggest you get out of here."

Bradley went to pass by Jensen, but Wells blocked him. He looked up at her brother, and Wren held her breath, waiting for the hit. "Can I get by, or is this really going to result in blows?

"Wells. Be an adult, please," Jensen said simply, and Wells rolled his eyes, stepping out of his way.

As Wells stepped next to Jensen, he watched Bradley, and she almost thought he would hit him, but then Vaughn said, "Oh, Brad, you forgot this."

Bradley's face scrunched up as he turned, but before he could even open his mouth to ask anything, Vaughn's fist crashed into his face, hard, and Bradley hit the ground just as hard.

Gasping, Jensen hollered, "What the hell, Vaughn?"

Shaking out his hand, Vaughn shrugged. "You told Wells to be an adult, not me."

"You knocked him out cold!" Wells yelled, and Vaughn shrugged. "On the runner! Shit, Alex is gonna be pissed!"

"How in the hell did you knock him out?"

"I tell you guys all the time, I'm strong as fuck."

Ignoring him, Wren reached out, taking Jensen's arm. He turned, looking down at her as her eyes begged for forgiveness. "Jensen, I'm so sorry. I didn't want you to find out like this."

He chuckled but without humor. "You mean, you didn't want me to find out at all."

"Yes, that," she said simply. "He's an asshole, he doesn't matter. I told you that. Only you matter."

Shaking his head, he looked down at the ground. "Wren, I'm so mad, I could fucking scream right now. Just let me go."

"Never. I'll never let you go. Please, don't be mad at me. I get it. I was an idiot—"

"You lied to me."

"But I didn't. I just didn't confirm or deny your theory because I couldn't, and I know that makes me a coward, and I know you're pissed. I'm so sorry. Please, Jensen, look at me," she begged, reaching for his face to pull him toward her, but when she saw his expression, she let him go.

His eyes were full of tears.

"Did you know he was going to be here today?"

Her brows came in as she shook her head. "I wasn't sure. I assumed so, but I didn't care. I swear it, I only care about you. Us. Our family."

Looking away, he closed his eyes as his shoulders fell. "The day of the Cup party, you didn't go because you knew he'd be there, didn't you?"

She pressed her lips together. She wasn't sure what he was getting at, but she was unable to lie, so she nodded. "Yeah, I didn't want to see him."

He nodded as a tear slowly rolled down his face. "And you wanted to fly home to be with my dad because you thought he'd be here, not because my dad was sick, right?"

It was like he'd slammed his goalie stick into her chest as she stared up at him. Was he fucking serious right now? How could he think that?

"I would never—"

"I'm over the lies, Wren—"

Wells took his shoulder, shaking his head. "Jensen, come on, bro. That isn't true."

"It makes sense. All she does is run," he said matter-of-factly. "Close people out or run, that's Wren's trademark, how she does things. Because people don't fucking change, do they, Wren?"

A sob escaped from her lips as she shook her head, feeling like she couldn't catch her breath. "No. I have. For you," she somehow got out, but Jensen shook his head.

"I thought so too, but—" He paused, wiping away the tear on his cheek before he looked down, inhaling shakily. "But this...this proves something completely different. Yeah, I'm out." Her heart shattered in her chest as she reached for him, but he was already turning before stepping over Bradley's body and heading down the aisle. Her parents moved out of his way, not making eye contact as she went to go after him, but both Wells and Vaughn stopped her.

"No, leave me alone for a minute," she protested.

"Yeah, he needs a minute. He's pissed," Wells warned, but Wren didn't care, pushing his hands away.

"I don't fucking care. He's my husband."

"If you want that, then you need to give him at least ten minutes to calm down," Wells demanded. "Listen, I know you love him, and I know you know him. But you haven't seen really angry Jensen. We have. He needs a fucking minute."

But she had to go after him. Her heart was breaking, and she'd be damned if she was going to let him do the one thing she was scared of. But when she tried again, Wells wrapped her up in his arms, kissing her head. "Really, Wren, give him a minute. Honestly."

"I can't! I love him, Wells. I can't," she cried, coming undone in her brother's arms as he buried his face in her neck.

"I know he loves you. He's mad, and he isn't going to listen. Just, please, listen to us," he begged, rubbing her back. "It's okay. I love you, it's fine. It will work out."

But would it?

As she cried into her brother's chest, clinging to him when she really wanted to cling to Jensen who was her constant rock, Vaughn asked, "What are we doing with this douche? Mom, should I drag him out and put him outside?"

It was the perfect time to laugh.

But Wren was pretty sure she would never laugh again if her worst fear was coming true.

That she had just lost Jensen.

* * *

GOD. He was an idiot.

He was a fucking dumbass.

How could he let this happen?

Why was he so fucking naïve!

Running his hands down his face, Jensen paced along the back of the venue on the water. While it was warm, the coolness off the lake was nice, but Jensen was shaking with anger. How dare she? How could she? Sleep with that guy? Bradley, whack-off-in-the-bathroom, Washington! He was a child, a fucking asshole, and he wasn't worthy of her. But she didn't think more of herself than to give herself to him! And then to have a kid with him? Fucking, really? Yeah, he couldn't give her a kid, but damn it, he would have been good to her. He was fucking good to her.

Damn it.

He was disgusted and couldn't believe it. What hurt the most was that she might not have thought she was doing it intentionally, but he knew she was trying to get out of her brother's wedding by going home due to the simple fear of seeing that bastard.

God, it hurt.

It fucking hurt bad.

His feelings were all over the place. He wanted to believe her. Believe in them. But he knew her, he knew her track record, and he would be naïve to assume she had changed. He didn't doubt she loved him and his family, he knew she did, but she would do anything to make sure he didn't find out about Bradley. He wasn't sure he could let that go. Also, Bradley? Really? That was his son's father? How the hell was he supposed to look at that kid…

This was what she didn't want.

This right here.

The thoughts in his head.

Swirling and making him feel like he was going to hurl.

"Fucking hell," he muttered as he sat down on a wooden bench, covering his face with his hands and leaning on his legs as they bounced with nervousness. Or fear. He didn't understand what he was feeling. A dread that was so unfamiliar, it hurt.

When he felt someone sit down beside him, he didn't look up as Vaughn said, "We need to stop meeting like this."

He couldn't even muster up enough energy to laugh. Swallowing hard, he moved his hands up a bit as he said, "Remember that time in the juniors when I was having the worst game of my life, and I let in six goals."

"I do."

"Seeing that puck behind me, sneaking in like a fucking asshole, was awful. I hate that feeling because I knew I could have stopped it —if I was quicker, you know? But that feeling, it gets me. It's like a drop in my gut, and I hate it. But this, what I'm feeling right now, is ten times worse."

Vaughn whistled, and Jensen shut his eyes behind his hands, seeing nothing but darkness, which was what he felt. "Well, I should have sent Wells, he's better with this kind of thing. But he was helping Winston get Bradley up and out, while Elaine tried to comfort a very upset Wren. I don't think I'm cut out for this kind of talk."

Jensen scoffed, shaking his head. "Just go, man."

"Nah, you're my bestie. I'll stay, try. If I ruin shit, then, eh, at least I tried," he said. "And by the way, I don't try, I win."

Jensen couldn't even roll his eyes, he just muttered. "You can go."

"No, can't. I'm here for you."

When Vaughn's hand came to his back, slapping it hard, Jensen shook his head. "I don't know what to do."

"Well, you could talk to her. I mean, you kinda just yelled and told her what she was feeling and doing. Didn't give her a chance to tell you differently."

"Because there is no point," Jensen said, dropping his hands. "This is what she does. She runs or she hides. She hasn't once just owned up to what she has done or what she is feeling—"

"Lie."

"Excuse me?"

He looked back at Vaughn with an eyebrow raised, and Vaughn shrugged. "Lie. She told you she loved you. Out of her mouth, to you, with no hesitation at what you said," he said simply, and Jensen looked away. "You say she hasn't changed, but I think she has. She isn't the girl I knew two months ago. Yeah, she still threatens me. But, dude, she does it with a smile. She looks at you with the same gooey look you always have for her. She set up a fucking nursery, for goodness' sake. She cares about what you think, what you want for her, and, dude, she loves your family. You know that. Come on, she wouldn't want to go home to be with your dad to get out of Wells's wedding because of that douche. She wanted to go for you, for your dad. You know that, so what's going on?"

Jensen's mouth trembled as he shook his head. He did know that. He knew all that, so what was it? Damn it. Why? As the tears burned his eyes, he inhaled deeply, his words coming out as a whisper, "It's too good, man. I got it all, and I knew... I knew it was too good, and here we are. I've got this fucker who can come and fight us at any moment for him, for the son I've decided is mine, the son she said was mine. And fuck, man, I mean, I'm... Damn it, Vaughn." He paused, taking a deep breath. "I'm scared that I'll keep giving everything to her, loving her, loving my son, and this fucker will come in and take it all."

Glancing to Vaughn, Jensen found his best friend staring at him like he was stupid or something. "Did you not listen to anything I said, Jenny? She told him to go take a hike."

"But he's the father—"

"No, he isn't. You are. We all know it. We all feel it, and that's it."

"But that's not how it works, Vaughn—"

"Who said? Because I don't have a relationship with my father, and who is my dad? Winston. He is who I consider as my father. Is he my blood? Nope. Same with you and Wells. I don't have a brother, I lost him. But thank God, he gave me you and Wells and, again, you guys aren't my blood. So I don't get it. I don't understand what you're upset about."

Shaking his head, his heart in his stomach, Jensen said, "It's different. Gunner isn't here yet, and this guy could take everything from me. He can give her more children. I can't, Vaughn. I mean, I'm hopeful, but I'm pretty sure I can't. And fuck, dude, she said I'm more man than him, but if that were the case, then I could give her a kid."

Jensen jumped as Vaughn threw his hands up with a shout. "Dude! She's yours. The kid, yours. Stop it. You aren't like this. You are a confident fucking man, and you aren't going to be like this," he announced, poking him in the arm. "When I felt like shit, you rallied with me and got me my girl. I don't have to help you get Wren because you've got her. Just get rid of this insecurity crap that doesn't have any relevance. What did she tell you? Did she tell you she wanted more kids?"

Jensen bit the inside of his cheek, his leg bouncing in nervousness as he looked out at the water. "I don't know."

"She doesn't. She didn't even want this one at the beginning, but she's changed—because of you. And if she does want kids, I know her, she'll adopt before she goes back to that guy because she wants you and only you."

Swallowing past the lump in his throat, Jensen kept his gaze fixed on the lake as its current pushed and pulled against the shore. Watching it, it reminded him of how it was with her at the beginning. She pushed him away, but he was always pulling her in. He wouldn't let go. Maybe he should have. Maybe this was a complete waste of time because now... Now knowing about this guy, he wasn't sure he could let it go.

But could he lose her?

"Guys, this thing is about to get started, and your best friend needs you to make this happen."

Running his hands down his face at the sound of Winston's voice, Jensen nodded before standing. He wasn't even the least bit ready, but he wouldn't let his best friend down. He'd deal, and then he'd figure out what he needed to say to Wren. Since he currently had no clue.

"Yup, onward to the wedding that I'm pretty sure isn't gonna happen," Vaughn laughed, smacking Jensen on the back. "But I know for sure you and Wren are good, so you know that too, man, okay?"

Jensen didn't answer because, for once, he didn't feel that way. He thought that the dude had been a one-night stand, that he really didn't matter to her, but they had known Bradley forever. He came from big money. He could easily take her to court and try for custody. That freaked Jensen out, not only for Gunner, but also for Wren. She wouldn't be able to handle that. She would rather just be with Jensen, with the possible chance of more kids, but he wasn't sure he would be enough to keep her.

Following behind Vaughn, Jensen saw Winston standing there. But instead of walking with them, he stopped Jensen, his hands landing on Jensen's shoulders. "Go on, Jo."

"Yes, sir."

360 | TONI ALEO

As Vaughn walked away, Jensen met the gaze of his second father and shook his head. "I'm sorry I lied to you."

"You didn't."

A little taken aback by that, he just held Winston's gaze. "I think I did."

"No, you called me, you told me you loved my daughter, that you wanted to marry her, and you loved your child. That's what I'm pretty sure you said to me. Is that what you plan on doing?"

Swallowing hard, Jensen looked down as he shrugged. "I want to, but—"

"There is no but, Jenny. It's yes or no."

Looking back up, Jensen felt his voice shake as he said, "I don't know."

Winston nodded. "You know, let me tell you something your dad said to me one time when I called him, mad as hell about my son being gay. After I calmed down, he said, 'Does it matter who he loves as long as he loves? Because loving someone is our job, is what we're programmed to do. It makes us happy, it makes us sad, but it's what we need to do to be complete. So how can you not want him to do what he needs to do to be complete?'" Pausing, Winston laughed. "I remember being so annoyed because he didn't under-stand—my son likes boys, ya know? And the more I thought about it, the more I realized I wanted Wells to be what I wanted. But I couldn't, you know? I lost my best friend because I wanted to change his programming, which isn't fair. And I know this isn't really making sense, but my point is, you're programmed to love Wren. We all know it, you know it, she knows it. Okay?"

Slowing nodding his head, Jensen cleared his throat. "Okay."

"Okay. Let's go do this wedding."

But before Jensen moved, he stopped Winston. "What do I say to her?"

Winston shrugged. "Tell her the truth because that's what she'll want. Give her your concerns, and I know you'll work out because she's too stubborn to give up, and she loves you too much to."

Jensen smiled. "You think she loves me?"

"I don't think it, boy, I know it. My girl doesn't light up like that around anyone but you, so, yeah. Let go of this bullshit, fix it, and go back to what you had." When he paused, he laughed. "Or she'll nag you like her momma nags me until she gets her way. That girl is stubborn like no other. Remember her with those bomb pops in the summer? She loved those things, never let anyone have any from *her* box. I'm pretty sure she knocked Vaughn's tooth out once because he took her box and tried to hide it."

Jensen chuckled, "She did."

"That boy. He's always been trouble."

Jensen grinned as he nodded. Clearing his throat, he asked, "Are you implying I'm the bomb pop?"

Winston thought that over. "I am. She doesn't let go of things she loves. So get ready, boy."

A grin pulled at his lips as Winston slapped his shoulder, walking with him up to the venue. When they reached the path that led to the back, they noticed everyone filing in, and Winston let out a long breath. "I'm not ready for this."

"Yeah, you are, because you love your son."

Winston nodded. "You're a good man, Jensen."

"Thank you, I learned a lot from you," he added, and Winston scoffed.

"No, son, you're your dad's boy. You're good, you love and forgive. I learned a lot from you two, and I'm thankful for that. But if you want to ever repay me for the years I fed and housed you, love my baby more than I ever can, more than her mom, more than anyone. Okay?"

Jensen nodded, blood rushing to his head as he gazed up at the man who had helped raise him. "Okay."

"All right, now I gotta go walk my son down the aisle."

As he watched Winston go through the door, his shoulders back, ready to tackle anything, Jensen wished he felt half of what the older man felt. But his insecurities were eating him alive, and he wasn't sure how he would be able to look at Wren and fix this.

If it was even fixable.

As he walked into the venue, following behind Winston down the hall, he saw Elaine running around like a chicken with her head cut off, yelling at everyone as Winston let his head fall back. "Lanie, fuck it. Come on, let's go walk our baby boy down the aisle."

Elaine stopped, looking up at her husband, and then nodded, her face breaking into a grin. "You're right."

She took his hand, and they walked to where everyone was waiting in the lobby to go in. When Wren saw Jensen, she came off the wall. Her makeup was gone, and he could tell she had redone it her way, which he felt bad about. He didn't like that she'd cried, but then, it was probably not preventable.

She came toward him, and he looked away as she whispered, "Jensen, please. Look at me."

"Wren, I can't right now. I'm trying to figure it out. Okay? I just need some time."

"Time? We're married, you don't get time. We're in this together. Me and you. Talk to me."

Meeting her fearful gaze, he shook his head. "Not now. We don't have time. This is about to start."

"I don't care. I need to talk to you."

"Not now," he asked once more. "Please."

"But you promised!" she snapped, her eyes welling up with tears once more as she held his gaze, her hands shaking beside her thighs. "You promised you wouldn't break up with me, leave me, and you said you don't make a promise you can't keep."

He bit his lip hard as his eyes fell shut, and before he could answer, Vaughn was calling him to go. Meeting her gaze, Jensen didn't say anything before heading toward his best friend with dread swirling deep in his stomach.

Because for the first time ever, he was worried he wasn't going to be able to keep a promise he had made.

# Chapter
# TWENTY-FOUR

atching his retreating back, Wren felt like her heart had fallen out of her chest and shattered on the ground.

What was happening?

Never in her life had she felt such pain.

The rejection from every guy ever didn't even come close to this. This was awful, and she didn't understand. Yeah, she may have lied about Bradley, and she was truly sorry for that. But did Jensen really believe she would pull some kind of shit like asking to go to check on his dad to get out of a wedding where there might be a chance meeting with Bradley?

Never.

"Jensen, really?" she yelled, and everyone in the lobby looked back at her. Alex's four little friends' eyes all widened in confusion as her brother rolled his.

"Wren, not here, please. Alex's friends—"

"No," she spat back at him as Jensen turned around, looking at her. "I get it, you're pissed and you have every right to be, but be mad at the right thing. I would never use your dad to get out of something. I love your father, I love you, I wouldn't do that!"

Jensen looked down before he nodded. "I know."

She went to argue, but then she paused as her eyes scrunched up. "Then what the hell is going on? Is it Bradley? Please. I don't want that dude. I want you."

"Wren, please, the music has started. We gotta go," Wells urged, and Jensen shrugged.

"We gotta go. We'll talk later."

With that, he turned. She didn't understand. This wasn't him. He was all about getting things fixed, but now, he was the one running from it. What the hell had happened? When someone reached for her, pulling her back, she looked up to see her father. Her eyes were wide while his hold was soft, pulling her to the back of the room. "Honey, just calm down. Let's get through this wedding, and then you two can talk."

"But, Dad, I need to fix this."

"I understand that, but we have a wedding to do," he said simply, cupping her face. "It will work out."

As her gaze held her father's, she shook her head while her eyes filled with tears. "Guess this all ruins my inheritance, huh?"

His face changed, his eyes narrowing. "What? You're married before your birthday. I see no problem."

"Even with everything you just heard?"

He shrugged. "I heard nothing except some asshole who hurt my daughter, but then someone else came along and fixed it all."

Her lower lip trembled. "I don't want to lose him."

"You won't," he said confidently. "You won't give up on something you truly want."

Meeting her father's gaze, she nodded slowly, hiccupping a sob as she whispered, "What if he tries to take my baby?"

Her father scoffed. "I wish he'd try. We'd ruin him. All of us."

Her heart sang, but only for a second before she looked up at her father. "Daddy, why haven't you brought up the inheritance? Not even once?"

His brows rose as his gaze bored into hers. "Because I never questioned you. I know for a fact that boy loves you, you love him, and that baby is his. I have no questions."

Her heart did a flip-flop in her chest because, unlike her father, she had a lot of questions, and they all revolved around Jensen. Before she could say anything else though, the music was indeed starting, and the doors opened. Standing in place behind Alex's man-maids, as he was calling them, she felt like she was about to cry her makeup off again. For so long, she couldn't fathom that someone like Jensen could love her. And then the moment she accepted it, and believed it deep inside of her, it all came crumbling down on top of her.

But she refused to put up with that.

And she didn't want to wait.

She needed to fix this.

She loved him.

And damn it, she knew he loved her.

When it was her turn, she walked out, her eyes on the prize. She didn't look anywhere but at him, standing in all his beautiful glory. When he finally looked at her, she held his gaze as she closed the distance between them before standing beside him, not missing that he tensed up.

"I can't wait."

"Wren, stop. After the wedding, I swear we'll talk."

"But that's not okay with me."

"Wren, dude, shut up," Vaughn snapped over at her, and she glared.

"Don't talk to her like that," Jensen whispered at him before looking to her. "I promise, we'll talk after this."

"Like you promised you'd never leave me?"

"Wren, I'm not leaving you."

"Oh, you're not?" she yelled, louder than she expected to, and when she looked up, Wells shot her a look that killed her dead three times over.

Whoops.

Lowering her voice to a whisper, she muttered, "It sure feels that way."

Setting her with a look, Jensen shook his head. "Please, we'll talk."

As the music changed, Céline Dion's "Because You Loved Me" blaring through the room, the doors opened once more, and Alex came out in a white suit with diamond-encrusted lapels, but Wren wasn't paying attention. All she could do was listen to the song. "I could seriously sing this song to you right now," she said, and Jensen's eyes widened.

"Please don't."

"But I could because I know you don't think I've changed, but I have. I promise you that—because of you. Your love fixed me, it did, and I love you, Jensen. I'd fall apart without you." His eyes drifted closed as Wells sent her another death glare that she promptly ignored as she started to sing along with the song, taking ahold of Jensen's hand. When a grin tugged at his lips, her heart sang for him. "I can sing loudly."

"Stop," he demanded, shaking her hand out of his. "Not here."

Pouting, she looked at where Alex was kissing his mom and then his dad before taking Wells's hands, coming to the altar. She understood that this was neither the time nor the place to try to convince her husband not to leave her, but she didn't like that she wasn't sure what he was thinking. Yes, he said he wasn't leaving her, but did he say it because he meant it, or because he just wanted her to shut up?

Reaching out once more, she laced her fingers with his, and when she saw his shoulders fall, so did hers. Was that good or bad? She didn't know, and when he glanced over at her, she gazed up at him, needing some reassurance. Just a simple squeeze, a kiss on the palm like he always did, or maybe even an actual kiss. Anything, but he just held her gaze, his eyes so damn unsure, and it was killing her. She couldn't lose him.

The minister began the service. "Alex and Wells's love story is like the 1996 Céline Dion *Falling into You* CD as they have told me. And knowing that, I know there is no reason ever to stop a love like this. Yet, I have to ask. Is there anyone here who feels this union should not take place? If so, please speak up at this time."

Wells was tense, sweat on his brow before he looked back at their dad. But the problem was, he didn't have to worry about their father.

Nope, he needed to worry about her.

She raised her hand, and Alex's eyes widened as she said, "See, I don't think it shouldn't take place, I was just wondering if we can take, like, an intermission?"

"Wren," Jensen snapped, and she held her hand up.

"Quick, I can't do this. Really, it's killing me——"

"Wren," Wells said through tight lips. "Are you having a baby?"

"I don't think so."

"Then shut up, and let me do this." She went to say something, but he snapped his fingers at her. "No."

She looked to her mom and dad, and they were both glaring at her. Feeling unsure about herself, she snapped her mouth shut as she crossed her arms over her chest and grumbled, "I'd let you ruin my wedding if you needed to fix your marriage."

"'Cause that makes no sense at all."

"This wedding is awesome," Vaughn said then, and the crowd all laughed, while Alex looked as if he was going to have a hissy fit.

"What is the problem?" Alex asked.

"She's having an issue. It's fine. Please go on," Wells said, waving off Alex's question before taking his hand once more.

"Are you sure?" the minister asked.

"Yes, please," Wells asked, and she didn't miss that he was sweating. She couldn't help but think that Wells didn't want to do this. But he *was* doing it, so she really needed to shut up and let him. It just didn't feel right. Something was off. She wasn't sure if it was her issue or if it was Wells and Alex, but she had this feeling in her gut that was driving her mad.

"Okay, wonderful. No objection to this beautiful union—"

"Actually, there is."

The voice was deep.

Very deep, and very sexy.

For a second, she thought it was Jensen, but it wasn't. When Wren's gaze fell on the tall, very handsome, dark-haired man with beautiful turquoise eyes who rose from the back row, she gasped loudly as Jensen muttered, "Holy shit."

As he turned, his eyes wide, Wells's mouth fell open as his ex-lover, Matty Haverbrooke, made his way down the aisle. Alex's face flushed with color as he glared at Matty and then at Wells.

"Wells."

But Wells wasn't listening as Matty stopped midway, his eyes on Wells. "I'm sorry, I am. And I don't mean to do this, but I can't let you marry him."

"Oh, snap," Vaughn said before shaking his head. "I knew I should have brought popcorn."

"Jesus, shut up," Jensen muttered, but then he noticed that Brie was eating a pack of peanuts from her purse.

Those two were meant for each other.

When Wells let go of Alex's hand, Wren's eyes widened even more as Alex yelled, "What? What are you doing?"

It was apparent that Matty wasn't sure of himself. He was nervous, his eyes wide and his shoulders back. Wren felt awful for him, but even she couldn't miss the way Wells's eyes had lit up the moment he saw him. "I know I did you wrong. I'm young, I'm stupid, but, Wells, I love you. I love you so much, and I can't do this.

I can't do life without you. Please. I know I have no right to ask this of you, but don't marry him."

Everyone in the audience was gasping. Hell, she was too! Holding her breath, she looked back to her brother. She knew how much he had loved Matty, but she also knew how broken he was when Matty wouldn't come out of the closet for him. When Jensen looked over at her, his eyes wide, hers mirrored his as she whispered, "What the fuck?"

"Right?" Vaughn asked, but Alex wasn't having any of it.

"No, we love each other. Get out of here! Someone remove him."

But Matty wasn't paying him any mind, his eyes locked on Wells. He looked pained, but still, so in love. It was tragic but beautiful at the same time. "I was wrong, I was so wrong. I let you go because I was a coward, and I swear to you, no more of that. I want to be with you, in and out of the closet. I want to love you because you came out of my dreams and made them real, Wells. You are every-thing I want and everything I need. I beg of you, don't marry him. Give me another chance, please."

Wells wasn't moving, nor was he speaking; he was just staring into Matty's eyes as a hush moved through the room. When Wren looked at her parents, both of them were gaping at the two men with wide eyes and open mouths. Everyone was pretty much stunned to silence.

Well, everyone but Alex.

"You left him. He doesn't love you! He loves me! Get out of here, you homewrecker! You can't have him!"

Once more, Matty wasn't listening to Alex as he closed the distance between himself and Wells, coming to stand on the stair below him, his head tipping back as he looked at her brother with nothing but a love in his eyes that was beyond overwhelming.

It was the way Jensen looked at her.

She didn't want to lose that.

Soon the tears were welling up in her eyes as Matty whispered, "I love you, Wells. You know I do."

"He doesn't love you," Alex yelled before looking up at Wells. "Wells, tell him. Jesus, are you mute?"

But Wells was still speechless, his eyes locked with Matty's as he moved onto the step with Wells, their bodies so close that if either of them moved, they'd be touching.

"Wells!" Alex yelled once more, but she was pretty sure neither of them was listening as they stayed locked in each other's gaze.

"Please tell me you still love me. Because no matter what I did, I couldn't stop loving you," Matty whispered, and Wren's heart ached at the look on her brother's face. He loved Matty, it was apparent, but he was scared.

Scared shitless.

Which was not a look she often saw on her brother.

"Wells! Damn it! What are you doing?" Alex exclaimed.

"I swear I'll never hurt you again. I'm sorry. But you are mine, baby, remember? You told me that. That I was yours, and I am," Matty begged. He didn't touch Wells, he just stood there, his eyes pleading while the room was tense and silent. He looked so damn big next to her brother. He was thick with muscle, but he was lean and looked gorgeous in the suit he wore. He had come to impress; the suit wasn't cheap, nor was the posh haircut and clean-cut shave. Matty Haverbrooke was one gorgeous man.

When Wells's eyes started to fill with tears, Wren went to save him. She had no idea what she was going to do, but before she could, Jensen stopped her. "This is all him." She looked at Jensen, her own eyes pleading as his hand slid off of her and into his pocket. "Let him do this."

"Do what? You better be kicking him out!" Alex yelled. "This is insane. Why are you just standing there? You don't love him, do you? What kind of best friends are you? This dude hurt him. Kick him out!"

His voice was so high-pitched and full of rage that Wren was wincing, but Matty and Wells weren't moving as Vaughn said, "We're the kind of best friends who want the best for our brother. Let him think!"

Alex went to argue, but her father's voice filled the room. "Son, that's enough. You need to say something."

Wells's eyes widened as he tore them from Matty to their father. He was terrified, and Wren wanted to wrap her arms around him, fix it for him. But she couldn't. This was all him, like Jensen had said.

Looking back to Matty, Wells's mouth trembled as he asked, "Your family?"

"Wells!" Alex cried, but Wells shook his head, waiting for Matty to answer him.

"Ha, told ya," Vaughn scoffed to her and Jensen, but they weren't paying attention as Matty nodded vigorously.

"I'm telling them. Even if you don't want me, I'm telling them. I promise. I just want you by my side when I do it because I love... I love you so much, Wells, please."

Wells paused, his lips trembling. "Why now?"

"It doesn't matter because you're marrying me!" Alex shouted, and Wren wasn't sure why the guy was still talking. It was obvious that Wells and Matty were in their own world.

"I wanted to tell you earlier, but I was scared. I'm still fucking scared, but I couldn't let you do this without you knowing that you changed my life. You make me want to be a good man, and I know I can do it without you, but I don't want to. You've made me want to fix things with my sister because of how much you love yours. I want to tell my brothers and my parents because I want to be myself. I want to be me instead of lying all the time. But, Wells, I want you beside me, with me, loving me. Please, say you will. Take me back, let me love you as you always loved me because, Wells, you own my heart. The whole damn thing. You know I don't do this kind of thing, but I can't stand by and watch you marry this guy. I can't."

When a tear rolled down Wells's face, Alex yelled, "Then leave!"

"I can't. I'm sorry, Alex, I am. But I love him," Matty said to him, but his eyes stayed glued to Wells.

"Wells, tell him to go!"

Swallowing hard, Wells looked back at Alex, and when he slowly shook his head, Wren covered her mouth to keep in her sob. "I'm sorry, but my heart beats for this man."

Matty let out the breath he was obviously holding before they wrapped their arms around each other, their mouths meeting in a familiar but beautiful way that took Wren's own breath away. She hadn't even noticed that Alex had stormed out or that his parents were yelling at hers. All she saw was the love that her brother felt, and soon she was grinning. He had loved Matty for as long as she could remember, and seeing them together, she could understand why.

It was a love like hers and Jensen's. But was that over?

When she looked to Jensen, she saw he was watching her, his eyes full of tears. The room started to clear out of Alex's family and friends, but she was pretty sure Wells was too busy kissing Matty to notice the ruckus going on around them. Everyone was yelling or asking what was going on. But she couldn't be bothered with them either because her world was staring at her with such uncertainty in his eyes.

But before either of them could say anything, Wells and Matty parted. Wells was laughing, wiping away his tears. "Shit, sorry."

"You don't be sorry, honey. It's obvious you belong with this boy," her mother said, coming toward them. "I'm Elaine Lemiere. You're Matty?"

Matty's face flushed as he nodded. "Yes. It's wonderful to meet you."

He held out his hand, but she ignored it, hugging him tightly as Matty grimaced, very unsure of himself. Wren's father came over then, holding out his hand. "I'm Wells's father, Winston. Matty, it's nice to meet you."

Exhaling hard, Wells shared a long look with Winston before smiles appeared on both their faces. Squeezing Matty's shoulder, Wells said, "I'm sorry, Mom. I can't get married today."

Elaine waved him off. "Then we'll have a nice, expensive dinner. Hope everyone is hungry?"

Vaughn laughed out loud. "I so won. I told everyone."

No one was listening to him as Wells smiled. "Unless you and Brie wanna get married."

Vaughn shrugged, but when he glanced at Brie, she glared. "Rodney isn't here."

He made a face. "Free wedding, babe." She made a face right on back, so he said, "But that doesn't matter because Rodney isn't here, and we couldn't fly him out in time, right?"

"Right," she deadpanned.

"Well, crap, guess expensive dinner it is," Wells said simply, but then Wren shook her head.

"No."

Everyone looked over at her, even Jensen as she looked up at him, her heart in her eyes as she said, "No, Jensen and I are getting married."

*　*　*

"WHAT?" Jensen's heart was pounding so hard, his vision was getting fuzzy as he held her gaze. "What in the world are you talking about?"

"I want to marry you. In front of everyone."

"But we're married."

"I don't care. I want it to be real this time because I want to." His heart stopped as she held his gaze hostage. "I fucked up. This whole time, I fought it, I fought it tooth and nail. But my fight was nothing compared to your love, Jensen. It's so pure, so beautiful, and I don't want anything else but your love. You. I want you. All of you, and I know I'm hard to deal with sometimes, and I'm stubborn and annoying, I don't listen well, and I've probably given you your fair share of frustrating moments, but, Jensen, if one thing is for sure, it's that I love you. I love you so damn much."

"Wren—"

"And yes, I know I lied. I know I should have been honest from the rip, but I hate him. I hate him so much because he made me doubt myself. He made me feel unworthy, and I hated me. I didn't believe in myself. I didn't think I could be a mom or a wife or anything. I was worthless, but you came along, and that changed. Everything changed. That fake marriage we had is now real, and I want to make that really real because I can't lose it. I can't lose you because I love you, Jensen. Surely you understand that."

He felt everyone's gazes on him as he looked down at her, tears gathering in her eyes as she stared up at him. Feeling a lump in his throat, he whispered, "I can't lose you."

"You won't."

But he wasn't sure. "I won't?"

Her eyes widened as she asked, "Why would you even think you would? I love you."

Swallowing hard, he shook his head, fighting back his own tears. "He can give you kids. You would be smart to go with him."

Her face turned red, scrunching up as she threw her hands in the air. "I don't want his kids, minus the one he already gave me," she said, taking his hands in hers and kissing each of them. "I only want yours."

"What if I can't—"

But she shook her head quickly. "Then we'll cross that bridge when we get to it. But we'll do it together." He looked away, but she reached up, guiding him back by his jaw, meeting his gaze. "I love you, Jensen Cade Monroe, so does *our* baby. We need to be okay—no, great—for this to work. We have to believe in each other. We have to lift each other up, and above all, we gotta love each other. We're good at that part, even the lifting part. We may need some work on the believing in ourselves part, but I know we can do it because we love each other. Do you love me?"

He scoffed. "Wren, I'll always love you, but I'm worried that I'm not enough—"

"Never. You're more than enough, all that I want and need. Don't ever think I need more. You're all I ever want to live for. No one else will ever do, just you. Believe in me. I know it's hard, because I wouldn't do the same for you at first, but I promise I have ever since I whispered I loved you on that dance floor. I fought it, I fought it so hard, but I think I always knew my heart was yours."

He could see it in her eyes. She meant every word, but he still wasn't sure. Could he do that to her? Take her, keep her to himself, when there could be more for her out there? A good man who could give her everything she wanted. Yet he couldn't imagine her with anyone else but him. Looking into her eyes, he saw his future. Holding her hand as she birthed their son, kissing her, telling her she was beautiful when she probably wanted to kill someone.

Diapers and throw-up, laughing because he'd probably gag. His son's first steps. Making love to her to celebrate their kiddo's achievements. Making love to her because he wanted to, which would be a lot since he always wanted to. Celebrating their milestones in their careers. Taking Gunner to school, hockey, college, and everything else, right by her side.

Life—he wanted to do life with her. Only her.

He knew he wanted her the moment he saw her, and he had her now. So why was he trying to push her away? Why was he trying to pull the kind of shit she had been doing to him? They had come so far, and there was no other way he wanted to go unless she was by his side.

"I want to grow old and gray with you, Wren Josephine Monroe."

Her eyes sparkled with tears as she reached up, taking his face in her hands. "So you'll marry me?"

He grinned down at her, dropping his head to hers. "I'd marry you a million times over just to see that smile."

As her face broke into an even bigger grin, the simple motion taking away his breath, his eyes fell shut as their lips met. Kissing her would never be normal; it would always blow his mind because, even though she was in his arms, kissing him, he still believed he was living in a fairy tale.

He finally had his queen.

"Heck yeah! Let's do this! Brie, get up here. You're the maid of honor, and Vaughn and I will go over here. Wait, can we turn that A into a J, you think?" Wells asked, and Matty nodded.

"Yeah, easy."

Smiling down at her as everyone moved around him, Jensen shook his head. "So this is happening."

"Yeah, I think it is. Oh, I wish your mom and dad were here," she complained, but Elaine held up her phone.

"FaceTiming Emma now!"

Before they knew it, a makeshift J hung on the other side of the W, while Wells and Vaughn stood beside him, and Brie stood beside Wren. The room had cleared out, leaving only their family, minus Jensen's parents. Wren still wore her suit, but he wasn't looking at what she was wearing, only into her eyes. Those green depths that took his breath away, and boy, was she gorgeous.

"Why are they doing this again?" he heard his mother ask as they laced their fingers together, pressing their foreheads together, getting lost in each other's eyes.

"Yeah, aren't they married?" his dad asked, and Elaine laughed.

"Oh, if only you knew. Today has been a mess, and my oldest decided not to marry the man he thought he was marrying. And then Wren and Jenny were fighting about some crazy crap and then they made up and now they're getting married."

"Oy. I'll need a glass of wine for the long version of that, eh?" Emma asked, her eyes filling with tears.

Elaine scoffed. "You mean three bottles?"

"Mom, can we get started?" he heard Wells ask, and then there was silence as Jensen stayed trapped in Wren's gaze while the minister repeated what she had just said earlier. Though, he was pretty sure neither of them was listening. He was too busy being lost in the only eyes he wanted to look into for the rest of his days.

"Jensen, would you like to say something?"

His lips quirked as Wren's did the same before he lifted his head up, wrapping his arm around her neck, and pulling her to him. "I have never in my life truly loved anyone but you. You were it for me. I've said that time after time, but having you, being with you, loving you...I swear it feels like a dream. A dream I never want to wake up from because I love you, and I'll never stop because my favorite thing about you isn't just your smile, Wren, but that I make you smile."

"Jesus, where is the tissue?" he heard his mom cry, and Wren's eyes started to cloud with her own tears.

"I promise I'll never love anyone the way I love you because I don't know how to love anyone else but you. I'm yours. Only yours and I'm ready for life with you."

"Shit, I'm gonna have to step my vows game up," Vaughn muttered, and Wells scoffed.

"Right?"

Jensen was still looking down at her as she whispered, "I love you."

And his grin grew as the minister asked, "Wren, would you like to say something?"

She was lost in Jensen's gaze, a tear leaking out the side of her eye before she declared, "One thing is for sure, I can't promise you an easy life. You know me and I'm tough, but I'll do my best not to disappoint you. I won't be the perfect wife because I don't know what the hell I'm doing, but I can promise you that I'll choose to love you, and only you, for the rest of my days. No one will ever love me the way you do, Jensen, and because of that, I'm going to love you the only way I know how." Her voice broke, tears falling as her lips trembled with a sob. "And that's with my soul. My whole soul is yours, because a heart can stop and a mind can forget, but a soul neither stops nor forgets. It only loves, and my soul belongs to you."

"Ah! She got that from me. Way to go, Wrenya!"

As her tears dripped down her face, his doing the same, Jensen's lips curved. "Your soul, Wrenya? The whole thing?"

"The whole thing. It's yours."

"Good, 'cause mine was yours from the beginning."

Her face lit up as she leaned into his chin. "Sorry it took me so long to join the game."

"Doesn't matter how we win as long as we do," he murmured as she backed up, looking up at him.

"And we will. Together. A team."

"Always, baby, always."

With that, he took his wife's mouth with his, and as he kissed her, Jensen knew that no Cup, no award, no nothing could ever add to his life the way Wren did. It hadn't been easy, and he knew it never would be. But the best things in life, he had always fought and worked for.

And Wren was the ultimate prize.

# Epilogue

"*I* am entirely too pregnant to be here."

Her husband looked down at her as he held his hand out to her before she took it, pulling herself out of the limo. "I don't understand why they pushed this back so damn far."

Jensen placed a kiss to the side of her mouth. "Venue conflicts, from what I was told."

She shot him a dry look, completely annoyed with the whole thing. She was supposed to be home, getting ready for Gunner's debut the following month. The last few weeks had been so busy for them that she didn't have everything done. Between going back to Canada, this time with Wells, Matty—whom she was still on the fence about but tolerated because her brother loved him so much— Brie, and Vaughn, and then the little vacation to Cancun Jensen had surprised her with, it was easy to say that nothing was done. Then there was the baby shower Elli had thrown for her, the birth of Benji and Lucy's baby girl, Charlotte, and the retirement party for Tate that Jensen had put on for him. Things were nuts.

Honestly, nuts.

"Don't they plan this shit out? Like, when you know you want to have the NHL Awards on said date, plan it, jeez. Now we're in Vegas in August when it's hotter than Satan's asshole," she complained as he waved to some of the fans who were calling out for him. He smiled shyly as he looked back down at her. She hoped she didn't look like a whale in her sparkly silver body-hugging dress that Jensen had picked out, but his eyes seemed to darken as he looked her over. Her hair was down, big curls to the side, trailing over her shoulder with a silver barrette holding it back. Her makeup was, of course, dramatic, as was the cut of the front of her dress. She was a little worried when the stylist busted out the tape, but her boobs were in their assigned seats and she was ready to go.

She just hoped Jensen liked it.

Which he had told her he did.

A million times since leaving the hotel.

"Vivid image, thanks," he muttered as he took her in his arms, holding her close as they started up the stairs of the venue. "By the way, I can't wait to slide this dress down those sexy, dangerous curves of yours."

Giggling, she leaned into him as they climbed the stairs. "Well, thank you."

"Hmmm," he muttered against her lips. "Think I can slide this over and get a peek at your boob?"

She laughed. "It's taped down." A challenge flashed in his eyes, and she smacked his moving hand. "Don't you dare."

He laughed, kissing her lips hard. "I love you."

"I love you."

"Good, be right back," he said with a wink before he kissed her hand and went to sign stuff for the fans. As she stood there, watching as he gushed over the kids, was great with the adults, and signed as much as he could, she couldn't help but think she couldn't love anyone more than him. He had been wonderful the last couple months. They were great and so happy. She still couldn't believe she had tried to keep her heart hidden from him. It was useless.

He owned it.

Her hand slid down the front of her belly where her son struggled inside of her for room, and her eyes drifted shut. She hadn't heard from Bradley since Wells's non-wedding. She wasn't sure what he was thinking, so Jensen made sure to hire a wonderful lawyer just in case. Since she had the texts from Bradley telling her to abort their child, her lawyer was confident they would be able to terminate his rights to Gunner if need be or if he ever tried to take her to court. Meanwhile, though, the plan was to have Jensen sign the birth certificate because Gunner was his, and that was that.

Coming toward her, Jensen wrapped her up in his arms as he kissed her. "Ready?"

"Ready," she said, leaning into him, and he grinned over at her.

"I love you."

"I know," she teased, and he kissed her once more as they headed into the theater that was full of all of hockey's best. Seated in the front by the greats of Jensen's generation, Wren leaned back in the seat, happy to be able to stretch her legs out in front of her. Her knees had been hurting, along with her hips. She wished the seats were bigger, but Jensen had already said they could leave after the Vezina Trophy.

She was praying it was the first award.

But Wren wasn't that lucky.

Nope, it was toward the end, and as they went through the nominees, she squeezed Jensen's hand when the nerves took over. But as always, Jensen was cool as a cucumber, laughing at her. But she couldn't help it. She knew that Emma and Antoine were watching, as were her parents, Vaughn, Brie, Wells, and probably Matty. She wanted so badly for Jensen to win. He deserved it. He was the best!

"You're insane," he muttered, and she stuck her tongue out at him as the guy on the stage opened the envelope.

"From the Nashville Assassins, Jensen Monroe."

Letting out a squeal, she somehow hopped up, clapping loudly, unlike the ladylike way hockey wives were supposed to do it, but she didn't care. She was proud of her man. Laughing, he stood, taking her face in his hands before kissing her hard on the lips. Parting, he kissed her nose as the room erupted, his stats and his highlights showing on the screen on stage. Pride shook her from her core as she watched everything while he climbed the stairs, accepting his award. She hadn't realized how big the Vezina Trophy was.

She had no clue where that was going in their apartment.

They really needed to buy a house.

She knew she was supposed to sit, but she didn't. She kept standing, that is until she felt a pain in her side that had her dropping into her seat.

Shit, that hurt.

"Wow, um, I'm very honored and very humbled. I love this sport, I love my job, and everything tied to it. I work for the best owner in the NHL, one who makes me feel like I'm part of a family instead of just someone on the payroll. I play every night with my brothers, a game we all love and have worked our butts off to get into." Everyone hooted and hollered, cheering him on, but Wren was hurting. Something wasn't right, and when warmth ran down her legs, her eyes widened.

Did her water just break?

Oh. Fuck.

"First, I'd like to thank my wife," he said then, and she directed her eyes up to the stage, meeting his. She knew damn well a camera was on her, so she didn't move. "I wouldn't be who I am today without her. Which is complete. I've known her for over fifteen years, and she made me chase her for fourteen years and nine months of that, but now, she's having my son, and she loves me. So it's okay that she made me wait because it was worth it. I love you, Wren Monroe."

"I love you," she somehow got out as everyone aww'd around them.

"Next, I want to dedicate this to my dad," he said, and she exhaled hard before she stood slowly, which of course, made Jensen pause, but she waved him off, trying to get the hell out of there so she could text him to meet her out front. But she only got two steps before a shooting pain hit her in the gut.

"Shit."

She didn't even know how it happened. She thought some other hockey player was holding her up, but it was actually her hockey player as people started to gather around them.

"Whoa, baby, what's wrong?"

She laughed through the pain to keep from crying. "My water broke."

People who heard her gasped as he shook his head, laughing as everyone started to fuss over her to get her out of there. But she was in pain and freaking the fuck out. How did this happen? She had a month! Was Gunner okay? Holy crap! She was having her kid in Vegas! Dammit! But then her husband's arms wrapped around her, not letting her go far. A much-needed wave of calm rushed over her before he muttered, "And you say you never get attention."

"You're lucky I love you," she said as they made it out the side door where they could get to a car faster.

With a grin on his face, he nodded. "I am. Now, let's go have us a baby."

* * *

"So Daddy won the Vezina yesterday, and let me tell you what that is. That's the award for the best goalie in the league, and Daddy is that. Did you know that, buddy?"

Jensen looked down into the face of his sweet boy, and he knew his heart was full. By the grace of God, Gunner looked like his beautiful wife, but he didn't miss that Gunner had Bradley's chin. Not that it mattered because unlike the fears he had been experiencing since he found out who Gunner's biological father was, he loved the kid with everything inside of him. It wasn't easy getting here, his insecurities were real, but all of that didn't matter now. All that mattered was this little human who was his and Wren's.

Holding his son close to him, he kissed Gunner's forehead as he rocked him, pacing the room while Wren slept. "You just wait. I'm going to teach you everything I know: how to play, how to be the best, and if you want to be a forward, that's cool. Uncle Vaughn will get you all set up. And if you want to play defense, that's great because Uncle Wells does that. I got you covered, man. You're going to be the best damn player ever. Better than the lot of us, you know that?"

Gunner just stared up at him, his eyes wide and so full of wonder. His eyes were a spellbinding blue, with a beautiful light hazel circle around the pupil that took Jensen's breath away. He was a damn cute kid, and Jensen still couldn't believe this little nine-pound bundle had come out of his wife. She had been so strong—okay, not really. She bitched the whole time, but she did it. He probably had some battle wounds, but they were worth it as he stared into his son's eyes. "So, like I told you when you were in your mama's belly, I'm going to love you more than anyone else, well, except Mama, in this whole world. I'm going to be your best friend, and you'll be mine. Unless you like your brother or sister more than me, and that will be okay. We'll get to that when it happens. If it happens."

A grin pulled at Jensen's lips as his body vibrated with excitement. He had gone back to the doctor when they had come home from Colorado, and the tests had shown that there was a slight chance he could father a baby. His sperm count was low, but it was at least something they could work with. Since both of them were too stubborn to accept anything other than a win, he figured it would happen. He wasn't sure when, or even if they would, but he might be able to give Wren more children. Not that she was asking after pushing a nine-pound child out her vagina. He was pretty sure she screamed she was never doing that again.

But in a way, it didn't matter. He had the best wife and the greatest kid.

What else could he ask for?

"Hey."

Turning around, he found his wife slowly getting up, moving her hair out of her face. "Is he okay?"

"He's perfect. Just like you."

She gave him a weak smile. "You're too good to me, Jensen Monroe."

"Never," he said with a wink as she ran her hands down her face.

"Does he need to be fed?"

"Nope, already did a bottle thing."

"Awesome, bring him here."

He did as she asked, coming to the bed and sitting beside her. He placed Gunner in the crook of her arm, and she kissed his forehead. "And I thought I was scared to do this. Look at this face."

"Right?"

Then she looked up at him. "Nope, still scared shitless."

He laughed, kissing her cheek as she leaned into him. "You got me."

"I do. You're so lucky, and you just wait till you meet all your family. They're gonna eat you up."

"They are," Jensen added as her phone went off. Reaching for it, he saw it was her mom. "It's your mom."

"Answer it."

"No, she'll ask me a billion questions I don't know the answers to, and then it will be like you're talking to her anyway."

She blew out a breath. "Fine, trade me," she said, and he hit answer before taking the baby as she answered, just as a knock came at the door. Her brows came together as the door opened and in came the last person he'd thought he'd see.

"Shanna," Wren gasped, her eyes widening. Jensen knew for a fact they hadn't spoken to each other since the wedding, but there she was with balloons and a basket of baby stuff. "Mom, let me call you back," she said before hanging up the phone and straightening her hair. "I didn't know you were coming."

"Yeah, I sort of just drove here when your mom posted the picture of him on Facebook. I wanted to see him and you." Setting the basket down, Shanna came toward them. "If that's okay?"

"Yes, of course," Wren said, waving her in. "I'm a mess. Jensen's not, and neither is Gunner, but please."

Jensen smiled as he went to Shanna, handing her his little man. She took him willingly, a grin covering her face as she moved the blanket down, running her finger along his chin. "He's beautiful."

"He is," Jensen agreed. "Looks like his mama."

Shanna looked up at him. "Thank God."

Jensen smiled. "Yeah. He's perfect. How are yours? Everyone healthy?"

She smiled back up at him before returning to look down at Gunner. "They're great, thank you for asking, Jensen."

Shanna rocked Gunner back and forth, and he just stared up at her. Jensen looked back at Wren to find her gazing upon them worriedly. Walking over to her, he wrapped his arm around her shoulder and kissed her temple. "You okay?"

She forced a smile as she nodded. "Yeah."

"He's lucky to have you two," Shanna said then, looking over at them.

"Thank you," Wren said softly.

Slowly nodding, Shanna took a deep breath before looking over at Wren once more. "I'm sorry for how I left it at the wedding. I shouldn't have done that, but I was upset."

Wren held up her hands, shaking her head. "No, I understand. I should have been honest, but I couldn't—"

"No, I understand. Either way, it was shitty of me, and I hope that maybe we can work on us."

Wren nodded eagerly. He knew she had felt awful and wanted to reach out to Shanna, but she didn't know what to say. Plus, they had all been so busy with trips and baby stuff that she really hadn't had time. "I'd love for that to happen."

Shanna's lips tipped at the side. "Maybe you'll let me see him sometime."

Wren smiled, and he knew she was going to say the same thing, but he spoke first. "Anytime you want, Shanna. You're always welcome."

Shanna sent him a small smile as she nodded. "He isn't going to bother you guys. Word is his wife is pregnant."

"You aren't talking to him?"

Shanna shook her head. "Not lately, but we're trying."

He knew Wren didn't know what to say, so he said, "Good for them. We wish them the best."

"Thank you," she said softly. "But don't worry. I made sure he wasn't going to do anything stupid. He doesn't need to. This baby isn't his, it's yours."

Emotion choked him as he nodded. "Thank you, Shanna."

"Of course," she said, coming over to him and handing him Gunner. "I'm gonna get out of here. I told Jay I'd be back tonight, so I need to go."

"Are you sure?" Wren asked and Shanna nodded.

"Yeah, I'll call you."

"I'd like that."

"Me too," she said as an exhale before the door opened, and then the whole family was in the room.

"Her boobs aren't out, are they?" Vaughn yelled.

"God, let's hope not!" Wells agreed.

"Shut up, boys. Oh, hey, Shanna. Where's my baby? There he is!" Elaine yelled, coming straight for them, and then it was like Wren and Jensen didn't matter as everyone gushed over their sweet boy. But Jensen didn't miss the way Shanna watched before she quietly slipped out of the room without a goodbye.

"That's gonna take time," Wren said then, and he hadn't realized she'd seen the same thing.

"Yeah, I think so too," he agreed, looking over at her, but it was only for a moment before their family was fawning over them.

"He looks like me," Winston said, tapping his chest. "Thank God."

"He does not. He looks like me," Elaine said.

"I see nothing but Wren," Brie gushed, moving her finger along Gunner's lips, her arms resting on her extended belly. She was getting so big, and it was really exciting because Jensen was pretty sure Vaughn was having panic attacks at the thought of being a dad. "He is gorgeous."

"Yeah, he is," Vaughn agreed. "Makes me want mine."

Jensen scoffed. "Have you decided on a name?"

Brie smiled happily. "We have. Julie!"

"Ah! I love it," Wren cheered, and Vaughn cleared his throat. "I came up with it."

Brie rolled her eyes as Wells said, "I'm pretty sure that name was thought of before you came into existence."

That had everyone laughing as Wells took Gunner from Brie and kissed his cheek. "Listen here, buddy. You have two cool parents, but your uncles are where it's at. We are so much cooler."

Vaughn nodded as Gunner just looked up at them like they were crazy, which they were. "We can help you play hockey, chase girls, all the bad stuff your dad never did."

"Give me my baby," Wren said then, holding her hands out. "You two are going to corrupt him."

Laughing, Wells brought Gunner to her. She took him, kissing his head before laying him on her lap. Reaching out, Jensen took Gunner's little hand, and man, his heart was full. He'd known he was going to love the kid, that was a given, but nothing compared to what he was feeling at that moment. That overwhelming love he usually only felt for Wren. But damn, Gunner was giving her a run for her money.

Looking over at her, he flashed her a grin. "Would you be mad if I love him more?"

She laughed as she shook her head. "Nope, 'cause I love him more than you."

"Good talk," he said, and they shared a long look full of nothing but love and heat.

But that was interrupted when Wells clapped his hands together. "So, I'm flying out to New York to meet Matty's parents tomorrow."

"Awesome, do they know?" Vaughn asked.

"That I'm coming? They have no clue."

Jensen laughed as Wren shook her head. "So it'll be a surprise?"

"One of many thus far," he joked, shaking his head. "During a trip they all took that summer, some shit had gone down. But none of them really talked about it since they all knew how upset Matty had gotten, which, in turn, upset Wells. "They probably hate me."

"Probably," Winston joked before wrapping his arm around Wells as they laughed together. "But once they meet you, they'll love you." Watching as they shared a moment, Jensen found himself grinning. Things were still a little weird between them, but he felt good about it. They might get back what they had so long ago.

The kind of friendship he prayed he had with Gunner.

* * *

LATER THAT NIGHT, after everyone was gone, it was just Jensen and Wren. He lay in bed with her, Gunner on her lap as he held her close, dusting kisses along her temple.

"I can't believe your mom called him a little cabbage. So what, we're the big cabbages?"

Jensen laughed against her temple, his eyes drifting shut. "I guess."

"She said he looks nothing like you and says we need another."

He smiled. "Guess we need to start working on that, eh?"

She scoffed. "Um, no. I just pushed something the size of a Zamboni out of my coot. You're going to have to give me time to forget that."

"You can forget something like that?"

"From what Elli said, yes."

"So, there is hope?"

She giggled, leaning into him as she slid her hand into his. "Maybe."

"I won't hold my breath or forget the image of your vagina roughly the size of my head."

She grimaced. "Don't remind me."

"At least you didn't see it."

"Thank God. Can you believe they asked if I wanted the mirror? Like, hell no, I don't want to see that! Just give me my kid."

"Some of us weren't that lucky."

Wren laughed out loud as she kissed his shoulder. "You were amazing. I'm sorry I ruined your award."

He grinned as he ran his finger along the back of Gunner's arm. "This is the prize I ultimately wanted."

She leaned her chin into his shoulder as he kissed her nose, feeling the love between them all over his body. Smiling, she said, "Your dad looked so proud."

"He did, and thank God he's walking some."

"Right? I was so happy to see him coming toward the phone."

"It was awesome."

She nodded, exhaling as she traced Gunner's lips. "I'm exhausted."

"Me too," he muttered into her ear. "Are we giving him to the nurses?"

"No."

He scoffed, shaking his head. "We're supposed to."

"I don't care," she announced, looking up at him. "He's ours."

"He is," he agreed, meeting her in the middle for a kiss.

She looked down at Gunner, running her thumb along the back of his sweet, soft hand. "Did this really happen?"

He smiled as he nodded. "It did."

"Who would have thunk it?"

"I almost dreamed it." Her lips curved as he kissed her temple. "But even dreaming could never come close to this moment."

"I love you, Jensen."

His heart exploded. "I love you."

Silence fell between them as they gazed down at their beautiful child.

"Hey, Wren?" he asked in a whisper.

"Yeah," she whispered back, tracing Gunner's cheeks with her finger. The baby was wide awake but drunk from all the milk he had consumed. For being almost a month early, the kid was healthy as a horse and eating as much as one too. He took after his mother in more ways than one.

"Are you happy?"

She looked up at him, and her eyes sparkled as she nodded. "Never in my life did I think I could be this happy." Leaning her nose to his, she smiled. "You?"

As his heart filled with such love and passion for the one who gazed up at him, completely exhausted and looking a hot mess, he nodded, feeling nothing but completion when he stared into her green depths. "I don't want what I'm feeling to ever change."

"It will." She gave him a wicked smile. "I'll piss you off and drive you completely crazy."

He laughed, nodding his head. "And I'll still love you."

She pressed her forehead into his chin, and his eyes drifted shut.

Jensen Monroe finally had it all.

*The End*

Keep reading on for a snippet of Wells and Matty's story!

# A NOTE FROM

*Toni Aleo*

Hello! I can't believe we're already to installment twelve of the Assassins series! Kind of nuts, but also superawesome. I hope you enjoyed this book. I absolutely adore this couple and had so much fun writing it. I love Wren, but I think I might love Jensen more. Haha!

So a lot of crazy things happened this year: signed an awesome contract with Waterhouse Press, then I had a small cancer scare, and also, my Predators lost in the Stanley Cup final. But through it all, I'm me. I'm a full-time writer, a mom to a gymnastics star and a gamer, also a dogmom, and then a wife to the love of my life. So yeah, I'm a happy camper. Things are good. Mostly because I have an awesome Life Manager, Lisa Holletta (Nope, still not how you spell it. But she loves me enough to let me misspell just that one word on purpose.) who keeps my business moving and grooving. I have awesome friends who stand behind me and a family that continues to believe in me. So thank you to all of them.

But a BIG THANK YOU goes to you. Yeah, you! With each purchase of my books, you help me live my dream, and there is not enough time to ever show my gratitude. So thank you. Thank you so very much!

I'm excited for the future. It's gonna be good! Especially with all of you behind me!

So thank you! Please go leave a review! And, hey, I love you!!

Love,
Toni

# About the
# AUTHOR

My name is Toni Aleo, and I'm a #PredHead, #sherrio, #potterhead, and part of the #familybusiness!
I am also a wife to my amazing husband, mother of a gamer and a gymnast, and also a fur momma to Gaston el Papillion.
While my beautiful and amazing Shea Weber has been traded from my Predators, I'm still a huge fan. But when I'm not cheering for him, I'm hollering for the whole Nashville Predators since I'll never give my heart to one player again.
When I'm not in the gym getting swole, I'm usually writing, trying to make my dreams a reality, or being a taxi for my kids.

I'm obsessed with Harry Potter, Supernatural, Disney, and anything that sparkles! I'm pretty sure I was Belle in a past life, and if I could be on any show, it would be Supernatural so I could hunt with Sam and Dean.
Also, I did mention I love hockey, right?

Also make sure to join the mailing list for up to date news from Toni Aleo:
http://eepurl.com/u28FL

www.tonialeo.com
toni.aleo@yahoo.com

# MORE BOOKS FROM Toni Aleo

**Assassins Series**

Taking Shots

Trying to Score

Empty Net

Falling for the Backup

Blue Lines

Breaking Away

Laces and Lace

A Very Merry Hockey Holiday

Overtime

Rushing the Goal

Face-off at the Altar

Delayed Call

Twenty-Two

In the Crease

**Bellevue Bullies Series**

Boarded by Love

Clipped by Love

Hooked by Love